SPINE TINGLING ROMANCE
FROM STELLA CAMERON!

ALMOST
AN ANGEL

Deb Stover

Pinnacle Books
Kensington Publishing Corp.

http://www.pinnaclebooks.com

PINNACLE BOOKS are published by

Kensington Publishing Corp.
850 Third Avenue
New York, NY 10022

First Printing: November, 1997
10 9 8 7 6 5 4 3 2 1

Printed in the United States of America

In memory of my mother, Susan Jackson, who taught me to love books, and for my father, Johnny Jackson,— a real life hero.

BOOK I

Prologue

1886, The Pearly Gates—almost.

I must be dead.

Terror seized Hilary Brown as her memory returned. Thirteen steps . . .

She remembered swallowing hard as the hangman slipped the noose around her neck. A blindfold mercifully blotted out the image of her brother's horrified expression. Why were the cruel men making Elliot watch his sister's execution?

A loud click. A thud. She fell . . .

Hilary stared in amazement at the robed woman before her. "Wh—who are you?" she asked, taking a step backward, but finding her path blocked by an invisible barrier. She shook her head, trying to discern how she'd traveled from Columbine to this strange place.

"Where am I?" She nervously wrapped a long strand of blond hair around her index finger. She couldn't deny it—the evidence was overwhelming. Closing her eyes for a moment, she tried to block her memories. A shudder swept through her and she bit her lower lip. She didn't *want* to remember.

The woman in white didn't seem in any hurry to answer Hilary's questions. She just sat there in a golden chair, leafing through a huge white book as if she had all the time in the world. An ethereal glow surrounded the figure, and when she finally glanced up, Hilary was mesmerized by the woman's beauty.

Hilary looked over her shoulder, then to each side. Nothing but vast emptiness surrounded them. They were suspended in space, just the two of them, the book and the golden throne.

Hilary had to ask, though she wasn't at all certain she wanted an answer. "Are you a . . . an angel?"

The woman nodded. "Yes, Hilary. I'm an angel. I'm called Sarah." Her voice was soft, yet it echoed through the void around them.

Hilary gulped. "I'm really dead." Was this Heaven? She hadn't always been good, but she hadn't exactly been bad, either. Fighting against something evil had caused her death. Was that how she'd made it this far—wherever this was?

There was only one way to find out. "So, is this Heaven?"

Sarah smiled. "Not quite, Hilary. I've been assigned to determine the nature of your afterlife." She sighed and glanced upward once. "We redirect souls here."

Hilary didn't like the sound of that. "Redirect? I thought Saint Peter—"

"You haven't made it quite that far, Hilary." Sarah glanced down at the open pages. "This book contains your entire life." She looked up again; her expression grew solemn. "Hilary, I'm afraid we can't admit you to Heaven."

Shivers raced up Hilary's spine. Was Hell anything like

Reverend Booth had claimed. If so, she wouldn't be cold much longer.

"However . . ." Sarah tilted her head to one side as if to study Hilary. "You lived under extraordinary conditions all your life. Perhaps we could be a bit more lenient—consider some options."

Options? Hilary's hopes soared. "I tried real hard to be good. And I took good care of Elliot," she said hesitantly. "Is that in there? Do you see it?"

Nodding again, Sarah smiled. "Your death occurred under very trying circumstances."

Hilary sighed, struggling with her memories again. "Yes, I remember." She looked up—she had to know. "Did Elliot . . . see all of it?"

Sarah met Hilary's gaze—a look of compassion crossed her features. "No. A kindly gentleman pulled him away just before . . ."

"Thank you for that." Hilary closed her eyes for a moment. At least Elliot had been spared seeing her last moment.

"Elliot's a good boy." Sarah smiled. "He'll definitely have a place here when his time comes."

Hilary nodded, wondering why there wasn't a place here for her, too. *Oh, how I wish I could undo some of my mistakes.*

Sarah peered at Hilary over the white book. "Perhaps we could grant your wish."

"My wish?" Hilary frowned. None of this made sense. "What wish?"

"The one you made a few moments ago." Sarah looked down at the book in her lap again, then closed it with a sigh. "It's a bit unorthodox, but, I believe we can do this."

Suspicious, Hilary tried to repress her question, but couldn't. "You mean I can stay?"

Sarah shook her head. "Not exactly."

"Oh."

A beautiful smile spread across Sarah's face. "You must earn your way here. A few moments ago, you wished you could undo some of the things you've done."

Stunned, Hilary took another backward step, then looked back to make sure she wouldn't fall. The invisible barrier was gone. Deciding it was safer to stand her ground, so to speak, she nodded. "Yes. I do remember thinking that."

"It's not within my power to return you directly to your former life, but I can put you in Transition."

"Transition?" Hilary wrinkled her brow and lifted her upturned palms. "I don't understand."

The angel smiled again. "It means you can live, in a manner of speaking, until the circumstances to return you to a time before your death are right."

"In a manner of speaking?" Hilary shuddered. "You mean I'll be a . . . a ghost?"

Sarah laughed. "We don't refer to souls in Transition in quite that way up here, Hilary," she explained in a pleasant tone. "There's nothing to be frightened of, but there are conditions and possible complications."

Hilary clenched and unclenched her hands. "Such as?"

"Those who knew you—your friends and family—won't be able to see you, even if you will it so." She smiled and blinked her beautiful eyes. "Transition must occur before the beginning of the twenty-first century, if you're to earn your way into Heaven."

"Twenty-*first*?" Hilary laughed in open relief. "That's over a hundred years from when I died."

Sarah's expression was solemn. "Time slips away. You must listen very carefully," she cautioned. "This is very serious. Your afterlife is at stake."

Suppressing her earlier optimism, Hilary reminded herself of her predicament. "I'm sorry. I won't laugh again."

"That's not all, Hilary." Sarah gave her a wry smile. "The situation is rather complicated."

"What do I have to do?"

"If you don't succeed before your time runs out . . ." Sarah paused, clutching the book of Hilary's life to her chest. "Well, I think you must realize where you'll go. It won't be here."

Hilary closed her eyes and nodded. The next century could very well be the best part of eternity. "All right. So, how do I get out of Transition?"

Sarah nodded, apparently satisfied with Hilary's attitude. "Good. I know you have strength—it's in here." She held up the book, then returned it to her lap. "You must find a liberator, a deserving person to serve. Your mission will be to help him or her through some personal difficulty. Whatever you do for this man, woman or child, must alter that person's life in a positive manner, and with love."

Frowning in confusion, Hilary tilted her head to one side and squinted. "Serve and help—I *think* I understand." She stared at her feet for a few moments. It didn't really matter, did it? She'd agree to anything to keep from going to Hell. "Yes, ma'am."

"If these conditions are met, and you're willing to serve this person, you'll be granted the opportunity to change the circumstances surrounding your death. You see? Your wish will then be granted."

Hilary's hopes soared. "You mean I'll be alive again?"

"Yes, but remember, you need to concentrate on the people of Columbine. There must be someone who belongs there—*really* belongs—for you to help before the end of the year 1999." She sighed with a shrug. "If we don't place a time limit on Transitions, some people would remain in this uncertain state indefinitely."

"I . . . I think I understand."

Sarah nodded, but held up a warning hand. "Beware,

Hilary,'' she warned. ''Temptation takes on many disguises. And if this miracle should happen for you—and I do hope it does—remember that hatred is a sickness, even when that hatred seems justified. Do you know who I'm referring to, Hilary?''

Fear and guilt gripped Hilary. She'd hated someone almost all her life. How could she forget that, even in death?

A knot formed in her stomach. ''I'm ready.''

Chapter One

Columbine, Colorado—present day.

"A ghost town?"

Zach clenched his teeth in frustration, then kicked the tire of the used Jeep he'd traded his BMW for. "Nothing but a damned ghost town."

To say he was furious was the understatement of the century. Pacing, he shouted every cuss word he could think of and invented a few more. He'd given up a sixty-thousand dollar a year job . . . for this?

Congratulations, Mr. Ryan. Your uncle's left you an entire town in the Rocky Mountains.

"Yeah, right." Defeated, Zach leaned against the side of his Jeep and sighed. "My very own town. Now just what the hell am I supposed to do with it?"

Zach looked around him, toward the far end of town, then closer. The word *Columbine* was painted on the side of the nearest building, if a structure with only one wall standing could be called that. The other three had partially collapsed. The porch was falling off and an old hitching post in front of the decrepit structure sat at a bizarre angle.

Across the weed-choked road sat a small log cabin. *Great, my new home,* he thought bitterly. He'd already noticed squirrels climbing in and out through the nearest window. He couldn't very well displace the little critters, could he? What would he do with a bunch of homeless squirrels, and what would a bunch of homeless squirrels do to him?

"Damn."

Zach kicked the ground and started walking through the town. His town—but he hadn't expected it to be deserted. What he'd expected was a community with at least a few habitable buildings and maybe even some people. Jeez, what a radical idea. He'd planned to live here in Columbine. It was going to be his permanent home—a place to hide from the past and from himself.

A damned ghost town.

Shaking his head in disgust, he paused at the dead center of the tiny hamlet and turned in a circle. Less than a dozen buildings and only three of them were in one piece. The structure in the center of town was built of native stone. Next to it sat a smaller building with bars on the windows.

"Marshal Dillon, where are you?" Zach shouted, listening to his voice echo against the surrounding mountains.

There was no answer.

No Festus to help him out of a tight spot.

Not even a Miss Kitty to ease his pain.

There was one more building on the far side of town. Zach walked slowly toward it, mentally gutting all his plans with each step. No gambling casinos. No ski resort.

No money.

He winced with this recollection. *Real smart, Zach.* He'd spent the last dime of his employee savings plan to relocate from Los Angeles to Colorado. His savings account could hardly be called that now. He'd count himself lucky if he didn't starve before winter set in, and what happened after that was anybody's guess. The Rocky Mountains, even a city boy like Zach Ryan knew, would be deadly at nine thousand feet above sea level.

"Great, just great."

Pausing in front of the last building, he frowned. It was in pretty good shape, relatively speaking. He rubbed his eyes and opened them again, half-expecting to find this structure in the same condition as the others. But it was still standing and whole.

He scratched his head and looked up at the windows on the second floor. Three of them were broken, but the fourth one was intact—an absolute miracle considering the condition of the rest of the town. Gazing up at the window, he noticed the way sunlight glinted off its shiny surface.

Clean unbroken glass?

Perhaps he'd been mistaken about the town being abandoned after all. His hopes soared as he tentatively stepped onto the porch.

So far, so good. He hadn't crashed through the wood floor. He glanced up. And nothing had fallen on his head. He was on a roll.

The door was undamaged, though old and badly in need of paint. On either side, a pair of windows flanked the portal, each one boarded over.

His hopes plummeted.

If someone lived in the building, surely they would have repaired all the windows, especially on the main level. He reached for the doorknob, noting the rusted plate where a keyhole stared back at him, a lonesome harbinger of disaster.

And stupidity.

Chuckling to himself, Zach couldn't help feeling hopeful as he bit the inside of his cheek and turned the knob. Nothing.

"It's locked. Locked? Who the hell are they trying to keep out?" One lousy building in the whole town that he might actually be able to do something with, and he couldn't even get inside to look at it. "The hell I won't."

Zach braced himself and turned the knob as he slammed his shoulder against the portal.

"Ouch!"

It didn't budge. He jiggled the knob, then dug into his pocket in search of something to jimmy the lock with. He removed his pocket knife, then worked on the lock for several minutes, accomplishing nothing other than snapping off the tip of the blade.

"Oh, damn. Damn!" He stood back and kicked the door, then grabbed his foot and jumped up and down in pain. The wood was downright petrified.

"By God, I'm an engineer and I *will* get inside without breaking anything else—including my foot," he vowed.

Limping off the porch, he headed toward the back of the building. But his quest came to an abrupt halt when he came face to nose with a bear, even taller than the invisible rabbit who'd been his companion for most of Zach's adult life. It was the biggest bear he'd ever seen. The Los Angeles County Zoo just didn't grow them in the giant economy size.

"Holy Mother of . . ."

He backed toward the door, but the huge beast seemed curious—or hungry—enough to pursue him, making noises deep in its furry chest that sounded nothing like Gentle Ben or Smokey. If this was a hungry bear, which Zach was predisposed to believe all such creatures were, he was as good as lunch.

Pinned against the formidable front door, Zach swallowed hard when the monster planted one huge paw on either side of his face and just stood there on its hind legs, staring at its prey. The beast sniffed and exhaled in Zach's face. Its breath smelled like something had crawled inside it and died.

And I'm next.

So this was his fate. Zach Ryan, aerospace engineer, would end his less-than-memorable life in the intestines of a gigantic black bear. He closed his eyes for a moment, waiting for the creature to take its first bite, but nothing happened.

Peeking through one eye, Zach thought it was too good to be true. The beast simply groaned, dropped to all fours and turned away. Maybe he didn't like the smell of Californians who'd lived in smog all their lives.

"Off with you, silly old bear," a woman's voice commanded as she prodded the beast in the haunches with a long stick. "Go find a tree and scratch your back. There's nothing for you here."

Zach blinked and rubbed his eyes in disbelief as the bear lumbered away from town and vanished into the woods. He heaved a sigh of relief, then turned his gaze on the woman who seemed to have appeared from nowhere.

She was a curious creature, wearing a calf-length red dress with a wide black belt laced up the front, accentuating full breasts and a small waist. Though he would have enjoyed permitting his gaze to linger on the swells of flesh pressed above the belt, Zach looked downward and discovered shapely legs encased in red and black striped stockings. Interesting fashion accessory.

Looking back up the length of her, he noticed a prominent scar on her neck, marring her fair complexion. The red mark formed a perfect, hideous circle around her slender neck. Not wanting to be rude, Zach dragged his attention from the scar. After all, she had plenty of assets to admire.

Her golden hair was pulled away from her face and held with a comb at her crown, while the back and sides hung in soft curls nearly to her waist. She looked like . . .

Miss Kitty.

He must be imagining things. Besides, Miss Kitty had red hair, not blond. This woman was like something out of an old John Wayne movie. Or a fairy tale? If she was Goldilocks, he sure as hell hoped Mama Bear and Baby Bear weren't lurking nearby, waiting to take up where Papa'd left off.

He took a tentative step toward her, noting the way the sunlight shone in her hair as she stood staring at him, the makeshift bear-prod still clutched in her hands. She blinked at him with a pair of the largest blue eyes he'd ever seen.

She was beautiful.

Then she smiled and he thought for certain he must be imagining her. This gorgeous woman couldn't be out here alone, could she? Dressed like a saloon girl?

"I helped you. Didn't I?" she asked eagerly, dropping her long pole as he approached. "I'm Hilary Brown. Welcome to Columbine, sir."

"Ms. Brown." Zach extended his hand, waiting for her to shake it, but she simply stared at him. Assuming Rocky Mountain women must not be as liberated as those in Los Angeles—thank God—he grinned crookedly and nodded. "Yeah, if you hadn't come along I'd have been bear kibble in another minute. Thanks. You an animal trainer, or something?"

She frowned, smiled, then nodded vigorously, obviously undecided. Her eyes lit up like a child's on Christmas morning. "I'm sure glad to see you. *Really* glad." She sighed and mopped her brow with the back of her hand.

"It seems like forever since there's been a human in Columbine."

Zach shook his head and chuckled. "You mean another human." *Unusual woman.* She was way too young to be one of the hippie rejects who'd ended up in the mountains after the sixties, though she could be the offspring of one. That was a definite possibility.

She gave a nervous laugh and waved her hand as if dismissing her strange remark. "Never mind that." Her voice was like honey, warm and rich, flowing over him as she stood smiling in the sunlight. "What's your name, stranger?"

Miss Kitty, all right. Zach glanced upward once, almost afraid to wonder what other adventures awaited him today. "Zach Ryan." He looked around him, then back to her. "Do you . . . do you live here in Columbine?" It was too good to be true. His town really wasn't abandoned, after all.

"Live? Oh, yes, I do." Hilary stepped onto the porch, pausing very near him. "Born and raised. I suppose you could call me Columbine's longest—only—remaining resident."

She moistened her lips with her tongue, then glanced at him from the corners of her eyes, lowering her brownish-gold lashes in an almost seductive gaze. The scent of honeysuckle drifted up from her hair. She was warm and sweet. And friendly.

How friendly?

Down, Zach. You have more urgent matters to attend than your libido. Like food and shelter?

He chuckled and took a deep breath. "Here? In this building?" He ran his fingers through his hair and paused with his hand on top of his head, trying to ignore the longing ache which began in his loins. He swallowed hard. "Alone?"

She nodded, pursing her full red lips into a pout. "All by my lonesome." Her smile was downright sexy as she stared at him with those gorgeous eyes. "You just visiting— or staying?"

Zach smiled, wondering if he'd imagined her subliminal invitation. "Staying." He grabbed onto the porch railing and thanked his lucky stars. If there was even one person living in this godforsaken town, that meant it was at least habitable—sort of. He puffed up with assumed self-importance. "I own it."

Hilary tilted her head to the side. "The *whole* town?" She whistled low and stared at him in obvious awe. "You must be powerful rich to own the whole town. Why, Sean McCune wasn't even that rich."

"Oh?"

"He owned the bank. Ornery old cuss. He even took Miss Nellie's away from my . . . my mother." Hilary shook her head sadly. "But that was a long time ago."

Zach drew his brows together in confusion. "Miss Nellie's?"

She pointed to the building behind him, and her face turned as red as her satin dress. "The saloon and . . . and . . ."

Zach's imagination filled in the details. The woman was a prostitute? No, she couldn't be. In a ghost town? He chuckled and scratched his head. Well, she certainly didn't have to worry about safe sex with no customers.

"So, Ms. Brown, what do you *do* out here all alone?" Permitting his gaze to wander to where her breasts spilled out above her dress, he knew what he hoped she did. This was one fine-looking woman, and it appeared she was the lone resident of Columbine, Colorado.

Until today.

Hilary sucked in her breath, still amazed she even had breath after over a century in Transition. She'd had no idea how *physical* Transition would be when Sarah'd first mentioned it. Of course, that was only true of breathing. She didn't feel hot or cold. Hunger and thirst were merely faded memories.

This man was probably her last chance. She was desperate. Eternal Damnation awaited her if she failed to serve the right person at exactly the right time. What did she have to lose? Whatever he wanted was his.

Anything.

Squeezing her eyes shut, she almost laughed at the irony of her situation. The very thing she'd been trying to avoid when she'd died might now be her only salvation. When she opened her eyes, she was aware of his piercing brown gaze on her bosom. Lord, he was a handsome man. She could do worse.

She almost had.

Wincing in painful recollection, she bit her lower lip and gazed at him with what she hoped was a guileless expression. She intended to invite him to ask anything of her, if it would meet the requirements to set her free.

"Doing? Why, waiting for you, Mr. Ryan," she stated honestly. "I've been out here all by myself, just waiting for you to come along and save me."

And that's the truth.

He lazily arched one dark brow as his gaze raked her. There was a devilish gleam in his eyes that made her gasp in shock as she recalled Sarah's words.

Beware, Hilary. Temptation takes on many disguises.

She swallowed hard. A handsome man with a devilish gleam in his eyes, after all this time? Was he too good to be true? But what choice did she have? She didn't even know what year it was, having lost track back in 1929 when the last of Columbine's citizens moved away.

"Save you from what, Hilary?"

He said her name like it was set to music. She liked his

voice. It seemed to crawl right inside her and rumble around before settling low in her middle. A warm sensation crept over her. It felt strange, so much time had passed since she'd felt much of anything.

Was he the right one—or temptation itself?

She stared at him in silence, taking in his chestnut brown hair and eyes, his broad chest beneath a strange shirt with no buttons or studs. The word "Lakers" was spelled out in bold letters across the front. His dungarees hugged slim hips and muscular thighs.

His shoes were the strangest things she'd ever seen— white, almost like slippers. The word "Reebok" was printed on each shoe. She had no idea what that meant.

Shaking her head, she commanded herself to redirect her thoughts to more urgent matters. Her life, or rather her afterlife. This must be the real thing. Time was running out and Columbine had been deserted for many years. There'd been no one here for her to serve—until now.

"What year is it, Mr. Ryan?" she asked in a soft voice, praying she had enough time left to earn her way to Heaven. She closed her eyes, anticipating his answer with trepidation.

"Are you serious?" His laughter echoed through the empty town. "What *year* is it?"

Hilary's eyes shot open and she tapped her foot in vexation. "I am very serious, sir. Please just tell me what year it is."

Zach stared at her soberly. Obvious concern replaced the devilment in his expression. "Ms. Brown, are you ill?"

How could she be ill when she was already dead? And if he didn't damned well hurry up, she was sure to burn in Hell after all. "Please sir, the year?"

Sighing, Zach looked down at his unusual shoes, then back at her. "It's 1997."

Simultaneously shocked and relieved, Hilary swayed.

The stranger's steadying hand snapped out to grip her upper arm. She gasped, then stared down at his hand on her arm. No one had touched her since the hangman's noose was slipped around her neck. She hadn't imagined it was even possible. Though she possessed the ability to make herself visible at will—though only to strangers—it had never occurred to her that she could *feel* a man's touch.

It was marvelous.

She'd missed the companionship of other people, and if this handsome man was the right person—and she succeeded in finding a better way to serve him than running off a pesky old bear—she'd soon be alive again. In her own time, with Elliot. Before . . .

"Are you all right?" His voice was quiet and filled with concern.

He gripped her other arm and rubbed them both with his warm palms. Warmth was something she hadn't felt since her death either. It was comforting, soothing.

And something more . . .

Nodding, she forced a smile. "I was just surprised by the year," she confessed. "Relieved, actually. I thought it might be later."

Zach shook his head and frowned again. He dropped his hands to his sides. "So, you really live here in this building?" He waved toward the saloon behind them. His gaze was warm and questioning as it held hers. "All alone?"

Why did he keep asking if she was alone? Of course she was alone. She was a ghost, spirit, or whatever. In Transition, stuck here, waiting for *someone who truly belongs in Columbine.*

Someone who owned the whole town most certainly belonged. Hilary's hopes multiplied, then plunged. What did she do now? Sarah hadn't explained how Hilary was to receive her second chance. She'd only been told the circumstances necessary for such a miracle to occur.

Oh, cherish the thought. To eat and sleep, and feel alive again would be heavenly—almost.

"1997," Hilary repeated, closing her eyes to wish with all her might that she would open them to the bustling Main Street of Columbine in the nineteenth century. Blinking, she groaned. "Darn it."

"Excuse me?" Zach touched her shoulder very gently. "Are you sure you're all right?"

"Yes, I'm fine." She trembled when his hand fell away again, feeling strangely bereft. He was the right one. She knew it, sensed it.

Hadn't Sarah said she should serve some deserving person? What did Zach Ryan need? "Why are you here?" she asked, desperate to learn his plans so she could find other ways to help him. It couldn't hurt.

Zach laughed, but it wasn't a happy sound. His expression hardened. "Chasing rainbows, I guess," he said in a derisive tone, then sighed. "I inherited the town from an eccentric uncle I haven't seen in thirty years." He rubbed his chin with his thumb and forefinger, appearing lost—forlorn. "I guess he bought it up little by little as people moved away and kept it for some ridiculous reason. Who knows why."

Someone who truly belongs.

Stunned, Hilary turned away. Was he temptation? Or her liberator? How could she be certain? The answer was simple—she *couldn't* be sure. It was a risk she'd have to take.

A flood of emotion threatened her resolve. Was this too good to be true? Hilary swallowed convulsively as tears stung her eyes. *Tears?* Yet another sensation she hadn't felt since her journey toward the light. Another sign? Or was she imagining things?

"You're crying," Zach said, touching her on the shoulder. He very gently turned her to face him, cupping her chin in his big hand. His expression was soft and caressing. "Why are you crying, Hilary?"

She shook her head. "I'm sorry." Taking a deep breath, she willed her tears to cease. She'd better make him feel welcome in Columbine, before he turned around and left her alone—again.

Lifting her chin, she forced a smile to her lips. "You must be tired from your journey. Let me show you the inside of the only decent building left in Columbine. Of course, the bank and jail might not be too bad, if you want to have a look."

Zach dropped his hand away from her face, wondering how this woman had gotten along out here by herself. And why was she wearing such a ridiculous costume? Though it was only September, he couldn't help but believe she'd be cold in the skimpy outfit once evening came.

But evenings were probably when she did her best work.

That gnawing hunger in his loins commanded his attention again, but he successfully crushed it. Maybe later. At the moment, seeing the inside of his new property must take precedence.

Imagine that, Zach Ryan, recovering alcoholic, owner of his very own saloon. Irony with a twist. Now his life was complete. Casting a furtive glance at Hilary's cleavage again, he amended that thought.

Almost.

"I'd love to see it." He nodded his head toward the building. "Do you have the key?"

"Key?" She furrowed her brow in apparent confusion. "Oh, I never use a—oh, uh . . ." Blushing, she reached into her deep cleavage and withdrew an old skeleton key. "Here it is."

She laid it into his outstretched palm. Zach closed his fingers around the warm object, unable to prevent his

thoughts and his gaze from straying to the tempting place
from which it had been retrieved.

Was she a prostitute? Though he'd never engaged the
services of such a person before, he was definitely considering his options where this one was concerned. There was a
niggling voice—a self-righteous one—in his sub-conscious,
telling him he shouldn't be interested in sleeping with a
woman who'd shared her body with countless men. But
he was a firm believer in safe sex, and Zach Ryan was far
from turned off.

Damn, what he wouldn't give to sample her wares.

Banishing his entertaining thoughts, Zach cleared his
throat and stepped onto the porch, inserting the key in
the lock. Within moments, the old door swung open on
squeaky hinges.

"Wow." He walked into the saloon and froze. It was
undamaged but filthy from years of dust accumulation.
How could Hilary live like this? Chuckling, he decided he
didn't care. His hopes soared. Somehow, he'd make a go
of it. There was hope for Columbine yet. Turning toward
Hilary, he blinked.

She was gone.

He looked down at his palm, the key still warm from
being cradled between her breasts. Instinctively, he closed
his fingers around the object, felt her warmth radiate into
him. He didn't know where she'd gone, but whether she
realized it or not, she had herself a new neighbor.

A very interested one.

Chapter Two

Zach wasn't surprised to discover the second floor of Miss Nellie's revealed several bedrooms, all decorated in elaborate detail. There were once-beautiful, antique brass beds in each room, all badly in need of polishing and exterminating. After all, what self-respecting house of ill repute would be complete without beds?

As he opened the door at the front corner of the second floor, Zach sighed. This room was clean, liveable in a relative sense, and obviously taken. The crimson wallpaper flecked with gold was peeling in several places, but the bedding was clean and fresh, nothing less than a miracle. All the other mattresses in the building were infested with a broad assortment of creepy crawlers.

Except for this one. Hilary's room . . . ?

Where'd she disappear to? He had a multitude of unanswered questions running through his mind, and Hilary was the only person who could answer them. The only person, period.

Frowning, Zach walked around the room, lifting various objects as he passed. He shouldn't snoop, but couldn't resist a little investigation into the mystery woman's habits and habitat. An antique silver brush and comb sat on her dresser in front of a cracked mirror. On the washstand rested a chipped white pitcher and bowl.

He'd already figured out there was no indoor plumbing, no electricity or telephone.

Sighing, Zach sat down on the edge of the bed. What the hell was he going to do with his inheritance? It wasn't as if he had a huge savings account at his disposal. It would take a small fortune to run utilities to this desolate area, assuming it was possible at all. Without electricity and telephone service, Columbine would remain just what it was— a ghost town.

"Gee, I wonder if there are any real ghosts in residence?" He laughed at himself, then wondered if he should tempt fate. A strange sensation swept over him, almost as if someone was in the room—watching him.

He turned to look over his shoulder. The rocking chair in the corner moved very slightly. A vaguely familiar scent tugged at his memory. He sniffed the air. Dust and honeysuckle.

Of course, this was Hilary's room, so it made perfect sense that her fragrance would linger even when she wasn't here.

Zach stared at the chair for several minutes, until the eerie impression passed. He didn't believe in ghosts— never had. But the chair had definitely been moving when he first turned. Now still, an unmarred coating of dust covered the wooden seat.

Running his fingers through his hair, Zach decided it was just his imagination. Stress, without a doubt. Lord knew he had reason to feel stressed. Unemployment and homelessness did that to a person.

Laughing cynically, he turned away from the chair. Ghosts? They wouldn't dare. Zach Ryan would have no ghosts in *his* ghost town.

The window he'd noticed earlier, the clean unbroken one, beckoned to him. He stood and walked over to pull aside the tattered lace curtain.

Hilary was outside. "What is she . . ." Zach tapped on the glass, then realized he might crack the only unbroken window in town. "Damn. What does she think she's doing?"

Hilary Brown was climbing into his Jeep, striped stockings and all.

Panic attacked from all sides as he rushed to the door and down the stairs. If she stole his Jeep, he'd be stranded out in the middle of nowhere. It was a long walk down the mountain pass—not that he could possibly hope to find his way out of this desolate area without the topographical maps stored *in the Jeep*. Columbine was nowhere near a paved highway. It had taken nothing less than a miracle— and a good compass—for him to find it at all.

Flying out the front door and down the dusty street, he didn't stop until he hit the hood of the vehicle with both palms and his body. "What the hell do you think you're doing?" he demanded when she looked up at him with a round-eyed innocent expression. He panted, still leaning against the hood. "Get out of my car."

Hilary slid from the driver's seat. "I . . . I'm sorry." She bit her lower lip and looked down at her feet. "I didn't mean to hurt anything."

Zach wrinkled his brow in disbelief. Hadn't she been about to steal his Jeep? Why else would she be sitting in it, snooping around? "What were you doing? Trying to hot-wire it?"

"Hot-wire?" Hilary frowned and shook her head, blinking as she met his gaze. "I didn't do anything to it. I said I was sorry."

Zach gnashed his teeth to silence his retort, then walked around to the driver's side and peered into the vehicle. Everything seemed fine. After releasing a ragged sigh, he bit his lower lip. Maybe he'd been mistaken. "I'm sorry," he said quietly, feeling thoroughly chagrined. "I must've been mistaken. I shouldn't have accused you of trying to steal my Jeep." *Especially since I was snooping around in your room just a minute ago.*

She cast him a tentative smile, one that made his guilt build like the rumors about the single-bullet theory.

"What did you call this?" She stepped around the vehicle and ran her fingers along the dusty hood to the front end. "A . . . a sheep?"

"Sheep?" Zach stopped in surprise, then laughed out loud. It echoed through the empty town as he stared at her in disbelief. What an intriguing creature this woman was. One thing was absolutely certain—she'd keep him entertained. As his laughter subsided, her silence prompted him to arch a curious brow. "Are you serious?"

A splotchy blush crept up her bare neck and covered her face. "I've been out of circulation for a while."

Clearing his throat as he considered how much circulating she'd actually accomplished in her lifetime, Zach struggled with his rising hormones again. This woman was driving him nuts. "It's a *Jeep.*"

"Jeep," she repeated, then smiled as if she'd accomplished something noteworthy. "I saw you roll into town earlier." Her eyes lit up when she met his gaze again. "Over the years, I've seen other carriages like this pass through Columbine. But no one ever stayed long enough for me to get a really close look. I did get to peek inside a couple of them when no one was around, though." She shrugged, an expression of obvious awe across her face.

"I still can't fathom how they go without horses or steam. It must be some kind of magic."

"Magic? Try internal combustion." Which was exactly how this woman made him feel. *Spark, fire, internal explosion.*

He mopped his brow and tugged on the neckline of his T-shirt, shifting his weight as he contemplated relief for something else that was about to explode.

Then another thought made Zach frown. This woman was so strange. Should he be concerned about her sanity? Good Lord, was Hilary an escapee from a mental hospital? She could even be some kind of criminal—a serial killer. She sure acted loony.

"How does it go?" she asked again.

"You're serious," he stated rather than asked. Sighing, he decided it was better to play along. He didn't want to push her over the edge, not that she had two feet on solid ground even now. "Get in while I move it closer to, uh, Miss Nellie's. Then you'll see how it goes."

Hilary's pupils dilated and her mouth formed a perfect circle as she climbed into the driver's seat behind the wheel and gripped it with both hands. She smiled and exhaled in obvious anticipation. "I'm ready."

He stared at her incredulously, but had to chuckle at her enthusiasm. She must have been a high school cheerleader. "Move over there." He pointed to the other seat and slid in after she'd repositioned herself. Her honeysuckle scent permeated the air all around him. He swallowed hard, then stared at this unusual but gorgeous woman.

He could do worse—even if she was crazy.

Sighing, he fished into his pocket for the key and started the Jeep. The guys at Alcoholics Anonymous would love this one. When he glanced at her again, he noticed she was holding on to the edge of the seat so tight her knuckles had turned white. Her eyes widened. *Yep, she's nuts. Certifiable.* "Better buckle up."

"What?"

He reached across her for the shoulder strap, barely grazing her breast with his elbow. The urge to follow his elbow with his hand was nearly overwhelming. She was, without a doubt, the curviest woman he'd ever been this close to. He ached to touch her, taste her lips—and more—to discover the secrets she kept barely concealed.

His gaze met hers, riveted as he felt her nipple harden against his elbow. The expression in her eyes was his undoing—she wanted him, too. The realization made his libido achieve lift-off.

Why should he resist? She'd already indicated her availability—her experience. But if she really was mentally ill, should he take advantage of what she offered? Not very gentlemanly of him. Maybe he'd been mistaken. Besides, she was so damned sexy.

Sliding the back of his hand along her breast, Zach shifted until he faced her, then he allowed his hand to come flat against the side of her breast. Her pink lips were moist and slightly parted, begging to be kissed.

"What . . . what are you doing?" Her words were barely more than a tremulous whisper. Her eyes enlarged with silent inquiry.

He smiled, leaning slightly toward her until his lips almost brushed hers. "What do you think I'm doing, Hilary?" he asked, then leaned closer to press his mouth against hers as empty air replaced the woman in his arms.

He fell against the seat, patting and turning, searching with eyes and hands for the woman who'd been there just a moment ago.

She was gone.

His breath came in rapid, terrified gasps as he waited for the thundering in his ears to subside. Could he have imagined her? She couldn't just be here one minute and gone the next. People just didn't do that.

People didn't.

Zach pushed himself upright. His heart pounded savagely in his chest as he gripped the firm steering wheel in an attempt to anchor himself in reality. "You're losing it, Zach."

He chewed the inside of his cheek and fought against self-denial. "Nah, no way. I don't believe in that stuff."

And what about the bear? Had he imagined that, too?

Not likely. The smell of the beast's horrendous breath would remain with him the rest of his life, and probably longer.

As would the sweet scent of honeysuckle wafting up from Hilary's golden hair.

She was real. He'd felt her, smelled her, almost tasted her. Combing his fingers through his hair as his confusion mounted, Zach considered all the perplexing possibilities.

Was she a magician? A David Copperfield illusion right here in Columbine? Of course. It was the only explanation. What else could it be?

Despite his best efforts, another possibility crept into his thoughts. He had to face it. Maybe he was slipping and these were all warning signs, danger signals. He felt cold as he considered the consequences if this proved true, but he really didn't want a drink. He hadn't given alcohol so much as a passing thought since Denver.

Not as long ago as he'd hoped.

"Damn." He ran his hand over his face and took a deep breath. It didn't matter if he wanted a drink anyway. There wasn't a bar—a stocked one—for thirty miles in either direction.

Thank God.

With a nervous laugh, he dropped the Jeep into gear and drove slowly toward Miss Nellie's. All sorts of bizarre thoughts raged through his mind during the ninety second journey.

"That was amazing," a female voice said from the passenger seat.

"What the—" Zach hit the brakes hard, kicking up a cloud of dust for his trouble. There she sat, smiling as if nothing out of the ordinary had happened. Vanishing seemed as insignificant to Hilary Brown as breathing did to Zach. "What the hell happened to you? Where'd you go? How'd you do that?"

She batted her eyes and smiled. "I just . . . just moved away for a few minutes."

Zach shook his head and drove the vehicle around to the far side of the building, then set the parking brake and cut the engine. "Moved where?" He struck the dash with his fist, then winced in pain. God, he was really pissed now. "More importantly, *how?*"

Leaning his elbow on the back of his seat, he faced her. "I want to know who, and what, you are." *Convince me I'm not Elwood P. Dobbs and you're not Harvey, the six foot rabbit, even though I'm as sober as the day I was born.*

Hilary ventured a peek at his expression. His fury was undeniable. She was supposed to help him, not make him angry. Maybe she shouldn't have disappeared like that. But when he'd touched her, the way she'd felt had been frightening. She wasn't accustomed to feeling so out of control.

She winced. "I'm sorry," she said quietly, forcing herself to meet his gaze. He was probably her last chance. She just couldn't make a mistake with him. At least, not any more mistakes.

"Sorry? You're *sorry?*" Zach lifted his eyebrows and glowered at her. "Just sorry—for scaring the holy hell outta me?"

Hilary giggled and touched her flaming cheeks with her hands. "You were really scared? Of *me*?"

He nodded. "Petrified!" He continued to stare at her in open fury. "I'm glad you think it was funny, but I didn't find it amusing at all."

"I . . . I didn't think about that—of scaring you." Her laughter grew louder, then she forcibly quelled it. "I've never frightened anyone before." She searched her memory. "At least, I don't think I have."

Zach drew his brows together and frowned. "And I suppose you think that makes it all right to make me the first. What's all this supposed to mean?" He tilted his head to the side and narrowed his probing gaze. "Are you a magician?"

Hilary laughed even louder. "No, of course not. How silly." She dabbed at her eyes and sighed as her laughter subsided. If either of them was a magician, it was Zach Ryan. Remembering the way his elbow had brushed against her breast made her feel warm and lissome all over. It had been strange and wonderful.

And terrifying.

"All right, if you aren't a magician, then how do you explain what just happened?" He leaned closer. "Hilary, I want an answer."

She looked down at her lap for a moment and sighed. *Now what, Sarah?* Hilary wished there was a way for her to communicate with the angel. She needed answers to so many questions. Was there really any reason she shouldn't tell Zach the truth? Her goal was to get into Heaven, so honesty was by necessity her only viable option.

"Hilary?" His stern voice sounded angrier by the minute. "Tell me exactly what's going on. We're not going anywhere until I have some answers. Now!" He touched her upper arm, his gentleness in direct conflict with the sound of his fury.

The wonder of the human touch filled her. He made her feel peculiar—more substantial. Even though she'd maintained a certain level of substance throughout her Transition, this was different. It was as if he shared a part of himself with her that made her more *real.*

But she wasn't real in a physical sense of the word. Was she? Sarah hadn't explained how she fit into nature's realm—if at all. What was Hilary Brown? Not a ghost, surely. She had too many physical attributes to be a real ghost. Didn't she? She breathed air and her heart thumped an erratic rhythm in her chest. She was dead . . . or was she?

Hilary met his gaze. A modicum of concern mingled with the anger in his brown eyes. She couldn't recall anyone but Elliot, and occasionally her mother, having shown concern for her welfare before.

Of course, Nellie Brown's maternal concern had always been given with a large dose of reluctance . . . and withdrawn entirely when Hilary'd needed it most. Hilary tried to suppress the surge of anger which swept through her. It was the hatred Sarah'd warned her about, still manifest after all these years.

"Hilary? I'm waiting for an answer."

The truth she told herself. Taking a deep breath, she turned to face him straight on. "Zach, I'm . . ." *What am I?* Again, she was stymied about her identity, the way she fit into the world—or between worlds. Being unable to define herself was an absolutely ridiculous situation. Getting angry about it certainly wouldn't help, so she gave him a helpless shrug instead.

Zach sighed and closed his eyes for a moment. "Who— or *what*—are you?"

Her laughter stopped straightaway. "I'm not sure." How could she explain this so he would understand? *She* didn't understand after a century. How could she expect someone who'd only known her a few hours to accept her situation? There was only one simple answer he might accept. "I guess I'm a—sort of a—ghost?"

Zach leaned against the door and simply stared at her. His expression was fathomless for several moments as he rubbed his chin with his thumb and forefinger. Finally, a sparkle began in his brown eyes. "A ghost?" One corner of his mouth twitched as he obviously suppressed a grin. "Halloween's still six weeks away, Hilary. It's too soon to go trick-or-treating."

"To go what?"

"Right. Pretend ignorance. You really expect me to believe you're a ghost?"

Hilary bristled. "Well, I *think* that's what I am. I know for certain I'm not an angel. I was almost an angel." She fidgeted and twirled a strand of hair around her index finger. "I'm just not sure. I told you that. When the angel, Sarah, sent me back to Columbine she didn't explain exactly what—"

Zach groaned out loud. "I don't believe this." He looked up at the sky and ruffled his hair with his fingers until it stood up on end. When he looked at her, his expression no longer held a trace of humor. "I quit my job and sunk every dime I had into coming to Colorado—for *this*?"

Hilary nervously chewed her lower lip, realizing his laughter hadn't originated from humor, after all. It had been a bitter, desperate sound. He needed help.

Help?

Her heart soared. Zach Ryan *was* the right person. She needed to help him through some personal difficulty. What did he need help with most? How could she do it? If she stayed close to him, maybe she'd find a way.

But the slightest thought of being close to Zach Ryan made her hungry for something she knew she shouldn't feel or want.

Something less-than-angelic, to say the least.

Hilary reached out to touch his arm. She needed the assurance he was really here. After so many years of loneliness, it was difficult to accept the fact that she was no longer alone. Trying not to tremble, she absorbed his warmth and substance. "What's wrong, Zach? How can I help?" *Please let me help*.

He covered his eyes and moaned. When he dropped his hands to his lap and looked at her, she recognized a helplessness that tugged at her heart.

And gave her renewed hope.

He laughed again. Bitterly. "I really don't think you'd understand." He turned and removed the key from the strange column, then dangled it in front of his eyes for a few moments. "This is really just perfect, though." He chuckled. "Hollywood couldn't have concocted a more perfect ending to a day like today. Indiana Jones would love it, I suppose. Perfect."

Frowning, Hilary squinted to study his handsome face. "What's perfect? And who's this Indiana Jones person?" She held her hands out in a gesture of helplessness. "I don't understand."

He suddenly closed his fingers around the keys and leapt from the Jeep. He ran around to her side, jerked open the door and gripped her hand, pulling her out to stand before him. His insolent gaze raked her. "A ghost, huh? Nope, I don't think so."

One corner of his mouth curved downward and he placed both his hands on her shoulders. His thumbs made little circles along her bare flesh at the base of her neck. Tiny shivers of excitement skittered down her spine.

Oh, Sarah, is this the temptation you warned me about?

The longing ache began as a slight tugging sensation deep in her belly. But as his caresses continued, the ache turned to all-out hunger. Her insides felt like a watch wound too tight. A spring of tension coiled in her tummy, just aching to burst with the slightest impetus.

But she was dead and shouldn't feel these things.

Zach's expression hardened—an unusual glimmer appeared in his brown eyes she hadn't noticed before. His face was so close to hers his breath was a warm caress against her cheek. She felt everything with an intensity, a terrifying sense of reality, which left her stunned.

"Ghosts are dead, Hilary," he whispered, inching his lips toward hers. "Dead people are cold. You're warm and sexy, just what the doctor ordered."

Her head swam with delicious, wanton thoughts as he barely grazed her mouth with his. Rivulets of desire originated in her center and scattered throughout her body. As he deepened the kiss, Hilary felt his probing tongue seeking entrance. She granted it, moaning in anticipation.

Zach wrapped his arms around her shoulders, pulling her hard against his lean, muscular body. The contact was explosive, rocking her very foundation as rational thoughts eluded her every effort.

Help him . . .

Hilary endeavored not to think about Sarah's words right now. They were dangerous and tempting. What had the angel meant about love? Surely not physical love between a man and woman.

He growled deep in his throat when she returned his hungry kiss with tentative explorations of her own. His tongue surveyed and tasted her, making Hilary's head reel with remarkable surges of pleasure.

There was no doubt, this must be temptation. It was by far the most tempting sensation she'd ever known—dead or alive.

Her breasts pressed hard against his chest. He brought his hand around to the side of her rib cage, stroking her aching flesh through her dress. Slowly, he inched his hand upward and forward until he grazed the exposed upper curves of her bosom with his callused fingertips.

She accommodated and recklessly encouraged his efforts as his tongue dueled with and stroked hers. Just when she thought she'd suffocate—if she weren't already dead—from his devastating kiss, he withdrew, only to repeat the entire wondrous process. She whimpered in his arms, trembled with desire. She wanted this, wanted him.

He lowered his hand to her breast. To Hilary's amazement, she felt its peak pucker and grow as he traced teasing circles around it with his thumb. She pressed her hips against him, the throbbing in her loins increasing to a nearly unbearable level.

Cupping her entire breast in his hand, he dragged his mouth from hers, then kissed his way down the side of her throat. She leaned her head backward, arching her body forward to offer more of her eager flesh.

Trailing his finger along the lace trim at the top of her bodice, Zach gently eased his fingers inside, compelling Hilary to draw a sharp breath. Within moments her bare breast was exposed to the cool mountain air . . . and at his mercy.

Muttering something unintelligible, he found the sensitive peak with his tongue while she gasped and pressed herself against him.

"Zach," she whispered when his lips closed over the tip of her breast and drew it deeply into his mouth. She immersed her fingers in the curling brown hair at his nape, then wantonly clutched him to her. A gasp of animalistic pleasure was the only sound she made or heard.

He nipped her with his teeth, suckled and kneaded her flesh. She couldn't have imagined in five centuries of Transition, let alone one, that a man's touch could feel anything like this.

Hilary's head reeled. She was stunned by her physical

reaction to Zach. This man was dangerous. No lingering doubt remained—he was wonderful, glorious temptation.

The hard, burgeoning ridge at the front of his jeans made her insides coil even tighter with an alien hunger. She was desperate to feel this man *do* things to her.

Anything he wanted.

Her dress felt tight and uncomfortable as he pressed himself against her through their combined layers of clothing. The emptiness deep inside her demanded satisfaction.

That thought brought her back to reality in a rush. How could she think, let alone *do,* something like this if she wanted to get into Heaven? Sarah would surely send her to Hell if Hilary succumbed to the evils of the flesh.

She'd be no better than her mother.

But the delicious waves of longing that swept through her didn't feel at all wrong. Having Zach pressed so intimately against her felt so very, very right. If only their clothing wasn't in the way.

No better than Nellie Brown.

Zach pressed her back against the hood of the Jeep, lifting the hem of her skirt and grinning lasciviously. "No panties," he murmured, stroking the inside of her thigh with the tips of his rough fingers. "And garters."

Hilary moaned when his caressing fingers grew bolder in their quest, stroking the tender flesh along the inside of her knee. She trembled in anticipation, trying all the while to force logic and reason back to her mind.

She must resist—this was wrong. "No," she murmured unconvincingly. Placing her hands on his forehead, she tried to push him away. "No." *I'm* not *like my mother.*

"Yes," Zach whispered, lowering his head to kiss her again while he found her exposed breast with his hand. "Oh, yes."

Why the hell not? Zach asked himself. No woman had ever tasted sweeter than this unusual creature. His mind and body were in a whirlwind of desire and a torrent of raw sexual need. The insistent throbbing between his legs required release.

Was she really a prostitute? Lord, he'd never considered this option before today, but he was a firm believer in being open minded. She'd made a sure sale without even trying. He was a pushover for her product.

There was no reason to hold himself back, despite her superficial protests. He had protection with him, and it was obvious she wanted him every bit as much as he wanted her. The way she moaned and pressed herself against him was evidence enough. He couldn't think of a single reason why he shouldn't indulge himself this once.

Maybe twice.

A maddening urge to take her right here on the hood of his Jeep possessed him. This macho stuff wasn't his usual style, but there was something about this woman that brought out the best, the worst and the beast in him.

Kissing his way back up to her swollen lips, he reached behind and cupped her buttocks, lifting her up and against him. Through his jeans, his insistent body sought the tender secrets she kept hidden within her skirt.

Ghost, hell. Hilary Brown was a warm, pliant and very eager woman, just what he needed to help him forget about this mess. Lord knew he needed a break after being stuck with a lemon like Columbine.

Zach closed his eyes in anticipation of tasting her sweet lips again, only to find his arms empty and his mouth coming into contact with the dusty hood of his Jeep. Spitting on the ground, he stepped away from the vehicle and looked around, frantically searching for any sign of Hilary.

She was gone—again.

His heart pounded in his chest like a road crew's jackhammer on the Santa Ana Freeway. A cold chill swept through his overheated body as the evidence assailed him.

Impossible.

He leaned against the wall behind him; his head hit with a soft thud. ''This can't be real,'' he whispered, swallowing hard. A cold sweat coated his flesh, dousing his arousal in a hurry. He closed his eyes and took several deep breaths, then looked at his Jeep again.

Was Hilary Brown really a ghost?

Chapter Three

Zach opened his eyes to glaring sunlight. However, the brightness of the sun bore no relevance to the temperature of the air. He shivered and tugged his inadequate blanket beneath his chin. It was cold. Damned cold.

"It's only September." He sat up in the back seat of his Jeep and squinted. "Where am I gonna sleep when it really gets cold? And snows?"

If he'd wanted to find out what it was like to live as a homeless person, he could've done that in L.A.—where it stayed warm. And never snowed.

He rubbed his chin and started to climb out to find a friendly tree, but an unexpected sound made him hesitate. It was a woman's voice—singing.

The song was unfamiliar, but her voice was lovely. He crawled out of the Jeep and walked around to the front of Miss Nellie's. When he gazed up, he noticed Hilary's window was open. He saw her move past it while she continued to sing.

The melody crept inside him and did a little dance, reminding him again of how close he'd come . . .

"Damn." He swallowed with difficulty and kicked at the ground in frustration. He could have been in her nice warm bed, but no. Instead, through the use of some mysterious technique Zach couldn't begin to decipher, Hilary Brown had vanished again, spurning his advances.

She was nuts—he'd already established that. But was she a nutty magician, or a nutty ghost?

Either way, she was the sexiest female he'd ever encountered. His body hardened with renewed desire and he cursed himself as a fool.

He had work to do. Either he'd fix the place up a little and try to sell it, or—just maybe—he could turn it into a resort of some kind. There was always the rather remote possibility that he could persuade some reckless investors to join him in the venture. Then he might be able to run utilities and renovate. He could turn the little town into a place people would want to visit. Maybe some courageous souls might even want to make Columbine their home.

Like he'd imagined before he actually saw the place.

Disappointment assailed him again, and Zach turned to walk toward the trees behind Miss Nellie's. There wasn't even an outhouse in the town, let alone a bathroom. But humans had been seeing to their natural urges and needs for centuries before the advent of indoor plumbing. Zach could handle this.

As he made his way back to town in search of something resembling breakfast, Zach suddenly remembered the bear. "Oh, shit," he muttered as his gaze darted from tree to tree. He hoped bears weren't early-risers.

The early bear gets the engineer?

Zach decided that a bear was definitely behind any one of the thousand trees within the scope of his vision—with company. Running scared was, without a doubt, the safer part of valor.

Bolting around the side of Miss Nellie's, he silently cursed himself for not checking for a back door earlier. Now sure as hell wasn't the time to conduct a search.

When he dashed through the front door of the old saloon, Hilary was standing at the base of the stairs staring at him. He huffed and puffed, leaning against the closed door in extreme relief.

She smiled.

Now why in the world would she smile at him after what had almost happened between them last night? Unless she was having second thoughts about her refusal. And about vanishing.

Zach couldn't help himself. Despite his earlier fury, not to mention being unreasonably terrified of her for a while, he returned her smile. It was impossible to remain angry with her for very long. She was too damned pretty and friendly. And such a talented magician. Maybe, if he ever got Columbine up and running, Hilary could perform. Of course, she'd have to come to grips with reality first.

"Good morning, Zach," she greeted him as if nothing had almost happened between them. She walked across the broad expanse of scarred flooring to stand in front of him. "You're out of breath. Have you been running?"

"Yeah, the bear. Shouldn't bears be going into hibernation soon?" Zach shook his head and chuckled at himself. He patted himself on the chest and took a deep breath. "Never mind. I guess it must be the altitude."

"Oh, you'll get used to it." She smiled again. "I was born up here, so it never bothered me. This happened to all the miners when they first arrived, though."

"Miners?" Frowning, Zach moved toward the bar and leaned against it while she walked around the room, touching things with her long slender fingers. He couldn't prevent mental images of those hands on his body from flashing through his mind. Damn, the woman oozed sensuality.

"Yes, Columbine was a mining town." She stopped near him and ran her fingertips along the bar. "But you must have already realized that. Didn't you?"

Zach nodded and released an exasperated sigh. "Yeah, I remember reading about it. But Columbine was a mining town about a hundred years ago."

"That's right." She smiled again and batted her eyes at him. "Remember, I was here. I'm a ghost—sort of a ghost."

Here we go again. He'd tried to tell himself that her vanishing act could have been ghostly, but it just didn't wash. *He* didn't believe in ghosts. It was ridiculous. Hilary Brown suffered from delusions.

Period.

And she was doing a damned fine job of trying to drag him right along with her. "Sure." He reached out to touch her arm, but she shied away. "A ghost. You can be Merlin the Wizard if you want. Whatever you say, as long as you point me toward food. I'm starving."

"Food?"

Count to ten, Zach. He ran his fingers through his hair again and looked upward. This was becoming more difficult by the minute. "I don't expect you to wait on me, Hilary. I can cook. I've been a bachelor all my adult life. I'll fix it myself." Silence. *"Food,* Hilary—as in breakfast?"

"Yes, I remember. I liked food." She sighed, then shrugged. "But I don't have any."

He barked a cynical laugh and covered his eyes for a few minutes. "Never mind. For some stupid reason, I thought there'd be stores and a nice hotel with a restaurant up here. Imagine that. Otherwise I would've brought food with me." Sighing, he moved toward the door. "I'll just grab a yummy, nutritious, not very filling, granola bar from the Jeep.''

When he stepped outside, Zach was pleased to find the sun had warmed the air considerably. The sky was bright blue. The mountain peaks in the near distance displayed a stark contrast between their treeless summits and wooded slopes. A white glacier glittered in the sun on one bald face. The little town of Columbine was surrounded by high peaks and pine forests. It was breathtaking. But why'd it have to be abandoned?

Except for one loony, gorgeous, woman?

He sighed and went to rummage through the back of the Jeep for a cereal bar. His stomach knotted angrily when he rewarded it with the dry fare. "Oh, for steak and eggs," he muttered, chuckling. "And I'd kill for a cup of coffee . . . or intravenous caffeine."

"Mmm, coffee," Hilary said dreamily, startling him. She was standing right beside him, but he hadn't heard her approach. "I haven't had coffee since before I died. I liked it with sweet cream. Matilda always made wonderful coffee. Of course, Mama always put whiskey in hers."

Whiskey? I'd better not think about that right now. I'm on a bizarre enough trip without chemical assistance. Zach bit his lower lip to prevent his retort. Her little game was getting old, except she couldn't be doing this deliberately. It made no sense—she had no discernable motive. She must be genuinely insane.

Yep—bonkers.

Either that, or she was telling the truth. *Okay, Zach, now you're losing it.* He cleared his throat, commanding himself to maintain control. He'd just try to play along as much as possible.

"Cream, yeah, but hot and black would suit me just fine." Zach put the last of the granola bar into his mouth, chewed furiously for a few minutes, then swallowed hard.

"I have more. You want one? It's better than nothing, which must be the alternative." He lifted a questioning brow, hoping she'd end her charade and produce a fully stocked kitchen somewhere in Columbine.

She shook her head. "I don't eat food, Zach." She laughed as if the mere notion of her eating was the most ridiculous thing she'd ever heard. "I haven't even felt hunger for a long time."

"Okay." Zach grinned to himself and straightened. Enough of this. It was leading nowhere fast. "Where do you get water?"

"I don't drink water, either." Hilary smiled in her infuriatingly sweet way. "But there's a clear stream about a hundred yards behind the saloon." She shuddered. "Of course, once winter comes you'll have to melt snow for water."

"Gee, thanks for reminding me." Zach turned and started walking toward the stream, then he caught himself whistling "Unchained Melody" and stopped short.

There's no such thing as ghosts.

He drew in a deep breath, took another step, then remembered the bear. Papa Bear, Mama Bear or Baby Bear? It didn't matter. They were all great big *hungry* bears as far as he was concerned. "Uh, Hilary?"

"Yes?" She stood beside his Jeep with the sun glinting off her golden hair.

Goldilocks. "Would you like to come along?" *And bring your bear prod with you?* Some macho mountain man he was turning into. Grizzly Adams would be ashamed.

She nodded eagerly and ran toward him. Zach was mesmerized by her bouncing figure as she approached. Swallowing was nearly impossible.

Breathing wasn't exactly easy.

It was a miracle he didn't pass out on the spot, the way his blood supply redirected itself in record time. He tugged at the neckline of his T-shirt when she paused beside him. "It's warming up fast."

Hilary smiled and nodded. "Even in the winter, if there's sunshine, it feels warm." She pointed through the trees. "Do you have a bucket?"

"Bucket?" Zach was so engrossed with this gorgeous woman at his side, it took him a few moments to comprehend what she'd asked. "Oh, I don't need one. I'll just fill my canteen. It won't hold much, so I'll just have to come back for more when I need it." He patted the container hooked to his belt.

"Would you like a tour of the rest of Columbine after you get your water?"

"Sure, what there is of it." Her eagerness was engaging, though she seemed determined to ignore what had almost happened between them. It was tough, but he'd give it a try. "Are you going to be my official tour guide?"

She nodded, walking slowly at his side. "Columbine used to be a busy place. It wasn't all good, mind you, but bustling." The expression in her blue eyes was solemn. "Of course, that was before the murders started, and Elliot found the mother lode. After that—"

"Murders? The mother lode? I remember reading about the big gold strike, but not the murders." Zach chuckled. "Man, I'll bet that discovery was something. I read up on Columbine after I found out about my inheritance."

She pursed her lips in an expression of obvious disapproval. "That big gold strike was the worst thing that could've happened to Columbine. The place was crawling with miners. They abandoned their families, gave up their entire lives just to find gold. They weren't all that way. There were some good family men, who brought their wives and children with them." She blinked rapidly as if fighting tears. "But some even killed each other over the wretched gold. It started before and continued after I died.''

After I died? Zach took a deep breath and shrugged. Arguing with Hilary about her status among the living would obviously be a waste of time. "That was a long time ago, Hilary."

"You still don't understand, do you?" She clicked her tongue and rolled her eyes. "Columbine is abandoned now *because* of that gold. They actually didn't hit the real mother lode until after I was gone. Poor Elliot." She sighed. "Of course, after I died it was—"

"Yeah, I guess so." Zach couldn't stand to hear her talk this way. She wasn't dead, so he certainly didn't want to hear the tale of her death. He noticed the sound of water rushing over rocks and quickened his pace. "Here's the stream."

"The aspen leaves are almost gone, now," Hilary said quietly while Zach stooped to fill his canteen. "They were beautiful a few weeks ago."

Zach looked around, noticing a few bright gold leaves fluttering in the gentle breeze. Mingled among the dark pine trees, the golden leaves seemed almost iridescent. The way each leaf fluttered individually was exquisite.

"Pretty," he agreed, taking a drink of cold water as he stood. "Sure hope I don't get hepatitis."

"Hepatitis?"

"From the water." Zach took another sip. "Sure you don't want some?"

Hilary gave him a wry smile. "I told you, Zach. I never eat or drink anything. I haven't for a hundred and eleven years."

"Ooookay. Have it your way." Zach smiled patronizingly and turned toward town. "I'm ready for my tour."

Hilary nodded and started walking. She loved this season. September was by far the sunniest month of the year.

Soon, snow would begin to fall and the entire area would be clean and white.

Would Zach stay with her through the winter? She glanced at him from the corner of her eye, noting the dark stubble that marred his handsome face. Even with that, he was the most appealing man she'd ever seen.

The thought of spending another winter alone made Hilary tremble. She couldn't stand it. So many lonely years in Transition . . .

Was Zach her liberator? Was he the person in need who truly belonged—the one Sarah had meant?

Would he try to kiss her again?

Hilary held her breath as she grew warm all over again. It was strange enough to feel warmth, let alone desire. She'd been dead so long such sensations seemed quite foreign to her, not that she'd had much experience with desire during her lifetime. Whenever Zach touched her, she started feeling things she hadn't felt since death, and many things she'd never experienced at all. She felt more substantial. More stable. Was all this some sort of sign?

Would she be given her second chance soon? Would she be able to help Elliot?

A wild thrill swept through her, then she looked at Zach again. For some reason, the thought of leaving him disturbed her.

But that's ridiculous. I hardly know him.

"So, tell me what this building was." Zach stopped in front of the small stone building in the center of town.

"The bank." Hilary placed one hand on her hip and tilted her head to the side. "The mighty Sean McCune's bank."

"Sean McCune? Interesting name. Sounds like he was probably quite a character in his day. Which was . . . when?" Zach's brows arched speculatively. "How many decades ago, Hilary?"

Hilary rolled her eyes. "At least ten, I'd say." She swallowed hard and fought the churning in her stomach. She almost felt hungry. How strange. "His son was horrible. Sean was pretty bad, but Baird's bad manners made Sean seem almost pleasant. But later, I discovered that Sean was . . . the more evil one."

"Baird and Sean McCune? I think I must've read something about them, but I can't remember what it was. The names are familiar. Were they Irish miners? I've read about some of their antics. Horrible, huh?" Zach's mouth twitched as if suppressing a chuckle. "And how would you know that? Oh, that's right. How could I forget that minor detail? You were here—or think you were—way back when."

"Are you making fun of me, Zach?" Hilary turned to face him, lifting her chin a notch.

Zach laughed out loud. "I'm sorry, Hilary, but you're so damned serious about all this."

She sniffed and elevated her chin another notch. "Of course. Why wouldn't I be? It's the truth."

Zach stopped laughing and just stared at her. The expression in his eyes softened to pity. "Never mind. I'm sorry." He turned and looked up at the tallest mountain. "Where does that trail lead?"

Hilary shuddered. "The . . . the Maggie-O."

"A mine?" Zach took a step toward the trail. "Let's go have a look."

"No!" Hilary grabbed his hand. "We mustn't."

"Why?" Zach turned to face her. "What's wrong, Hilary?"

She trembled as memories assailed her. The murders. The ghost.

Hilary really should laugh at the irony. After all these years, she hadn't ventured up to the Maggie-O but once. That terrible day, a few weeks after her own death . . . If only she'd been able to make herself visible to those who'd known her during her natural life. Like Elliot.

"What is it, Hilary?" Zach's expression filled with concern. "You look as if you've seen a . . ." He bit his lower lip and drew a deep breath. "You won't believe this, but I almost said ghost."

She nodded, then looked away. "I didn't see it, but others claimed it was there. A long time ago."

"Another ghost?" Zach clicked his tongue. "My, Columbine's filling up fast. Is this a friend of yours? Do you go haunting together?"

"It's not funny." Hilary trembled and hugged herself, seeking non-existent warmth. "I wish it were."

"I'm not laughing anymore, Hilary." He rubbed her arm with his hand. "Not now. I didn't realize how upset you were about this. I'm sorry."

She looked up at him and saw concern and pity. If there was one thing Hilary Brown hated, it was pity. Offended, she thrust aside memories of the Maggie-O ghost and turned toward the far end of town. It was past time to change the subject. "The small cabin on the left was the schoolhouse." She paused and faced him, anticipating a challenge. "I was the teacher."

Zach's eyebrows shot up and his lips twitched again. "And was this the uniform you wore to school each day, teacher?" He touched the red ruffle on her sleeve.

Hilary shuddered. His taunt brought back a flood of memories she'd hoped never to experience again. "How dare you insult me? Of course this isn't what I wore to school. This isn't even mine. I was forced to wear it when . . ." She turned away, but his grip on her upper arm halted her movement. "Just let me go, Zach."

"Hilary, you've got to stop lying to yourself about all this," Zach said soberly. There was no trace of humor remaining in his tone. "You can't be dead. Ghosts are nothing but figments of over-active imaginations. There's no such thing."

Hilary blinked back the tears which stung her eyes. *Tears again—what's next?* "Zach, I told you last night I'm not exactly sure I'm a *real* ghost. In fact, I don't think that's true at all. I just couldn't think of any other way to explain it to you. There isn't a word I know of to describe what I am." She sighed. "I'm dead. I was . . . was . . ."

She shuddered as the distressing memories tore at her anew. Her death had been such a horrifying ordeal. The sensation of plummeting through the trap door with the noose around her neck was vivid. Elliot's terrified expression just before she'd been blindfolded . . .

Inadvertently, she touched the mark on her neck and swallowed hard. She struggled against the rising terror which threatened to destroy her resolve. "Please, it's too painful. I don't want to talk about this."

Zach touched her shoulder. "I'm sorry." She heard him sigh loudly. "I didn't mean to upset you."

Hilary trembled when his hand made contact with her bare shoulder above the taffeta sleeve-ruffle. Again, she felt peculiar when he touched her. It was terrifying yet exhilarating.

She nodded, then swung her head to stare at his hand against her fair skin. She raised her gaze and met his. He stood so very close; incredibly heady sensations swept through her.

Why couldn't she have found a man like Zach Ryan when she was alive? Why now, when it was too late—much too late?.

"I need to start working on Miss Nellie's." Zach looked down the street. His expression seemed tormented. "Winter'll be here soon, and this is the only building worth anything as far as I can tell. And that's debatable." He chuckled and shrugged, letting his hand fall away from her shoulder. "At the very least, I need to clean up one of the rooms today so I'll have a place to sleep tonight. I froze my butt off last night."

Hilary nodded and looked away. Unspoken words hung in the air between them. She could fill in part of them. He'd slept in his Jeep last night, cold and alone because she was a coward. "Yes, winter will be here soon," she said, realizing how inadequate such a statement was, when compared to the reeling emotions sweeping through her. Would she have another long, lonely winter? Or would Zach stay?

"I stopped in Divide and talked to a realtor yesterday morning on my way up here," he said, chuckling. "I thought the poor guy was going to have a heart attack, laughing so hard, when I told him what I'd inherited." His expression darkened. "Now I know why."

"Realtor?" Hilary walked alongside Zach, watching his inspiring profile, and the magical way his brown eyes sparkled and crinkled at the corners whenever he smiled. "What's that?"

Zach cast her a look of open disbelief. "Ah, Hilary." He looked upward and sighed, then lowered his chin to his chest. His lips moved slightly as if he was talking to himself. "Ten." He released a breath in a loud sigh. "A realtor is someone who helps people buy and sell property, for a percentage of the selling price."

Hilary froze, tugging on his sleeve to keep him from walking away. "Zach? Are you planning to . . . to sell Columbine? Miss Nellie's? My home?"

He shrugged. "I may not have any choice, Hilary." He stopped and faced her, reaching out to brush the backs of his fingers along her cheek. "Unless I can find some foolish investors, I won't be able to afford the cost of having utilities run up here—if it's even possible. It wouldn't surprise me to hear Ma Bell laugh her ass off at the notion."

"Utilities? Ma Bell? Who . . ." She chewed her lower lip in confusion, wishing she understood all the strange things he talked about. "I don't—"

"Of course, you don't." Zach rolled his eyes and dropped his hand to his side with a sigh. "Dammit, Hilary."

"I'm sorry, but I really don't understand." Apprehension filled her. How could he even consider selling her home? What would happen to her if someone came in and tore down Miss Nellie's? Where would she go? Sarah hadn't mentioned what would happen to Hilary if something like that were to happen.

"And I can't explain it to you." Zach slapped his thigh and grabbed her hand. "C'mon. Let's go back to Miss Nellie's. I wanted to at least clean the place up a little before the realtor comes."

"Someone's coming up here?" She allowed him to lead her into the saloon, making no effort to pull her hand from his grasp even after they were inside. "Really coming here—to Columbine? Today?"

Zach squeezed her hand and nodded. "I already told you, Hilary. I asked a realtor to come up and look the place over—just in case."

"In case you decide to sell it." Hilary's hand fell dejectedly from his grasp. She turned away, desperately needing some time to herself to think. "I'm going upstairs for a while." What was she going to do? The man she'd thought of as her liberator could become her executioner.

All over again.

"So, what do you think, Mr. Ralston?" Zach stood back, waiting for the man to complete his appraisal. "Think someone might be interested in investing up here? It's gorgeous country."

The man shook his head and sighed, tugging at the

waistband of his jeans. His huge belly hung out over a wide
belt buckle boasting the word "Coors" negating any doubt
as to the cause of his rotund abdomen.

"I gotta tell you, Mr. Ryan," he said. "These places
aren't worth the taxes owed on them. If folks want to open
gambling casinos, Cripple Creek's not far from here. I'm
sure you must realize you're a long way from civilization
here. *And* utilities."

"Yeah." Zach scratched his head, wondering what he
was being punished for, then recalled with a flinch of
anguish the night of his brother's death. He took a deep
breath and forced the devastating memory away—for now.
"Oh, believe me, I've already thought of all this."

"Without utilities, you can't do anything up here. No
casinos, ski resorts—nothin'." The man walked around
the main room of Miss Nellie's, then withdrew a pad of
paper from his pocket and made a few notes. "I might
know one client interested in a place this desolate. He's sort
of a Howard Hughes type. Real eccentric." He shrugged.
"Never hurts to ask."

"Well . . ." Zach glanced up the stairs, thinking of Hilary.
"I'm not sure I want to sell it. Maybe he'd like to be an
investor, though." He chuckled. "Color me nuts, but I'm
kind of attached to Columbine." *And its lone resident.* "Did
you knock on the door of that front bedroom upstairs?
It's in pretty good shape."

Ralston chuckled. "I knocked, but nobody answered, so
I went inside. You're right, it's not bad, but it still don't
have a telephone, electricity, running water—or a toilet."

"Nobody was in there?" Zach looked anxiously up the
stairs again. "You're sure? You didn't see an attractive
blonde wearing a red dress?"

"I'd remember an attractive blond in a red dress." He
laughed and rolled his eyes. "Especially in a place like

this. You know, legend has it that this was a whorehouse. Just imagine . . ."

Zach bit back his anger. Ralston didn't mean to insult Hilary personally, because the man didn't know she existed. Mentally counting—*again*—Zach shook the real estate agent's hand and sent him on his way. For some reason, he felt a desperate need to find Hilary—to make sure she was all right.

Once the realtor and his monster four wheel drive were out of sight, Zach rushed up the stairs two at a time. "Hilary?" he shouted, dashing into her room without knocking.

"Is he gone?"

There she sat in the middle of her brass bed, her pink cheeks streaked with tears. Her eyes were red and puffy from crying.

"Yeah, he's gone." Zach took a step toward her. He felt like an ass. Hilary was driving him even crazier than she was. She made him feel and think things he hadn't realized he was capable of anymore.

She'd managed to reproduce an emotion buried deep within him—something he hadn't felt since before his brother's death.

Compassion for another human being.

He couldn't bear to hurt her. But what the hell was he supposed to do? Keep Columbine and pay taxes on it just so she could stay up here alone, pretending to be a ghost?

Or stay up here with her?

Zach swallowed hard. That had definite possibilities. She looked so frightened and innocent sitting there, with her skirt spread out around her crossed legs. There was an incredibly sexy pout on her full lips, making him burn to kiss it away.

But her eyes.

They were tormented, pleading, as she gazed up at him. *Damn.* If he were to leave Columbine, what would become of Hilary? She had to eat and have water to drink, heat to keep her from freezing this winter, whether she realized it or not. That was what worried him most of all—she really didn't comprehend her own needs for survival.

Hilary really thought she was a ghost. To her this was real.

"Are you going to sell it?" she asked in a small shaky voice. Her lower lip trembled until she bit it with her straight white teeth.

Zach swallowed and followed his gut instinct to shield her from the truth—for now. "No. I've decided to try and make this work. I'm not going to sell it, Hilary." *I'm the one who's gone nuts.*

She was in his arms so fast it staggered him. Zach stared down at her smiling visage as she clung to him, her arms wrapped around his neck, her breasts pressed enticingly against his chest.

Who gives a damn which one of us is nuts?

"Oh, thank you, Zach." She laid her head against his shoulder. Holding her felt right—too right. "I don't know what I would've done if you'd sold it to someone who might tear it down. The angel didn't say what would become of me if something like that happened."

Angel? Zach swallowed. God, she worried him. Why did he have to care so much for a crazy woman? He barely knew her. Closing his eyes for a moment, he savored the fragrance of honeysuckle wafting up from her shining hair. She was so soft, so lovely.

He kissed the side of her neck, exposed when her hair fell to the side. "Sweet," he murmured, kissing lower until he found the curve of her shoulder.

He rubbed her back with his hands, feeling himself harden with desire for this bewitching creature. She was a powerful woman. Sex appeal oozed from every pore on her petite frame.

God, how he wanted her.

She seemed to melt against him as Zach's self-control withered like the aspen leaves fluttering away on the breeze outside. He dipped his hands lower, massaging her buttocks through the satin, feeling his pulse escalate and thud dangerously in the side of his throat. His loins were on fire.

He felt like an enthusiastic pre-pubescent with his first erection. With one significant difference—Zach knew exactly how to handle this natural phenomenon.

She tipped her face up to meet his lips and Zach groaned when she trembled in his arms. His exploring tongue delved deep into her warm, moist mouth. She returned his kiss, accepted and responded to it.

He smothered a tiny moan from her throat as she pressed herself even harder against him. Where pliant met firm, there was an aggravating yearning for more—much more.

His self-control was slipping away like water down an open drain. He moved his hand to the side of her ribcage, gently massaging the taut flesh beneath her satin dress. She deepened their kiss, persuading him to move his hand forward, just enough.

He held the weight of her breast in his hand, aching to bare it to his starved senses. She seemed just as enthusiastic, as he maneuvered his fingers beneath the lace to find her swollen nipple.

Her weight sagged in his arms and she moaned again. Zach's hopes soared. A nagging voice told him to go slow, not to take advantage of Hilary's vulnerability. Was she strong enough to handle this? Would he hurt her by making love to her?

No. Her response told him she wanted this as much as he. He wouldn't—couldn't—hurt her.

He swept her into his arms and crossed the room, bending to lay her gently on the bed. Her luminous eyes gazed up at him and he saw longing mingled with fear, giving him pause as he considered the magnitude of what he so desperately craved.

"I want you, Hilary," he whispered in a ragged voice as he remained standing beside her bed.

Her gaze searched his. He watched her eyes fill with moisture and a tear trickled down her cheek. Her lower lip trembled and she looked down at her lap.

Then Hilary Brown simply dissolved into millions of minute particles right before his eyes. Colors blended together, then converted to a cloud-like substance before she vanished entirely.

Again.

Zach looked around him, frantically searching for the woman. She couldn't be a ghost. *He* didn't believe in ghosts.

The woman he'd held in his arms couldn't possibly have been dead. She was too warm and passionate. Just thinking about her voluptuous body, the way soft met hard when they were kissing and straining against one another, made him shudder with renewed longing.

She'd vanished three times. Once, he could laugh off—twice, maybe. But three times? And what about the way she'd sort of dissolved into nothingness? Definitely not David Copperfield's style. He raked his fingers through his hair.

Could she really be a ghost?

A real ghost?

"I can't handle this." *I need a drink.* "I've gotta get out of here."

He ran down the stairs and into the twilight, having lost track of how late it was growing. He was tired, hungry and in desperate need of a shower and shave. Tired and hungry were warning signals to an alcoholic. A hot meal and a warm bed would help him see things more clearly in the morning—help him stay sober. He'd come back tomorrow and get to the bottom of this mess.

Outside, he looked to the west, noticing the sun sinking fast behind the highest peak. Darkness would cloister the tiny valley in only moments. He sure as hell didn't relish the idea of spending another night up here. But driving out in the dark wasn't exactly an appealing prospect, either.

What was he supposed to do? Stay in Columbine with a sexy ghost—if she was a ghost—in the dark?

Dangerous memories filled his mind. Warm, smooth whiskey sliding down his throat and settling in his belly. The burning sensation that preceded the inevitable satisfaction spreading through his body. Yes, he needed a drink in the worst possible way.

He pulled his keys from his pocket with trembling fingers and climbed into the Jeep. Starting the engine, he backed around the corner of the building and headed out of town the way he'd come in, praying he wouldn't get lost in the dark. There were at least a dozen sheer drop-offs between Columbine and the main highway.

But anything was better than being cold, hungry and terrified in this hellhole.

This haunted hellhole.

At least he had headlights. That was a whole lot more than Columbine had to offer.

"A damned ghost," he muttered—still unconvinced—to himself. He leaned over and reached into the glove compartment for the topographical map he'd used to find the property in the first place. "I suppose every self-respecting ghost town should have at least one."

Hilary swiped angrily at the traitorous tears that slipped down her face. She was dead. Dead people weren't supposed to cry. They weren't supposed to feel the powerful emotions Zach had conjured within her either. It wasn't fair.

Leaning her forehead against the cool windowpane, she watched with a sinking feeling as Zach drove away from Columbine.

No doubt, forever.

She rubbed her forehead and glanced heavenward. "Oh, Sarah, what am I supposed to do now?" Her last opportunity to earn her way out of Transition was gone.

There was no answer to her plea—there never was. Hilary paced the confines of her small room, praying for an end to her nightmare. Transition had turned into her Hell. It was time for it to end.

One way or another.

Chapter Four

The deer came out of nowhere.

Swerving hard to the right, Zach barely missed the graceful creature as it bounded out of sight, into the safety of the dense forest on the *up*hill side of what passed for a road.

Zach was rewarded with the downhill side.

Mercifully, the Jeep hit a pair of trees only a few yards off the road, bringing the vehicle to a very sudden stop. The Jeep's headlights—Zach's only salvation—shattered into a million useless, glittering shards against the twin pines.

Instinct and memory told him he was very near a steep drop-off. Just how far down, he had no idea. He couldn't see his hand in front of his face, much less find his way back to civilization. If he managed to keep from falling into a canyon, he'd count himself lucky.

Are bears nocturnal creatures?

His gaze darted around, searching for any moving shapes

in the darkness. Nothing. Only stillness and the faint sound of the wind rustling through what remained of the aspen leaves.

The darkness was blacker than anything he'd ever known. Having grown up in the suburbs of Los Angeles, he'd always thought of night as a sky with a surreal glow from a meticulous blending of dust particles, smog and artificial light. Sort of a grayish shade of yuck.

But this was *b-lack*.

His heart gave a lurch of protest when he unbuckled his seat belt and eased one foot to the ground. Good. At least he wasn't just hanging over the edge.

But how far away was the edge?

And, more importantly, how far down was the bottom?

Keeping one steadying hand on the vehicle, Zach inched his way to the back and opened what passed for a trunk. Fumbling around in the dark, he found a flashlight and flipped it on.

The narrow beam of light gave him a gargantuan amount of comfort. At least now he could see the ground near his feet. It was an incredible relief, being able to ensure his next step wouldn't be into a deep ravine.

"Damn, it's cold." He pulled a blanket out and wrapped it around his shoulders. It had never occurred to him that he'd need a coat this early in the season. And as the wind began to howl through the trees, he realized how foolish that assumption had been.

The temperature continued to drop as he stood in the middle of the old mining road. Shining his flashlight in both directions, he weighed his options.

Columbine was less than a half mile back up the road. He shuddered, recalling Hilary's latest vanishing act. Returning to the possibly haunted town filled him with uncertainty.

But Hilary was warm.

And he was cold.

Damned cold.

If he continued down the mountain, he could become hopelessly lost. That was more than a remote possibility. Gazing up at the sky, he noted with a frown that the moon and stars were no longer visible. A few moments ago, they'd seemed so near he thought he could reach up and pluck one from its velvet bed.

Clouds meant precipitation.

Snow?

"Oh, God—not that, too." Zach shivered, tugging the blanket tighter around his shoulders. It couldn't snow this early in the season. Could it? Yeah, it could. Considering the way his day'd been going, anything was possible.

Even sexy ghosts?

He really didn't have much choice. The enigmatic Hilary Brown? Or the unknown wilderness?

She had to be a magician. Optical illusions were obviously her specialty. For her, it was a gift. For him, it was a torment. But he knew she wasn't a real ghost. He'd been a fool to run away.

Deep in his gut, though, he knew that he'd been running toward something even harder than he'd been running away. A drink. A lousy bottle of blended whiskey. That had been much more profound to his alcoholic mind than his fear of non-existent ghosts. With an internal shudder, Zach sought and found his willpower, forcing his thoughts toward other matters.

Like Hilary.

The memory of the way she'd felt, tasted and reacted to his kisses made Zach's temperature rise a few degrees.

That settles that.

Turning toward Columbine, he started the uphill climb just as the first flakes of white appeared in his flashlight beam. One became ten. Ten became fifty.

He stared into the meager light as the flakes started to sting his face and cover the blanket.

"I'm in for it."

Hilary waited.

Surely Sarah would see the wisdom in ending Hilary's exile. She was lonely and tired. Enough was enough. A hundred and eleven years of waiting for the right person to come to Columbine was too much for anyone. She was beyond ready to surrender it all.

Even eternity.

She'd lived her eternity. Alone and miserable, with no one to talk to and nothing to do.

Until Zach Ryan.

Hilary covered her face with her hands, then jerked suddenly. Something compelled her to peer into the darkness outside the window.

It was snowing.

That wasn't terribly unusual for September.

Hilary sighed. Another long winter alone.

Again, when she leaned against the window, the tugging sensation made her jerk upright. It wasn't exactly a voice. It was more of a . . . an instinct. Someone—*something*—communicated with her.

Sarah?

Without hearing anything specific, Hilary allowed herself to follow her instincts. She walked down the stairs and into the night. Snow swirled around her. It clung to her hair and eyelashes, heavier with every passing moment.

She turned to the far side of town, then walked along the road. Somehow she knew this was what she should do. She resisted the impulse to fly through the storm. She might miss something important.

Was it Zach? Was he lost in the storm?

She shook her head in bewilderment. The snow and cold didn't affect her. That was really the only advantage to her condition. But why didn't she feel the cold weather, when Zach's warmth had been so clearly discernable? Did people in Transition have selective perception? If only she could have elected not to feel Zach's touch.

Hilary continued to walk, ignoring the snow and wind whipping around her. The calling, the pulling sensation, grew stronger with every step.

A narrow beam of light shone through the darkness just ahead. She broke into a run, then dropped to her knees beside the snow-covered light. It was a strange cylinder with a light glowing on one end. She gripped it in her hand and knew instantly it belonged to Zach.

A strange sense of purpose possessed her. She picked up the cylinder and straightened. Sweeping the area nearest her in every direction, she gasped when the beam fell upon the slumped figure.

"Zach." She ran to the still form, rolled him onto his back and stared at his startlingly white face. *God, don't let him be dead,* she prayed, feeling his chest for the faint rise and fall of his breathing. His heartbeat was barely detectable through his snowy clothing.

She must transport him back to Miss Nellie's. But how? Moving herself from one place to another with the blink of an eye was easy. Practicing the subtleties of disappearing and such had been her only means of entertainment over the years.

But how was she supposed to move Zach?

He was far too heavy for her to carry. When he'd held her in his arms earlier, she'd noticed how tall and muscular he was. She barely reached his shoulder.

The wind gave an unholy howl. She had to try. If she didn't move him to shelter, he'd surely die.

Hilary wrapped her arms around him and closed her

eyes, concentrating hard on making them both transcend the bonds of the fourth dimension and move to Columbine, into her warm room at Miss Nellie's. She didn't open her eyes or release him for interminable moments.

A sensation of floating encompassed her. This was a good sign, but she dared not look. She'd never transported even herself such a great distance, let alone a passenger. But something was definitely happening.

The floating sensation became more pronounced. Hilary tightened her grip on Zach's shoulders, flattening herself against his prone form. The warmth she'd noticed emanating from him earlier was conspicuously absent.

But his heart still thudded slowly in his chest.

She felt softness suddenly envelop them. Opening her eyes, Hilary heaved a sigh of relief. They were in her bed—Zach was safe.

"I did it," she said in wonder, lifting herself slightly to gaze down at his pale face. The strange, tubular light was still clutched in her hand even as she continued to hold him. She used it to make certain Zach hadn't suffered any injuries, then realized she no longer needed the device. Sunlight bathed the room in a soft, gray light.

He groaned and shifted slightly beneath her.

"Zach?" she said softly, lifting his short brown curls from his forehead. She didn't think he'd been in the cold long enough for her to worry about frostbite. He'd probably just passed out from exhaustion. But if she hadn't found him . . .

Hilary bit her lower lip and squeezed her eyes shut for a moment of silent thanks to God and to Sarah. They must have sent her to Zach. How else could she have known he needed her help, let alone found him in the dark stormy night?

In repose, he looked more like a small boy than the virile man she remembered so distinctly. She ran her fingertips along his cheek, smiling when he turned his face toward her hand. His warm breath and soft lips teased and tantalized her open palm.

Though she knew he wasn't purposely trying to seduce her now, his inadvertent impact was every bit as powerful as his deliberate one. Lying against his long hard body brought them into such intimate contact, she grew warm and languid with desire.

"Hilary." His voice was barely more than a whisper. Dragging her gaze from his mouth, she met his smiling eyes. "Thank you," he murmured.

She started to push away, but he reached around her. "Don't disappear again." His expression was solemn, pleading. "Please."

Blinking back the stinging sensation in her eyes, Hilary nodded. "All right."

He reached out to caress her cheek, making a pain of longing shoot right through her. Why did she have to feel such human emotions now? During her lifetime, she'd longed to find a man who could make her feel the way Zach Ryan did with virtually no effort.

"You're beautiful."

She started to shake her head, but his expression deterred her. His eyes relayed to her the truth of his statement.

"Thank you," she murmured, looking quickly away as she struggled with her warring emotions.

What did she have to lose at this point? If she gave herself to him now, she'd go to Hell knowing what it felt like to be loved by a man. As it was now, she'd go to eternal damnation anyway. Try as she might, Hilary couldn't think of a single reason not to indulge herself.

It was her last chance.

"Are you injured?" she asked, meeting his smoldering gaze.

His grin was charismatic. "No, Hilary. I'm not hurt. Just cold, but definitely in a certain kind of pain."

She gasped, felt her face flood with heat—another non-ghostly sensation, she was sure. A giggle bubbled up from her chest. Despite her lack of experience, she knew exactly what kind of pain he was feeling. She shared his discomfort.

"I don't care anymore if you think you're a ghost." Zach shrugged as he watched her through hooded eyes. "Look where running away from you got me."

"Serves you right." He was so handsome. Her breath caught in her throat when he reached around to cup the back of her head and pull her face down toward his. "What . . . what are you doing?"

His lips captured hers in a kiss so soft, she imagined it was something like a butterfly landing on a flower petal. She wanted more. Deepening their kiss was a simple matter. Hilary opened her mouth to receive his exploring tongue, returning his tantalizing investigation with tentative efforts of her own.

She wanted Zach. Hilary had spent her life, and lost it, trying to avoid this very thing.

But, somehow, this was different.

She was giving herself to Zach because she wanted to, and because he needed her. *He needs me.* Joy and a sense of purpose filled her. Perhaps this wasn't what Sarah'd had in mind, but it was sure a lot more fun than the last century had been.

She knew what she must do.

Zach was on fire.

Saint Bernards carrying brandy couldn't hold a candle to Hilary Brown.

This woman—or whatever she was—drove him nuts. She'd saved his life twice. Now he wanted nothing more than to bury himself deep inside her. He knew she'd be a fiery lover—the passion she displayed each time he touched her was explosive. There was definitely nothing ghostly about this warm, vibrant body pressed so enticingly against his.

Forcibly banishing thoughts of the way she'd disappeared before in his arms, Zach ran his hand down the back of her dress. He hadn't wanted a woman this desperately since adolescence. He was sure she wasn't a ghost, but she was decisively magical.

Try as he might, he couldn't determine how to get her out of the strange dress. There wasn't a trace of cold left anywhere in his body when he dragged his mouth from beneath hers to nibble on the delicate lobe of her ear. "Help me, Hilary," he entreated, gasping when she lifted her face to meet his gaze.

Her blue eyes darkened as she released the laces at the front of her dress. Several hooks were hidden beneath the wide belt. Within a few moments everything fell open, revealing her beauty to his hungry gaze and starved senses.

"You're gorgeous."

Easing the dress from her shoulders, she permitted it to fall about her waist, completely exposing her breasts to him. His gaze was riveted. Pale, almost luminous skin, curved over her full breasts. Rosy nipples, puckered like tiny twin buds, beckoned and tempted him.

She leaned slightly forward, straddling him. Zach had to get rid of his clothes fast. He couldn't wait much longer.

Reaching for her tiny waist, he eased her backward enough to permit him to sit up in the bed. It wasn't easy to maneuver himself around on the soft featherbed, but he was incredibly motivated.

She swung her leg across him and stood, permitting her dress to fall to the floor with a whisper, where she kicked it away. Zach froze. Here she stood, wearing nothing but

black and red striped stockings with garters, and enough
blond hair to form a veil over them both while they made
love.

Every man's wildest dream.

His gaze traveled down her length, worshipping her
breasts. They were large and firm, with nipples hard and
upturned. Looking lower, he noted her flat tummy and
flared hips. A golden triangle of hair reminded him of his
goal.

And she was a natural blond.

Sunlight chose that moment to flood the room, bathing
her in a golden glow. He jerked his T-shirt over his head
and tossed it to the floor. Kicking off his Reeboks, he
reached down and peeled off his wet socks. When he fumbled with the buttons at the front of his jeans, he hesitated,
searching her gaze for confirmation. "I want you, Hilary.
Are you sure . . . ?"

To his relief and amazement, she nodded, then sat on
the edge of the bed to release the fly of his jeans herself.
Her fingers barely grazed his erection through the fabric
as she eased the denim downward.

Before he lifted his hips to assist her, Zach fished into his
pocket to retrieve a square packet, silently congratulating
himself on his good judgment. With a grin, he helped her
rid him of the burdensome garment. All that remained
were his black jockeys.

Her eyes grew round as he eased the stretchy fabric
lower. She rested her hand on his abdomen, just above
the part of him that screamed for release. She looked so
innocent. Though he felt sure it was an erroneous perception, he hesitated.

"Do you . . . do you want this, Hilary?" he asked again,
praying she wouldn't back out. Not now.

She bit her lower lip and nodded. "Yes," she whispered,

sliding her fingers downward until she joined him in pulling away his briefs.

The waistband caught on him, making Zach wince. "Oops." He grinned sheepishly, then deftly released himself from the confining garment.

Her eyes grew even more round.

She acted as if she'd never seen a naked man before. But she was experienced, wasn't she? She certainly kissed him as if she knew exactly what she was doing.

Then the thought of her with other men barged into his thoughts, threatening his modern liberated male persona with a vengeance. He didn't like it. Not one bit.

But he still wanted her—bad.

"Hilary?"

He reached for her and pulled her toward him. Sighing, she met his mouth with a ravenous kiss that stole his breath. This was more like it.

Her naked breasts teased his bare chest, making Zach ache to taste her again. He kissed her rashly, twirling and stroking her tongue with his until he withdrew, gasping for air. He nibbled his way down her throat. She lifted herself slightly as he urged her over to straddle him again.

Except this time there were no barriers to separate her flesh from his.

He wanted desperately to claim the prize she kept within her golden triangle of hair. Her warmth pressed against him, but he resisted the urge to bury himself in her just yet. It was too soon.

Hilary moistened her lips. "Show me the meaning of all this, Zach. Very soon."

Her invitation fueled his desire. Zach raged with a hunger he'd never known before. It didn't matter that she thought she was dead—a ghost. Nothing mattered except the exquisite way she fit against him, reacted to him.

A soft moan left her parted lips when his tongue toyed

with her tender nipples. Her position astride him kept
Zach acutely conscious of his pulsing erection pressed so
intimately against her. He wanted to be inside her. Now.

The urgency he felt with Hilary was terrifying.

But it was a heady, all-consuming kind of terror.

She leaned forward as Zach pulled a pillow behind his
head. He cradled her sumptuous breasts in his hands,
bestowing equal attention to them both. Her flesh was a
hungry whisper against his tongue. She drove him mad
with wanting her.

"Zach," she whispered, gasping as his mouth ardently
joined with her nipple.

His thumb and forefinger teased the other until he felt
like screaming from his own raw need. She was hot against
him, not cold like death.

She entwined her fingers in his brown hair, pressing her
breast more fully against his insatiable mouth. Since the
first moment he'd seen her, he'd thought of this, of tasting
her, of having her. He couldn't get enough of her.

He moaned as she ground her hips against him without
taking him inside. "I don't know how, Zach," she whispered, making him wonder for a fleeting moment what
she meant.

Growling, Zach fell back against the bed and rolled Hilary to her back. He hovered over her, then began to stroke
her inner thighs with his callused fingers. She arched her
hips as he kissed her navel and moved his fingers upward,
inch by devastating inch.

He found her sensitive core at the juncture of her thighs.
Hilary groaned and thrust herself against his hand, showing him that she was feeling the same waves of heat that
swept through him.

His mouth tarried, then displaced his fingers as he slid
between her thighs and dropped her legs over his shoul-

ders. She gasped, sounded stunned by the intimacy of his actions.

Madness consumed him. Zach desperately wanted this to end, yet knew he'd die if it ceased too soon. She grabbed handfuls of his hair, holding him against her as his fingers dipped beneath to probe the part of her he ached to fill with his swollen, eager body.

She tilted herself against his hand, held his mouth to her and wept with the wonder he ached to share. Zach sensed her explosion, knew when she fragmented into completion.

Hilary sighed as he kissed his way back up her body, lingering to stroke her breasts again with his tongue. He wanted to catch her before she landed in reality again, immediately returning her to a state of intense longing.

Gravely aware of his unrelenting male body pressed against her thigh, he persisted with her delectable breasts. When she reached downward and found his throbbing tip and stroked it with her silken fingers, he winced in agony. Kissing his way back up her neck to nuzzle her ear, he deftly placed his erection in the palm of her hand.

He sucked in his breath with a jolt as she closed her hand around him. He was so hard, so ready, like a loaded gun, hammer back and ready to fire.

His gut coiled into a painful knot; he had to be inside her. It was time—way past time. She squeezed him tighter and drew her hand up to the tip, then slowly back down. Zach growled.

"Now Zach," she pleaded, easing her legs around his waist to pull him against her. "I want—need—you."

"God, woman," he muttered hoarsely, rising up to maneuver himself nearer.

He hesitated just long enough to tear open the small packet he'd removed from his pocket earlier. He'd almost forgotten. She was driving him far beyond caring about safe sex.

Hilary pulled him against her. He felt her slick folds open, eager to favor his engorged male body. A thrill of anticipation charged through him as he inched his way inward.

She purred low in her throat, a sexy sound he'd expect in an erotic dream. It was obvious from the way she angled her hips to meet him more fully that she was as eager as he. Zach grunted in surrender as he filled her with one powerful stroke.

He froze above her, his body buried deep within her, knowing something was amiss. A virgin? The resistance had been unmistakable. He'd torn his way through it, having never anticipated its existence. He took a deep breath in an attempt to bring himself under control. No woman had ever driven him to such carnal hunger before.

As her body surrounded his with a voraciousness that left him breathless, Zach forced the puzzle of her virginity to the back of his mind. Besides, it was too late to worry about that now. There were far more pressing matters.

She was hot and tight, surrounding and swallowing him with a passion which rivalled even his own. Zach began to slowly move within her, savoring each tiny contraction of her body. He felt like a bomb ready to explode. Ticking away.

She matched his rhythm, undulating her hips to meet his thrusts as they grew more and more urgent. He watched her face, relished her fluctuating expression. The veins on her slender neck became more prominent; her delicate nostrils flared slightly. She moaned and whimpered incoherent sounds of pleasure as he moved against her.

Slipping his hands beneath her, he cupped her buttocks as his thrusts became more urgent. He couldn't last much longer. She was too much. Too good. Damned good.

When she cried out beneath him, he knew she'd found it—the miracle he also sought. Her body contorted, swallowed him, made him gasp and groan. He released himself with an explosion unlike anything he'd ever known.

"Oh, God, Zach," she gasped, then he covered her mouth in a kiss while the throbbing between them quieted.

He slumped against her, buried his face in the pillow to inhale her sweet honeysuckle fragrance. Who was this mystery woman? She couldn't be a ghost, not that he believed in such phenomena. She was too warm, too passionate, to be dead. It just wasn't possible.

Rolling to his side, he propped himself on one elbow to study her delicate features. Her magnificent breasts rose and fell with her rapid breathing, more evidence that she couldn't be a ghost. Her large rosy nipples were still swollen and tempting.

A ghost who breathes? Cries? Makes love so beautifully?

He cupped her face in his hand, stroking her cheek with his thumb. She was perfect.

A languorous smile spread across her face. "That was . . ."

He grinned and arched a brow. "What?"

"Wonderful." She sounded like a cat who'd just lapped up a bowl of cream. "I never knew."

"Yeah, I noticed." He kissed the tip of her nose. "Why didn't you tell me this was your first time?"

She reddened beneath his probing gaze as he continued to stare at her. Her only response to his question was a shrug.

"I would have been gentler," he said with a hint of remorse. "Did I hurt you?"

Her blush deepened and she shook her head. "Only for a moment."

He released a breath. "I'm sorry." His hand moved from her face to the side of her neck. "Tell me, Hilary . . ." He traced a thin blue vein down her neck from the red scar, across her chest and drew circles around her nipple. "How is it that a ghost can breathe air? How can a ghost have a heart that beats like a drum when I do this?" He grazed her nipple with his lips and teeth. "Hmm?"

Hilary gasped as he drew her nipple into his mouth. "I . . . I told you."

He granted similar consideration to her other breast, earning him her immediate response. She moaned and wound her fingers in his hair.

He lifted his face only slightly. "Tell me who you really are," he urged. "Tell me."

She groaned and arched against him. "Hilary," she whispered. "Hilary Brown."

"Tell me the truth. Who—what are you?"

"I'm not sure." Her voice was deep and throaty. "I died a long time ago."

Zach lifted his face to gaze at her. He wanted to see her expression, to discern whether or not she was lying to him. Perhaps she really believed her ridiculous claims. If that proved true, then she really was insane.

Gorgeous, sexy and insane.

One hell of a combination.

"When did you . . . die?" he asked, stroking the inside of her thigh as he watched her wavering expression. "Hmm? When?" Would her story remain consistent? He slid his hand higher.

"1886."

Zach froze for a moment, then resumed caressing her while she moaned and stared at him. "And you're a ghost?" It just couldn't be true, yet how could he forget the way she'd vanished? He moved his hand higher still.

"In Transition," she murmured. Her breathing quickened and her face was flushed with desire. "Dead—in Transition."

What the hell does that mean?

"Zach . . . inside me . . . again?"

Lord, how could he refuse such an invitation? Delaying his interrogation, he protected them both and granted her request. She was wet and wild, right on the verge of orgasm when he entered her.

She cried out and wrapped her legs around his waist as they both achieved almost instantaneous, and definitely explosive, climaxes.

"You're one helluva woman, Hilary Brown."

She smiled up at him. "And you were worth waiting for, Zach Ryan."

"Now, pretty lady," he murmured, holding her chin firmly in his hand. His tone was uncompromising—he hoped. "You will tell me exactly who, and what, you are."

Chapter Five

Hilary swallowed hard and nodded. How could she make him understand? For that matter, *why* did she want to? *Accept it, Zach. I'm dead.* "I told you who—what—I am."

Zach shook his head, his eyes dark and penetrating. "You didn't tell me anything I can *believe*, Hilary. You haven't explained how you just disappeared on me three times." He leaned closer. "And, just for the record, I don't believe in ghosts, or the living dead. And I'm not at all certain I believe in angels, not after some of the *hell* I've already been through."

She closed her eyes tightly and sighed; she felt so helpless. "I already told you, I don't know exactly what I am." A shudder commenced in her belly and spread through her. Only a moment ago she'd been so happy and secure in his embrace. Now he was interrogating her—treating her like a criminal.

One who'd been hanged for murder.

If he wanted the whole truth, then she'd just give it to

him. What difference did it make? "Fine." She lifted her chin a notch, then tugged the sheet up over her bare breasts, hoping to diminish her vulnerability. "I'm Hilary Brown, born right here in Columbine, in 1860. Columbine was nothing more than a mining camp then. My mother was Nellie Brown. My father was a miner—he walked out on us one day and never returned. After that, Mama made a living the only way she thought she could, I guess. She ran her business out of a tent, then a cabin. Eventually, she became the proprietress of Miss Nellie's." She bit her lower lip, struggling against the old resentment and humiliation. "Miss Nellie's House of Ill Repute. A whorehouse."

She covered her face with her hands, furious for feeling ashamed of her origins even now. Taking a deep breath, Hilary lifted her gaze to meet his. "I refused to become a . . . a harlot, even though my mother expected it from the moment I turned fourteen. It wasn't easy, but somehow, I always managed to avoid it. At least, for twelve more years I did."

"1860?" Zach rolled his eyes and stared long and hard. "This is ludicrous, Hilary. You don't look a day over twenty-five, let alone a hundred and something." His expression was one of total incredulity. "You can come up with something more realistic, can't you? I mean, you don't really expect me to believe any of this."

"It's the truth." She tugged on the sheet again as if it might provide a barrier between her and the pain of her past. "I was a schoolteacher. I told you that, too."

"Yeah, right." He lifted a brow and picked up a strand of her hair, twining it around his index finger. "A schoolteacher."

"Yes." She looked away, then glowered defensively as she faced him again. "A teacher. A good one."

He chuckled. "All right, if you say so. Go on."

"The town didn't offer lodging as part of the teacher's

compensation. Huh! It was hard enough to convince them they needed a school at all. So, I was stuck here at Miss Nellie's. Besides, there was my brother to think of. He needed me."

"Yeah, you mentioned him earlier."

"I remember. He was . . . special. I always took care of him—raised him." Hilary scooted back until she sat up straight with the sheet clutched beneath her chin. "Our mother certainly couldn't—didn't—take care of him. She was a drunk."

Zach winced and closed his eyes. "Oh." He reopened his eyes and nodded. "I'm listening."

"The bank foreclosed on Miss Nellie's, but Sean McCune let her stay and run the place. Somehow she managed to keep part interest in the business."

"How fortunate, but this is all fiction, of course." Zach clicked his tongue. "Hilary."

She sniffled and looked down at the footboard of the brass bed, deciding to ignore his interruption. He wanted the truth, he was going to get it. All of it.

"Mama was determined that I take over the business. She said she wanted to retire and get married." Hilary's gaze locked with his. "She did get married—to the banker, Sean McCune."

"Sean McCune again?" Zach frowned and rubbed his jaw with his hand. "So, he married your mother, even though he'd already foreclosed on the saloon."

Hilary bristled beneath his inquisition. Why couldn't he simply believe her? "Yes. Lucky me. And that was the beginning of the end."

"I read up on Columbine's history before I left California. It was a pretty notorious little town. I suppose you could have done the same research. It stands to reason you'd have access to more local history at libraries here in Colorado."

She narrowed her eyes and scowled at him. "I was here, Zach. That's how I know what happened." *And how I know what happened* after *I died.*

"Sure." He stared at her as if he were trying to read her thoughts. "I remember reading something else about the McCune family. What did you say the other one's name was?"

Hilary shuddered and her stomach lurched. "Baird." Her throat ached every time she thought of the man who'd cost her everything.

"Yeah, Baird." Zach rubbed the whiskers on his jaw with his thumb and forefinger. "I remember. There was a big scandal. I read that he was murdered by a jealous woman."

That did it. Hilary was furious. "A *jealous woman?*" She sputtered for a few moments, searching for words venomous enough to describe how she felt. "I'll have you know I *know* what happened to him. I was here. He was Sean's son. Sean was always mean, but Baird was nothing but scum—pure scum."

Hilary's stomach clenched at the mere thought of that night. "When I refused to quit teaching and take over Miss Nellie's, Mama and Sean turned the place over to Baird. Of course, Mama was always so drunk she didn't know what she was doing half the time." Her lower lip trembled and she bit it to quell the traitorous movement.

Zach's expression was softer now, though she could tell he still didn't believe her.

"It's all true, Zach," she insisted, miserable that he thought her a liar. "I wouldn't lie to you." *I killed a man— right here in this room.*

Zach snorted. "Sure you wouldn't. And neither would the lawyer who sent me on this wild goose chase." He grimaced and leaned on one elbow. "I'm sorry, you didn't deserve that. It isn't your fault." He reached toward her and brushed the loose strands of hair away from her face.

"Go on, Hilary. I want to know everything you . . . think happened."

Hilary tried very hard not to cry. She took a deep steadying breath and rushed on. "Baird arranged for a customer to visit my room one night after I'd gone to sleep." One telltale tear trickled down her face and she swiped it angrily away. "This isn't fair. Dead people aren't supposed to cry."

Zach took her hand in his. "I'm listening, Hilary." His voice was soft, encouraging.

Did he believe her? She met his gaze and saw sympathy in his eyes, but not faith. She wanted desperately for him to accept her story. It seemed strange that it was so important to her, since she would either vanish back to her own time to right the wrongs, or go to Hell in a few years. Whether or not Zach believed her was totally irrelevant where her afterlife was concerned.

But for some unknown reason, it seemed critical.

At least he hadn't walked away from her—yet. That was something. Drawing a deep breath, she seized strength from his hand holding hers. She must tell the truth, whether he chose to believe her or not.

"The man—the customer—was very drunk. He came to my room while I was asleep," she explained, suppressing the shudder that threatened her resolve. "I was terrified." Her voice fell to a whisper. "He—he . . ."

Zach squeezed her hand even tighter. "What happened?"

She met his gaze again, finding courage in the soft brown eyes. "He tried to . . ."

"The son-of-a-bitch." Zach's voice was ominous; a muscle twitched in his cheek. He ran his hand down the front of his face and groaned. "What am I saying? This is your imagination talking."

"You believe me. You don't want to, but you do. It isn't my imagination, Zach." Hilary's hopes soared.

Zach simply shrugged. "Just finish your story, Hilary."

"Very well." She summoned every ounce of grit she could. "He tried to get into bed with me—said Baird had sent him. He was very proud of the fact that he'd paid extra for the honor of . . . of 'deflowering the prissy teacher.' The man was furious when I told him to leave. He started to shout."

Hilary squeezed her eyes tightly shut to prevent her tears from escaping. When she reopened them to meet Zach's gaze, she knew he wanted to believe her.

But he still didn't.

"Then what happened?" he asked.

The secret she'd carried for over a century . . . She cast him a furtive glance. Dare she trust him? What difference did it make anyway? The person involved was long gone from this world. He was in Heaven, where he belonged. Yet, even now, she couldn't bring herself to tarnish his memory.

"Baird came up here. He said we were disturbing the other customers." Her vision blurred, but she couldn't even blink. "It all happened so fast." She was transfixed, seeing the entire scene play back before her eyes as she retold the tale.

"He had a gun. After the customer left with a full refund, Baird turned on me. He laid his gun there on the dresser." Her breath caught in her throat as she remembered those next few, fateful moments . . .

"Baird unfastened his trousers, said he was going to 'break me in good.' He wanted to teach me a lesson I'd never forget."

Zach clenched his other hand into a fist as his entire body tensed at her side. "Then?" he urged.

"I ran over and grabbed the gun. Before he could take it away from me, I shot him dead. That faded stain over by the door was his . . . his blood. You see, Zach? I killed

Baird McCune to protect myself." Her voice cracked as she visualized Baird's prone figure sprawled on the floor, blood pooling around what remained of his head. Her stomach lurched, protesting the gruesome image.

"The Sheriff came to arrest me," she continued when Zach remained silent. "He and Sean made me wear that hideous red dress. It didn't belong to me, of course, but that didn't matter to them. Sean said it was fitting for a murderous whore like . . . like me." Her voice diminished to almost nothing as the disturbing memories charged through her mind.

Zach nodded. "I think I'm beginning to understand this a little better."

"Are you?" Hilary turned a pleading expression in his direction. "Really, Zach?"

"You must have read about all this somewhere. You need professional help, Hilary." Zach's expression grew solemn. "You need a doctor, and as soon as I make enough money we'll go to Denver and find the best psychologist in the state."

"*Read* about it?" Hilary shuddered—something tore at her insides. She needed him to understand, but he didn't—couldn't. It had taken her all this time to accept it herself. "Zach, I'm telling the truth. You asked earlier how I got the mark on my neck." She touched the rope burn and turned icy cold. "It's from the hangman's noose."

Zach flinched and touched the mark on her neck with his fingers. "I believe you're telling the truth as you imagine it." He smiled indulgently and patted her hand in an infuriating manner. "I don't want you to worry about anything. I'm going to take good care of you until we can get you to a doctor."

"Take care of *me*?" she repeated as if they were the foulest words she'd ever heard. "Zach, that isn't what I need or want. I'm already dead. Besides, I'm here to help you."

"Help me?" He chuckled and caressed her breast through the sheet, obviously not taking her seriously at all. "This is the only help I need or want from you, Hilary Brown. You have a delectable body and a sweet nature. I enjoy your company and I can't get enough of you." His magnetic voice fell to a ragged whisper as he nuzzled her neck, tracing tiny circles with his tongue.

She tingled inside, trembling from the onslaught of passion evoked from his touch. "Zach." Hilary felt deflated as she fought the waves of longing he created within her. How could she make him understand?

Trying to ignore his lips on the side of her neck and his thumb stroking her breast, she swallowed hard. She took a deep breath when he covered her nipple with his warm mouth through the sheet. "I think you're the right one—oh, God that feels good. Sarah said I had to stay here in Transition until the right person came along for me to help."

Lifting his face to gaze into her eyes, Zach looked skeptical. "Sarah? Oh, yeah—the angel." The corners of his mouth twitched in obvious amusement. "Sure, I see."

"Zach." She punched him on the arm when he laughed outright. Why was it so crucial to her that he understand? What difference would it really make to her future? "None of this is funny. Not to me."

"Like I said before, don't worry about it." His tone was patronizing. "We'll get you a doctor as soon as I make some money on this place." He looked around the room. "I suppose the only feasible thing to do is fix it up and sell." He laughed derisively. "I don't know who in their right mind would buy it, though. The realtor mentioned someone not in his right mind, though. So, there might be some hope."

Hilary felt as if he'd struck her. "I thought you decided not to sell Columbine." She clutched his shoulders, searching his expression with her gaze. "Promise me you won't sell it, Zach. At least not before I'm . . . I'm gone." *God, please not that.*

His expression grew solemn. "Gone? Where are you going?" He pushed away the damp sheet, ran his fingers down the curve of her bare breast and toyed with its taut, incredibly sensitive peak. "I don't want you to leave, Hilary. I want you to stay right here . . . with me."

His voice was honey poured over hotcakes. It melted inside her like butter, flowing and filling her with need. His touch was the dynamite the miners had used in their infinite quest for the mother lode. He displaced his fingers with his warm lips, caressing and teasing until she moaned with longing.

Undeniable in the midst of her confusion was one painfully prominent fact—Zach Ryan only wanted her body. Would he still want her if she managed to convince him she was really dead?

That he'd made love to a dead woman?

He didn't care about the truth at all. Her eyes stung as she struggled to hold back the tears threatening to burst forth, even as her body continued to betray her by responding wantonly to his seduction.

"I want you to believe me," she said very softly, looking down at his mouth on her breast. His whiskers scraped her, accentuating the delicious waves of yearning. His teeth nipped at her, making her shudder with the emphatic need for more of what he could offer.

She was going to Hell. All hope of ever making it to Heaven vanished in a flash of introspection. Conceding the battle at long last, Hilary sighed in resignation. She'd just as well enjoy what little time she had left in Transition. Soon it would be over.

Really over.

His hand dipped between her thighs, caressing her there until she surrendered to the hunger. He was powerful, able to control her with so very little effort. It was frightening.

Amazing.

He was an artist generating something beautiful when he made love to her. Hilary felt pretty in his arms, so complete and wanted. But as she succumbed to the shattering pleasures of the flesh, reached the summit of physical bliss again with Zach buried deep inside her, she felt strangely bereft.

He still didn't believe her.

She bit her lower lip in frustration as he leaned on one elbow to gaze at her.

"I told you my story, now how about yours?" she urged. "It's only fair."

He grinned crookedly, gently stroking her upper arm with his fingers. "Not much to tell." His expression darkened. "I was a flight test engineer for a big aerospace company in California."

"California?"

"The gold rush is over, Hilary." Merriment danced in his eyes. "Anyway, when the lawyer read my crazy uncle's will, leaving me an *entire* town in the Rocky Mountains, I thought I'd found my own personal gold mine." He snorted in obvious disdain. "What a fool."

"I don't believe you could ever be a fool." *Except about believing me.* Hilary touched the side of his face, liking the feel of his rough whiskers rasping against her palm. She'd missed simple pleasures—eating, drinking, smelling, tasting, feeling.

"You don't, huh?" He shook his head and raked his fingers through his hair until it stood on end. "I quit my job to move here. That rates real high on the stupidity meter. Hell, aerospace engineers are a dime-a-dozen right

now. We're being laid off right and left, and I *quit* my job
. . . for this.''

"I'm sorry Columbine isn't what you expected.'' Did he
realize that if he hadn't come here he never would have
found her? Did he care? Did it matter? "What's aerospace?''

"Aerospace, Hilary—airplanes?'' He smiled, then
searched her face, his manner softening as he caressed
the side of her cheek, then tilted her face until her gaze
met his. "But I found you, so I guess it was all worth it.''

Her mouth gaped open in complete shock at his declara-
tion. "Really, Zach?'' She closed her eyes for a moment
and kissed his palm, then laid her cheek in it and stared
at him in wonder. "I'm glad you're here. Maybe that's
selfish of me, but I'm very glad you came.''

Zach stared at her for several minutes in total silence.
A barrage of peculiar feelings bombarded him from all
fronts. This woman was insane, yet he adored her already.
Less than two days with her had him hooked. The mere
notion of being without her was unfathomable. Besides,
what did he have to return to if he left Columbine?

Not a damned thing.

"It's funny.'' He chuckled, still touching her face. "I'm
glad I came here, too. I sure wasn't at first, but now . . .''

Her face glowed as she smiled at him. Zach gasped at
the naked emotion he saw in her gaze. This was happening
too fast, he cautioned himself. More than too fast—it was
ludicrous.

Yet his feelings couldn't be defined or denied.

Since his parents had died suddenly in a boating accident while he was in college, Zach had been on a downhill
slide. Then his brother, Jake . . .

He clenched his teeth and closed his eyes, desperately
trying to blot out the pain of that horrible night. He'd

been so drunk he hadn't even realized what had happened until the next day . . . when the doctor told him.

Your brother's dead, Zach. The police will be here to question you later. You shouldn't have been driving. Your blood alcohol level was . . .

And Zach had been totally alone all this time. Except for fast cars, more than a few willing women over the years, and his drinking buddies from work, he'd been totally, completely alone in the world.

By choice.

He'd killed his own brother with his stupid drinking. He took a deep, shuddering breath, held it for several seconds, then released it in a loud whoosh. When he opened his eyes, Hilary was still staring at him, her lovely face etched with concern.

Why did this eccentric, beautiful woman affect him so radically? Dare he possibly consider this something real and lasting—permanent?

Permanent? Yeah, right.

Mentally, he shook himself. He had to break this baffling spell she'd cast upon him with her inviting smile and friendly nature. Not to mention her body. He was becoming way too serious, too damned fast.

Zach kissed her soundly on the lips. "Mmm, you taste good," he murmured, then looked down when his stomach rumbled. He shot her a sheepish grin.

Hilary giggled. "I may taste good, but sounds to me like you need something a bit more substantial to eat."

"One granola bar yesterday just wasn't enough for a growing boy like me. Such a shame to leave this bed, but I believe you may be right." He sat up and stretched lazily. "Besides, we need to keep up our strength for more of this. And for working on this building. I'll go find us both something to eat. I'm way beyond granola bars now." He swung his legs over the edge of the bed and pulled on his jockeys and jeans. "Where's the kitchen? I know what you told me yesterday, Hilary, but no more games. I'm starving."

"Uh . . ." Hilary shook her head and laughed. "No one's used the kitchen here for a very long time. Remember?"

He cast her a look of what he hoped was tolerant disbelief and lifted an eyebrow. "Where's the kitchen, Hilary?"

"Downstairs, in the back, but I don't think you'll—"

"I'll just run down and see what I can throw together." He bent over and kissed her forehead. When he straightened, the expression he saw smoldering in her eyes was mesmerizing. It was filled with promises—promises he planned to help her fulfill. "Don't you move from this bed. Stay right where you are."

Zach blew her a kiss and closed the door behind him, whistling as he made his way down the stairs. Hilary Brown was the most delightful and perplexing woman he'd ever known. In less than forty-eight hours she'd made him think, feel and do things he'd never dreamed. She was the kind of woman he could spend his life with.

Whoa, Zach, slow down.

He paused at the base of the ornate staircase. He wasn't being rational at all. His reaction to Hilary was nuts.

She was nuts.

The woman thought she was a ghost or an angel. Which was the least rational of the two? A smile tugged the corners of his mouth as he recalled the angel in his arms this morning. Just the thought of her delectable body made him harden with renewed longing.

His stomach growled again, reminding him of his mission. "Need to keep up my energy." He looked around the main room of the saloon again. "And I need to get to work on this dump if I ever plan to make any money on it."

With a pang of guilt, he recalled Hilary's reaction to his

intention to sell Columbine. He didn't really want to part with it, either—at least not without a fight. He sure as hell had his work cut out for him.

He opened the front door to peer outside. The snow had already melted away beneath the bright sun. The air smelled clean and fresh; a chill still lingered in the morning air, though the sun felt warm on his face. Inhaling deeply, he turned toward the back of the building in search of the kitchen.

As he passed the bar, something caught his attention. He froze. There was a slight movement—or seemed to be one—in the mirror behind the bar. It was spellbinding, yet amorphous. For some unexplainable reason he couldn't drag his gaze from it.

He stared at the mirror for several moments, then walked around behind the bar. There were several old whiskey barrels and beer kegs, a few broken bottles, but nothing moving.

Nothing alive.

"Looking for more ghosts, Zach?" he chided himself.

Chuckling, he started to turn around, then stopped—paralyzed. His breath caught in his throat as he stared into the huge, warped mirror that ran the length of the room behind the bar.

A shape—a face?—wavered in the silver. It was vague, but there. Squinting, he moved nearer, but the wavering form didn't become any clearer. The eyes drew his scrutiny as they twisted and changed shape behind the warped silver.

Hilary.

It couldn't be. The image continued to fluctuate. Whoever or whatever, it seemed trapped. He took a step back, bumping into the bar, his hand clutching his throat. His heart pounded in his chest to the rhythm of the words that played over and over again in his mind.

I'm dead, Zach—in Transition.

Impossible.

He shook his head and reached behind him for something solid. The bar felt rough and real beneath his grasp, anchoring him in reality—he hoped.

He blinked to clear his vision, then stared again at the warped silver. Nothing.

"My imagination." Heaving a sigh of relief, he chuckled at himself. "You're tired and hungry, Zach," he admonished. "Get a grip."

"Is everything all right, Zach?"

Turning, he saw Hilary standing at the top of the stairs. She had the sheet wrapped around her body, tucked beneath her arms as she stood staring at him.

"I thought I heard voices."

He swallowed the lump in his throat as he stared at her. Who was she? *What* was she?

And why did he care so damned much?

He was lost.

"Hilary, I . . ."

"What is it?"

She came down the steps toward him. "Are you sure you're all right?"

He closed his eyes as she caressed the side of his face. He was terrified by the onslaught of vivid emotions sweeping through him. She felt good—right.

This was insane.

She was insane.

"I'm fine." He cleared his throat and covered her hand with his. He'd been imagining things. Hilary was here—not in the mirror. "Where'd you say the kitchen was?"

"Zach, why can't you believe me?" She gave him an indulgent smile. "See for yourself if you must, but you'll find nothing but cobwebs and dust in the kitchen."

Zach followed her to the back of the saloon, but just

before he stepped from the main room, he felt compelled to turn back to the mirror.

Coldness wormed its way through him as he stared at the glittering silver. It seemed to taunt him. Again, he saw movement within the reflection, but it was vague. Indistinguishable.

He repressed a shudder of pure, illogical terror. Cold sweat beaded his brow as he stared long and hard at the mirror. What was it? Who was it?

More importantly . . . He dragged his gaze to her.

Who and *what* was Hilary Brown?

Chapter Six

Zach looked stunned. "What the hell is this, Hilary?" His gaze swept the room once. Twice. "I don't believe it."

"The kitchen." Hilary stared at him. "You asked me to show it to you, Zach. I'm sorry, but this is it."

"This is even worse than the rest of the place. How are we supposed to eat? How have you managed to survive up here all alone?" He looked at her suspiciously. "For that matter, how long *could* you have really been in Columbine without some sort of working kitchen? You have no transportation. Did someone dump you up here—abandon you?"

Yes, an angel abandoned me up here. Hilary bit her lower lip and grimaced. "I've tried to explain this, but you refuse to accept the truth. I know it's hard. If someone had tried to convince me of this when I was alive, I never would've believed it. If I disappear again will you believe me?"

"No, please . . . don't." He closed his eyes, then sighed as he opened them. "I don't believe in ghosts, Hilary."

He shook his head and rolled his eyes in obvious frustration, then turned his attention to the room again.

"Part of the floor's rotted through," he said steadily. "A cast-iron stove, cobwebs in every nook and cranny—nice touch. Ah, and of course, the pots and pans hanging from the ceiling. So Americana." His eyes darkened as he surveyed the ceiling again. "See the cracks on that beam?" He pointed at the ceiling.

Nodding, Hilary pulled the sheet tighter around her. He was really angry with her now. If only she could make him believe her.

"One of those crossbeams could fall." He firmly gripped Hilary's bare arm and guided her back to the doorway. "It isn't safe in here."

He stood, silently staring at her for several minutes. She could tell from the way the muscles in his cheek and jaw clenched that he was gnashing his teeth. "I'm sorry you're disappointed, Zach."

"If I didn't know any better . . ." He chuckled nervously. "My sense of reason tells me you couldn't possibly have been up here for very long. You being here at all grows more and more puzzling. Please just tell me—did someone bring you up here and leave you?"

"I tried to tell you—"

"We'll just have to go to town for groceries," Zach interrupted, obviously determined not to hear the truth again. "I have enough money left to buy some of the supplies we'll need. I sure can't survive on cereal bars much longer." He visibly shuddered. "And I'm not one for hunting. I hate the thought of shooting a defenseless animal, except for maybe that bear. Nah, not even him. Of course, he doesn't have much to worry about, since I don't even have a gun."

She liked that about Zach. He wouldn't shoot an animal even to feed himself. Suddenly, she realized exactly what he'd said before that. "Town?" Hilary tugged on the sheet again. "What town?"

Zach shrugged. "Divide was the last one I passed before turning up the old mining road. I'll have to check the map." He turned to lead her out of what had once been a very busy kitchen. Then he paused to stare at her again. "I wish you'd tell me just how long you've really been up here alone, Hilary. And what have you done for food all this time?"

She looked at the floor and squeezed her eyes shut. "I've told you at least ten times already, Zach."

He gripped her shoulders with both his hands. "Look at me, Hilary." His voice dropped to a low, urgent whisper. "Look at me."

Lifting her gaze to meet his, Hilary struggled with the emotions surging through her. This man was turning her inside out. In the less than forty-eight hours she'd known Zach Ryan, she'd committed at least one sin—more than once—that could very easily keep her out of Heaven. She fought the image of Sarah's face when the angel had first denied Hilary admittance to Heaven. The second time would be even worse—permanent.

She was doomed.

Damned.

After all this time, the thought of having a liberator was simply too good to be true. Whoever kept track of such things up in Heaven had probably given up on Hilary Brown long ago. She was a lost cause.

Another horrible thought assailed her. What if she remained in Transition forever? If they'd forgotten about her . . . "Oh, not that," she whispered. "Anything, but that—or damnation." Though it would be nice to remain with Zach for as long as possible.

She was stuck in her earthly Transition for the time being. What eternity had in store for her was anybody's guess. She'd just have to make the best of the situation until something happened.

But not *too* soon.

There was nothing left for her to do except stay with Zach. Was it possible to have the remainder of her years here with him, loving him?

A thrill shot through her. At long last—over a century after her death—Hilary Brown had found love. Real love.

Could a ghost—or whatever she was—live with a man as his what? Wife? There was nothing in the world she wanted as desperately as to spend her Transition with Zach. Of course, she was assuming Sarah wouldn't choose to shorten Hilary's time because of her obvious inability to resist temptation.

"Hilary Brown, you're driving me nuts." Zach laughed and rolled his eyes toward the ceiling. "But you do need help from a doctor. I want to make sure you understand that."

Hilary sighed in defeat and held her hands out plaintively at her sides. "What can I do to prove the truth to you, Zach?" she asked. "I'm really dead. I'm a . . . a ghost. I was put here, like this, because I wasn't quite good enough to go to Heaven, but not bad enough to go to Hell—at least not right away."

"No, Hilary." Zach rubbed her shoulders with his strong hands. "You're confused, that's all. I'm going to get you help."

"I don't *need* any help, Zach." Hilary sighed and lowered her gaze. "But I'd like to stay here with you—if it's all right?"

"All right? I can't begin to imagine being here without you, Hilary." Zach chuckled. "Hell, I can't believe this is happening to me. When I drove into this hellhole day before yesterday, I thought my life was over. I'd lost it all. Then I saw you chasing away that monster bear."

He threw his head back to laugh. It was a gleeful sound that drew Hilary into its spell. Soon, she was laughing along with him. This wasn't anything like the bitter laugh she'd heard coming from him yesterday.

Hilary tilted her head to study the man she loved. She had no idea what they were laughing about. "What is it, Zach?" She relished the way his hands felt on her bare shoulders. Warm and rough, yet soft at the same time. Each passing hour with Zach left her feeling less ghostly and more alive. "What's so funny?"

"I am. You are. *We* are." He pulled her against him. "This is crazy, Hilary, but I'm nuts about you. I really am. I can't imagine life without you." He laughed again and kissed the side of her neck. "I want to help you get well." He lifted her chin in his hand and gazed into her eyes. "I want you to stay with me, be with me, Hilary Brown."

She stared at him in amazement. Tears stung her eyes and her lower lip trembled. This man, whom she loved with all her heart, wanted her to . . . to what? Marry him? Was he proposing marriage to a dead woman? "Zach, I can't."

He nodded. "Yes, you can." He paused for a moment. His expression caressed her. "I know you're not married, because you were a virgin. So why can't you live here with me, for as long as we're able to stay here, that is?"

Hilary's face flooded with heat. "Zach."

"Hilary." He kissed the tip of her nose. "All you have to do is stay with me. Be with me, and let me raise the money to help you get well. Stay. Say you will. Say yes."

She squeezed her eyes shut against the pain. "I can't stay forever, Zach. Sooner or later, I'll be taken away—my Transition will end." Her tears flowed freely now as she tried to tear herself from the protective yet tormenting circle of his embrace. "Why can't you understand? Didn't you wonder why there was no virgin's blood in the bed this morning? Think, Zach. I'm dead—a dead person can't bleed. Want me to walk through a wall? A door? Disappear?''

"No, Hilary." He pulled her against him again and kissed the top of her head. "Sweet Hilary. You're confused, but I'm going to get help for you. If you stay here with me, I can get you a doctor soon."

Her hopes plummeted. "Oh, no." She pulled free of his embrace and turned away. "You don't really want me. You have some sort of heroic need to rescue me from myself. That's just like a man. Are you trying to be my knight in shining armor?"

Zach touched her hair from behind. "It's much more than that, Hilary," he said in a ragged tone. "Please try to understand."

"No."

"Hilary, I care about you. We just met, but I feel as if I've known you forever. I really do." He stepped in front of her and cupped her chin in his large hand again. "I *want* you. Yes, I want to help you, but it sure as hell isn't heroic." He laughed. "It's purely selfish on my part."

His words were so sweet.

Hilary leaned into him, savored the solid feel of his chest. Laying her head against his shoulder, she wondered if this could really happen for her. But what about Zach? If he loved her, and she desperately wanted to believe that he did, then he had a right to know she would only be around until the turn of the century.

After that . . .

"Zach, I care about you, too," she whispered, moaning when his lips found hers in a kiss so tender it made her tremble. When he lifted his face to gaze into her eyes, she melted against him. "Yes, Zach. Anything. Everything you want."

Zach spun her in a circle. "Yes!"

Laughing, Hilary fought the perfidious tears that threatened her resolve yet again. This was all she had left. She'd spent over a century waiting for her liberator.

Returning to her old life just wasn't to be. Zach Ryan was real. He wanted her—she loved him. Even if this was wrong—a sin—it was almost heaven.

For the next few years, nothing else mattered.

Zach was worried.

Hilary was even more confused than he'd thought.

"Why can't you wear something else?" he asked while he reluctantly ate another granola bar. No amount of coaxing had convinced Hilary to join him in his light repast. "Don't you have other clothes?"

Sitting on the edge of her bed, Hilary shook her head. "They rotted away or became nests for mice years ago." She laughed. "That horrible red dress is all I have; it's what I died in. I guess it's in Transition, too. It doesn't age and neither do I."

Zach looked at his feet and took a deep breath. She needed help—bad. Question was, could she really wait until he managed to come up with enough money to get her help? As it was, they'd be lucky to have enough money to see them through the winter months ahead. Of course, with her pitiful appetite, food wouldn't be as expensive as it could have been. But this thought far from soothed him.

"Wear a pair of my jeans and a T-shirt," he suggested, pulling the items from his backpack and laying them across the foot of the bed. "The jeans'll be too long, but you can roll them up."

Hilary's mouth formed a perfect circle. "Maybe you should go alone, Zach. Except when I went after you last night, I haven't left Columbine since 1886."

Practice your relaxation exercises, Zach. Remember biofeedback?

He tensed the muscles in his neck, then relaxed them, took a long breath, then released it. What was it his grandmother had always said? *God, grant me patience, but hurry the hell up about it.* He had to keep his cool. Hilary needed him.

"Then I'd say it's past time you had an outing, Miss Brown," he said in a light tone, seating himself on a red velvet ottoman which had long ago seen better days. "Try on the jeans, Hilary. I think they'll fit."

"Women really wear men's clothing now?" When he nodded, she sighed, dropped the sheet and pulled his T-shirt on over her head.

Zach forced down the dry granola that lodged in his throat when he saw the way she filled out his T-shirt. It was white—wrong choice.

"Uh, Hilary?"

"What?" She held the jeans up in front of her, staring at them as if she'd never worn pants before.

"Don't you have a bra or panties?" Zach's pulse raced as he stared at her nipples, clearly defined through the white fabric. She'd be a wet T-shirt contest queen. When she shook her head, he reached into his backpack and removed a red and blue plaid flannel shirt. "Try this on over the T-shirt."

Following the direction of Zach's gaze with her own, Hilary's face flushed crimson. "Oh!" She tugged the proffered garment on over the revealing T-shirt. "Thank you."

Zach grinned and wolfed down the rest of his breakfast, such as it was. The flannel shirt helped hide the red ring around her neck, too. What had caused the scar? A horrible thought made the last of his breakfast stick in his gullet.

Had Hilary tried to hang herself? She didn't seem depressed or suicidal. Just confused.

Correction—very confused.

"I'm sorry there's nothing else here for you to eat,

Zach," she said in her smooth voice, rescuing Zach from his nightmarish thoughts.

"Sure you don't want one of these? They're pretty good." He knew he was badgering her, but she had to eat. Hell, he wanted to see her eat for his own sanity. Judging from her voluptuous curves, she hadn't been starving before he came. Maybe he was being paranoid for nothing. She seemed healthy . . . if only physically.

Hilary sat down on the edge of the bed to pull on the jeans. His view of her bottom half was his undoing. His libido leapt into overdrive and his blood pressure hit the roof. "Oh, boy." He reminded himself they had to get to town and back before dark, so there wasn't time to do what he wanted to so desperately again. Not that he had the strength, considering he was half-starved.

"There." Hilary buttoned the fly and looked at him expectantly. "How do I look?"

"Good enough to eat." *Right now, every day, all day.* Zach tugged at the neckline of his T-shirt and stood. "Do you have other shoes?"

She sat on the edge of the bed and pulled on the leather shoes she'd worn with the red dress. They were heeled and laced up the front to just above her ankles.

Zach tried not to chuckle, but this was too much. "I think that look went out of style a few years back, but what do I know about women's fashion?"

"Pardon me?" she asked, standing to stare at him with a bewildered expression.

"Nothing." He reached for the door. "If we're going to be back before dark, we'd better get started." Zach noticed some letters and numbers carved in the woodwork around the door frame. He paused, running his fingers over the old letters. "What's this?"

She stood beside him and traced the letters with the tip of her finger. "Mine." She blinked rapidly when he turned to stare at her. "My brother and I used to measure each other here every year on our birthdays. Mama never cared."

"That's right. You mentioned your brother before." Zach winced inwardly. He hoped she wouldn't ask about his family. He wasn't ready to share that experience with anyone yet. Not even Hilary. "I see your name right here." He traced the letters in the wood.

Maybe she had lived here before. Had her family lived in Columbine during Hilary's childhood? The markings indicated her growth over a period of years. The dates were also scratched into the surface, but they were difficult to read. He squinted and held his hand up to where her height would have been at that time.

Hilary looked up at him and he noticed the tears in her eyes. "What's wrong, Hilary?" He captured a tear with the tip of his finger, then kissed her on the forehead. "Why are you crying?"

"My brother." She touched the other name lovingly. "Elliot."

Zach followed the direction of her movement. "He was younger?"

She nodded, then her hand dropped to her side. Her smile was sad. "In his mind, he was much younger."

Frowning, Zach watched her turn away and run her fingers through her hair. He sensed she wouldn't welcome any questions just yet about her family either. He was very curious about how long it had been since people really lived in Columbine. It would have to wait until later—he didn't want to upset her further, and it was getting late.

"We'd better go, Hilary," he said quietly. When she turned to face him, her tears had ceased and she was smiling, but he could tell it was forced. "Are you ready?"

Hilary's eyes grew round as she stared at him. "Are you sure about this?"

Zach opened the door and they stepped into the hall. "About going to town?"

"I guess." Her voice trembled slightly as she descended the stairs at his side. "Like I said, it's been a long time since I left Columbine."

"I'm sure." Zach's heart swelled in his throat. He just had to help Hilary. "Do you have a copy of your birth certificate, Hilary? Passport? Any kind of identification?"

Disappointment filled her gaze, even though she tried to look away. "I don't think I ever had a birth certificate."

"Driver's license?" *Dumb question.* "Never mind."

She paused at the bottom of the steps to look at him. "Do I need identification just to go to town?"

"No, not for that." He shrugged. "I have an idea, but I think we're going to need some kind of ID to pull it off. I'm going to call my old benefits advisor out in California. I still have medical insurance for six months. Maybe you can get coverage as my significant other."

Hilary drew her brows together and she frowned. "Your what?"

Zach mentally kicked himself. "Uh . . ."

"I'm not familiar with that term, but I know enough to be sure I don't like it." She took a deep breath and lifted her chin a notch. "I'm not a . . . a . . ."

Zach took her hand in his. "Hilary, I know that better than anyone. Remember?"

Blushing, she nodded and smiled. "All right." She squeezed his hand. "Let's go to town."

"That's the spirit." *Bad choice of words.* "Uh, we'll have to walk to where I left the Jeep last night. And, Hilary?"

"Hmm?"

"Thanks for saving my hide last night."

"You're welcome."

Her smile was radiant as they strolled out into the sunshine. The heavy wet snow was gone, leaving behind moist earth and a few lingering patches of green grass. Only the highest peaks remained white.

They walked out of town, down the road he'd driven on last night. If he remembered correctly, he hadn't been more than half a mile from town when he'd hit the trees.

Something suddenly occurred to him that he should've considered much earlier. His black and white engineering mind had been preoccupied with sex. Glancing at the beautiful woman at his side, he was reminded of exactly why he hadn't been thinking clearly.

"Hilary, how did you know I was in trouble last night?"

Hilary blushed and turned her head so suddenly her blond curls covered her face for a moment. "I'm not exactly sure, and that's the truth."

Zach contemplated the events which had led up to this point. Besides the fact that he had no idea how she'd known he was in trouble, there was the very real problem of moving him from the accident to Columbine. Until now, he hadn't even considered it.

"Hilary?"

"Yes?"

"How'd you move me?" He laughed, but he knew it was a nervous sound. One way or another, he had to squelch that little voice in his subconscious that still wanted to believe her ridiculous tales. "I'm one helluva lot heavier than you, and I'm pretty sure I didn't walk back. I think I'd remember if I had."

Hilary sighed. "What's it going to take to convince you, Zach?" She stopped and jerked her hand from his. "Shall I disappear again for you? Or, maybe I could walk through a tree?"

He rubbed his eyes with his thumb and forefinger, reminding himself how fragile her mental state was. He shouldn't quiz her like this. It was obvious she couldn't handle it.

But he couldn't imagine how she'd managed to move him so far by herself. For the time being, he'd have to play along, patronize her as much as necessary to keep from pushing her off the deep end. If she wasn't already well on her way. "Convince me of what?"

"Zach, I'm dead. And I do have some . . . powers."

"Powers?" He couldn't suppress the shudder that started in his spine and included his entire body before it was finished. "Like disappearing?"

She nodded. "Exactly. And transporting myself from one point to another by closing my eyes and just thinking about it."

He chewed his lower lip for a moment and reached for her hand again. "I don't think it's much farther. Let's go."

Hilary blinked back her biting tears. Wouldn't it really be easier for her if he thought she was a crazy woman? For some reason, she couldn't stand for him not to understand and accept her true identity. She wanted him to welcome her as she truly was.

Dead.

Zach continued to hold her hand until they rounded a curve in the road and saw the Jeep. She stood to the side while he walked around it, muttering to himself and shaking his head.

"I think it'll run, but both headlights are shot." He furrowed his brow and the little lines at the corners of his eyes seemed more pronounced as he contemplated his predicament. "But, like I said earlier, we have to get back before dark. I'm not risking another close call like last night. Jeez, all these years on the Southern California freeways—my insurance agent is going to love this."

Smiling, Hilary didn't bother asking him to explain what he was talking about. None of it made sense to her. She simply nodded, wondering if she could move the Jeep with her powers. It was so near the edge, half-way down an embankment that gave way to a sheer drop-off of at least five hundred feet. However, the trees were doing a good job of keeping the Jeep secure for the moment.

Zach stooped to pick up a stick while she concentrated on the heavy conveyance. She closed her eyes and visually pulled the Jeep toward her, onto the road and away from the cliff. It was exhausting, but she felt it working.

She opened her eyes just as he straightened. He looked at the Jeep, then at her.

"What . . . ?" He frowned, his eyes wide and confused. "Wasn't it over there?" He walked closer. "See the broken headlights here, next to the trees?" He looked up at her. "Did you *do* something?" he asked in a monotone which barely resembled his usual voice.

Hilary smiled nervously. "I moved the Jeep for you," she explained with a shrug. "It worried me, being so near the edge."

Zach walked around the Jeep and touched the hood. When he looked at her, his eyes were filled with suspicion. "I don't understand any of this, Hilary."

There was an unspoken question in his tone. How could he continue to deny the obvious? "I've been telling you the truth all along." Would he leave her once she managed to convince him of the truth? The next few years without Zach would be unbearable. He was a potent nectar—once tasted, she couldn't bear to live without him.

But she wasn't living now.

He shrugged helplessly. "Forget I asked. I don't want to know how you moved the Jeep. All right? Just get in."

He helped her into the Jeep and fastened her seat belt. Again his arm brushed her breast, but Hilary didn't vanish. She savored every tiny bit of contact she could have with Zach. It was exquisite, so perfect; almost frightening.

His gaze locked with hers as he half-leaned toward her.

When his lips brushed hers, she felt her insides turn to warm liquid.

"I'm sorry I was brusque. You're beautiful," Zach whispered when he lifted his lips from hers. "Whoever—whatever—you are."

"Thank you, Zach." Blinking back her tears, Hilary watched him straighten and fasten his own seat belt. The muscles in his forearms rippled with the simple effort. When he turned the key, his Jeep made a horrid groaning sound, then sputtered and roared.

"Good." He smiled and pushed the black rectangle on the floor with his foot until the noise grew louder. "That's a relief."

Hilary grimaced and gripped the edge of her seat when he maneuvered the stick that stuck up from the floor between them, then he made the Jeep move backward. She much preferred her method of travel. She could just close her eyes, think about it and it happened.

A giggle bubbled from her chest as she considered how strange her talents must seem to Zach. What was even more incredible was his ability to maintain his staunch refusal to accept the truth, even after witnessing irrefutable evidence. Imagining how she would have reacted before her death to meeting someone who had such gifts, Hilary's laughter ceased.

"All right." Zach drove the Jeep slowly forward, down the steep incline. "If you'll open the glove compartment, Hilary, there are some maps of the area in there."

"Glove compartment?" Her gaze swept the metal directly in front of her, where Zach had pointed. A small button on what appeared to be a door drew her attention. When she pressed the button, the door fell open, startling her when several rolled maps fell out at her feet.

"If you'll unroll this one for me, please?" He touched

the largest of the maps. "I think I can find my way around. I hope."

His grin was magical. Hilary returned it and obeyed his request. "Here it is."

Zach stopped the Jeep and took the map from her hands. "It isn't very far to town, but it's not much of a road until we get to the highway," he said quietly as he studied the map. "We shouldn't have too much trouble getting back before dark."

Hilary nodded as he handed her the map. She returned it to the glove compartment and leaned back in the seat. Zach made the Jeep move slowly down the mountain. She watched in awe as his feet worked the strange pedals and the stick in the center. When he turned the round black thing in front of him, the conveyance changed directions. It was quite miraculous.

Her mouth gaped open when they emerged from the trees. A long road covered with a smooth substance stretched before them in both directions. It was a long gray ribbon, winding its way down the mountain.

She gripped the edge of her seat even more tightly as Zach turned the Jeep onto the surface. He increased the Jeep's speed as she continued to stare in amazement.

"You okay?" Zach asked, reaching over to give her hand a squeeze.

Hilary nodded, unable to speak. She felt as if they were floating—no jarring or bouncing like in a wagon. The top of the conveyance fluttered and flapped in the wind as they sped down the road.

"That's the one problem with rag tops," Zach said above the roar. "Noise."

She nodded again and held her breath as he began to slow down. Several buildings appeared around the next curve in the road. Hilary blinked and swallowed hard.

People.

It wasn't a large town by any means, but several people walked along the sidewalks. They passed two vehicles similar to Zach's, then he pulled into a large flat area. He brought the Jeep to a stop, then turned it off.

"Here we are."

She nodded again, but didn't move or release her grip on the seat.

"Are you sure you're all right, Hilary? *Hilary?*" He touched her face, gently coaxing her to turn toward him. "Hilary, what's wrong?"

"That was fun!" She laughed, then gasped in joy. "Can we do it again?"

"Do what?" His brows came together, forming a ridge of concern on his forehead. "You mean drive?"

"Yes, it was ever so much more exciting than last time. Will it go as fast when we ride back?" Hilary reached for the stick in the middle and wiggled it from side to side. "What's this? How does it make the Jeep go?"

Zach laughed out loud. "If you like, I'll teach you to drive later. In Columbine, where there's no traffic." He shook his finger at her and chuckled again. "With any luck, the only thing you might hit is a big black bear. Nah, I didn't mean that. I wouldn't even wish that on him."

Was she serious? Zach stared at the gleeful expression on her face as she looked around the town. Her eyes were wide with fascination. She was like an innocent child, just now exposed to the world.

At her age?

Batty, Zach. Mad. Several bricks shy of a load.

He almost gagged on the lump of apprehension in his throat. Hilary needed more than psychiatric help. She needed love and patience.

But most of all . . . she needed watching.

He didn't dare let her out of his sight while they were in town. The citizens of Divide, Colorado, weren't ready for Hilary Brown. No one was. He chuckled low and climbed from the Jeep to open her door.

Taking her hand, he kept it close to his body as she walked at his side. When the automatic door swung open to admit them to the grocery store, Hilary squealed and stepped back.

Zach followed her retreat, allowing the door to close again.

"What . . . what made it do that?" she asked in a shaky voice. "It opened by itself."

Zach's stomach lurched. She was worse off than he'd thought. Maybe she did have amnesia. She certainly had no memory of the real world.

But she knew her name and a richly detailed, fictional past. Maybe she was a writer who'd fallen into character and been unable to escape.

"Hilary, let me show you." Zach led her slowly toward the door again. "When we step on this black mat here, the door will swing open by itself." The door opened on cue. "See?"

Nodding, she allowed him to guide her through the door, looking quickly over her shoulder when it closed behind them.

"When we leave, the other door will let us out the same way." Zach squeezed her hand and rolled his eyes. This was going to be more difficult than he'd thought. "Come on. We'll get some food. I brought a barbecue grill and outdoor cooking utensils with me just in case. Good thing. Tonight, we eat steaks. I don't care about cholesterol."

She stared in silence as he led her through the store, filling the shopping cart with canned goods and other non-perishable items. He splurged on a couple of T-bones. Two days of fasting had left a huge empty hole in his gut that demanded satisfaction.

"I dunno about you," he said with a chuckle, "but I

need my coffee tomorrow morning. I'm suffering from caffeine withdrawal. Guess we can heat water and make instant. I don't think cream's a good idea, but we can get you some non-dairy creamer."

"Coffee?" Hilary looked left, then right down the frozen food aisle. "What's this over here?"

Zach ignored the teen-aged boy who paused to gape at Hilary. She was quite a sight in his snug-fitting jeans, with the flannel shirt open in the front to expose the white T-shirt and her voluptuous curves. Irrational jealousy surged through Zach. Resisting the urge to reach over and button her shirt, he clenched his teeth, then turned the shopping cart away from the frozen food aisle. They had no way to keep anything cold anyway.

"Zach, why—"

"This way, Hilary." He cursed himself for snapping at her, but her naivety was getting old. He knew she wasn't pretending. Not even an Academy Award-winning actress could have pulled this off. She was too consistent.

Sighing, he turned to apologize near the coffee urn.

But she was gone.

"Oh, no—not again." Zach abandoned his cart and did an about-face, retracing his steps until he found her in the frozen food aisle. She was running her fingers along the frosty containers of vegetables and ice cream. Pausing, he felt a protective wave sweep through him. She needed his love and understanding, not his hot temper.

"I'm sorry," he said quietly, touching her arm as she picked up a container of ice cream.

"What's this, Zach?" she asked. Her eyes were round with wonder. "Is it real ice cream? Already made?"

Zach smiled. His heart swelled with affection for this incredible creature. She was such a delight. "Do you like ice cream, Hilary?"

She nodded and smiled. "I only had it once on the

Fourth of July. I remember it was the best thing I ever tasted in my entire life.''

''Really?'' He touched her face with the back of his hand. ''The very best?''

She flushed beneath his stare and met his gaze. ''Almost.''

Her tongue moistening her lips created an image in his mind that made Zach shudder with longing. ''What flavor do you want?''

''Flavor?'' She was still staring at him. ''Touch my arm, Zach.''

''Huh?'' He straightened and stared at her. ''Touch your arm?''

''Yes, please.''

He complied with her request, then watched her tentatively reach out to touch one of the cartons. ''That's what I thought.''

''What?''

''When you touch me, I can feel hot and cold.'' She moved her hand away from the carton. When she turned to gaze at him, her expression was smoldering. ''And other things.''

Oh, God. I don't know if I can wait 'til we get back. He looked down at her hardening nipples, dark and tempting beneath the tightly stretched white fabric. Forcibly, he turned his attention back to the ice cream. ''Vanilla? Strawberry?'' He peered at her through partially closed eyes. ''Chocolate? Yes, you look like a chocolate lover.''

The image of covering Hilary in chocolate ice cream and kissing it off made thoughts of debauchery explode in his mind. ''Damn.''

''Are you all right, Zach?'' She touched his arm while he reached for the container she held, then he retrieved an additional one from the bin.

''Nothing a couple of half gallons of this stuff won't

cure," he quipped, battling the ideas wreaking havoc on his composure. "I'll get some ice and put it in the cooler. But we'll have to eat it right away. Soft serve." *Oh, God.*

She smiled like a small child on Christmas morning. "I don't know if I can eat. I haven't even tried since . . . But I'd like to try. Mmm."

Mmm. "We'd better hurry if we want to get back before this melts." *And before I make a complete fool of myself in public.*

"All right."

Zach felt like a dirty old man while he put the ice cream in the cooler in the Jeep. He had to forcibly remind himself to call California. "I need to find a pay phone."

"Pay phone?" Hilary frowned when he took her to the side of the building.

He dug in his pocket for a quarter and his wallet for a credit card. When he finally found the number of the benefits office in California, he punched in the digits, glancing askance at Hilary's stunned expression as he did.

Tilting her head to the side, she stepped closer and pushed a button with her long slender finger.

"Don't, Hilary." He grabbed her hand before she could push another button, then replaced the receiver and started over. "You messed up the number. It's long distance and the middle of the day. It'll cost a bundle I don't have."

Her lower lip trembled. "I'm sorry."

She turned and walked toward the Jeep just as a voice sounded in Zach's ear. He watched her while asking the necessary questions, looking away only once to read the numbers off his insurance card. When he turned back, she was nowhere in sight.

"Damn."

"Excuse me, sir?" the voice on the phone asked. "Did you say Colorado?"

"Yes, Colorado." He leaned as far away from the wall

as he could without breaking the connection. No sign of
Hilary.

"How may I help you, sir?"

"Uh . . . uh . . ."

"Sir?"

"I gotta go."

Dropping the phone, Zach ran around the corner of
the building. He froze for a split second when he saw her.
She was standing in the middle of the highway, watching
cars whiz by on both sides. Her expression was one of total
awe—like a kid who'd been denied access to toys and
candy her entire life.

She turned and started back toward him. The smile on
her face was so innocent, so beautiful, that it made him
ache inside.

The distant roar of an eighteen-wheeler barreling down
on the small town of Divide made him look away. *Oh, my
God.* His blood turned cold. "Hilary, stop!"

But he was too late.

The driver hit his horn, making Hilary hesitate in the
path of its huge wheels. The next few moments made Zach
realize what it meant to be responsible for someone he
cared about.

Loved.

He ran as fast as he could, but the truck met Hilary
before he even reached the curb. He screamed. The ragged
sound wrenched itself from his gut, his very soul, as he
squeezed his eyes shut for a moment of pure terror, then
forced them open as the vehicle roared past. The truck
driver was still trying to stop, applying the squealing brakes,
obviously overheated from coming down the mountain
pass.

The sight before Zach rocked the foundations of his
sanity.

Hilary Brown stood in the middle of the lane the semi had taken on its way through town. There was no way it could have missed her. He took a step toward her.

She was still standing.

Smiling.

"I missed her!" The frantic driver rushed to the scene. His face was red as he held his hand over his heart and sighed in obvious relief. "My God, I thought she was a goner for sure."

Zach still stood staring at the woman who slowly approached them.

Still smiling.

"I just don't see how I coulda missed her." The driver removed his cap and scratched his bald head. "There was no way I could stop. Thank God she's all right. Still don't understand it, though. It's a miracle, plain and simple."

Zach nodded, too stunned to reply when Hilary stopped in front of him and took his hand in hers. "Zach, did you see how fast that big thing was moving?" she asked, her voice filled with ingenuous reverence.

The driver shook his head and replaced his hat. "Miss, I'm real sorry, but you're old enough to know not to be standin' out in the middle of the highway like that." He sighed raggedly. "I just thank God you ain't hurt. It's a miracle, no other explanation."

Still unable to speak, Zach nodded when the driver announced his intention to park his rig and take a very long lunch break.

Zach blinked once.

Then he locked his gaze with Hilary's.

"What the hell happened out there, Hilary?" he demanded, jerking his hand free from hers. He was shaking inside. "What *are* you?"

Hilary took a step back. "I've told you what I am, Zach."

She trembled and looked down at her feet. "I'm sorry. I didn't mean to frighten you."

Zach took a deep breath and counted to ten. Twenty. "We'd better go back to Columbine before anything else happens."

Chapter Seven

Hilary was terrified.

Zach was all she had. She loved him more than anything or anyone she'd ever known. She'd abandoned all hopes of going to Heaven for that love.

The return trip to Columbine passed in total silence. The excitement of riding in the fast-moving Jeep no longer appealed to her.

Tears streamed down her face as he parked the Jeep at the side of Miss Nellie's and carried the groceries in without a word to her. He came back once for the strange box he'd put the ice cream into, then he just left her sitting there.

Crying.

She sat alone in the passenger seat for several minutes after he'd gone inside. What could she do to repair their relationship? She couldn't stand for him to remain angry with her. She loved him so much that it hurt.

Then another thought made her brighten. *Now he'll have to believe me.*

She dabbed her eyes with the sleeve of Zach's flannel shirt and climbed out of the Jeep. Sighing and lifting her chin in determination, she walked through the front door of the saloon, without bothering to open it first, and found him at the bar unpacking the food. The expression on his face was haggard.

"Zach?"

She noticed his jaw twitch, but he didn't look at her. "Zach," she repeated, determined to make him speak to her.

He sighed and sat a jar of coffee down with a thud. "What do you want?" His tone was clipped and he still didn't look at her. "You want to tell me some more ridiculous stories? Maybe you could walk through a wall or something. Now *that* would be impressive." He laughed derisively.

He obviously hadn't noticed the way she'd entered the saloon. "I wanted to talk about what happened in town." She took a step toward him, praying he'd look at her with those soft brown eyes. "Please look at me."

When he finally looked up at her, the expression on his face made her stomach lurch and her chest tighten. But the pain in his eyes gave her hope. If he was hurting, that meant he really loved her. Didn't it?

"I'm sorry about what happened." She went to the bar and stood on the opposite side, placing her hand over his. "I didn't know."

Zach snorted in obvious disbelief. His face was very red. "God, I need a drink. Hell, I need about twenty drinks." He squeezed his eyes closed for a moment. "You actually expect me to believe you had no idea being run down by a semi-truck would hurt you, Hilary?" He pulled his hand from beneath hers. "You're farther gone than I thought."

"Zach, I'm . . . I'm already dead." She walked around the bar and touched his shoulder. "The truck went *through* me, not over me. Don't you understand that? I didn't feel a thing."

He nodded. "Yeah, I saw it, but I still don't believe it. I've touched you, Hilary—felt how solid you are. Remember?" His gaze was anchored to hers. "You're a magician. It was an illusion—an optical illusion. That's all it could have been. The only plausible explanation. You've fallen into the magical world and can't find your way back."

Tears trickled down her cheeks and she shook her head. "There's nothing I can do or say to make you believe me, is there?" *Even though I love you?*

Zach sighed and lowered his gaze for a second, then looked into her eyes. "Hilary, I want you," he whispered in a helpless tone. "God help me, but no matter how sick you are, I still want you, can't get enough of you. I *care* about you." He shuddered and closed his eyes again. "You scared the bloody hell out of me today."

"Oh, Zach!" She threw herself into his arms. She felt his heart hammering against her as she breathed in his musky scent. "I care about you, too. I wish you could believe me, but I guess it doesn't matter as long as you really care."

"Damn you, woman." Cupping her chin in his hand, he lifted her lips to meet his. A growl low in his throat rumbled into Hilary as his hands roamed urgently over her body.

She felt languid, yet tense with desire as he cupped her buttocks and lifted her against him. His rigid manhood pressed against her, making her ache inside for the full allotment of love.

Zach released her with a groan. He stared at her—they both gasped.

"Ice cream. Now," he muttered. His eyes glittered with a powerful passion as their gazes met.

"Ice cream?" she echoed in confusion as he reached into the box on the bar and removed a carton of ice cream.

He tore off the paper lid with one hand. "It's soft and sweet, just like you." There was a desperate, hungry, look in his eyes.

She smiled in anticipation as he slipped the flannel shirt from her shoulders, then lifted the revealing T-shirt over her head. She kicked off her shoes and wriggled out of the breeches he'd loaned her, while he did the same with his. The physical barriers were removed, permitting heated skin against skin.

She giggled when Zach reached into the ice cream container and scooped out a handful. He held it to her lips. She hesitated, afraid. It had been so long since she'd tasted food or drink. She touched his arm, anchoring herself in the strange near-real world he pulled her into with his nearness. Dare she sample the sweet, melting confection he offered?

Hilary took a tentative lick of the cold, creamy substance, moaning with pleasure when it filled her mouth. Zach's expression as he watched her sensuously eat the melting confection from his fingers, created a surge of molten longing within her. The sweet chocolate and Zach's gaze were pure decadence.

As were her thoughts.

Chocolate melted and dripped between them, covering her breasts and abdomen. Zach scooped her into his arms and placed her face up on the bar beside the open carton. He delved into the carton again, but this time he rubbed the cold, creamy substance across her breasts as she gasped in shock from the cold against her skin. Cold she shouldn't feel at all.

"A la mode has never been like this before," he whispered, grinning lasciviously.

Then he did something marvelous. He kissed and licked the ice cream from her neck and chest. He explored the valley between her breasts, making her moan beneath him. His search for her nipple, concealed in the ice cream, drove her mad. Then to compound her torment, he reached into the carton with his free hand to scoop more ice cream out for her other breast.

He laved her chocolate-covered nipple with his tongue, covering her breast with his warm mouth. The contrast of sweet-hot coldness with his heated lips was devastating. She pressed herself against him, offering him more of herself for their mutual pleasure.

He kissed his way downward as his thumbs continued to tease her pebbled nipples. She arched against him and he reached with one hand for more ice cream, placing a generous scoop on the triangle of hair between her thighs.

The ice cream began to melt on contact, stunning Hilary as it dripped between her thighs. He chuckled lecherously, lifting his gaze to meet hers for an instant.

"I can't waste all this delicious chocolate." Kissing her lower abdomen, he turned her slightly, then dropped her legs over his shoulders.

Hilary gasped when his mouth sought and found the most sensitive part of her body. The aroma of chocolate mingled with her own scent as Zach tasted and explored her at his leisure.

She moaned and pressed herself against him as he continued to possess her. What madness was this? The stark contrast of cold ice cream with his warm mouth drove her crazy with desire. If he accused her of insanity now, she'd be unable to deny it.

She was so hot inside. How could she be dead and feel something so glorious? Her body tensed, proceeded to a level of pleasure Hilary never could have imagined, then she simply shattered. Tiny pinpricks of rapture fixated and tantalized every inch of her body.

"Oh, Zach." Floating back down, she gritted her teeth in anticipation as he kissed his way back up her abdomen, laving her tender nipples again. "I want you."

Growling, Zach leapt onto the bar and slid between her thighs. He pressed himself against her womanhood until she opened for his entrance.

Hilary gasped when he slid his full length into her, sheathing his pulsing manhood within her inadequate body. Instinctively, she wrapped her legs around his waist, urging him even deeper with each thrust. She couldn't get enough of him—ever.

Each time he withdrew and returned, Hilary went higher and higher toward that summit Zach had shown her before. She nuzzled his neck and pulled with her legs as he thrust his magnificent male body into her.

She cried out in pleasure when the joy came again and again. His mouth covered hers in a devastating chocolate kiss, swallowing her cries of rapture as he tensed and shuddered against her.

She heard Zach's groan as her body contracted around his pulsing shaft. Something was different this time, then she recalled the strange sheath he'd worn when they'd made love earlier.

Panting, he lifted himself to gaze into her eyes. "I'm sorry," he whispered.

"Sorry?" The last thing in the world she wanted was for him to regret this glorious experience. "Don't be sorry."

"I'm not sorry this happened." He smiled and kissed the tip of her nose. "I was so fired up I forgot to protect you."

"Protect me?" Hilary frowned. "I don't understand."

He shrugged, then kissed her again. "You drive me crazy, Hilary Brown."

She felt as if she would explode with the wonder of it all as he eased himself from her and helped her off the bar. "I'm so glad you came here," she whispered, leaning against him for a few extraordinary moments.

He turned to face her, running his gentle fingers along her back. "I was terrified today when I thought . . ."

Hilary felt his heart thudding in his chest. She lifted her gaze to his. "I'm really very sorry for frightening you."

"It's all right, now." He sighed. "You're safe and that's really all that matters. That . . . and us."

Hilary felt a surge of guilt. Somehow she had to make Zach understand that their time together was limited. But how could she accomplish such a feat when she couldn't even convince him she was dead?

"I don't understand how this happened so fast." Zach pulled her close and sighed. "All I know is that I care about you and want you forever."

"Oh, Zach." Hilary blinked against her stinging tears, but to no avail. The watery turncoats slipped down her cheeks. "Forever?"

He chuckled and eased himself away, grinning when their sticky bodies seemed reluctant to separate. "I think we both could use a bath."

"A bath?" Hilary tilted her head to one side. How long had it been since she'd had a warm bath? Not since two days before she was hanged. Too long. All these simple human sensations and experiences were so foreign to her now—but still very appealing.

"I can heat the water over the grill. It'll take a while, though." He shook his head and chuckled. "Maybe, one of these days, I can rig a solar water heater. If I can design a navigational computer, I think I should be able to handle that."

Hilary had no idea what he was talking about, but smiled anyway. "I remember there being a tub in the kitchen. We could fill it in there and—"

"Not safe. Remember the beams?" Zach turned to the sacks on the bar. "I'll bring it in here to fill." He waggled his eyebrows at her. "Not as if there's anyone around to see us."

Hilary laughed. This was all so dangerous. She'd actually tasted food, drank water, felt hunger and passion. Were these warning signs? Could Sarah—

No, not now. She couldn't bear the thought of leaving Zach, not even for her afterlife. It was wonderful to see him happy again. She'd almost lost him. "Zach, you're happy."

He stared at her. An expression of wonder possessed his features. "Yeah, I am." He shook his head and laughed. "Day before yesterday, when I drove into Columbine, I thought my life was over. Then I met you."

Hilary warmed inside at his words. "I . . . I make you happy?" It was too wonderful to be true.

"You make me *very* happy." He leaned over to kiss her lips, then turned his attention back to heating water. "I'll set the grill up out back, so I won't have to carry the water so far. Then after our baths, we'll have steaks. Lord, I'm hungry. You're wearing me out."

She blushed as his gaze caressed her. "Can I help with something?"

He smiled at her. "I think some towels might be nice. I left my backpack up in your room. You should find a couple in there."

Pleased she could help, Hilary slipped on his over-sized flannel shirt and started up the stairs. She paused on the landing to stare at him. He looked up and their gazes locked. There was an unfathomable emotion deep in his brown eyes. It made her feel terrified, but happier than she'd ever been, all in one pithy moment.

"Hilary." His voice echoed through the saloon. "I forgot to mention something earlier. Something I want—need—to tell you."

"What's that?" She was almost naked, and sticky with chocolate, but didn't care about anything but Zach. His gaze held hers captive with its intensity.

He smiled as he spoke. "I love you."

Hilary felt dizzy with joy. She clutched the bannister with both hands. Tears trickled down her face and she smiled. It was true—he *did* love her. *Thank you, God.* "I love you, too, Zach."

He nodded. "Good." His smile lit his face and her heart. "Then we'd better get cleaned up. First thing in the morning, we're going to figure out some way to fake a birth certificate for you and elope."

"Elope?" Her throat constricted.

"Get on with you, woman." Smiling, he pointed up the stairs with one hand while he used a rag to wipe chocolate ice cream off the bar with the other. "I'll start the fire out back and carry the water. If you hurry, we can share the tub. Of course, I'm assuming that pesky old bear won't find me first." He laughed, then blew her a kiss.

He was magnificent. He was hers. A sudden chill made her shudder.

At least for a while.

When Hilary entered her room, a strange sensation washed over her. Her head began to spin and she gripped it with a feeling of pure terror. The room went black and she felt weightless.

Somehow, she knew.

Sarah.

*   *   *

Where the hell was she? Had she vanished again?

Zach opened every door in the decrepit saloon, then searched the other buildings in Columbine.

Hilary was gone.

There was no sign of her. Even her red dress had vanished. He held the flannel shirt, still smelling of chocolate ice cream and Hilary, in his hand. The pain of remembrance burned in his throat.

How could she just leave?

He walked down the stairs in the saloon again after searching the entire second floor a third time. Twilight blanketed the town, leaving him alone and bewildered. He stared at the bar, where he'd made love to Hilary just this afternoon.

Chocolate had never tasted sweeter. He loved her, but it was a losing battle.

That woman, whatever she was, made him crazy. In two days she'd managed to turn his entire world inside out. He wanted her more than anything or anyone he'd ever known. This kind of desire was all-powerful.

Terrifying.

She'd said she loved him. If that was true, then why would she leave?

As he descended the stairs, Zach paused, his gaze riveted to the monstrous mirror behind the bar. An eerie feeling swept through him.

Again, he saw movement within the silver. He swallowed hard, then walked quickly toward the bar. Squinting, he moved around the bar to touch the smooth surface. Movement, very slight but real, was undeniable within the warped silver. He'd begun to think the first time had been nothing but his imagination.

Colors blended together, then merged to form an image—a face.

Hilary.

"No, it can't be." His heart pounded in his chest as he touched the impression with his hand. What was happening to him? Was Hilary's insanity contagious?

But the face in the mirror continued to waver tauntingly before his terrified gaze. "Hilary?"

You're nuts, man.

He combed his fingers through his hair, then ran them across his stubbled chin. This was real. He needed a shave. This building needed renovating. His belly was empty.

Hilary was gone.

Or was she? The image coalesced. It *was* Hilary, but she looked different. Her hair was parted in the center and pulled back in a severe style. An unflattering dress came up high beneath her chin. She seemed to be calling for help, but no sound reached him. There was only her terrified visage, trapped in the glass.

"Hilary!" He clawed at the smooth surface, tried to touch her, reach her, but there was nothing. Only cold, hard silver.

Was she really a ghost? "No." Zach drew a deep breath, forcing away the bizarre thoughts. Renewing his resolve, he looked around the room, but his gaze returned again and again to the mocking mirror—the face.

He had work to do. And his first order of business was to get rid of that blasted mirror.

Hilary was upstairs. She had to be. He'd simply overlooked her somehow.

What a lie. A gut-wrenching sadness enveloped him. The crazy mirror was making his imagination run rampant. That was it. He saw things in the mirror that couldn't possibly be real. Looking down at his feet, he spied an old brass spittoon, empty and heavy enough to do the job.

Zach swallowed hard, bent down and picked up the tarnished brass. Its weight helped to steady him, to brace his nerves against what he must do. He held it in his hands for several seconds as he watched the face again.

Hilary's expression looked desperate as he watched her. Her mouth moved again and again, but still no sound came forth. She was trapped in the mirror, begging for release.

Emancipation.

Clenching his teeth, he reared the spittoon back over his shoulder, then hurled it at the mirror, covering his face when it shattered and splintered all around him, showering Zach with glittering silver shards.

A strange sensation washed over him. He felt weightless, lighter than air. Reeling, Zach groped for the bar, seeking support that wasn't there. Emptiness engulfed him.

His fall didn't terminate at the rough, pine floor. Trapped in a void, he floated toward some unknown destination. It was as if the floor beneath his feet had simply vanished, leaving him suspended in a dark, empty place, determined to draw him in against his will.

A woman's scream reached his ears as a light appeared above the void. Hilary's scream? Had he freed her from the mirror, or harmed her in the attempt?

Am I dead?

Zach reached upward, groping through the abyss for the blessed light. It was the only thing tangible surrounding him as he continued to descend into the terrifying pit of blackness.

His descent suddenly halted as his head began to spin. Gripping his middle, he closed his eyes in an effort to halt the vertigo and its accompanying nausea. But the spinning merely increased in velocity, terrifying him with its bizarre and unknown purpose.

He must reach the light. Somehow, he knew it was his only hope. It would lead him to deliverance.

To Hilary?

The air was sucked from his lungs as a pain ripped through his chest. He couldn't recall having ever been so frightened of anything. This experience was without precedent, a mysterious journey through a fathomless atmosphere.

Zach continued to spin and reach for redemption when he sensed he was beginning to rise toward the light. He could no longer see it, because his eyes were tightly shut against the whirling.

What was happening? Where was Hilary?

As if in answer to his myriad of questions, another scream echoed through the void.

His.

BOOK II

Chapter Eight

"Throw some water on him, boys."

Zach grabbed his head and groaned, struggling to pry his eyes open to determine the identity of the intruder. Though definitely female, this voice was rough and grating, not soft and lyrical like Hilary's.

Hilary.

Where was she? Was she all right?

Zach pushed himself upward, wincing when his head and back were doused with icy water. "Shit." Shaking his head, he rubbed the water away from his eyes amid gales of raucous laughter.

"Well, stranger," the grating voice continued, "we were beginnin' to wonder if you was ever gonna wake up at all."

Zach blinked, trying to focus on the strange woman. His gaze traveled upward, taking in the dress, so much like Hilary's. This woman was short and buxom, with blond hair piled high on her head. Feathers of some type were stuck in the elaborate mane. And her face . . .

She was an older version of Hilary.

Zach's heart hammered his chest as he pushed himself to his feet, swaying once until he gripped the bar for support. The bar? It had been old and splintered when he'd last seen it. Now it was polished to a high gloss, with a shiny brass rail around it.

And the mirror.

He took a step backward, nearly collapsing again for his trouble. Ignoring the jeering laughter all around him, Zach stared in horror at the silver mirror which ran the length of the wall behind the bar.

Intact.

"I broke it," he whispered, shaking his head in denial. A vivid picture of the glittering shards sprinkling down around him filled his mind. The spinning. The light. "What happened? Where am I?"

The woman didn't join the men in their laughter as she touched Zach's arm. "You all right?"

Swallowing hard, he turned to face her again. It just couldn't be. He must be unconscious—delirious. Maybe he had a concussion.

"Who are you?" he asked in a voice that barely resembled his own.

The woman chuckled and shook her head. "I guess we oughta be askin' you that question." She led Zach to a table and pulled out a chair. "Nobody even saw you come in. Ned there found you behind the bar when he opened up this mornin'."

Zach glanced up at the one called Ned, a huge bald man with a striped shirt and a handlebar moustache. Standing behind the bar with his arms folded over his chest, he glowered at Zach.

"How'd you get in here?" Ned demanded in an angry voice.

Zach raked his fingers through his hair. "I was—I don't

know." He licked his parched lips, trying to sort through the bizarre situation. Where the hell was Hilary?

The big man started around the bar, but the woman held her hand up to halt him. "I sure don't remember seein' you last night with one of the girls," she said, shaking her head. Her brow was wrinkled in obvious confusion. "But it sure as hell ain't the first time and probably won't be the last. I can't keep track of everybody who comes in and outta here."

Zach sat in the chair and held his head in his hands. His gut was still churning. He placed his hand over his empty stomach. It rumbled audibly.

"Tell Matilda to serve up some breakfast for me and . . ." The woman frowned and leaned closer to him. "What's your name, handsome?"

"Zach." This couldn't be happening. Unless they were ghosts. Ghosts like Hilary? He believed her now. What choice did he have? The evidence, combined with everything else he'd denied since first meeting Hilary, demanded acceptance.

He looked up suddenly, glancing around the room at the rough-looking men who stood in a semi-circle, staring at him.

Ghosts—all of them?

Suddenly, he started to laugh. Recalling how disappointed he'd been to arrive in Columbine and discover it abandoned, he had to laugh. This was ridiculous, falling right into the "be careful what you wish for" category. How appropriate—a ghost town full of real ghosts.

"Zach what?" The woman sat in the chair next to him and stared while he laughed. "I ain't ever seen you around Columbine before. At least, not in here. And everybody comes to Miss Nellie's sooner or later."

Miss Nellie's? His laughter died a quick, clean death. This was impossible. "I just arrived day before yesterday."

Where was Hilary? Who was this strange woman? Could she really be . . . ? "This is weird."

The woman gave him an indulgent smile. "I'm Nellie Brown, part-owner of Miss Nellie's," she announced proudly. "The most popular place in town, I might add."

The small group of men all cheered in agreement, making Zach grab his head. It ached. Bad.

Miss Nellie.

"How'd you get here?" he asked, not sure he really wanted an answer.

She laughed. "I expect you've been on one helluva drunk, son." She rolled her eyes dramatically. "Musta been a good one." She winked in an exaggerated way. "Woman trouble, no doubt."

Woman trouble, wasn't that the truth? Zach was so confused. Dare he ask about Hilary? Was she here—wherever here was—too? Was this a fifth dimension or something? It reminded him of an episode of *The Twilight Zone.*

The mirror.

He took a deep breath, then released a ragged sigh. "Miss Nellie." He tried to clear his mind so he could concentrate on this bizarre turn of events. "What year is it?"

"Year?" Miss Nellie threw her head back to laugh. "Son, you're in sad shape."

"You don't know the half of it."

A large woman placed two plates overflowing with steaks and eggs in front of them. She filled a pair of cups with black coffee, then looked toward Miss Nellie.

"Thanks, Matilda." Nellie gave the woman a nod of dismissal as she reached for a bottle of amber liquid on the table. "Eat up, Zach. It's on the house." She poured a generous portion of the amber liquid into her coffee, then extended the bottle to him. "Hair of the dog? Might make you feel better."

Zach froze. A good stiff drink might bring him out of this nightmare in a hurry. And into another one. He squeezed his eyes shut as he considered his options. If this was a dream, then a drink wouldn't hurt. If it wasn't . . .

"No, thanks." Wondering if he'd regret his answer, he rubbed his eyes. "The year?" Zach tried to ignore the fragrant food, but his stomach didn't share his mind's priorities. Reaching for the coffee first, he took a tentative sip. It was hot and strong, bracing him for whatever he had to face. "Please?"

The woman's expression grew solemn. "You're serious, ain't you?"

Zach nodded.

"It's 1886. The month of September." Miss Nellie leaned back in her chair, sipping her coffee and staring at Zach.

1886? Zach's stomach lurched, protesting the strong coffee on its empty lining. He needed food and sleep. He'd wake up later to learn this was all nothing but his overactive imagination, a nightmare. It was probably all that chocolate ice cream on his empty stomach. And when he woke up, Hilary would be at his side.

In the twentieth century.

Claiming she was a ghost?

"Oh, God."

"Are you sure you're all right?" Miss Nellie leaned on her elbows and stared long and hard at Zach. Her expression was almost maternal as she reached for the whiskey bottle and refilled her coffee cup. "Maybe we oughta fetch Doc Simon."

"No, I just have a headache." Zach tried to digest the bizarre facts thrusting themselves to the forefront. If it was really 1886, then Hilary'd been telling the truth. Was it possible? Had the Hilary Brown he'd made love to, and fallen in love with, been a real ghost?

A dead-woman-ghost?

"Oh, my God." Zach groaned again and rubbed his hand over his face. He couldn't think straight. Food would raise his blood sugar and fortify his senses. He needed brain food, definitely. Or maybe a lobotomy. Electric shock treatments?

His stomach rumbled again. Resigned, he reached for his fork and started to eat. For several minutes, he silently shoveled food into his mouth, feeling himself become stronger with each bite.

"You were hungry," Miss Nellie observed with a crooked smile when he set aside his fork. She peered at him over the rim of her coffee cup, then lowered it to the table to fill it a third time, but not with coffee. "Now, tell me, Zach, how is it that a big handsome man like you can't even remember what year this is?"

How could he explain something he didn't understand himself? "I'm . . . I'm not sure." Dare he ask about Hilary? He needed to find her, ask her what the hell had happened to him.

If she was a real ghost, could she have known this was about to happen? He scratched his head, mulling over his foggy memory of lying in bed with her, discussing how she'd died. And there was the question about how she'd acquired the red scar around her neck.

His stomach burned in protest. Hanged.

Except for the small gathering of rough-looking men, the saloon was nearly empty. Early morning probably wasn't their busiest time of day.

Shaking his head in total confusion, Zach scanned his surroundings. Polished furniture instead of broken antiques. Overhead, a crystal chandelier glittered in the morning sun shining through the *un*broken windows which flanked the front door.

The same door he'd had trouble opening when he'd first arrived in Columbine.

An image of Hilary flashed through his mind. She was standing in the street with a long stick in her hand, dressed in that peculiar red dress. The bear was lumbering away after she'd prodded it in the haunches.

"Damn."

"Well, so you don't know how you got here, or what year it is," Nellie said thoughtfully, staring at Zach as if trying to read his mind. "Tell me, Zach, what do you know?"

Footsteps sounded on the staircase, making Zach turn to discern the identity of the newcomer. His pulse raced at the sight that greeted his hungry gaze.

Hilary.

But it was the Hilary from the mirror.

Parted down the middle, her hair was pulled back in a bun at the base of her neck. She carried a bonnet by its strings in one hand; a stack of books occupied the other. Her clothing was plain and completely covered her arms and throat.

But it was still Hilary.

"Hilary!" Zach jumped up and rushed over to grab her wrist. "What happened to you? To us? Where'd you disappear to? How'd we get here?"

Her blue eyes grew round and frightened as she tried to pull away from him. "Let go of me."

"Hilary?" Zach was frantic. "Listen to me. You were in the mirror. How'd you get out? What happened? Please tell me."

Her eyes were huge and terrified when he met her gaze. "Let go of me." She pulled and twisted, struggling to get away from him.

"Let go my sister," a hesitant voice commanded from the door that led to the kitchen.

Zach glanced over his shoulder. A tall teenager with long straight hair stood staring at him. The youth's fists were clenched at his sides and a spattered white apron was tied around his waist. There was an almost vacant expression in the boy's blue eyes.

"Elliot."

The sound of Hilary's voice made Zach return his gaze to her. He stared at her in desperation. "You don't remember me." Seeing her look of pure terror, he released her wrist. She took a step back, but her frightened gaze never left his face. "I'm Zach. Zach Ryan."

She lifted her chin a notch. "I've never seen you before in my life." She turned toward the door. "I'm late for school."

"What kind of game are you playing now?" He stared after her in horror. Where was she going? How could she drag him into this nightmare, then pretend she didn't know who he was? She *had* to remember him.

"Hilary?" He ran after her, gripped her shoulder and she screamed.

"Let go of me." She twisted and freed herself from his grip. "Mama, do something."

Nellie Brown threw her head back and laughed. "Well, well, seems this stranger might have come in with one of the girls last night, after all."

Hilary's face reddened beneath her mother's scornful glare. A tear trickled from the corner of her eye and she looked at the floor. "I beg to differ with you, Mama, but I'm not one of your girls," she said in a clipped tone. The look on her face was haunted. "And I've never seen this man before in my entire life."

Not in life, but in death? Zach stepped away just as Elliot's large hand grabbed the back of his collar. The youth lifted Zach off the floor.

He was too overwhelmed to pay Elliot much attention.

Zach simply hung limply from the youth's powerful grasp. Why was she doing this? Of course she knew him.

But the pained expression in her eyes tore at him. Zach wouldn't hurt her again, even though she was his only link with reality. He recalled her sorrowful confession about her mother's profession and her own struggle to maintain her distance from it.

All true?

He tore his gaze from Hilary's frightened expression and glanced at Elliot's face, noting the slack jaw and innocent look in his eyes. Then he remembered Hilary's words about her younger brother.

Elliot permitted Zach to stand on his own two feet again. Nellie's head wobbled as she reached for the bottle— *again*.

His gaze shot from Hilary to Elliot, then back to Miss Nellie. So many things were beginning to make sense, or become more confusing, depending on one's perspective.

Nellie Brown was a drunk, an alcoholic, just like him. She was practicing and he was recovering. But the difference wasn't as great as he'd have liked.

Zach's guilt forged itself to the front of his mind with a vengeance. His own brother had died because of alcohol. When Zach looked at Elliot's innocent expression again, he wondered if alcohol could be responsible for the boy's retardation. Was Elliot a product of Fetal Alcohol Syndrome?

"You gonna leave my sister alone?" Elliot stood there, waiting for an answer.

"Elliot, I'm all right." Hilary touched her brother's forearm. "Thank you for helping me, though."

"I won't hurt Hilary," Zach said with total honesty, trying not to let himself wonder if Hilary had known this was about to happen. His gaze locked with hers. "I promise."

Elliot nodded with a smile. "Good."

"Get back to the kitchen, Elliot," Nellie Brown ordered in a slurred voice. "You got dishes to finish. Besides . . . nobody wants a . . . an idiot for a hero." The woman looked away. Her guilt was manifest. "Don't you know that?"

"Oh, Mama." Hilary stared in horror and disgust at her mother's back.

The patrons in the bar laughed and hooted, praising Miss Nellie for her crass insult of her own son.

Zach's stomach lurched. My God, how could the woman treat her own child so cruelly? But he knew it was her guilt talking. He looked away from Nellie, who was busy with her cup again, and saw the pain on Elliot's face. The boy's shoulders drooped and he walked slowly toward the kitchen.

So many things Hilary had claimed were turning up to taunt him. Was she lying now about remembering him? "Hilary, I can't believe you really don't remember me."

"I've never met you," she said in a strained whisper, lowering her gaze when he looked at her.

If this was all true, did that also mean that Hilary Brown would be hanged for murder? He went cold at the thought. He had to make certain that never happened. If she didn't remember him, then she probably didn't remember that, either.

Zach's gaze met hers, searching her face for answers to a myriad of questions. But she was staring after her brother's retreating form. The naked love he saw in her eyes for her brother mocked him. How could all this be pretense? No magician, not even Hilary, could pull off such an illusion. Even David Copperfield with the aid of television cameras couldn't be this real.

God, Hilary, I love you.

Then she turned in his direction and their gazes joined. A flicker of something deep in her eyes gave him hope. Whatever miracle had caused this bizarre twist of fate might yet lend a helping hand. Surely, something this powerful must be an act of God. What other explanation could there be?

Zach's head throbbed. He'd never been a religious man by any means. But this little adventure was putting what shallow faith he did have to the test.

The ultimate test.

"Excuse me." Hilary moved toward the door.

Zach longed to run after her, but he didn't. She'd been hurt by her mother's harsh words and he'd been the cause. He wouldn't risk that again. But when he was able to speak with her alone, he had to make absolutely certain she didn't remember him. There was still the horrendous possibility that she was somehow involved in this mess, that she'd dragged him into this nightmare deliberately, for whatever reason.

"So, Zach." Nellie stood, staggered over to him and dropped her arm across his shoulders. "Tell me how it is you know my prissy daughter."

Zach watched the front door close behind Hilary. He felt a great sense of loss with her departure. But there would be another occasion to speak with her, somewhere away from Nellie Brown, when he would learn the truth.

"Didn't you hear me?"

Zach shook himself and turned to face his hostess. "Uh, no. I guess not."

The woman rolled her eyes and clicked her tongue. "I wanted to know how you knew my daughter." She laughed. "Hilary ain't easy to get close to. Especially not by a man, if you know what I mean."

How mistaken could a human be? Nellie would be amazed to learn what a passionate love her daughter was. Zach winced, recalling his last time with Hilary, the sweet taste of chocolate mingling with the musky scent of her desire.

A deep sense of loss pervaded him. He looked up and saw Elliot staring at him from the kitchen door. There was a sorrowful longing in the youth's expression. It tugged at Zach, drew from him a surge of brotherly concern he hadn't felt in a very long time.

"Not talkin', eh?" Nellie laughed and patted his shoulders. "Well, it's about time a handsome young man showed Miss High-n-Mighty a thing or two."

Zach steeled himself and met Nellie's gaze. "Hilary's a lady," he said steadily, surprising himself with his words. He looked back toward Elliot and saw the flicker of approval flash across the boy's face before he turned to enter the kitchen.

Zach had arbitrarily assumed Hilary was a prostitute when they'd first met. He owed her an apology.

He owed her a great deal more than that.

She'd tried very hard to tell him the truth, yet he'd refused to hear her pleas. Even after seeing a semi-truck pass right through her.

"I just don't believe any of this."

"Believe what?" Nellie urged Zach back to the table.

"Where and when I am." He chuckled and shot a glance toward the door. "Where the devil is Artemis Gordon when you really need him?"

Hilary looked over her shoulder as she rushed toward the small log building at the edge of town. The strange man was nowhere in sight.

Breathing again, she leaned against a rough wall near the door. Her heart pounded in her chest like a bird batting its wings against a cage. Placing her hand over it, she closed her eyes for a moment.

Why had the stranger affected her so? It was almost as

if she knew him from somewhere. But of course, that was impossible.

The only men she'd ever had the occasion to meet were the miners of Columbine. They weren't all bad, but they were all single-minded in their pursuit of gold. Some of them were family men—good, God-fearing husbands and fathers.

But most of the men of Columbine were rough and disorderly, responsible for and to no one but themselves. These were the segment of the population who frequented Miss Nellie's establishment, the ones Hilary avoided like ticks in springtime.

I'm not like my mother. Her frequent assertion to herself filled her mind as her breathing returned to normal. She would never be like Nellie Brown, no matter what.

She'd rather die.

Patting her hair, Hilary entered the small building. Split logs served as seats for the seven children who regularly attended. Their mothers had fought hard for the funds to operate the school.

Hilary smiled cynically when she recalled how outraged some of those women had become upon discovering the identity of Columbine's first schoolteacher. The daughter of a notorious prostitute? Teach *their* children?

She was the only one in Columbine free to seek employment who was also qualified as a teacher. It was nothing less than a miracle Hilary was able to read and write at all, let alone teach school.

Sighing, she recalled the old man who'd lived out his final years as Columbine's undertaker. Old Silas Flint had been an educated man. Fortunately for Hilary, he'd also been lonely. He'd been resistant at first to her suggestion that he teach her reading, writing and arithmetic in exchange for her doing his mending and laundry.

Silas was gone now, but his legacy would live on in the

minds of every child Hilary reached with the gift of knowledge.

She was a teacher—not a harlot.

Forcing such thoughts at bay, she moved about the dim interior of the log cabin which doubled as a church on Sundays. She made certain the seven slates were clean and ready for a day's work. The children would arrive shortly. She straightened her shirtwaist and looked outside. It was a mild autumn day.

"Mornin', Hilary."

She winced at the sound of that voice. It's nasal twang flowed over her like pond scum, made her feel dirty and ill-at-ease. It was almost as if the owner of the voice touched her in some vile manner with every syllable he uttered.

Turning, she faced the intruder and folded her arms. "Mr. McCune." She started to turn away, but his voice halted her.

"I heard tell Pa's plannin' to boot Elliot if Nellie don't marry up with him real soon." His laughter was caustic. "Won't that weddin' be somethin'? Then the two of us'll be brother and sister. And I could be a real . . . affectionate brother. Imagine that."

Elliot was the constant target of this man's ridicule, even though Baird McCune was Elliot's half-brother. Hilary stiffened as her gaze traveled from the top of Baird's greasy brown hair, down to the soiled dungarees. He was a startling contrast to his impeccable banker-father. "If you don't mind, Mr. McCune, I'd rather not imagine that."

"Well, it don't make much difference what you'd rather, now does it?" He stepped onto the small porch near the door and grabbed her wrist. "One of these days, you're gonna learn some manners, Miss High-n-Mighty. One of these days . . ."

Hilary held her breath, attempting to avoid breathing in his sour stench. The man made her flesh crawl. It was amazing that Baird could actually be related to her gentle Elliot. "I must prepare my lesson plan, Mr. McCune," she said carefully, avoiding his probing gaze. "If you will excuse me?"

"Not yet, I ain't." He stepped in front of her. "When are you gonna give up this teachin' stuff and join your ma's stable? I'd be real gentle with you, Hilary. Make it real good for you . . . especially the first time."

Hilary wrinkled her nose in disgust as her stomach twisted. If he didn't move away from her soon, she'd lose her breakfast in his face. Now that she considered the possibility, it seemed rather appropriate, all things considered.

Pulling her hand, she tried to free herself from his brutal grip. She knew a purple bruise would encircle her wrist from his harsh treatment. Why couldn't the man just leave her be?

"Please, Mr. McCune," she whispered, still avoiding his gaze. "The children will be here soon. *Your* son among them. Let me go."

Leaning closer until he was right in her face, he laughed. His gaze dropped to her bosom, making Hilary want to crawl in a hole and die. She swallowed convulsively.

"Prissy teacher lady." He straightened and flung her wrist away in one smooth motion. "One of these days . . ."

His laughter crawled up her spine as he turned at last to walk away. Hilary was unable to suppress a shudder of revulsion. She gulped fresh air and closed her eyes to compose herself.

When she opened them he was there—the man she'd seen with her mother this morning. His brown gaze was almost pleading as he stared at her. She felt a surge of compassion for the stranger, then quickly chastised herself for such foolishness. She didn't even know him.

"Good morning," he said quietly, pausing in front of

the step. "I came by to apologize for my . . . my abruptness when we met earlier."

Hilary was momentarily taken aback by his chivalry. "That's very kind of you, sir. Apology accepted." She bestowed a smile on him, marveling at how his eyes lit from within when she did. Unexpected warmth swept through her.

"Well, I guess I'd better go look for a job and a place to stay." He shrugged with a chuckle, though there was no humor evident in his tone.

"You're not a miner?" Hilary tilted her head to the side to study the handsome stranger.

He smiled. It was easily the most beautiful smile she'd ever seen—full lips over unusually straight white teeth. He wore a black shirt with no buttons or studs down its front. A peculiar bird-like creature adorned the front of the garment, with the letters "B-1B" beneath it. His shoes were even more bizarre. They were white and soft. She'd never seen a man in white shoes before.

"No, I'm not a miner, at least not yet." An emotion flickered across his face, then he frowned. "A miner, that's a switch."

"Pardon me?" Hilary was struck again by the man's good looks, and by the profound sadness in his expression.

"Never mind." He rolled his eyes. "I guess this situation gives the term dislocated worker an entirely new meaning."

"Dislocated worker?" Hilary shook her head in bewilderment. "I'm sorry."

"No, *I'm* sorry." Regret clouded his features when his gaze met hers again. There was something almost desperate about his eyes. "I . . . I guess I'll be on my way."

"Wait." Hilary could have kicked herself for stopping him. What had come over her? She was always a target for men in town because of her mother's reputation. She must be more careful. "I was just wondering . . ."

He arched a brow and tilted his head to the side. "Wondering what?"

"How you know me?" She frowned. "I'm quite certain I've never met you before."

His eyes darkened as his gaze dropped slowly down the front of her, then back up to her face. Her flesh grew warm and a strange tugging sensation started low in her middle. It was disconcerting, almost as if he was touching her.

The intensity of his gaze was mesmerizing. Hilary trembled, feeling as if he knew her deepest secrets.

"I do know you, Hilary," he said quietly, stepping onto the small stoop. He paused less than a foot away, gazing down at her face. "I know you from another place, another time. And when you're ready . . . I'll explain it to you."

Hilary was riveted. Try as she might, she couldn't drag her gaze from his. He held her captive with some sort of commanding spell. It was the most powerful and bewildering experience she'd ever known.

He must be mad.

She took a step backward as her hand went to her starched white collar. Her heart did an unusual flip-flop. She turned hot then cold, terrified then captivated by this strange man. Why?

"Mornin', Miss Brown," a happy voice chimed as a child bounded onto the stoop.

Hilary was brutally jolted from her daze. Her face flooded with heat as she looked down at Jacob McCune. Three other children followed the boy into the building, signaling to Hilary it was past time for her return to reality.

She glanced back at the strange man. He was smiling the most devastating smile she'd ever seen. It made her feel warm all over . . . and something else she couldn't define.

"Until later. Maybe, if we're lucky, we'll get to the truth

then.'' With a nod, he turned away, whistling an unfamiliar tune as he walked toward the center of town.

"Merciful heavens, I don't know what came over me.'' Shaking her head, Hilary turned to enter the building.

But before she went inside, she couldn't resist one more look at the mysterious newcomer.

Who was he?

And more importantly, how did he know her?

Chapter Nine

Zach stood in the center of town and turned in a full circle, retracing the steps he'd taken when he'd first arrived in Columbine. Was this real?

Am I dead?

He felt his arms and chest with his hands, deciding he must be alive. If he were dead, the tremendous pain in his head wouldn't be troubling him any longer.

Right now it felt as if someone was playing "Wipe-Out" on his temporal lobe.

A freight wagon came barreling down the middle of the road, forcing Zach to take a diving leap to avoid being run down. He crawled to the boardwalk in front of Miss Nellie's and sat, rubbing his aching head.

The entire incident reminded him of Hilary's close encounter with the semi-truck. His stomach lurched. Why hadn't he believed her? Only a fool—a very stubborn one—could deny her claim after seeing what he'd seen.

If only he'd listened to her pleas, maybe he wouldn't be sitting here right now.

In 1886.

He recalled the pained expression on Hilary's face when he'd repeatedly rejected her ghostly proclamation. All along, she'd simply been striving to convince him of reality—that she'd been in something called Transition. Transition from what to what?

From one time to another? Could Hilary have known this was going to happen? That they were going to be thrust back in time?

God, no. The woman couldn't be guilty of such treachery. The Hilary he knew—or thought he knew—wasn't capable of anything so despicable.

Or was she?

Did he really know her? He hadn't believed a word she'd told him in his own time. Why should he believe her now?

Zach, you're losing it.

He swallowed hard and continued to hold his head in his hands, ignoring the people walking behind him. He had to face the truth, at least what appeared to be truth. He'd wasted far too much time denying it already. The only way to determine his course of action was to face facts as they were presented to him, rather than trying to deny and alter them to suit his sense of reason.

Zach Ryan had traveled back in time.

Groaning, he ran his hands over his face and stood. He squinted against the bright sunlight and took a deep breath. He could be mistaken, but maybe his headache was a bit better now that he'd accepted his fate.

Well, not exactly accepted.

There just didn't seem to be any other alternatives to consider at the moment.

He looked at the people going about their business all around him. Ladies wearing skirts that swept the dusty street when they walked, with bonnets tied beneath their chins, and baskets clutched in their hands. Some of them had children in tow, happy little faces eagerly skipping through the streets of Columbine.

But men outnumbered women at least four to one. Miners were everywhere. Hilary'd been right—they were a ragtag bunch. Dirty and unshaven, with straggly beards and unkempt hair sticking out from beneath battered hats, they talked and argued among themselves, and stared at him with open curiosity as they passed. More than a few of them ducked into Miss Nellie's.

This scene was very different from the vision of Columbine he'd been greeted with a few days ago. Hilary'd said it had once been a bustling community. Well, this was definitely what he'd call bustling.

"Hilary pretty."

Zach turned toward the sound of the voice. It was Elliot, leaning against a post no more than a few feet away from where Zach lamented his puzzling situation.

He couldn't—refused to—let Elliot see pity in his eyes. Thanks to his mom, Zach had been raised knowing people with disabilities deserved as much respect as the next person.

"Yes, Hilary's pretty." *The most gorgeous woman I've ever known.* Struggling to his feet, Zach offered the youth his right hand. "You must be Elliot."

The teenager stared vacantly at Zach's hand for a few moments, then grinned as he grasped it and pumped heartily. "Yep, Elliot. Who are you?"

Zach flexed his fingers when Elliot finally released his hand. *Yikes, what a grip.* "Zach Ryan."

"You . . . know Hilary?" Elliot blinked as he waited for Zach's answer. "She's my . . . my sister. She takes care of me."

Zach remembered with a jolt the expression in Hilary's

eyes when she'd traced Elliot's name with her fingertip in the door frame yesterday. *Yesterday?* He shook his head in bewilderment.

"Hilary's very lucky to have such a strong brother, who loves her as much as you obviously do, Elliot." Zach meant every word, as he tried desperately not to think of his own brother.

Elliot shifted his weight and reddened, then nodded vigorously. "Yeah."

"You wouldn't know where I might find a job around here, would you? Or maybe there's an issue of *Wall Street Employment Weekly* in town?" Zach chuckled. "I seem to have left home without any money." *At least not any recent issue.*

Elliot furrowed his brow for a few minutes as if contemplating the matter. "Shorty." He nodded and a bright smile split his face. "Shorty."

"Shorty?" Zach lifted his brows in curiosity. Laughter started in his chest. "All right. Who is this Shorty?" *And what kind of job would a person called Shorty have to offer?*

"C'mon." Elliot pointed toward Miss Nellie's. "Shorty's here."

Chuckling, Zach shrugged and turned to enter the establishment, then froze.

He didn't own it now.

Digesting this bit of reality, Zach pushed open the door and went inside. "This is the nuttiest thing that's ever happened to me," he whispered as he followed Elliot to an empty corner table. Time travel was even crazier than believing Hilary was a ghost. And he was sober. This was one escapade he couldn't blame on alcohol.

Elliot's excitement was obvious. "You wait here," he said, gulping air. "I'll get Shorty."

"Take your time, Elliot." Zach grinned. "I've got all the time in the world." *Except the time I'm supposed to have.*

As Elliot walked away in search of this mysterious Shorty, Zach's gut twisted into a painful knot. Jeez, what really happened? He replayed the events in his mind.

Hilary'd been there one minute, then she was gone. The next thing he knew, he'd broken a mirror in a fit of temper and traveled back in time.

"You're losing it, Ace." Zach looked around the saloon. There were several filthy, noisy men at the bar. Zach didn't order anything to eat or drink, remembering all money carried a date. Just how the hell would he explain a coin from the future?

"Damn." He rubbed his hand over his face and sighed. "What am I going to do if this Shorty person doesn't have a job for me?"

He had to laugh. In his time, he'd accused Hilary of being insane. Now he was the one people would consider crazy. It served him right. It really did. Talk about poetic justice.

"Howdy, stranger."

Zach glanced up at the small man who made himself at home by pulling out a chair and taking a seat. Elliot pointed at him and sat down between them.

"Afternoon," Zach greeted, wondering if it really was afternoon. He'd lost all track of time. The thought made him laugh again. He'd lost track—or control—of time in a big way.

Taking a deep breath, he looked at Shorty. The man was over sixty if he was a day. Most of his teeth were missing and he smelled as if he hadn't bathed in years, if ever.

"So, Elliot here tells me you've come to try your luck at minin'?" The man nodded and cast Zach a toothless, welcoming grin.

Zach sent Elliot a suspicious glance, then leaned back in his chair until its front legs came off the floor. He had to do something for money. "I haven't really decided."

He tilted his head to the side to study the man's face. "Why do you ask?"

The man emitted a wheezing chuckle. "Well, I got me a claim on the far side of town, but I can't work it no more." He slapped his hip. "Rheumatiz."

"I see." Zach lowered the front of his chair to the floor. He had to do something with himself until he found a way out of this mess.

With Hilary.

"Name's Shorty Lamb." The man extended a grubby hand across the table.

Zach hesitated a moment, wondering what sort of insidious disease he might contract, then accepted the man's handshake with a sigh. Elliot beamed in approval. "Zach Ryan. Pleased to meet you, Mr. Lamb."

"Just Shorty." The man grinned and nodded again. "See, what I need is somebody willin' to work my claim for part of the take." He coughed and patted his chest. "You got an honest face. Most of these fellas in here'd rob me blind." He leaned closer. "I got one of the richest claims."

Zach leaned forward to better hear the old man. The smell of Shorty's breath almost sent him off the edge of his chair. No wonder he didn't have any teeth. They'd all abandoned ship because of the rotten stench in the man's mouth. "I'm listening." *I'm being asphyxiated, but I'm listening.*

Shorty looked to both sides, then smacked his lips. His voice was very low, his expression secretive. "I think I'm gettin' close to the mother lode."

Mother lode? Zach's memory went into overdrive. When he'd first received word of his inheritance, he'd conducted massive research on Columbine's history. There was a significant gold discovery made in the 1880's but he couldn't recall the year. Could this really be it?

But that discovery had been the beginning of the end for Columbine. Miners swarmed the area, raping the land and the town in their quest for gold, even more so than they already were.

A catch twenty-two if ever there was one.

"How 'bout it, Zach?" Shorty waited, still leaning on the table. "You're young and strong. That's what the job needs."

"Not so young," Zach said, picturing his last few hours with Hilary. Losing her made him feel old—sort of dead, really. His throat closed and he struggled with a burning sensation behind his eyes, which he refused to identify. He glanced at Elliot, who was still grinning at them as if he alone were totally responsible for creating a binding friendship between them.

"Elliot, Ned needs you up at the bar to fetch another keg," Nellie said as she staggered past the table without stopping.

Elliot frowned, then pushed himself to his feet. "I'll be back." He waved as he went behind the bar to speak with Ned.

"All right. So, you need me to do the work while you reap the profit." Zach lifted his brows demonstratively as Shorty guffawed. "Is that about it?"

"Somethin' like that." Shorty shook his head as he continued to laugh. "Gotta admit, that sounds mighty appealin' to me, but somehow I don't think you'll cotton to it much."

Zach smiled. "That's right." He leaned back in his chair. "I don't."

"Fair enough, I—"

"Whiskey, Ned," a boisterous man demanded as he walked into the saloon.

Zach looked up at the new customer. He was of medium height and build, with thin brown hair. Turning his atten-

tion back to Shorty, Zach noticed the older man glowering
at the new arrival.

"Chicken shit bastard," Shorty muttered, still staring at
the man who was now bellying up to the bar and downing
a shot of whiskey. "Acts as if he owns the town."

"Who is he?" Zach was only mildly interested, though
he couldn't help but wonder why Shorty hated the newcomer so much.

"Baird McCune." Shorty said the name as if it tasted
vile on his lips. "Son of that scalawag, Sean. It's hard to
say which is the worst of the pair."

A maelstrom of memories struck Zach. He straightened
in his chair, remembering Hilary's heartfelt confession of
the events which had led to her hanging.

"My God." Zach started to stand, then thought better
of it. He needed as much information as he could possibly
collect if he was going to help Hilary. He had to do something to prevent her death.

What about her neck? Was the mark there, now? He
needed to see for himself, though he knew the answer. Of
course, it wasn't there. Hilary may have been a ghost in
his time, but she was alive in this one.

He couldn't lose her now—not after traveling through
time to find her again.

"You all right, Zach?" Shorty waved his hand in front
of Zach's face.

"What?" Zach cleared his throat. "Why do you hate
McCune so much, Shorty? What'd he do to you?" Good
God, the man Hilary'd supposedly murdered—or was
going to murder—stood less than twenty feet away. Zach
was unable to suppress a shudder as he glowered at the
man's back.

"Damned yella' belly." Shorty side-glanced at McCune
again, then faced Zach straight on. "He walks around here

pickin' on Elliot like the boy weren't nothin' but a stray cur. His own flesh'n blood."

Zach heard a roaring in his ears. *His own flesh'n blood?* What did that mean? "They're related?"

Shorty snorted in derision. "Well, ever'body knows they are, but old Sean ain't admittin' it."

"What do you mean?" Zach leaned on his elbows to better hear Shorty's story.

"Sean McCune is Elliot's paw." Shorty shrugged. "Not that he'll admit it."

"Let me get this straight." Zach rubbed his eyes with his thumbs. God, he was so tired. "If Sean's Elliot's father, then Baird is—"

"His half-brother." Shorty shook his head and clicked his tongue. "Elliot's got a lot more goin' for him than Baird in my book."

Zach smiled. He liked Shorty Lamb. The man was honest and straightforward. "Yeah, I agree."

"Since old Sean owns the bank, Baird thinks he can run the town, see. He hides behind his paw's money."

"Hides from what?" Zach leaned closer, finally growing immune to Shorty's breath.

Shorty scratched his chest for several moments. "Well, a few years back he foreclosed on Miss Nellie's while Sean was laid up with the pneumonia."

Zach leaned back, narrowing his gaze to study Shorty's expressions carefully. He was convinced the little man was telling the truth. "Go on."

"Well, the old man was fit to be tied when he come around and found out what Baird was up to." Shorty chuckled and wheezed. "See, everybody in town knows Sean and Miss Nellie's had a thing goin' for years. Since before Elliot."

Zach nodded. Hilary had told him all about Sean and Nellie's "thing." He rubbed his whiskered jaw with his thumb, finding something real and stable in the rasping sound it made. A disturbing memory shot to the front of his mind. "They're not engaged, are they?"

"Who? You mean Sean and Miss Nellie?" Shorty slapped the table and laughed as if that was the funniest thing he'd ever heard. "Nah, not that I know of, that is. Old Sean's a slippery weasel."

"Good."

"Huh?"

"Oh, nothing." Zach sighed and glanced at Baird again. The man was drinking heavily and talking loud with the miners. He was a braggart, plain and simple.

He remembered Hilary's story about Baird coming into her room.

"Damn." This was just another example of his stupidity. She'd tried so hard to make him understand ... Zach shook his head and searched his mind for answers. Whether or not Hilary had known she and Zach would be swept back in time, he had to prevent the events that would lead up to her shooting Baird.

And her being hanged.

Even if he had to shoot the bastard himself.

"So what about my offer?" Shorty leaned back in his chair. He folded his arms across his middle and belched. "More room outside than there is in."

Zach chuckled and sighed. He liked the old coot. Only God knew why. Besides, he was going to need money to eat, and ...

To take Hilary and Elliot away from Columbine.

This realization stunned Zach, but gave him a sense of direction all in one blast. "Yeah, Shorty." He offered the stunned old man his hand. "Pardner."

Shorty nodded in satisfaction, though his expression made it evident he was surprised by Zach's sudden, affirmative answer. "This'll be a fifty-fifty split. No funny stuff."

"I wouldn't dream of it." Zach pushed himself to his feet. "Why don't you show me where the mine is now? I'll need some supplies and a place to stay, too."

Shorty got to his feet, limping as he walked around the table. "That ain't gonna be a problem. There's a cabin out there. 'Course, Sean keeps tryin' to buy the whole claim from me, but I ain't sellin'. I don't use the cabin no more. Moved to town before winter sets in." He patted his hip again, as if in explanation. "There's a cook stove with pots and pans there already. All you gotta take with you's the food."

"Why, you stupid ass, why don't you watch where you're goin'?"

Zach looked quickly toward the bar, where Elliot stood with his head lowered to his chest. "I'm sorry. I didn't see."

Zach hesitated to stare at Baird, waiting for the man to make a move against Elliot. An overwhelming urge to strangle Baird with his bare hands right here and now swept through Zach. He quelled it with growing reluctance as Elliot continued to suffer the man's taunts.

"Stupid idiot." Baird brushed the droplets of whiskey from the front of his soiled shirt. "Walked right into me with your big clumsy—"

"S-sorry." Elliot turned to walk away from the vicious man, his brother.

Baird moved toward Elliot just as Zach rushed over to place a protective arm across the boy's shoulders. "Hey, Elliot, where you been?"

Elliot blinked when he turned his gaze to Zach. "Right here."

Shorty Lamb limped over to the pair. His expression when his gaze met Zach's was one of open approval. "Elliot," he began, "we need your help today. Nellie, Elliot's goin' with me."

"Take him. It'll keep him out of our hair for a while."

Elliot smiled and nodded as Zach and Shorty led him from the saloon.

Zach's head reeled. How much time did he have? If he found enough gold to move Hilary and Elliot far away from Columbine and Baird McCune, they'd be safe. Maybe when he went to her with his pockets lined with gold and told her the truth, she'd leave with him.

She had to.

"Here she be." Shorty brought his wagon to a stop in front of the smallest cabin Zach had ever seen.

It was no bigger than a child's playhouse. "I see it, but what exactly *is* it?" Zach grinned, then hopped down from the wagon. He'd never ridden behind a horse before. In fact, he'd never even been this close to one before.

"Nice horsey," he muttered as he skirted around the animal to walk to the back of the wagon. As he passed, he couldn't help but wonder if horses bit people. He pulled a bag from the back of the wagon. "Let me put this stuff inside, then you can show me the mine."

Shorty nodded and eased himself off the hard bench seat. "Oh, settin' on that wagon seat makes me powerful sore." He rubbed his haunches as he limped around to the back of the wagon and removed a jug. The old man yanked out the cork and took a long pull of the jug's contents. "Ah, that hits the spot."

"Medicine, eh?" Zach grinned at the old man's indignant expression. "Just kidding, Shorty."

"Just remember who's the boss, boy." Shorty's lips twitched as if he had to struggle to prevent a smile. "I want you to know a few things 'fore I heads back to town."

"All right, boss." Zach lugged the flour and beans inside, while Elliot followed him with the coffee and sugar.

"Thanks for advancing me enough money to buy these supplies, Shorty." *Especially since I don't know how long I'm stuck here.*

Shorty belched, but didn't respond to Zach's gratitude as he limped into the cabin behind Zach and Elliot.

"Now I know how the passengers felt in *Cocoon.*" Zach whistled as he looked around his new—very temporary— home. "Man, this place is tiny."

"It's easier to keep it warm this way." Shorty seemed unruffled by Zach's reaction to his little cabin. "The place I got me in town is lots bigger, harder'n hell to heat come January, though."

Just the thought of January made Zach shiver. His California blood better acclimate itself real damned fast. The extent of his winters had been a bit of Christmas rain. He was really in for it now.

"The Maggie-O is just behind here," Shorty explained, taking another drink from his jug. He smacked his lips and stood near the door. "By the way, since I ain't a spring chicken no more, in case anything happens to me, Elliot here's my heir. You gotta problem with that, Zach?"

"Nope." Zach struggled with a nagging memory. There was something important about the Maggie-O, something Hilary'd tried to tell him in the future, when he wasn't listening to her. *Damn.*

"You ready to have a look-see?"

Zach took a deep breath, glanced at the grinning Elliot, then nodded. At least the little cabin was clean, a whole hell of a lot cleaner than its owner. He had cooking utensils, food and a stove. There was firewood stacked right outside the door against the log wall. At least he wouldn't starve or freeze this winter. He hoped.

"So why Maggie-O?" Zach asked, following his new partner and Elliot around to the back of the cabin.

"Maggie nice," Elliot said with a smile as he lumbered along between Zach and Shorty.

"Yeah, she was nice all right." Shorty belched again. When he turned to face Zach, his expression was wistful. "Maggie was my wife."

The past tense in Shorty's admission was self-explanatory. "I'm sorry. How long have you been a widower?"

"Oh, about four years now, I reckon." The small man punched Elliot on the upper arm. "She was crazy 'bout this youngun. Hilary, too."

Zach swallowed the lump in his throat. Maggie Lamb must have been quite a woman, especially to put up with this smelly old man. "Did you have any children?"

Shorty nodded. "We had us four." He sighed and looked across the mountains, stopping to take a few deep breaths. "The three girls got hitched and moved away. Last I heard, the youngest was in Californy. 'Course, that was before Maggie'n me come here."

"Ah, California."

"You been there?" Shorty seemed impressed, as did Elliot.

"Yeah." Zach patted himself on the chest and took a deep breath. "I used to live there."

"Never heard tell of anyone comin' back from Californy," Shorty said with a chuckle. "I thought ever'-body was always headed in that direction."

Elliot nodded and laughed along with Shorty. Zach just stared in silence as he contemplated whether or not he'd ever see California or the twentieth century again.

Was he stuck here, in this time, forever?

"So you done much minin', Zach?" Shorty asked as he led them up a trail on the north side of the cabin. "The face of this mountain here blocks the winter wind. Let me tell you, it's a blessin'."

"Yeah, I'll bet." Zach cleared his throat. "I guess you

have a right to know the truth. I've never done any mining, Shorty."

Shorty stopped short and turned to face Zach. "Now why in tarnation didn't you tell me that back yonder?" Shorty spat on the ground and glowered at Zach. "My first partner was Maggie's brother, Abe. He know'd plenty 'bout minin', but he was kilt 'bout two months back."

"Killed?" Zach ventured a peek at Elliot, who was nearly doubled over in laughter. Surely not about Abe being killed? "What's so funny, Elliot?"

"No miner."

Elliot kept laughing, though Zach didn't see anything at all funny in this situation.

"Well?" Shorty stood there with his hands on his hips, his lower lip thrust out, and his eyes blazing.

Zach's lips twitched. For some inane reason, he wanted to laugh with Elliot. "Shorty, you tell me something," he said with a shrug. "Would it have made any difference to you if I had told you I didn't know anything about mining?"

Shorty looked from Elliot to Zach. "No, I don't reckon it would." He stomped his foot and sighed. "Elliot, what in the world is you laughing at, boy?"

"You." Elliot pointed at Shorty and continued to laugh.

"Do I have two heads, or somethin'?" Shorty patted his head in an exaggerated manner. "Three eyes?"

"I was 'memberin'." Elliot dabbed at the tears running from his eyes. "Maggie said you was . . . no miner, either. Abe said so, too."

Shorty's face turned red, then purple while he struggled with his obvious fury. Zach couldn't help himself. He started laughing with Elliot and couldn't stop. Before he knew it, he and Elliot were hanging onto each other and guffawing at Shorty.

"Ain't funny," Shorty muttered and turned to walk toward his claim. "If you want your split of the gold, Zach, you'd best stop that tomfoolery and get your young ass on up here."

Zach cleared his throat and climbed up the steep trail behind Shorty. His ass sure didn't feel very young right now. The altitude was still getting to him. "How much farther up the mountain is this place, Shorty?"

"Not far. Like I was tellin' you before, Abe was Maggie's brother." Shorty turned a sharp corner and pointed at a limestone cliff. Beneath it was a dark, gaping hole, obviously man-made. "There it is. The Maggie-O."

Zach stared at the wooden frame built around the mouth of the mine. "How is it you have this claim up here all by yourself?"

"I reckon you ain't all dumb. Abe asked me the same thing." Shorty reddened again, then nodded. "Yep." He removed his hat and scratched his head. "Ever'body else thinks the mother lode is *down* the mountain. But I know better. An' I think I ain't the only one who's figgered it out."

Zach nodded and shrugged his shoulders. "I suppose it's worth looking, anyway." He shaded his eyes and glanced at Elliot. "What do you think, Elliot?"

"Here." He nodded matter-of-factly. "Gold. Abe said so."

Gold.

Despite his common sense, Zach's pulse raced at the prospect of actually discovering gold. Could Columbine turn out to be a worthwhile inheritance after all? Even though he didn't actually own it at this particular time? The thought made him shudder, then shake his head.

As he followed Shorty through the mine entrance, Zach's engineering persona kicked in. He made mental notes of how and where the shaft needed reinforcement. That should be his first order of business, if he had enough time. But he didn't, since he had no idea when Hilary's crime would be committed.

Zach cleared his throat of the lump of emotion lodged in it. "How far back in the shaft is the mother lode, Shorty?" he asked with a shudder. He didn't relish the thought of going very far back in the shaft without proper equipment. Come to think of it, he wouldn't have liked the idea even if he had the most modern technology of the twentieth century at his disposal.

"I ain't sure, Zach, but it can't be too far back." He pointed at the cave wall, just inside the mine entrance. "Abe found it just before he got hisself kilt. But before he showed me *exactly* where it is."

"I just can't understand why you don't have some competition up here." Zach squinted in the darkness, stepped closer, then ran his fingers along the wall. "Why do you think this is the mother lode, Shorty? I don't see anything but rock."

"Abe told me." Shorty chuckled and wheezed. Elliot laughed as well.

"Abe again?" Then a memory flashed through Zach's mind. Hilary's terrified expression when he'd wanted to explore this very mine. She'd claimed there was a ghost up here . . . and she'd mentioned murders.

"Shorty." Suspicious, Zach narrowed his gaze as he studied the man. "Exactly, *how* did Abe die?"

Elliot and Shorty exchanged glances, then the smaller man shrugged. "Well, guess now's as good a time as any to tell you," Shorty said with a sigh. "Mine's haunted . . . and old Abe was murdered."

Murdered? Haunted? A shiver raced down Zach's spine. Had he been whisked away from his own time only to be haunted by a different ghost in this century? A murderous ghost? "Murdered by whom?"

"Lots of mines is haunted," Shorty explained as if this

conversation was as typical as talking about the weather. "Folks in town thinks the ghost murdered Abe, but I ain't so sure."

Zach squinted in skepticism. "Then that's what keeps people away from this mine and this particular ghost?" *God, I don't believe this. Not another one.* Though he felt certain this ghost wouldn't be anything like Hilary. She'd been one in a million.

Trillion.

Shorty chuckled. "Well, I reckon you could say this ghost is sorta mysterious. But I still don't think it kilt Abe."

Elliot merely smiled, looking around the mine. "Never . . . see it," he said in his slow way.

"Never?" Zach swallowed hard. Then this ghost definitely was nothing like Hilary'd been. His memory of the morning Hilary'd dissolved into tiny colored particles while sitting on her bed at Miss Nellie's assailed him. "Shit."

"Ain't nothin' to be scared of, Zach." Shorty patted Zach on the back. "Besides, it's the mother lode. It'll be worth it."

"Yeah, that's easy for you to say." Zach chuckled. "What a mother of a load it is, too." He took a deep breath and looked around at the timbers that supported the mine entrance. "Tell me again why you're so convinced this is the real thing, Shorty."

"You'll see for yourself when the time comes."

Time. There was that word again. Zach turned to follow Shorty and Elliot from the mine. He had no way of knowing whether or not he was stuck in this time, or if he'd be able to find his way back to the future. He wasn't even sure he cared to return—not without Hilary.

"All right, let me get all this straight. Elliot's your heir now. Right?" Zach chewed his lower lip as he contemplated the situation. Niggling suspicion slithered through him. "Shorty, was Abe your heir, too?"

Shorty nodded. The old man's faded eyes were shrewd as they looked knowingly at Zach. "I think you're startin' to figger this out, Zach." He nodded approvingly. "You're smarter'n I thought."

"Gee, thanks." Zach glanced at Elliot. If he was right, the boy'd need protection.

What the hell have I gotten myself into now?

The uncertainty was disconcerting, to say the least. As they made their way down the path toward the small cabin, Zach tried to force the image of Hilary from his mind.

Hilary as Goldilocks. Hilary as Miss Kitty. Hilary the magician. Hilary in his arms.

Hilary in front of the semi-truck.

Hilary vanishing before his eyes. Hilary gloriously naked and covered with chocolate—her rapt expression when she'd reached her climax.

Hilary's terror-stricken face trapped in the silver mirror.

Chapter Ten

Hilary searched everywhere for Elliot. Where could he be? It wasn't like him to leave without letting her know where he was going.

As usual, by the time Hilary'd returned from school, her mother was too drunk to be of any value to anyone, including herself. Nellie Brown couldn't remember where her youngest child had gone, or with whom. And it was obvious, at least in her present condition, that she didn't care.

As a rule, Hilary tried to avoid the saloon during the evening hours. But someone might know where Elliot had gone, so she took a deep breath and girded her resolve. Closing her mother's bedroom door, Hilary lifted her chin and started down the stairs.

The usual crowd was scattered around the noisy saloon. Tobacco smoke drifted up and stung her eyes. The scents of sweat, whiskey and beer mingled to create a sickening stench that made her stomach lurch in protest.

But she must find Elliot.

Her gaze darted around the room, hoping for a glimpse of her brother. But of course he wasn't here. Like her, Elliot didn't spend any more time in the saloon than absolutely necessary.

She glanced from face to face, wondering who might know where Elliot had gone. Three of her mother's "girls" were working the floor, hanging onto various men. They wore feathers in their hair and lip rouge. One woman had a small black patch glued to her cheek beside her too-red mouth. More of her bosom was displayed than concealed as men drooled and pawed at her body.

And this was what Nellie Brown expected from her own daughter.

Hilary suppressed a shudder and reminded herself of her mission. She must find Elliot. He was so naive and gullible sometimes. The miners ignored him for the most part, though a few of them occasionally played cruel tricks on him. Once they'd even sent him on a fake errand that had resulted in Elliot falling down a ravine and breaking his arm.

Hilary chased away her nagging worries and looked around the room again. Ignoring the catcalls and whistles, the groping hands that plucked at her skirt as she made her way through the main room, Hilary leaned on the bar. "Mr. Carter," she called to the bartender over the din of voices raised in raucous celebration. Problem was, even the participants didn't know what they were celebrating.

"Yeah?"

"Have you seen Elliot this afternoon?" Hilary was growing more worried with every hour that passed. "Mama has no idea where he's gone and it'll be dark soon."

Ned Carter had made it very evident in the way he treated Hilary that he didn't approve of her refusal to join her mother's profession. He'd even offered to introduce Hilary to what he'd referred to as the fine art of pleasing a man, on more than one occasion. Her refusal of his offer had set the tone for their relationship ever since.

"I ain't his keeper," Ned said with disdain as he wiped out a glass and set it behind the bar. "But he was in here this mornin'."

Hilary sighed. "Do you remember seeing him with anyone?" This was going nowhere.

"Yeah." He nodded toward the end of the bar, nearest the door. "Baird." The bartender grinned knowingly.

Hilary groaned internally as she looked toward the end of the bar. When she returned her gaze to Ned and saw the mocking expression in his eyes, she knew he was looking forward to watching her deal with Baird McCune. Her distaste for the man in question was common knowledge in Columbine. "Very well. Thank you."

Hilary moved to the other end of the bar, realizing every gaze in the place was on her. Baird's constant pursuit of Hilary, and her open vehemence toward him, were favorite topics of conversation for the town gossips. It was a volatile combination, one people would probably pay money to see come to a boil. Well, today wasn't the day. She just needed information about Elliot.

"Mr. McCune?" She held her hands folded in front of her as she waited for him to speak. His gaze exploited her as it passed over her bosom, then dipped lower. "I understand you spoke to Elliot this morning." *Your half-brother.*

He snorted and shook his head. "Yeah, I saw the idiot. What of it?" Baird held a drink in one hand and steadied himself with the other. He was very drunk, not atypical for him on any day.

"I can't seem to find him," Hilary rushed on, praying for the patience to see this through. "Do you know where he's gone, or who he may have left with?"

Baird grinned and reached out to touch her arm. Hilary jerked away. The man made her flesh crawl. She felt as if she needed a hundred baths every time he walked by, let alone touched her.

"Please, Mr. McCune." She reminded herself this would only take a few minutes. "Do you have any idea where Elliot might be?"

"Nope." He reached toward her again, but she avoided contact by shifting to his opposite side. "Don't know where he went, but I did see him talkin to some people this mornin'. He left with them."

Hilary recognized the expression in those hideous eyes. Baird would try to exact some form of payment for his information, whether it was worthy of compensation or not. "With whom did he leave?"

"Well, you might just need to freshen my memory a bit, teacher," he whispered, placing his glass on the bar and pushing himself away. "Maybe a little kiss'd help me remember."

"Please don't do this, Mr. McCune," she requested in the most dignified voice she could muster, acutely aware of the multitude of gazes on her. "You know Elliot can't be out alone like this. Tell me where he is."

Baird reached out to grab the back of her neck, then dragged her against him, covering her mouth with his foul-smelling lips. Her stomach recoiled at the intimate contact as she pulled against him and twisted in the attempt to free herself.

She wrenched herself away, but he staggered toward her. Hilary backed into a table, then inched her way around it until she'd managed to place the furniture between herself and her leering stalker. "Please just tell me who Elliot left with this morning, Mr. McCune." It was all she could do to prevent herself from screaming in horrified revulsion, let alone continue to plead with him for information she wasn't even certain he possessed.

Baird started around the table and Hilary darted in the opposite direction. But he out-maneuvered her by turning so suddenly she ran into him. "Gotcha."

"No." Hilary turned her face to the side as he tried repeatedly to kiss her. Several of the patrons in the saloon cheered and snickered from behind her.

"Let go of the lady," an ominous voice commanded from the front of the saloon.

Hilary gasped in relief as Baird released her. He took a step away before turning toward her rescuer. She watched in dread as he held his hands to his sides in a curved manner, indicating his readiness to draw his weapon should he deem it necessary.

She didn't want blood spilled because of her. She glanced quickly at her savior, stunned when she recognized the stranger who'd insisted he knew her this morning. "You," she whispered, backing quickly toward the bar.

Then she saw another figure behind Zach Ryan. "Elliot!" She ran to her brother, ignoring the unfurling tension between Mr. Ryan and her tormentor. "Where have you been? I was worried."

"You interrupted me, stranger," Baird said in a slurred voice, wavering as he stood with his hands still poised in readiness. "I don't much like that."

Hilary drew Elliot away from the door and Zach Ryan. If bullets started flying, she didn't want him hurt. For that matter, she didn't want Zach Ryan shot either. "Don't do this," she pleaded, looking toward Baird as she spoke.

"Hell, you ain't even got a gun." Baird sneered in open disgust, obviously dismissing the newcomer as no threat to him. "What the hell kind of man walks around town without a gun?"

"Supporters of the Brady Bill." Zach took a step toward

Baird McCune, then he paused with both fists on his slim hips. His eyes sparkled dangerously as they narrowed in intense scrutiny of his opponent.

Hilary silently prayed the pair of men wouldn't harm each other over her. "Please, Mr. Ryan." She took a step toward him and placed her hand on his arm. "Don't pursue this on my account. It isn't worth it. I'm quite accustomed to Mr. McCune's bad manners."

Baird threw his head back and laughed, but Hilary felt the moment of crisis pass. The muscles in Zach's forearm twitched beneath her hand, making her aware of him as a man again. Feeling defensive and uncertain, she broke contact with him. "Thank you," she whispered for him alone.

Zach nodded very slightly in her direction. "I'm sorry for keeping Elliot out so late," he said quietly, watching Baird stagger toward the bar and pick up a glass. "He told me a little while ago that you'd be worried if he didn't get home by dark."

Hilary sighed and smiled as he turned to face her. "I do worry about him." She glanced nervously toward the door, where Elliot still stood smiling at her. "Have you had your dinner, Elliot?"

"Zach cooked." Elliot nodded.

"Thank you again." She bestowed another smile on Zach, then returned her gaze to her brother. "You'd better go on upstairs now."

Elliot yawned. " 'Night, Zach. 'Night, Hilary."

Zach watched with a lump forming in his throat as Elliot walked slowly up the staircase. He felt Hilary's gaze on him, and when he turned to look at her his heart flip-flopped in his chest. This gorgeous woman was driving him crazy—all over again.

"Thank you again, Mr. Ryan." Hilary smiled sweetly.

He studied her fluctuating expression, searching for

answers to a myriad of questions. There was no evidence in her demeanor to indicate she could possibly be pretending not to know him. Her blue eyes were wide and innocent, just like before. He knew Hilary well enough to realize she would be unable to hide behind a mask of innocence. Deceit would disclose itself candidly in her expression. He hoped.

Still, no matter how he tried to convince himself, he couldn't completely dismiss the slight possibility that she'd somehow known he'd be swept backward in time with her. But Hilary Brown was his only connection to his identity, and he was still crazy about her. Or maybe he was crazy, period.

"Would you step outside with me for a minute, Miss Brown?" he asked, casting her what he hoped was a friendly smile. His gut balled into a knot of controlled tension. He wanted desperately to just blurt the truth to her, but he'd tried that once already and it hadn't proven effective at all.

Hilary nodded slightly and allowed him to hold the door open for her. Zach was aware of Baird McCune's angry gaze on his back as they left the saloon, but he quickly quelled his concern for such matters as the fresh mountain air revived him.

"It's chilly this evening." He glanced at Hilary, who was bathed in moonlight.

Except for the noise from Miss Nellie's, the town seemed deserted, almost like the Columbine he'd previously known. But not quiet enough to suit him. He swallowed hard, remembering how enjoyable it had been for he and Hilary to have the entire town to themselves.

It was almost comical, now that he thought about it. He'd been furious to learn Columbine was a ghost town. And now . . .

"It does get cool up here at night." Hilary's voice

sounded faraway as she looked at the sky. "Very soon it'll begin to snow. Most of the miners leave for the winter months, though, because it's nearly impossible to mine in deep snow." She laughed softly. "Their absence makes the cold and snow almost tolerable."

Zach chuckled. "I'll bet." God, how he wanted to touch her. It was hell being so near and not being able to touch Hilary—his Hilary.

But she wasn't his Hilary anymore. She was the woman before her death—the one he'd never known. How could she save herself if she didn't remember? What a cruel twist of fate this was turning into.

"I was wondering." He hesitated, searching for words. How did men ask for dates in the nineteenth century? It wasn't as if he could ask her to a movie, after all. "Could I call on you sometime, Miss Brown?" *I sound like I just stepped out of a Roy Rogers movie.*

Hilary's head snapped around as she turned to face him. He saw her eyes widen with surprise in the moonlight. She was a pale, colorless form in the darkness. But he was able to fill in the details. The details that drove him mad with desire just standing near her.

"I . . . suppose that would be all right." She lowered her gaze. "Elliot likes you."

Zach warmed internally at her words. He sensed it meant a great deal to her to have her brother treated with respect. "I like him, too." She was so close—he couldn't endure not touching her. He noticed the familiar floral scent of her hair. "You smell like honeysuckle."

She patted her hair. "I—yes." For a few glorious moments, her gaze seemed riveted to his, then, with a tiny gasp, she turned away. "It's getting rather chilly now. Perhaps I should be going in."

Don't go, Hilary. Help me learn how to survive in this strange world. Stay with me forever.

But he couldn't say those words to her, no matter how desperately he wanted to. Not yet.

"Hilary." He touched her shoulder, felt her tremble beneath his hand. His heart swelled in his chest as if it would burst if he couldn't say the words burning in his mind. "I . . ."

She half-turned toward him and gazed up at his face. "There's something strange about you," she said finally, continuing to stare into his eyes. "I feel as if I know you, but I know I don't. It isn't possible. I've never been anywhere but Columbine."

And Transition. He remembered her stunned reaction to his words this morning. Dare he tell her? No, it was too soon. He must win her trust, her love, all over again.

"Maybe there's something pulling us together," he ventured, wondering how that bit of cosmic drivel sounded to a nineteenth century schoolteacher.

Hilary giggled. "Some kind of invisible force?" She shook her head. "I don't believe in ghosts and tall tales, Mr. Ryan."

Hilary Brown doesn't believe in ghosts? The irony of the situation made Zach chuckle. "If you say so."

She turned toward the saloon. "I . . . I'd like to go in through the back door, if you don't mind."

Zach sighed. "I understand." It was terrible for Hilary and Elliot to have to live at Miss Nellie's. He'd seen their mother's drinking problem with his own eyes. Lord knew he should be able to feel compassion for the woman. But it was hard, seeing Elliot the way he was, and wondering if Nellie's drinking had anything to do with it.

"It's very difficult to be in the saloon in the evenings." She lowered her gaze. "I'm sorry. I shouldn't burden you with this."

"Don't be sorry. I really do understand." Zach took her arm in his as they stepped off the boardwalk and went to the back of the building. He paused for a moment near the spot where he'd parked his Jeep, remembering the first time he'd kissed Hilary.

He still wanted her—needed her like an airplane needed flaps and rudders. He felt incomplete. She'd fallen into his life like rain, sweet and clean—refreshing. He needed that again.

His body flamed with desire as he held her arm tucked modestly in the crook of his elbow. He remembered how she'd tasted, felt, responded to him when he'd made love to her. When he'd covered her sumptuous body with chocolate ice cream . . .

"Didn't you hear me, Mr. Ryan?" Hilary asked when he stopped walking. "Mr. Ryan?"

"Huh—what?" Zach shuddered with barely suppressed desire. "I'm sorry. My mind was wandering." *Not only my mind.* He reached up to touch her smooth cheek with his fingertips, and was pleasantly surprised when she didn't shy away from his contact. She closed her eyes as he stroked her satiny skin. The expression that passed over her face was like the Hilary he'd known—the Hilary who'd been brimming with passion and love.

For him.

Unable to deny himself any longer, Zach lowered his face and barely brushed her lips with his. She immediately stepped back, breaking the contact and the magic. Her eyes were wide with surprise, almost as if—dare he hope?— she remembered something.

"You . . ." She touched her cheek where his hand had been a moment ago. "Goodnight, Mr. Ryan."

Zach sighed, then cleared his throat, which suddenly felt very full. "I'm not going to apologize for kissing you, Hilary."

He saw her hesitate just before she turned toward the back door. She stood with her back to him, a pale form against the darkness. "I don't want you to apologize, Mr. Ryan. Not at all," she whispered without turning to look at him, then rushed up the steps and through the door.

Zach stood there in the darkness for countless minutes. He clenched and released his fists, flexed his fingers repeatedly as he struggled with his warring emotions. One part of him wanted to rush inside and carry Hilary away against her will. Another part—with a very loud voice—wanted to go inside and drown his sorrows at the bar. But he wouldn't—couldn't—succumb to alcohol. He had to protect Hilary.

How much time did he have to win Hilary's love? To get her away from Miss Nellie's and Columbine? How long before she would be forced to shoot Baird McCune?

And be hanged?

Zach was no miner.

If Shorty hadn't been so adamant about the location of the gold, Zach wouldn't have even bothered. The fact that where he'd been told to concentrate his efforts was just inside the entrance helped matters considerably. If he'd been expected to venture back inside the dark mine, where the air quality and integrity of the shaft might have been in question, Zach would've abandoned his efforts before he'd even started.

After a week of banging and scraping away at the wall, and carting what seemed like a ton of rock outside to the sunlight, Zach hadn't found anything even remotely resembling gold.

Real or fools'.

He should be designing and testing airplanes, not digging in a wall of rock with a pickaxe. He mopped the perspiration from his brow, then stepped outside for some air.

The mild autumn weather seemed to be holding for a while. He shuddered internally as he recalled the night he'd almost frozen to death.

He gazed overhead as an eagle winged its way upward. The giant bird soared with such ease. Seeing the wings spread in flight tugged at Zach's lifelong love of flying. Airplanes had been an integral part of his life since the age of three, when his father had taken him up in a single engine Cessna just for fun.

And what fun it had been.

At that tender young age, Zach Ryan had known his life would revolve around airplanes. He'd obtained his pilot's license at seventeen and logged many hours in the air alongside his father. But that had been long before the boating accident took both his parents' lives. Before Zach had turned to the bottle for solace. Long before Jake's death.

The eagle vanished behind a peak and the chasm of silence swallowed Zach within its empty embrace again. Los Angeles should know such silence, just once. It was the most peaceful feeling he'd ever known.

And the loneliest.

The wind whipped up the face of the mountain, reminding Zach of the updraft such terrain often created. Images of gliders drifting through the canyon below flashed through his mind.

Could he design and build one?

His pulse raced. He took a step nearer the edge of a steep drop-off about twenty yards from the Maggie-O. The wind continued to tease his hair and whistle around his ears. It was a perfect launch-site for a glider.

Orville and Wilbur, look out.

But what would he use for materials? It wasn't as if fiberglass and plastics were readily available. There was wood, fabrics of various sorts. It was worth a try. But not

to change history—just for himself. The Wright brothers
could still have their glory.

Of course, he dare not test it from this particular place
the first time. It was a long way to fall if it didn't work.

A very long way.

Zach chuckled and ran his fingers through his hair as
he turned back to the mine. He stared at the hole in the
side of the mountain for several minutes. Shorty Lamb
must have been imagining things. Zach hadn't discovered
anything to indicate there was gold up here at all, let alone
anything as substantial as the mother lode.

And he certainly hadn't seen any ghosts. At least, not
in this century.

He hadn't been to town for a week. Hadn't seen Hilary's
smile for a week.

Zach's heart did a little flip-flop. He was being careless,
not checking on Hilary sooner. What if the circumstances
which had led—would lead—up to her shooting Baird
McCune had already occurred during Zach's absence?

"God, not that."

Zach laid his tools down and turned, but before he left
the mine, an eerie sensation crept over him. He felt a chill
surround him, then a very slight breeze encircled him.

The hairs on the back of Zach's neck stood on end as
he was mesmerized by the sensations whirling around him.
He wasn't alone.

There was someone, or some*thing,* in here with him.
Was it the ghost? He saw nothing, heard nothing. But the
sensation of not being alone remained. He dragged in a
deep breath.

"Who are you?" he asked, wondering why he wanted to
know. Instinct told him he might be much better off not
knowing the identity, or the actual existence, of any ghost
haunting the Maggie-O.

There was no answer to his question, but the sensation

of cold and a presence remained for several chilling moments as he stood transfixed. He felt almost as if the ghost was trying to communicate with him. It was similar to the experience of being sniffed by a dog trying to determine whether or not Zach was friendly.

It was frustrating as hell not being able to make certain the presence was present. The eerie sensations and the chill could be nothing but his overactive imagination.

Zach didn't move. He didn't dare. If there was a ghost, he didn't want to do anything to anger it. Then again, if this was nothing but his imagination, what harm was there in standing still and waiting, making certain?

As suddenly as it had begun, the phenomenon ended. The air warmed and the slight movement in the air ceased, as did the sensation of being watched.

Zach stroked his chin. Was he imagining all of this? Had his experiences with Hilary primed and conditioned him to believe every unusual sensation or occurrence was something supernatural?

"Weird." He scratched his head contemplating how far he'd come in embracing the unexplainable. He was an engineer. He dealt with facts and figures, not instincts and superstitions. To him life had always been black and white, with no room for variance.

But Hilary, though she didn't realize it, had shown him how much more there was in the world beyond the tangible and the believable. He was paying for his refusal to accept the truth now. With interest.

His throat constricted. His experiences with Hilary's ghost had taught him many things. Nothing was impossible—nothing at all.

She'd been dead, but now she was alive. If that wasn't a miracle, he didn't know what was. They'd both traveled back in time and Hilary was alive.

And doesn't have the vaguest idea who I am, or what we shared.

He swallowed the lump in his throat and took a deep, steadying breath. With determination in every step, Zach walked down to the cabin and washed himself as much as possible without a hot shower. Shaving with a straight razor was a new experience, but he managed to only cut himself four times. He put on the clean shirt he'd purchased with the advance Shorty'd given him, and shut the cabin door with a sense of purpose.

Winter was coming. Even though the sun was shining and the air was warm, Zach smelled, sensed, the impending change of season.

He laughed to himself as he walked down the twisting trail toward the town of Columbine. A city boy like Zach Ryan smelling winter in the air? Except for that one precarious episode when Hilary'd come to his rescue, he had no idea what winter was.

And wasn't at all sure he wanted to know.

Unless he could keep warm the way he had that night . . . He'd never forget that morning after his near-death in the unanticipated snow. Hilary'd given herself to him totally.

The image of her fair skin bared before him exploded in his mind, enlivened his senses. His breath caught in his throat as he remembered every detail of Hilary's body. The expression in her blue eyes when she'd given herself to him, the moment in the saloon when he'd told her he loved her.

He paused on an outcropping of rock, then stood on a large boulder and squeezed his eyes and mind closed on the painfully pleasant images. So sweet.

When he reopened his eyes, he gazed down at the lively town of Columbine. People walked along the busy streets, each one occupied with his or her business of the day. Children's laughter drifted up to remind him that this thriving little community wasn't a ghost town—yet.

He sighed, long and slow. Was there a way to prevent Columbine's downfall? Could he do anything to alter history enough to ensure the continued growth and existence of Columbine, Colorado? Was it possible to alter history? Then he was again reminded of something far more important.

He had to prevent a death.

Hilary's.

Chapter Eleven

Elliot wiped the plates and set them on the counter. "Zach not afraid of the ghost."

Hilary froze in mid-step as she crossed the kitchen with a stack of plates. She stared in disbelief at Elliot. "What did you say?" She couldn't have heard him correctly. "What's this nonsense about ghosts?"

Elliot chuckled and shook his head. "Real." He stuck the tip of his tongue out as he concentrated on scrubbing a dirty pan. He was slow but meticulous in everything he did. "Zach not afraid."

Hilary reconsidered her opinion of the mysterious Zach Ryan. What kind of gibberish was he filling Elliot's mind with? "Elliot, there's no such thing as ghosts." She walked over to stand beside him while he finished wiping out the large iron kettle.

He sighed, then reached up to hang a pot from its hook on the ceiling. "Yes."

Hilary closed her eyes for a moment and wondered how

she was going to convince Elliot not to believe everything people told him. Her brother seemed to be suffering from some kind of hero-worship where Mr. Ryan was concerned. She must put a stop to it before it got out of control.

"We'll talk about this later, Elliot." She patted his arm and smiled. "I'd like you to come to school with me in the morning. All right?" That way she could make certain Elliot wasn't being filled with more of Mr. Ryan's tall tales.

Elliot brightened, but shook his head. "Mama wouldn't like that." He sighed and looked down at his feet.

Hilary chewed her lower lip. He was right. Their mother yelled and screamed about what a waste of time it was for Elliot to go to school, because—according to Nellie Brown—he couldn't learn anything. He was useful here in the kitchen, though. Hilary suspected that was the real reason for their mother's strong feelings against educating her son. He was a dishwasher she didn't have to pay.

No doubt, Sean McCune liked that idea. Hilary suppressed the shudder which always accompanied her thoughts of Elliot's father.

"Zach flies."

Hilary froze, then arched her brows in incredulity. "He does *what?*" This was really getting ridiculous. Next thing she knew this Zach Ryan would be telling Elliot he could walk on water, too.

Elliot nodded his head vigorously, then followed his sister to a table near the kitchen door and sat down. "He flies."

"Flies? Like a bird?" Hilary closed her eyes and sighed, then rubbed her chin with her thumb and forefinger. She opened her eyes to study her brother's innocent face. He was so naive. He'd believe anything this Mr. Ryan decided to tell him.

Well, she'd just have to discuss this matter with Zach Ryan. How dare he spread tall tales to someone who couldn't possibly understand they were being given in jest? That made him no better than Baird.

Hilary hit a mental snag with that thought. Zach Ryan was definitely *much* better than Baird McCune. She fingered her cheek where he'd touched her. A tingle crept up her spine with the memory.

"Hello." The male voice startled her from her thoughts as she and Elliot both turned toward the back door of Miss Nellie's kitchen. It was a quiet time of day, too early for dinner and too late for lunch. Matilda was gone and their mother was probably passed out in her room.

"Zach." Elliot beamed and pulled out the chair beside him. "Sit."

"Thanks, Elliot." Zach stepped inside and looked up at the ceiling. "This is more like it."

"Excuse me?" Hilary frowned, trying to ignore the way her pulse raced as she watched Mr. Ryan walk toward the table. "What's more like it?"

Zach's face reddened as he sat down in the chair between her and Elliot. "Oh, nothing." He grinned. "You wouldn't understand. *I* don't understand it, to be perfectly honest."

"Elliot, would you mind going over to the dry goods to pick up a bag of sugar?" Hilary pulled some money from her apron pocket and passed it to her brother. "And buy yourself a peppermint stick."

"All right." Elliot nodded and pushed away from the table. He took his hat from a peg near the back door and put it on over his shaggy hair. "Sugar and peppermint."

"Right." Hilary smiled at her brother. She needed to cut his hair later. "Come right back, though."

"I will."

Zach turned to Hilary with a grin after Elliot left them alone. He raised an eyebrow and tilted his head to the side. "If I didn't know better, I'd say you were trying to get me alone, Miss Brown."

Hilary's face flooded with heat at his words. "I was," she confessed without thinking, then bit her lower lip in vexation. "I mean, I wanted to talk to you alone . . . about Elliot."

"Oh."

He seemed disappointed. Hilary's heart did a little flutter as she involuntarily brought her hand to her throat. She'd left the top two buttons of her bodice undone while helping Elliot with the dishes. Self-consciously, she closed them, all the while aware of Zach's gaze riveted to her throat.

His eyes were wide, almost frightened, when her gaze met his. "Is something wrong, Mr. Ryan?"

He reddened again and cleared his throat. "I—you don't have . . ."

"Yes?" Hilary frowned. "Are you ill?"

"No." He sighed and his color returned to normal. "It's just, I knew a woman who had a red scar on her neck." He tugged at the collar of his shirt. Perspiration beaded his brow. "I'm sorry. Forget about it. You have a beautiful neck."

Hilary couldn't help but wonder about this man's stability. He'd already filled Elliot's mind with bizarre tales. And now he was struggling with some memory which was apparently quite painful—about a woman.

"Are you married, Mr. Ryan?" Why had she asked him that? But she held her breath, waiting for his answer.

His gaze possessed hers. Those soft brown eyes were filled with something unfathomable. His expression absolutely stole her breath.

"No, Hilary," he said quietly, reaching across the table to cover her hand with his. "I'm not married. I was engaged, though."

Her heart soared, though she had no idea why. But he'd loved a woman before. Did he still? "Engaged?"

Zach's eyes clouded for a moment, then burned with an intensity that made her tremble. He nodded. "I was." He released a loud sigh and his hand closed over hers. "She . . ." He winced. "She died."

Hilary felt horrible. She'd been feeling jealous of a dead woman. Besides, she had absolutely no reason to feel jealous of anything or anyone connected to Mr. Ryan. He was nothing but an eccentric, captivating stranger.

"I'm sorry." She tried to withdraw her hand, but his held hers. There was a warm tingling sensation from the contact. It made her think and want things she'd only imagined before in her dreams. Recently, her dreams had become far more graphic than anything she'd ever experienced in the past. Especially since Mr. Ryan's arrival in Columbine. "Very sorry."

Zach nodded, lowered his gaze for a moment, then looked at her again. "Do you like ice cream, Hilary?"

What a strange question. "Why would you ask me something like that?" She couldn't keep herself from giggling. "But yes, I love ice cream. I only had it once. It was the most . . . sinfully, decadently delicious, wonderful thing I've ever tasted."

"Oh, God." He swallowed hard enough to cause his Adam's apple to bob up and down in his throat. The perspiration coating his brow increased. "I was afraid of that."

She laughed again. "How silly." Hilary cleared her throat and brought herself under control. Mr. Ryan was having a very unusual effect on her. She must remember herself. "Mr. Ryan, I really needed to speak with you about Elliot."

Zach nodded and took a deep breath. "I'm crushed. That must be the real reason you sent him on that little errand." His smile was friendly and open. "All right, I'm listening."

Warmth crept up her neck to flood Hilary's face. Why did this man have such a powerful impact on her? It wasn't as if he was *doing* anything to her. Like when he'd kissed her the other evening.

"Yes, well." She cleared her throat and realized her hand still rested beneath his on the table. Hilary thought she should pull it away, but couldn't quite bring herself to break physical contact with him just yet. "Uh, Elliot seems to have some rather bizarre ideas." She took a deep breath and forced herself to meet his gaze. "I think they're coming from you."

Zach gave her a crooked, boyish grin and nodded. "Such as?"

Hilary's heart thudded and raced. There was something deliciously suggestive about the way he looked at her. It made her feel warm and tingly inside. *Get control of yourself, Hilary. You're a grown woman, not a young girl.* But the thoughts she was having about this man were very grown-up.

"Elliot was talking nonsense about a ghost." She leveled her gaze with his and summoned a serious expression. "Do you know anything about this, Mr. Ryan?" *His lips are so full and enticing.* She held her breath as the agitated sensations increased within her. This man was making her crazy—but why?

He paled slightly beneath his tan. "A ghost, huh?" He rubbed his chin in a contemplative manner. "Well, yeah. I guess I know where he got the idea."

"Yes?"

Zach tried to drag his gaze from hers. *Damn, but this woman must have been made just for the purpose of tormenting the hell out of me.* "You don't believe in ghosts, Hilary?"

She moistened her lips with her tongue. An image of Hilary standing naked before him, sensuously licking chocolate ice cream from his fingertips shot through Zach. His hormones were alive and well. Time travel hadn't hindered the little devils one whit. He wasn't sure at the moment whether to feel relieved or disappointed.

"No, of course not." Hilary shifted uneasily in her chair and tried to pull her hand from beneath his, but his fingers closed over hers before she could accomplish the task.

"Your hand is very soft." He gently stroked the outer edge of her hand with his thumb and felt a tremor run through her. "Soft."

Hilary's eyes grew round and color crept into her face as he watched her and continued to caress her hand. "Yes, well . . ."

"Ghosts. Weren't we talking about ghosts?" Oh, the ghost stories Zach could tell her. He almost laughed, imagining her reaction to being told they'd made love in the twentieth century while *she* was a ghost, or in Transition, though he still didn't understand exactly what that meant.

"I . . . I asked if you knew where Elliot may have gotten the idea that there were ghosts." She closed her eyes as his thumb crept to the underside of her wrist.

Zach's pulse took off like a NASA rocket. Just this innocent contact with Hilary was driving him nuts. Knowing how passionate and creative she could be in bed wasn't helping matters any either. His memory was wreaking havoc on his libido.

"Ghosts, Mr. Ryan?"

"Zach. Please call me Zach." *Call me anything you want.* He smiled and watched her through hooded eyes. He noticed her gaze on their hands. It was obvious she wanted him, though she didn't really understand it yet.

"Zach." She glanced up, then quickly lowered her gaze and bit her lower lip. "Please tell me what you told Elliot about ghosts."

Zach suppressed a shudder of raw, almost violent, sexual hunger. He was on fire with wanting Hilary, remembering vividly how open and loving she'd been. "I didn't tell him anything."

"You didn't?" She looked up suddenly and tilted her head to the side. "Then, who did?"

"Shorty." Zach put his other hand on the table and started stroking the inner curve of her wrist with the tips of his fingers.

"Mr. Lamb." Hilary closed her eyes again and he noticed her soft intake of breath as his fingertips crept up her wrist to her forearm. "Do you know, exactly, what Elliot heard?"

"Just that there's a ghost in the Maggie-O." Zach's gaze was riveted to her expression. He felt and shared the sensations she was experiencing. "I haven't exactly *seen* anything myself."

Hilary opened her eyes and gazed at him. There was an inner sparkle in the blue depths that set Zach's imagination in motion.

"Haven't seen it, but . . . ?" She smiled. It was a woman's smile, one that could drive a man crazy in any century.

Zach forced his thoughts back to the subject they'd been discussing. "Felt something." He bit his lower lips and lowered his tone. *I feel something right now.* "You know how it is when you feel something very powerful, but you can't explain it, even to yourself?"

Hilary gasped and suddenly pulled her hand away from his caresses. "Oh." Her face reddened and she brought her hand to her mouth as she stared at him. "Yes, I suppose I do." She blinked several times and took a deep breath. "But what about the flying, Mr. Ryan—Zach?"

"Flying?" Zach scratched his head. "I'm afraid I don't understand what you mean."

Hilary laughed. It was a musical sound. "Elliot said you know how to fly." She shook her head and shrugged. "He has an excellent imagination. Perhaps you said something to trigger it?"

Zach swallowed hard. His hands still rested on the table where they'd been in intimate contact with Hilary's only a moment ago. He felt strangely bereft without her hand beneath his. "I may have." How could he explain to her that he'd drawn a picture of an airplane for Elliot in the dirt? "I talked to him about air—I mean, flying machines."

"Flying machines?" Hilary grimaced and folded her arms across her chest. *Flying machines?* Why would you fill the boy's head with such nonsense?"

"Good imagination?" Zach chuckled and rubbed his freshly shaven jaw with his thumb. Had she noticed he'd cleaned up for her? Did she care? "All right, I've thought about trying to build one." That was no lie.

"Build a flying machine?" Hilary laughed and sighed in an almost maternal way as she pushed to her feet. "Fine, Zach. You build your flying machine, but don't expect Elliot to ride in it."

Zach pushed himself away from the table. He stood and took a step toward her. "Deal." He reached up to brush her cheek with the backs of his fingers. "Soft."

She closed her eyes for a moment and smiled again. "You said that already," she reminded him as she opened her eyes.

"It bears repeating." Zach wanted to kiss her so desperately, he ached. "May I kiss you, Hilary?"

She gasped and looked down at her feet. Biting her lower lip, she side-glanced at him through her brownish-gold lashes. "No one's ever asked me such a question before. I'm not sure how to answer."

Zach took a step closer. "From your heart, Hilary." He placed a hand on each side of her face and gazed into her eyes. "Tell me what you want—really want."

"Yeah, Hilary," a grating voice suggested from the doorway. "Tell old Zach here what it is you really want." Drunken laughter filled the room.

Zach closed his eyes and counted to ten. "Forgive me," he whispered as he stepped away from Hilary's horrified expression. He turned to face Nellie Brown, seeing himself a few years ago. It sickened him. Then he reminded himself the woman was ill. And he should know better than anyone how tough it was to beat this particular, insidious disease. "Mrs. Brown." He inclined his head toward the inebriated intruder.

"C'mon, Hilary. I wanna hear this, too." Nellie laughed as she staggered across the room and sat a glass down on the table. "Miss Priss just about got herself a real kiss. Whooeee!"

Silent tears trickled down Hilary's cheeks as Zach looked from mother to daughter. How could Nellie treat her own child this way? Then he remembered the way she'd treated Elliot the other day in the saloon. The woman's cruelty wasn't reserved for her daughter alone. He suspected it was more self-directed than anything else.

"Hilary, I—"

But Zach's words were left unfinished, hanging in the air between them as Hilary bolted from the room. He clenched his fists at his sides as Nellie Brown laughed. When he turned to face her, it was all he could do to prevent himself from slapping her puffy face.

Then he looked at her—*really* looked at her. What he saw was a creature to be pitied, not hated. He relaxed his hands and shook his head. Drawing a deep breath, he took a step toward Nellie Brown—one step closer to facing his own past.

The woman stared at his face. Zach could only hope his expression was as serious as he intended.

"What are you gonna do?" No humor remained in her voice.

"I'm not going to hurt you, Nellie," Zach said slowly.

"Though a big part of me would love to. But see, I know how you feel."

A flash of insecurity appeared in the woman's faded blue eyes. "How I feel? How the hell could you know how I feel?" Her insecurity was displaced by hard, cold hatred—no doubt, also self-directed.

"Because I've been there," Zach said with a fierceness he couldn't suppress any longer. He reached out and gripped the woman's upper arms and stared into her eyes. "I'm powerless over alcohol. It almost killed me once—and it *did* kill someone I loved." He winced and drew a quick breath. "But I'll be damned if I'll stand by and watch you berate Hilary and Elliot through your drunken stupor. Has it occurred to you that the people who don't seem to mind you being drunk like it because it suits their own selfish purposes? Your customers? Your employees? Sean McCune?"

Nellie's eyes widened, and for a few moments she looked as if he'd struck her. Then the coldness returned. "Sean don't think I'm so bad," she said with a wicked laugh. "The old coot's done asked me to marry him." She laughed again. " 'Course, I ain't so dumb that I don't know he just wants my half of Miss Nellie's. I'm still part-owner."

Zach felt as if he'd been hit by a train. Nellie Brown's engagement preceded Hilary's death. God, if only he knew the date of Baird's murder. He looked long and hard at Nellie. "When is the wedding?"

"Oh, I ain't give him my answer yet." She laughed again and swayed slightly.

"Don't answer him, Nellie," Zach pleaded, still gripping her upper arms. "Let me help you sober up, and stay sober for a while, before you give him your answer."

She laughed, then stopped suddenly. Her lower lip trembled and she nodded. Tears glistened in her eyes. "If you can."

Zach swallowed the lump in his throat as the memory of his own decision to finally get help for his drinking problem surged to the front of his thoughts. He'd hit bottom, killed his own brother before he'd seen the light. Maybe, with any luck, Nellie could be helped before tragedy struck.

Before Hilary shot Baird McCune.

Would postponing the engagement also halt the series of events which led up to the shooting? He couldn't be absolutely certain. But it was damned well worth a try.

"What do I gotta do?" Nellie trembled and she looked down at her feet.

Zach released her arms. "Let's sit down at the table."

Nellie sat down with a loud sigh. The fumes from her breath were nearly powerful enough to push Zach off the wagon himself. He wrinkled his nose, then sat across the table from her. Sitting at the table with Hilary had certainly been more pleasant.

Zach sighed and patted the woman's hand. "Never touch another drop of alcohol as long as you live."

She looked up in shock. The expression on her face was probably something like Napoleon's at Waterloo. Zach's mind strayed for a moment from the very serious topic to a bit of trivia he hadn't considered before.

"Who's president now?" he asked without thinking.

"Who gives a damn?" Nellie scowled at him and hit the table with her open palm. "Tell me what I gotta do to stay sober."

"Sorry." Zach was properly chastised. He'd deserved that. "I told you. The most important thing is to admit you're powerless over alcohol. You have to think of it as your worst enemy. Believe me, it *is*. It's pure poison. And if you let it, sooner or later it's going to kill you." *Or someone you love.*

Nellie laughed, then her lower lip trembled as if she was going to start blubbering. *God, just what I need—Nellie Brown on a crying jag.*

"Why don't you go up to your room and take a nap," Zach suggested as he stood to help Nellie to her feet. "After you've sob—rested, we'll talk again."

"Sean's comin' over." Nellie swayed against Zach as they moved toward the door.

Zach hesitated, gripping Nellie's elbow to steady her. "When?"

"I dunno."

"Well, you rest first." Zach rolled his eyes as he led Nellie through the near-empty saloon and up the stairs. He hadn't ascended this staircase since his journey through the mirror. *Great, just like Alice chasing her white rabbit. Or maybe my journey through the looking glass was more like the one Jefferson Airplane had in mind.*

Except he was sober.

More sober than he'd been in his entire life.

"Which room is yours?" he asked the staggering woman.

She pointed to one across the hall from the door Zach knew led to Hilary's room. He clenched his teeth as they passed her closed door. His thoughts were suddenly filled with memories of what he and Hilary had shared behind that door. He directed his attention back to getting Nellie situated in her room.

As soon as he managed to open her door, Nellie staggered across the room and fell face down on the bed. She groaned once, then the only sound in the room was her snoring and the ticking of a clock on the mantel.

He remembered this room from his initial inspection of the building, over a century from now. The window'd been broken out; several birds had taken up residence in

the beams around the ceiling. The mattress of the ornate
bed had been occupied by some sort of rodent and its
extended family.

Shaking his head, he backed out of the room and closed
the door. When he turned around, he froze. Standing in
the open doorway across the hall was Hilary. Her expression was one of obvious shock and betrayal.

Damn, she thinks I've been *with her mother.*

He took a tentative step toward her. "Hilary, I—"

She closed the door in his face.

Zach stood in the hall outside her room for several
minutes. He heard her muffled sobbing, knew she was on
her bed, the same bed he'd shared with her ghost. He
couldn't bear for her to think he'd actually slept with her
mother.

Lifting his hand, he knocked gently on her door. He
heard her stand and move around the room. He knocked
again.

"I'm coming. Just a minute."

Footsteps sounded as she made her way to the door. He
held his breath while she turned the doorknob and swung
the barrier open wide. A look of total amazement crossed
her face.

"I was expecting Elliot." She looked down at her feet.
"What do you want?"

Zach reached up and gripped the edge of the door,
anticipating having it slammed in his face. Indecision
flashed through him, but he banished it. "I need to talk
to you, Hilary." He looked beyond her, into the room.
"Privately."

Hilary shook her head. Her eyes widened even more.
Then her expression hardened and she glanced at the
closed door across the hall. "You've already been with my
mother. Wasn't that enough?" Her voice was wretched.

Zach's mouth fell open in shock. He'd suspected she

thought as much, but to hear the words leave her lips was too much. "No, Hilary," he said through clenched teeth, pushing his way into the room. "I haven't *been* with your mother, or any other woman since I met you." *Except you.*

"I saw you coming out of—"

"You saw me coming from her room," he finished, then reached for her hands. She jerked hers away, making him cringe. He captured her gaze with his. "But I was only helping her upstairs because she was drunk. You're the only woman I want—ever."

Stunned by his passionate statement, Hilary gasped and took a step back. Was he mad? She was reminded of that first morning, when he'd claimed to know her. The vehemence in his tone was so genuine.

"You must go." She looked away from the hungry expression in his eyes as he walked slowly toward her. "Remember, I'm *not* one of my mother's girls."

He touched her shoulder, ran his fingers up the side of her neck. A chill swept through her at his touch, then a flame chased it away, a flame of longing so intense she thought she'd weep from the sudden emptiness which filled her.

He reached to the back of her neck and released the pins from her hair. It cascaded around her shoulders and down to her waist. When she looked up and met his gaze a fleeting image flashed through her mind. She was in his arms. Naked. Kissing him. It seemed so real.

Her knees felt suddenly weak as his grip hardened on the back of her neck to hold her head as his lips met hers. Hilary moaned, but the sound was swallowed by lips that would permit no protestations. Her head spun and the room seemed to close in on her. Only she and Zach existed in this make believe place. She had no idea where they were, what was happening or what the consequences would be once it ended.

All she knew was that this man *belonged* here with her.

His tongue invaded her mouth, stroked and dueled with hers as she leaned against him. Her breasts flattened against his muscular chest, yet she felt as if she couldn't get close enough to him.

His kiss was demanding and thorough. She felt as if she couldn't breathe, yet didn't need to. He was feeding her everything she could ever want or need with his devastating kiss.

Her limbs were no longer a part of her body as he moved his hand around to the side of her rib cage, then inched it slowly upward. She ached inside, craved something she'd never experienced before. It was maddening.

And spectacular.

His thumb gently brushed against the tip of her breast through two layers of clothing. Hilary's knees buckled beneath her, but his other arm wrapped around her even more tightly, holding her upright and against him.

As he made her breast ache and swell in his hand, Hilary became conscious of the long hard ridge at the front of his dungarees. Her middle coiled into a knot of hunger as she became aware of, and internally acknowledged, this part of him. A minuscule flicker of common sense tried to forge its way to her conscious mind, but to no avail. He deepened the kiss and his thumb became more bold as it drew circles around her puckered peak. Involuntarily, she thrust her pelvis hard against his, shocked when he groaned and reciprocated.

She was lost. Whatever this man wanted from her was his. The strength to resist him wasn't hers to wield. He was too powerful. This hunger he'd created within her was far too demanding to deny.

"Hilary," Elliot called as he swung open her door and stepped into the room.

Hilary was stunned when Zach wrenched himself away

from her and crossed the room to close the door behind Elliot. Her brother simply stood looking from one to the other of them, then shrugged as if there was nothing strange or inappropriate about Zach being in Hilary's room. For once, Hilary was thankful for Elliot's simple ways—God forgive her.

"Zach, something awful . . . happened." Elliot sat on the edge of Hilary's bed, apparently oblivious to his sister's mussed hair and rumpled clothing. The boy seemed agitated and upset.

Hilary met Zach's gaze from across the room. There was a wolf-like gleam in his eyes. She squelched the flame of desire he'd created within her and walked over to her dressing table and turned her back. She fumbled with her long hair until it was back in its demure knot at the base of her neck.

When she turned, she was aware that Zach's gaze had never left her. Her face flooded with heat.

"What, Elliot?" Zach finally asked her brother, still looking at her.

"Sheriff Tyler found the . . . the ghost."

The moment was lost. Zach immediately turned all his attention to Elliot.

Hilary sighed, but decided it was for the best as she walked around to the other side of her bed to watch her brother's face. "Elliot, there are no ghosts," she said in a voice which belied the true state of her nerves.

Elliot's gaze darted around the room, then he looked at Zach. "Sheriff found him."

Zach kneeled in front of Elliot. The expression on his face was patient, without a trace of mockery. "Tell me about it, Elliot. What did the Sheriff find?"

Hilary thought at this moment that Zach Ryan was the most wonderful man she'd ever known. No one had ever treated Elliot with this much respect, with the possible exception of Shorty Lamb.

"Sheriff went up to . . . the Maggie-O." Elliot sighed and ran his fingers through his long, straight hair. "He brought back a . . . dead man."

"Who was it?" Zach stood and waited for Elliot's answer. "Was it Baird McCune?"

Hilary took a step closer to Elliot and touched his shoulder. "Who was it, Elliot?"

"Not Baird. I dunno." Elliot shrugged. "I heard Baird say it was the ghost."

Hilary looked sharply at Zach. His expression confirmed that he was as concerned over this as she.

"It couldn't have been a ghost, Elliot," Zach said in a steady voice. "If it was a ghost, it wouldn't need to be brought to town. Ghosts are already . . . dead."

"Oh." A look of utter confusion, then horror crossed his face.

Hilary met Zach's gaze—her stomach clenched and burned. They both must have reached the same conclusion.

She saw Zach's Adam's apple bob up and down in his throat, then he said, "It must be . . ."

Hilary filled in the name. "Shorty."

Chapter Twelve

Zach left Elliot and Hilary in her room and went downstairs to see what he could learn from the gossiping miners. There were at least three times as many men in the saloon now as there had been when he'd escorted Nellie upstairs less than an hour ago.

"Heard his neck was wrung like a chicken's. Just like old Abe's," one man said, waving his hands in the air. Then he lowered his gaze to the bar in front of him. "Poor old Shorty."

"Yeah, he was a good man," another man agreed, shaking his head.

Zach took a seat in the corner and just listened. He wanted to be as inconspicuous as possible. It was difficult to keep his mouth shut when he had so many unanswered questions. Shorty'd been his friend, his benefactor, for a very brief while. At least now the old man's rheumatism wouldn't cause him any pain.

"Where'd they find him?" another man asked, shaking

his head in obvious sorrow over the loss of life. "Was he *in* the mine?"

"That's what Sheriff Tyler said," Ned offered from behind the bar. "Heard he was lyin' inside the entrance with his head durn near twisted off."

Zach suppressed a shudder. Shorty must've gone to the mine looking for him. If only Zach had been there . . .

"Damn," Zach muttered under his breath. Then he recalled the eerie sensations he'd noticed earlier this morning in the mine. The chill . . . the moving air . . .

A shiver raced down his spine. The fine hairs on the back of his neck stood on end. Shorty'd said the ghost of the Maggie-O was mysterious. Murder was considerably more than simply mysterious.

"What in tarnation was he doin' out there by himself?"

"That's what I'd like to know."

Zach turned to look at the pair of men who walked slowly into Miss Nellie's. They were both wearing black jackets with vests beneath them. A star was pinned on the lapel of the taller man; a holster sporting a pearl-handled gun was slung low on his hip.

The other man was older, with thick silver hair and a moustache. He had an air of authority about him. And affluence. Zach knew without being told he was looking at the infamous Sean McCune.

"Evenin', Mr. McCune," Ned said in what could best be described as a "teacher's pet" manner.

"Ned." The silver-haired man nodded and looked around the room. "Where's Nellie?"

Ned raised his eyebrows. "She's sleepin' it off, sir."

McCune sighed and nodded. "It's just as well. She was fond of Shorty."

"We all were," Zach said without thinking. *Oh, shit, I've put my foot in it now.*

Sean McCune turned toward Zach. He arched a woolly

brow and sauntered over to the table. The sheriff followed close behind, kind of like a puppy dog begging for a handout.

"I don't remember seein' you around before." McCune paused beside Zach's table and waited. He made no effort to introduce himself, offer his hand, or anything else that even remotely resembled courtesy.

"I don't remember meeting you before, either," Zach returned with what he hoped was a shit-eating grin. "I don't believe I caught your name."

A muscle twitched in McCune's jaw and the sheriff stepped around to the side, offering Zach an unobstructed view of his glare.

"Mr. McCune asked who *you* were," the lawman said arrogantly.

A suck-up if I ever saw one. "Did he?" Zach leaned back in his chair and grinned again. "Maybe there's something wrong with my hearing then, because I don't recall hearing him say anything of the sort."

McCune rolled his eyes and groaned. "A smart-ass. Just what Columbine needed." He sighed and shifted his weight. Extending his hand, he said, "Sean McCune. And you are . . . ?"

Zach stood to shake the man's hand. This was Elliot's father. And Baird's father. "Zach Ryan."

"Ryan." Sean rubbed his chin for a few moments. "Don't recall ever hearing that name in these parts before. So you're new in town?"

"Isn't that his line?" Zach pointed at the man who wore the star, but he sure wasn't pumping gas. The lawman's face was turning redder by the minute. "At least, it always was with John Wayne."

"I don't recollect ever hearing that name around here either." McCune arched his brows in open curiosity. "So, Ryan . . . you knew Shorty?"

"We were partners." Zach looked at the sheriff. "He needed someone to work his mine in exchange for half the take."

The sheriff tilted his head to the side. "I'm Sheriff Tyler." He didn't offer his hand. "And all mining claims, including changes like takin' on a partner, are supposed to be recorded in my office."

Zach stiffened. Was he a suspect? "Shorty probably didn't get around to it." He shrugged. "I'm not going to take his mine. His heir's welcome to it."

"Heir?" McCune laughed. It wasn't a pleasant sound by any stretch of the imagination. "That old coot didn't have an heir."

"I wouldn't be so sure of that," Ned called from behind the bar.

Sean turned toward the bartender. "Why's that, Ned?"

The big bald man walked around the bar and approached Zach's table—uninvited. "I heard Shorty in here one day talkin' to Elliot." He glanced from Zach to McCune. "He named Elliot as his heir."

McCune laughed again. "Well, is that so?" His smile was replete with avarice.

"Something wrong with that?" Zach narrowed his gaze as he stared straight into Sean McCune's eyes.

"No, not a thing." McCune sighed. "It's fine with me."

The man was lying. He'd known all along that Elliot was Shorty's heir. "What makes that fine, Mr. McCune?"

Sean reddened slightly, then turned toward Tyler. "What time did you say you thought Shorty was killed?"

"The undertaker said sometime today."

"Had to have been after noon," Zach said, wondering how all these developments fit in with what Hilary'd told him about the Maggie-O in his time. "I was in the mine this morning working. There was no sign of Shorty before I left for town." *Only a ghost—or something.*

Sheriff Tyler took a step toward Zach. "And how do we know you ain't the one who wrung poor Shorty's neck? Maybe you wanted all the take, instead of just half."

Zach met his stare. He felt like he'd just been cast in a Clint Eastwood movie. *The Good—me. The Bad—Sean and Baird McCune. The Ugly—Sheriff Tyler.*

Except he was more of a Chill Wills than a Clint Eastwood type. Especially when it came to guns and horses. Zach Ryan didn't know the first thing about either one, and didn't want to.

"Because I didn't," Zach said in a steady voice he barely recognized as his own. "I liked Shorty. He treated me right."

"Yeah, we'll see." Sheriff Tyler suddenly glanced down at Zach's feet and burst out laughing. "Will you look at them shoes?"

Sean McCune followed Tyler's suggestion and his lips twitched. "Interesting."

Zach wondered what their reaction would be to learn how much he'd paid for his Reeboks. Damned fine pair of shoes, as far as he was concerned.

Baird came into the saloon. "Hey, Pa," he said, swaggering toward Zach's table.

"Jeez, I must look lonely over here," Zach muttered, choosing to ignore the cold looks cast in his direction.

"Figger out who done in old Shorty yet?" Baird didn't seem to be drunk for a change. "Reckon it was that ghost Shorty was always talkin' about?"

Zach suppressed a shudder. He recalled the day Hilary'd given him a tour of Columbine, the ghost town. She'd been adamant in her refusal to take him up to the mine then. He rubbed his chin as he considered the situation. This must've been her reason for refusing to take him up there.

And the ghost.

Who was the ghost of the Maggie-O? Had it killed Shorty? If so, why?

I wonder how this ghost feels about me? Zach again recalled the bone-chilling sensation he'd had this morning in the mine. It must've been the ghost. What else could it have been? Again, Zach was amazed by how easily he was able to accept such bizarre ideas.

Because of Hilary, who didn't believe in ghosts.

"So you're livin' out at Shorty's cabin then, Ryan?" Sheriff Tyler asked in an official-sounding voice.

Zach nodded. "That's what Shorty wanted me to do." He looked toward Ned, who still stood behind Sean McCune. "According to Ned here, Elliot is Shorty's heir. If that's so, I think you'll find the boy wants me to stay on."

Sean smiled in a smug way that made Zach itch to break his jaw. "We'll see about that. Is Elliot here?" He faced Ned as he spoke.

"Upstairs," Zach answered. "He was with his sister. He was pretty upset about Shorty."

Sean's gaze narrowed. "You were upstairs?"

Zach nodded, but offered no explanation. Many men ventured upstairs at Miss Nellie's. That's what the girls, excluding Hilary, of course, were paid to do. They entertained men in their rooms. Let the old man think whatever he wished. The only opinions Zach cared about belonged to Hilary and Elliot.

Sean McCune stared long and hard at Zach. It was obvious he suspected Zach of something. Just what was anybody's guess.

The silver-haired man turned to walk away, obviously disgusted with the entire conversation. That suited Zach just fine. He rocked back on the heels of his trusty Reeboks and grinned at Sheriff Tyler.

"Don't leave town," the man said as he turned to follow McCune. "I wouldn't wanna have to come lookin' for you if I have any questions. I might get riled up."

"Heaven forbid."

Baird scowled at Zach, then followed his father over to the bar. He glanced over his shoulder once, but Zach didn't budge. He kept his gaze riveted to the back of the man Hilary'd already been hanged once for shooting.

But no. That wasn't right. They'd traveled back to a time *before* the incident. It hadn't happened yet.

Zach Ryan hadn't been born yet.

He sank down into his chair, alone. What would become of him? Would he stay here with Hilary in the nineteenth century? Would he be whisked back to his own time once he'd managed to stop her execution?

If he managed to pull off such a miracle at all.

He had to. The thought of Hilary . . .

No. Panic threatened to take control of Zach's sense of reason. He had to remain calm, think clearly. Hilary's life was at stake.

Damn. I wish I'd paid closer attention to what she tried to tell me in my time.

Perhaps then he'd recognize the warning signs. Of course, Sean had already proposed to Nellie. That was his strongest clue that time was running short. What could he do to prevent the vicious cycle that could cost Hilary her life?

Again.

Hilary left early for school. She'd been so preoccupied with developments at Miss Nellie's, then with Shorty's murder, that she'd neglected her lesson plans. The children deserved a teacher who had her wits about her every day.

The sun was barely visible when she left Miss Nellie's by the back door. She loved early morning. There was a light frost on the grass and rooftops around town. Winter was on its way, no mistake.

She tried not to think about Shorty's murder. Why would anyone want to murder an old man? To her knowledge, Shorty Lamb had never harmed a soul, and she certainly didn't believe the nonsense about a ghost in the Maggie-O having committed the dastardly deed. But Shorty's brother-in-law had been killed up there in the mine a few months back.

"Nonsense." She took a deep breath and quickened her pace. As she neared the edge of town, an eerie feeling swept through her. She glanced quickly over her shoulder, but saw no one. Yet the sensation of being watched prevailed as she approached the schoolhouse.

As she stepped onto the stoop and pulled the latchstring, a hand reached out and clamped over her mouth. "Hilary, be quiet," a familiar voice whispered.

She breathed a sigh of relief as he lowered his hand from her mouth. "Zach," she whispered, turning to face him. "What are you doing here?" *And why did you grab me and frighten me?*

"I've been here all night," he confessed. His eyes were bloodshot and there were dark circles beneath them. "Watching your window."

She swallowed hard. "Why? I'm not in any danger. Am I?"

He shuddered and closed his eyes. "This is driving me nuts, Hilary."

When he opened his eyes to look at her, the intensity of his expression pilfered her breath. Suddenly, she was frightened. Of him? No, not him—exactly. She searched his eyes for some clue to the cause of his anxiety.

"What is it, Zach?" She barely knew him, yet felt a link

with him that terrified and thrilled her at the same time. "Is it Shorty?"

"I have to get you away from here." He pressed his fingertip to her lips when she opened her mouth to speak. "Listen to me, Hilary. Leave a note on the door canceling school for the day. Come with me to the cabin and hear me out. Please? Give me a chance to explain."

She stared into his eyes. They seemed so sincere. Trusting him, as she so desperately wanted to, was insane. She shook her head in pointless self-denial. "I don't know why I'm agreeing to this, but I'll come with you. Elliot believes in you for some reason. I guess I do, too."

"Thank God." Zach closed his eyes for a moment and murmured something. Then he pulled an unusual object from his pocket. "Here, write a note and leave it."

Hilary took the thin cylinder in her hand. There was a button on the end. When she pushed it, a small metal head popped out the other end. "To write with?" she asked, turning the object over in her hand.

"Yes. Please hurry." Zach seemed almost frantic.

She passed the object back to him. "I'll need chalk for the slate." She stepped inside and scratched a note on a slate, then propped it near the door where the children would see it when they came to school. She hated canceling classes like this, but an agitated voice in her subconscious refused to be quelled. Whatever it was Zach Ryan needed to tell her, she must hear him out.

"You ready?" he asked impatiently, shoving his hands into his pockets. "We really should hurry."

Hilary frowned. Why was she agreeing to this lunacy? "I'm ready, but what about Elliot? Is he safe?"

Zach's brow furrowed in obvious concern for a moment. "I'm not sure. For now, as far as I know." He sighed and chuckled, a cynical sound. "If only I hadn't been so damned stubborn."

"What?"

"Never mind." He took her elbow and led her back through town and along the twisting trail that led up to the Maggie-O.

She glanced ahead of them several times, thinking of Shorty Lamb. Who—or what—had murdered the old man? She bit her lower lip in frustration and fear, though she knew she'd be safe with Zach. Hilary had no idea why or how she knew this, but she was certain.

The tiny cabin was just ahead, built very near the trail that led to the mine. The mountain sheltered the cabin from the winter winds. She remembered Maggie and Shorty Lamb when they'd first moved to Columbine. She and Elliot had been very young. The couple had seemed like the grandparents they'd never known. Good people, both gone.

"Here we go." Zach opened the door and waited for Hilary to enter, then he followed her inside. He left the door ajar and opened the shutters over the window to permit the light and air inside. "I know it's still a little chilly, but I need a little space. This place makes me downright claustrophobic."

"What is it you wished to speak to me about?" Hilary was suddenly struck with how scandalous and risky it was to be alone—so totally alone—with a man she barely knew. A man who'd kindled her primitive blood to a flame with the slightest impetus, on more than one occasion.

He came up behind her and placed his hands on her shoulders. "This is going to sound crazy to you, Hilary," he began in a hoarse whisper. "But you must try to listen to all of it."

She nodded, suddenly feeling as if this man held her future in his hands. *Preposterous.* "I'm listening, Zach."

"Sit over here." He led her to the crude table and bench. "It's a long story."

He sat on the edge of the narrow bunk built into the wall, only a few feet away from her. "All right," he said with a nod, but she had the impression it was a signal for himself.

"This is the most bizarre thing that's ever happened to me, and I'm sure you'll feel the same way." He took a deep breath and leaned his elbows on his knees, rubbing the back of his neck with one hand. "The only way to do this is just do it." He flashed her a crooked grin. "God, now I sound like a Nike commercial."

"What?" Hilary was beginning to have serious doubts about Zach's sanity. He was behaving very strangely. "What's that?"

"Nothing. I was thinking out loud." He sighed, then his expression grew somber. "Hilary, I'm from the future."

Hilary jerked her head up and stared at him with growing unease. "Zach, I don't believe such nonsense." She snorted in derision and started to get to her feet. "I should have known better than—"

"Don't go, Hilary." He gripped her hand and pulled her back down to the bench, then he resumed his seat on the bed. "I need you to listen. It's important. If you won't do it for yourself, then do it for me . . . and Elliot. Please?"

She sighed, silently berating herself for falling for his sincere approach again. "Zach, I think you must have lost your mind if you really believe this."

He winced. "I deserved that. But it gets much worse, Hilary." He looked upward and shook his head. "Here. I just thought of something that might help convince you." He reached into his pocket and withdrew a coin. "Look at the date on this quarter."

Hilary took the strange coin and turned it around in her fingers while she read the date. "It says 1991," she read aloud, then pressed her lips into a thin line of disapproval.

"Really, Zach? Where'd you get this? It's some kind of terrible joke."

"God, talk about role reversal. Hilary, I'm trying to tell you." He reached into his pocket and withdrew more coins of different denominations. "And this." From his hip pocket, he removed a leather pouch. He unfolded it and took out a card made of a strange substance. "Here."

Hilary took the card in her hand, more interested in what it was made of than the words on it. Then she turned it over and saw Zach's face behind the shiny coating. "It's a picture of you." She smiled. "May I keep it?"

"Sure, I don't need it. God, I'm tired." Zach took a deep breath and rubbed his eyes.

"Maybe you should get some rest," she suggested. "That's probably what's wrong with you."

"There's nothing *wrong* with me!" He leapt to his feet and paced the small cabin. "Aren't you listening? Read the card, Hilary. It's my driver's license. A license to drive a car—an automobile."

Hilary tilted the card so the words were plainly visible. "I see your name and a lot of numbers. It says *Operator's License.*" She shrugged. "What does that mean?"

He stooped beside her and pointed to some of the numbers. "This is my birth date."

Hilary stared in disbelief. "Zach, you don't really expect me to believe this, do you?" She giggled. "This is some sort of joke."

"No joke, Hilary," he said in a wretched voice. "This is one helluva payback for me not believing you."

She frowned. "What didn't you believe?"

A muscle twitched in his jaw. His brown eyes grew misty as he stared at her. "When you told me you were a ghost in 1997."

Hilary gasped and dropped the card. "You're frightening me, Zach."

"Good." He lowered his gaze for a moment, then looked directly at her. "I didn't mean that. I'm sorry. Listen, you have to hear the entire story, Hilary." He reached for her hand and pulled her up to stand in front of him. He cupped both sides of her face with his warm hands. "I love you. We first met in 1997, here in Columbine."

She tried to pull away, but he didn't release his gentle but firm hold on her face. "I don't want to hear this." She trembled beneath his touch.

"Yes, you will. Your life is at stake."

"My life?"

Zach nodded. "Now will you sit down and listen?"

She'd much rather stand here with his hands on her face, but she nodded in agreement. "All right." When he released her, she returned to her seat. "I'll hear all of it." *But right now I'm so drawn to you I'm not sure I can think clearly.*

"Thank you." Zach began pacing again. "I inherited the entire town of Columbine from my uncle. When I first got here, I found a deserted town. There was only one person in Columbine. You."

Hilary sighed. "In 1997?" Why was he doing this—making up this bizarre tale? What purpose could it serve?

"That's right." Zach nodded and sat on the bed to gaze into her eyes. "You were living in your same room at Miss Nellie's, but you were the only person in town. Except, you weren't exactly a person."

Hilary scoffed. "Oh, that's right. You said I was—"

"A . . . a ghost." Zach shrugged and held up his hand when she started to sputter in disbelief. "You said you'd hear it all."

"I don't believe any of this." She covered her face with her hands, then nodded. "Go ahead. Get this over with. Though, I can't imagine what you're trying to prove with this."

"Believe me, when I tell you I couldn't accept it, either. I came up with a logical explanation for everything you did to try to convince me you were dead." He laughed and gazed up at the ceiling. "You even vanished right in front of me on three separate occasions."

"Did I fly and walk through walls, too?" Hilary blinked rapidly and bit her lower lip. "No, Zach. This isn't true. It can't be."

"Yes, it is true." Zach reached for her hands, but she eluded his effort. "You told me the story of how you died. I only wish I'd paid more attention to all the details. See . . . you were hanged."

"Hanged?" Hilary heard a roaring sound in her ears. This couldn't be happening. She'd finally found a man who really interested her, only to learn he was insane. "Zach, you need help."

"Which is precisely what I told you in my time."

"Your time . . ."

He nodded. "You were hanged, Hilary." He shuddered, then rubbed his hands over his face again. "For shooting Baird McCune."

Hilary tried to steady her breathing. That part of his story didn't sound as impossible as the rest. Many times she'd considered how much more pleasant her life would be if Baird McCune would cease to exist.

"So, according to you, I was hanged for shooting Baird." She clenched her hands together in her lap and drew a deep breath. "When?"

Zach swallowed loud enough for her to hear. "This year sometime." He lowered his gaze for a moment. "I don't know the date, but there's only a few months of 1886 left."

Hilary nodded. "I don't believe you, but if this were true—I'm not saying it is—it would have to happen shortly.

Hangings and such aren't at the top of our list of priorities in the dead of winter." *This is so crazy, Hilary.* Why was she even listening to him?

"I thought of that." He stood again and began to pace. "You tried and tried to make me believe you. You mentioned an angel."

"A ghost *and* an angel. This is interesting." Hilary folded her arms across her abdomen. "Go on."

"You can't imagine how weird this is. It's a case of complete role reversal."

"Role reversal?"

"A term from my time." He grinned with a shrug. "Women vote and even run for office, by the way."

"Really?" Hilary almost fell into his trap. "In this fictitious world of yours?"

"Real, Hilary." He stooped beside her and gripped her hands in both of his. "This is all true. The angel offered you the chance to return to your own time to prevent your premature death. But when she sent you back here to your time, apparently you lost your memory of the next hundred years. So, you don't even know enough to save yourself."

"Zach, I've really heard quite enough." She tried to pull her hands free, but he held them fast.

"No, you're not leaving here." He squeezed his eyes shut for a moment. "Don't you see? I don't know when this shooting is supposed to take place. If you shoot Baird, you'll hang. It's that simple. You're staying here with me, where I can protect you. Even if I have to tie you to the bed."

She gasped as her mouth fell open in shock. "I can't stay here with you." She struggled against the gagging lump in her throat. "It's indecent."

"Hilary Brown," he said in a hoarse tone. "We fell in

love in my time. We made love. You were the most passionate lover I've ever known.''

Heat suffused Hilary's face. Her heart thudded and
raced, seeking liberation from this insanity. She leaned
away from him. ''You're mad. I've never been . . . with a
man.''

He nodded. ''I know.'' He reached out to cup her face,
but when she flinched, he dropped his hand to his side.
''I know that because you were a virgin when I—''

''I *am* a virgin,'' Hilary said, closing her eyes for a
moment against the embarrassment, but it didn't help.
The heat in her face increased. Her cheeks were probably
the shade of ripe apples. ''This conversation has to end
now,'' she insisted, trying to rise to her feet. He gripped
her shoulders and held her down. ''Please let me go, Zach.
You're frightening me.''

''I can't let you leave here.'' His eyes glittered, his expression tortured. ''You're staying here with me, where I can
make sure you're safe.''

''What about Elliot?''

A shadow passed over Zach's face. ''I . . . I'll go after
him later in the week.''

''Zach—''

''Hilary, you must listen to me—believe me.'' His voice
was desperate. ''Please just promise you won't leave me
again.''

Please just promise you won't leave me again. He needed
her. For some reason, she couldn't bring herself to walk
away from this man when he so desperately needed her.

When he pulled her to her feet before him, she knew.
Hilary Brown was ready to commit herself to this very
attractive, very insane, man. Her own sanity was definitely
in question.

''You'll stay?''

He cupped her chin in his hands. She nodded, realizing she'd agreed to do much more than merely stay with him. "With you."

He lowered his mouth to cover hers.

She was lost.

Chapter Thirteen

Zach tasted her with desperation bordering on frenzy. This was Hilary, his love. He'd known her as intimately as he'd ever known any woman, yet this was different. This was their first time all over again.

Her body grew pliant and molded against his. His blood thickened, heating to a level of passion that wouldn't be silenced. He swelled and hardened as she pressed her softness provocatively against him.

Anticipation fueled his hunger. Memories wreaked havoc on his libido as he deepened their kiss, savored the innocent explorations of her tongue as she returned his kiss with her awakening passion. Hilary Brown was becoming a woman right here in his arms.

Again.

He cradled her against him, then lifted her into his arms. Placing her on the narrow bunk, he gasped at the naked emotion blazing in her blue eyes. She was exquisite.

And she was his.

Strengthened with the knowledge that Hilary wanted him as much as he wanted her, Zach took a few steps toward the door and kicked it shut, dropping the board in place to deny any intruders entrance to their sanctuary. As he passed, he closed the shutters as well, until only a small amount of light entered the tiny cabin through minuscule cracks between the logs.

When he turned to face Hilary again, he froze. She was unwinding her hair and spreading it with slender fingers to frame her upper body. His gaze drifted downward to her voluptuous breasts, where she began to unbutton the front of her dress. It was clear she was determined to see this through.

A momentary pang of guilt halted him. Zach stood staring at her for several minutes while she shook her hair free and eased her arms from her sleeves. Her bare shoulder gleamed alabaster in the dim light. He sucked in his breath as she swung her legs to the dirt floor and permitted the dress to fall in a pool of gray at her feet. A thin shift was all that separated his hungry gaze from her delectable breasts.

He took a tentative step toward her as she lifted her foot to the bunk and rolled her black cotton stockings down and slipped them off her slender feet. Inch by agonizing inch, she disrobed before him.

He unbuttoned his shirt and slipped it from his shoulders as her torturous performance continued. Lace-trimmed pantalettes followed the stockings. When she picked up the pile of clothing at her feet and gingerly placed it on the table behind her, granting him a glorious view of her backside, Zach kicked off his shoes and shed his socks.

His memory of their *first* time, in that other world, assailed him. She'd disrobed for him then, too. But he'd erroneously assumed she was an experienced woman. This time he knew better.

He took another step toward her as she turned to face him. She held her hands out, beckoning to him. In less than an instant she was in his arms. Only her shift and his jeans separated their hungry flesh as he held her against him.

Slowly, methodically, he began to massage her lower back, savoring the feel of her breasts pressed so enticingly against his chest. Her nipples were burning embers, boring into him, making him ache to taste their sweetness.

He could never get enough of this woman in any form. Whether it be her ghost or the real Hilary, alive and well and loving him, Zach knew she was his. They were destined to be together.

He'd never believed in such nonsense before he met Hilary. But now he knew destiny wasn't nonsense at all. Here was living proof. That mirror behind the bar at Miss Nellie's, which he'd cursed with vehemence in his own time, had delivered something precious to him. Hilary— a reflection of his heart.

He cupped her buttocks in both palms and lifted her slightly against his erection, showing her exactly what she was in for. Her reaction was his undoing.

Hilary wrapped her legs around his waist, making Zach nearly explode with a surge of raw sexual hunger. He groaned, sought her mouth with his and probed for that hidden release he knew was waiting.

As their lips clung together, he lowered her to the bunk again, running his hands along the sides of her rib cage as he reached for the hem of her shift. He lifted the garment up until she ended their kiss to slip the shift over her head. She shook out her blond curls and gazed up at him. Her blue eyes were pleading, burning with naked desire.

"You're so beautiful," he whispered, lying beside her on the bunk. He tracked a line where a thin blue vein ran from her neck to her breast. The velvety feel of her skin beneath his callused fingertip made him shudder.

So sweet.

He kissed her cheek, the lobe of her ear. Then he trailed tiny kisses down the side of her unmarred neck to the curve of her shoulder. She moaned as he cupped her breast with his hand, then gently teased her flowering nipple with his thumb. When he displaced his thumb with his mouth, fusing his lips against her breast, she gasped and pressed against him.

"Zach." Her voice was a whispered catalyst for his starved senses.

He cupped her breast and teased her with his fingers as he tasted the other. Soon, he pressed them together and gave identical consideration to them both as she writhed and arched against him.

"Sweet," he murmured between breasts, loving her response, loving her.

He spent an eternity tasting her, savoring her reaction as she pressed against him, gasped and moaned in ecstasy. This was his Hilary. He adored her, drowned in her fragrance, relished his anticipation of tasting all of her, feeling her surround him with her warmth, her love.

He reached down with one hand and freed himself from his jeans and briefs, then slid them off by wiggling and twisting. Soon, his throbbing erection was free and very ready.

Inch by inch, he kissed his way downward toward the triangle of golden brown curls. He teased her flat abdomen with his tongue, swirled circles around her navel as she trembled beneath him and wound her fingers in his hair.

The fragrance of her desire intrigued him, urged him

downward until he lifted her legs over his shoulders. Ignoring her murmured protests, he tasted her.

Hilary saw pinpoints of light as she stared up at the ceiling. She'd had no idea it would be like this. As his mouth possessed her woman's flesh, she lifted her hips to meet him. His tongue was magic, inflicting her with a maddening combination of torture and pleasure.

But it was wonderful.

She needed him like a flower left in the hot sun needed water. He was an essence of her life she hadn't realized was missing, until now.

She grasped the back of his head as his mouth brought her higher and higher toward something wonderful. Hilary didn't know exactly what it was she sought with such desperation, but she was certain she'd die if she didn't find it.

Soon.

Then something extraordinary happened.

Hilary's senses, her heart, her mind, everything joined in a miraculous explosion of pleasure unlike anything she'd ever imagined. Blackness shrouded her vision, and for one delicious moment, consciousness seemed to elude her.

A flash of heat coursed through her veins as he kissed his way back up her abdomen, caught her before the ecstasy passed, to bring her up to a state of intense longing yet again.

This wasn't over yet. And Hilary wasn't sure she ever wanted it to end.

His lips claimed her breasts again, making her insides coil with a hunger she imagined was something people would kill to satisfy. It was terrifying, all-powerful.

She was drunk with the heady power of arousal as he kissed his way up her neck to her mouth. Initially, she was surprised to taste herself on his lips, but she soon forgot such details as the hard core of him pressed insistently against her thigh.

The sudden urge to touch him possessed her. She inched her hand between them until she found his hot, smooth tip. It was slightly damp, throbbing and hard. A flash of hunger swept through her lower abdomen, like a tense spring, wound too tight, about to burst with the slightest impetus.

This impetus—Zach.

She wrapped her fingers around him, savoring the smooth-hot feel of him. Groaning, he inched his way upward until she felt his entire length.

"Oh, God, Hilary," he whispered, the ragged sound tugging at her primitive womanly instincts to make it all better. For both of them.

She wrapped her legs around him, pulled him toward her. His gaze met hers for a brief moment. She saw his silent question and answered by guiding him nearer, toward her.

"Make me yours, Zach," she pleaded, angling her hips to meet him partway.

Zach growled in surrender and pressed himself against the folds of her womanhood. Hilary felt herself contract and throb in anticipation. She wanted, needed, this.

Miraculously, she opened and surrounded him, drawing him deeper as he inched his way slowly into her body. She wanted him inside her—completely.

When he gritted his teeth and thrust himself upward, Hilary was stunned by the sharp, burning pain. She bit her lower lip to prevent herself from crying out as her flesh tore to accommodate his.

After a moment, he kissed her forehead. "I'm sorry, love," he whispered, then began to move very slowly, torturously, within her.

Hilary soon forgot her pain. The sensations of having Zach fill her, then retreat, only to fill her again made her spiral toward that summit she'd found earlier. But she sensed this would be even greater than before. There was something about having him buried deep inside her, a part of her, that made this all the more spectacular. It made her feel complete.

"Oh, God," he muttered in a ragged whisper. His movements became frantic as he thrust and burrowed within her.

Hilary met him, positioning herself to take him more completely within her as he moved faster and faster. Each time he plunged into her, she went higher and higher, felt herself grow nearer to completion.

They became one, merging and arching together in an age-old rhythm. Hilary felt the beginnings of fulfillment as she mindlessly surrendered to the desperate need this man had created within her. Her body quivered and contracted around his heated shaft, swallowing him with a fury over which she had no control. Primitive instincts commanded and ruled.

When the explosion came, it unhinged her. Hilary's body became liquid fire. Her blood heated and pooled around Zach's as the sensations washed over her. She splintered, fractured, shattered—each particle a mindless rendition of pure, erotic satisfaction.

Zach unleashed his passion in all its fury. She accepted him, answered his silent plea for gratification. He came into her then, like a fire seizing a timberland too long denied precious rain. Hilary met him, welcomed his possession, answered again and again.

He flinched and shuddered, then slumped against her. Their breathing came in rapid gasps as heartbeats slowed and temperatures resumed some semblance of normalcy. Hilary ran her fingers down his sweat-slickened back, kissed the side of his neck, heard his moan of pleasure.

She felt so right, lying here beneath Zach, entwined as

lovers. The remorse she'd expected didn't come. He lifted his head to gaze into her eyes.

"Hilary, I love you," he said in a soft voice. His gaze was reverent as it held hers. "I love you now and forever."

His lips brushed hers as he slipped his weight to her side. Hilary touched his cheek. His brown eyes were so sincere. He couldn't be deliberately lying about his wild tales. He was suffering from delusions. Perhaps they'd go away, or maybe Doc Simon could help him. All she knew was that she wanted him, needed to be with him.

Loved him.

As impossible as it seemed, after knowing Zach such a short time, Hilary had found love. Real love. Her heart soared, then plummeted as she reminded herself of his probable insanity. How could she commit herself to someone with such a precarious grasp on reality?

Yet how could she not?

She bit her lower lip and met his gaze. He stroked the side of her face with the tips of his fingers, pushed her errant strands of hair behind her ears. She was transfixed, mesmerized by the intensity of his gaze.

"I love you, too, Zach," she murmured, feeling a surge of giddy excitement course through her at hearing her own words. "I really do." She surprised even herself with the truth. It felt wonderful.

Yet terrifying.

"God, Hilary." Zach cradled her against his chest. "You can't begin to guess how happy it makes me to hear those words from your lips. When I first awakened in this time, I thought I'd never hear you say it again."

In this time.

There it was again. Zach, her beautiful Zach needed help. He needed her. Hilary touched his face. She should hear his entire story, try to understand what brought him to this. Perhaps it would empower her to bring him back to reality.

"Tell me, Zach," she urged, continuing to stroke his cheek. "Tell me how this miracle of yours came to pass."

A look of uncertainty flashed across his face. "Are you sure you want to know?" He shook his head. "You have to believe in miracles to understand it. I didn't. That's why I almost lost you."

His words touched something buried deep within her. "Miracles." She smiled inwardly, wanting desperately to believe him, yet knowing it was impossible. Time travel? Ghosts? It just couldn't be.

"I guess finding each other now is a miracle," she said, hoping to pacify him with her words, yet meaning them with all her heart. "I never thought I'd be lucky enough to find someone like you. No, not like you—only you."

Zach grinned. It was a boyish grin that melted her heart. "I do love you." He hugged her close and kissed the top of her head. "I want to take you far away from here, before . . ."

"Before what?" Hilary gazed into his eyes when he lifted his face to look at her. "Tell me."

"Before you shoot Baird McCune and are hanged for it," he blurted out, then shuddered as his face blanched beneath his tan. "God, Hilary. Can you ever forgive me for not believing you when you tried to tell me?"

Hilary's stomach tied up in knots at his words. He was so confused. "I forgive you," she whispered, hating herself for lying to him. But she loved him so much it hurt. She couldn't bear to see him struggle with reality the way he was. "Do you remember anything else about the angel you mentioned earlier?" If she was going to help him, she needed to hear as many details of his ludicrous story as possible.

Zach chuckled. "I teased you something fierce," he confessed, running his fingers through his hair until it stood on end. "I really don't know much else, because I didn't listen to you, didn't believe you. What a fool." He chuckled in derision. "God, if only I'd listened to you."

She stroked his cheek and nodded. "Tell me."

He shrugged. "I wish I could, but that's about all I know. You said something about being in Transition."

She nodded and ran her fingers along the lobe of his ear. "I'm glad you brought me out here, Zach," she confessed. "If you hadn't, I still wouldn't know the meaning of . . . love."

"And I do love you, Hilary."

"I was afraid I'd feel dirty after. But I don't. I know what the difference is. It's really very simple—it's love that makes it right. All my life I've tried so hard *not* to be like my mother." She felt warm from within, warm with love. "Thank you for loving me, Zach." She pressed herself against him. "I liked the things you did to me." Her face flooded with heat and she averted her gaze, but only for a moment.

"Not as much as I enjoyed doing them. And *you* could never be anything like your mother." He arched his brow and grinned lecherously. "And the next time will be even better."

She felt like a kid at the candy counter. This was all so new to her, so decadent. It was incredible. "Next time?"

He nodded as he lowered his lips to hers. A warm glow began in her loins and spread slowly. "Oh, Zach," she murmured as he kissed his way down her throat to the curve of her breast. She watched in awe as he covered the tip of her breast with his lips and fused his mouth to it. A thrill shot through her at the sight of his tanned face against her pale flesh. It seemed so right, so natural.

The slow-burning passion built to an inferno within a few minutes as he touched and caressed her with his talented hands and lips. Hilary felt like a musical instrument; Zach was the musician, formulating a symphony of sensations with a proficiency that stole her breath. Such talent should be illegal.

"Marry me, Hilary," he murmured against her breast, then lifted himself to gaze into her eyes.

"What . . . what did you say?" Her heart did a little somersault at his words.

"I asked you to marry me." He grinned and inched up toward her face. "Marry me—*now*."

"Now?" Hilary stared at him in bewilderment. "Right now?"

He hesitated. "Tomorrow we'll go after Elliot and get married. We're not going anywhere until I've shown you how pleasant the second and third time can be."

"Third?" Hilary grinned and moistened her lips with her tongue. "Show me, Zach."

"Will you marry me, tomorrow?"

Hilary stunned herself. "Yes."

She fell through a hole—trapped—unable to break free. Hilary screamed, yet no sound came forth. Then a bright light led her through a tunnel of darkness. She must reach the light—salvation.

Darkness was everywhere, surrounding and enveloping her in an empty void. There was nothing, nothing tangible. There was no up, no down.

A beautiful woman in a white robe smiled at her. She showed her a book, the book of Hilary's life. In it was everything she'd ever done, both good and bad.

But she wouldn't let Hilary stay. The angel said Hilary had to perform a task first. She must help a deserving soul through some personal crisis. Hilary was frightened, but she agreed. She'd do anything to keep from going to Hell—eternal damnation.

Why was she here? She was dead, but why, how?

Then she touched her neck, felt the raised ridge which encircled her entire throat. She'd been hanged. As she glanced down at her dress, a scream tore from her soul. She wore a harlot's gown, a red satin dress which barely covered her breasts.

Hilary Brown had been hanged as a murderess and a whore.

"No!" she screamed, sitting upright in the narrow bunk, clutching at her throat for breath. Her neck felt as if it was squeezing the breath from her, strangling her. Perspiration streamed off her face and dripped between her breasts.

"It's all right, Hilary," Zach mumbled sleepily from her side, sitting up and pulling her against him. "You must've had a nightmare."

She nodded and swallowed convulsively. Just a nightmare, not real. The story Zach had told her earlier must have fueled her imagination enough to create the images she'd seen. Yet they'd seemed so real, as if she'd really experienced them.

No, it couldn't be.

Her heart raced and hammered against her chest, but her breathing quieted, the strangling sensation passed. She was all right. Alive. She glanced down at herself. There was no red dress. She hadn't been branded a whore.

"I'm sorry." She laughed at herself, but it was a nervous sound. "You go back to sleep. I'm all right, now."

But Zach continued to hold her against his chest while he rubbed her back and shoulders. He kissed the side of her neck, his breath warm and reassuring against her bare flesh. "I love you, Hilary. We'll go to town in the morning and get Elliot. He can be my best man."

Hilary smiled against his shoulder. "Elliot will like that." She suppressed the shudder that was born in her belly. By holding her breath for a moment, she brought herself under control again. "I love you, too, Zach. I'm glad you made me come out here with you."

She stretched out beside him, cradled in the protective

circle of his embrace. The reassuring sound of his heart beating against her ear quieted her. She needed answers. Why had she dreamed in such vivid detail? The terrifying part was that she'd filled in details Zach hadn't mentioned earlier. Like the red dress.

"Zach?"

"Hmm?"

"Tell me again." She took a deep breath.

"What? That I love you more than my own life?"

"Mmm. That's nice, but I wanted to hear more about what you were telling me this afternoon." She bit her lower lip, wondering if she was really ready to hear this story. Heaven forbid, it could trigger another nightmare. But for some inexplicable reason she needed to know. Maybe to make sure he didn't know all the details her imagination had provided on its own.

"You mean about the angel?" Zach tensed at her side. "Are you sure?"

She nodded against his shoulder. "I need to hear it again." She took a deep breath, then sighed. "Tell me every detail you can remember."

"All right."

He stroked her hair with his hand, still holding her against his chest while he spoke. His voice rumbled through his chest and into her. It was soothing and reassuring. Hilary waited.

"You said she, the angel, couldn't admit you to Heaven." He sighed and touched her cheek. "My beautiful Hilary, turned away from Heaven."

She kissed his palm when it ventured near her lips. "I do love you so."

He kissed the tip of her nose. "This angel made you a deal," he continued. "Just like Monty Hall."

"Monty who?"

"Never mind." He laughed. "Uh, she put you in Transition, made you a ghost, I guess. You told me she gave you until the end of the twentieth century to find a deserving soul in Columbine to serve, to earn your second chance to prevent your hanging."

Hilary shuddered, though she still couldn't believe his story. But *he* seemed so convinced this bizarre tale was true, it frightened her.

"The first time I laid eyes on you, I thought you *were* an angel." He chuckled. "You rescued me from a hungry bear." He shook his head and laughed again. "There you stood, in the middle of the street, holding that long stick in your hand. You sent that bear packing, though."

Something tugged at Hilary's subconscious. It was frightening. She almost suspected it was something she'd purposely forgotten, pushed away because it was too painful for her to deal with. *That's ridiculous, Hilary.*

"A bear, huh?" she asked, quelling her nervous stomach by taking a deep breath.

"Yeah, you were a sight, let me tell you." He chuckled again. "Miss Kitty from *Gunsmoke,* I thought at first. Then I decided you looked more like Goldilocks."

Hilary giggled. "Because of the bear?"

"Right."

"Was Miss Kitty a woman you knew?"

Zach laughed out loud and hugged her close. "No, silly. She was a character from a television show."

"Television show?" Hilary frowned. "What's—"

"Something that hasn't been invented yet." He rubbed her back again. "No, I thought you were Miss Kitty because of the way you were dressed."

"Dressed?" Dread descended over her, made Hilary feel cold from within. Her heart pounded mercilessly again and she took a deep, steadying breath. "How was that, Zach?" *God, please no.*

She felt him swallow, heard his deep breath. Then he

sighed. "When you were hanged, Sheriff Tyler or Sean McCune, I'm not sure which . . ." He shuddered. "Are you sure you want to hear this, Hilary?"

The roaring in her ears made it difficult to hear Zach. But she knew what he'd said—sensed what he was about to say. Yet she had to hear it. "Please just tell me all of it."

"They made you wear a red dress, like the ones your mother wears."

Chapter Fourteen

Zach watched Hilary's profile as they walked to town. He was worried about her. She seemed withdrawn and tense this morning. Was she having second thoughts about marrying him?

A knot formed in his gut. He had to get Hilary away from Columbine—fast. She was in danger. Anytime now the events which originally led to her hanging could repeat themselves. Zach wouldn't—couldn't—let that happen.

Even if he had to kill Baird McCune and face the hangman's noose himself.

Suppressing a shudder, he gave her hand what he hoped was a reassuring squeeze as they entered through the front door of Miss Nellie's. Ned looked up from his station behind the bar and arched a curious brow. His expression was one of open disdain.

"Out all night, eh?" He flashed her a look of pompous satisfaction. "For somebody who talks so High-n-Mighty, you sure ain't picky 'bout who you—"

"That's enough," Zach said, clenching his fist as he observed Ned's changing expression.

The bartender shrugged. "Have it your way."

"Where's my mother?" Hilary asked with a trembling voice, betraying her uneasiness. "I need to speak with her about something."

Ned whistled low. "She sure is actin' strange."

A warning bell went off in Zach's head. "Strange how?" If Nellie was drinking, she'd be susceptible to Sean McCune. Then Baird would take over management of the saloon, just like before.

No. "Where is she?" Zach held his breath, waiting for the answer.

"In the kitchen."

Hilary and Zach went into the kitchen together and stopped short. There stood Nellie Brown, cooking breakfast and carrying on a conversation—a *real* conversation— with Elliot. The flashy clothes, feathers, rouge and painted lips were gone, leaving behind an attractive middle-aged woman. She was pleasant.

And definitely sober.

Zach gave himself a mental high-five. Though Nellie had a long way to go before she'd be over the rough part, this was a beginning. A very positive one.

"Mama?" Hilary took a tentative step toward her mother. "What are you doing?"

Nellie turned around and smiled at Hilary. "Where have you been, Hilary? I was worried."

"You were?"

Zach stepped forward and held Hilary's hand. "Good morning," he said to Nellie, smiling in open approval. "Smells good in here."

Nellie nodded in Zach's direction and blushed. "Good morning, Zach." Lowering her gaze, she turned to Elliot.

"Elliot, get two more plates down for your sister and Zach, please."

"Are you all right?" Hilary sat down at the table, still staring in obvious shock at her mother. "You seem so . . . different."

Nellie reddened again as she dished food onto four plates. "Different? I reckon that's gotta be an improvement." Her hands trembled as she poured coffee and gave a nervous laugh. "I should seem different. I'm not drunk this morning."

Hilary sighed audibly and nodded. A frown marred her smooth brow as she lifted her shoulders in a questioning manner. The expression in her blue eyes was skeptical. "I can see that. I'm glad."

Nellie nodded and sat down between her children at the table. "It's been one helluva long time since I sat down to table with my family." She took a ragged breath and patted Elliot's hand. "Way too long."

Elliot beamed. "Ma's better."

"Much better, Elliot," Nellie said, reaching for her coffee with both hands.

Zach knew Nellie's trembling would worsen before it improved. Lord, didn't he know it? He frowned, wondering what he could do to help maintain Nellie's newfound sobriety. Then he remembered his own experience. No one could do it for her—Nellie had to want it, and do it, for herself. But a little support couldn't hurt.

Hilary's anxiety seemed to increase as they sat around the table. She barely touched the food on her plate as Zach sampled Nellie's cooking and glanced around the table. Maybe history'd been altered enough to prevent the events that could lead to disaster. Maybe.

"I think we should tell your mother about our plans, Hilary," Zach suggested, deciding it was best to include the entire family in the wedding, if possible. Everything would be official and out in the open that way. He was fairly certain he wouldn't be asked for identification in order to marry. In 1886, a man's word should be acceptable. Well, he'd just have to alter his birth date by a hundred years or so.

"What plans?" Nellie looked from Hilary to Zach, then smiled. "I knew it that first morning when I saw the look in your eyes, Zach. We're gonna have us a wedding."

Hilary nodded and reddened beneath her mother's happy but curious gaze. "Yes, we are." Hilary glanced at Zach. "We're going to be married today, if possible."

"We'll make it possible." Zach fought the churning in his gut. Every time he considered the urgency of their situation, his stomach gave a lurch of protest. "It has to be today."

Once he and Hilary were married, all he had to do was keep her out at the cabin until he found the mother lode. Then he'd have enough gold to take her far away from Columbine.

And Baird McCune.

But what about the strange events at the mine? Shorty's murder? He felt cold inside as he remembered the terror on Hilary's face when she'd refused to visit the Maggie-O with him in the twentieth century. What was up there?

Nellie leaned back in her chair. "Well, the preacher was in town yesterday, but I don't rightly know if he's still here." She shrugged and smiled. "He usually heads down to the flat land before winter sets in."

"I can go see," Elliot offered, pushing away from the table. The tall boy grinned at his mother and sister. "A wedding."

"And Elliot?" Zach stood and offered Elliot his hand. "I'm in need of a best man. Would you be willing to help me out? It's an important job."

Elliot grinned and nodded. "Sure."

The youth left by the back door. Hilary smiled at Zach in open appreciation, then turned her gaze on her mother. "Mama, I really am very happy to see you so . . ."

"Sober." Nellie Brown took another sip of coffee. "It ain't easy, honey. Let me tell you, your man here, he helped me see the light, though. Lord willing, I'll stay sober. We don't know much about Zach, but I can tell he's a good man."

"Thanks. But it's all up to you, Nellie." Zach took a bite of fried potatoes. "Mmm. I hope your daughter cooks as well as her mother does."

Nellie blushed. "Well, I don't know when the last time was a man complimented my cooking. I've had men compliment lots of other things about me over the years, but I think this is better." She shook her head. "Seems I been missing a lot more than I thought."

"Will you come to the wedding, Mama?" Hilary's tone was uncertain. It was clear she had mixed emotions about her mother's presence at their wedding.

"If you'll let me be there." Nellie reddened and nodded. It was evident that she understood her daughter's misgivings. "I can't think of nothin' I'd rather do, Hilary." The older woman covered her face in her hands and wept.

Zach lowered his gaze. He felt like an intruder on a very personal moment. He should excuse himself, yet he was afraid to. The thought of letting Hilary out of his sight terrified him.

"So we're having a wedding." Nellie dried her tears, took a ragged breath and slapped the table.

"Today," Zach repeated, wanting to make certain everyone understood his intentions. He and Hilary would be married today, one way or another. Even if he had to carry her down the mountain to find a minister.

Hilary and Nellie both looked at Zach.

"In an awful hurry, ain't you?" Nellie asked with a wink.

"I reckon since you kept my girl out all night, it's the least you can do, though."

Hilary blushed and lowered her gaze. Zach felt her tense at his side, but she didn't speak. He suspected her old fear of ending up like her mother was returning. With a pang of remorse, he recalled how she'd been afraid of feeling like Nellie Brown after she'd made love with Zach. But she hadn't felt that way. At least, she'd said she hadn't.

Nellie sighed and lowered her gaze. It must have been as obvious to her as it was to Zach that it would take more than one day of sobriety to make up for years of parental neglect. "As soon as Elliot gets back, we'll see about getting it done, then."

Hilary nodded and squeezed Zach's hand when he found hers in her skirt. "I'd like to clean up and change into a nicer dress before the wedding, Zach."

He flinched. "You look fine to me."

Nellie laughed. Her faded blue eyes seemed brighter— younger than before. "Must be love."

"See, I look awful." Hilary blinked rapidly. Her eyes were glassy and her lower lip quivered. "You'll survive a little while away from me while I take a bath and change into my good dress."

Zach clenched his teeth. He hadn't wanted to let Hilary out of his sight until they were well away from Columbine. But he couldn't very well deny her the luxury of a bath on her wedding day. "I guess I could do with a shave myself." He rubbed his chin. "Is there a barber in town?" He still had some of the money Shorty'd advanced him.

Poor Shorty.

"There's a barber straight across from the schoolhouse. He pulls teeth, too, if you've a need." Nellie stood and started clearing plates. "Matilda'll be here in a while to take over in the kitchen. Then I'll go up and change into somethin' nicer."

Hilary stood and moved toward the door. She hesitated, as if struggling with a decision. "I'm proud of you, Mama," she finally said, then moved toward the door.

"Aw, get on with you." Nellie reddened again, obviously aware of her daughter's reluctance to accept the change in her.

Hilary faced Zach. "I'll meet you down here in about an hour."

A whole hour? Zach swallowed the lump in his throat. "Sure. Don't go anywhere else, though. I'll be back from the barber by then."

"I'm not going anywhere." Hilary turned her cheek to his kiss, then left the room.

Zach couldn't resist the overwhelming urge to watch her get safely up the stairs. He held open the swinging door separating the kitchen from the saloon, just far enough to watch Hilary ascend the stairs.

"I sure can't figure out how you knew my daughter when you first come to town, Zach. But I can see you love her," Nellie said in a quiet voice. "Don't you think you're bein' just a mite overprotective?"

Zach turned to face Nellie, letting the door close behind him as he did. Hilary was safely up the stairs, but that was no guarantee he'd be able to protect her while she was out of his sight. After all, Baird's shooting had occurred in her bedroom . . . right here at Miss Nellie's.

"No, not at all, Nellie," he stated with total honesty. In this situation, there was no such thing as overprotective. "I love her and just want her to be happy . . . and safe."

Nellie smiled in open approval. "Ain't much more a mother could want for her daughter, then. Lord knows I've been a pitiful excuse for a mother. A cat's a better mother than I've been. I even tried to make her come into the business. God forgive me. Imagine, me wantin' her to live the same hell I've lived." She wiped at a tear that trickled down her cheek. "Hilary ain't ever gonna forgive me, though. I can see it's too late for her. But maybe Elliot can."

Zach touched the woman's shoulder. "I'm sure of it. But don't give up on Hilary."

"Now, if I can just keep away from the whiskey."

"You and me both." Zach nodded. "Amen."

Hilary paced her room and chewed her lower lip in frustration. Why had she dreamed in such detail?

More importantly, why had the dream included information Zach hadn't revealed? There was really only one explanation, yet she couldn't accept it. It just wasn't possible.

Could Zach be telling the truth? About her death? Ghosts? Angels? Time travel?

"No. It just can't be." She sat down on the edge of her bed and placed her chin in her palms. "It isn't possible, Hilary. Don't be so naive."

She looked down at her blue muslin dress. It would've been nice to have a real wedding dress and a fancy ceremony. Tears stung her eyes, but she blinked them away. None of that mattered. All that mattered was that she really loved Zach, whoever he was, wherever he'd come from.

And the bizarre possibility that his story was true.

If only there were some way to make certain. She searched her mind for answers to the unexplainable, then glanced up at the small clock on the mantel. It was time to go downstairs and meet Zach.

Time for her wedding.

She stood and brushed out her skirt, then walked over to the mirror. Zach had asked her to wear her hair down. She smiled, remembering how he'd made love to her. Color crept up her neck to flood her cheeks, giving her a blushing bride look if ever there'd been one.

She was being silly. Zach's story couldn't be true, and the coincidence in her dream with the red dress was just that—coincidence. Nothing more.

Taking a deep breath, she moved toward the door. She knew the blue dress matched her eyes, and her golden hair hung in waves past her waist—for Zach. She'd tied a blue velvet ribbon around her head to hold her hair away from her face.

She was ready.

Ready to commit the rest of her life to a man who thought she'd been hanged for murder. Then been refused admittance to Heaven by an angel. Zach Ryan actually thought she'd been a ghost in the twentieth century.

That she'd saved him from a hungry bear.

And fallen in love with him—twice.

"God, this is driving *me* crazy." Hilary paused near the door and rubbed her forehead. Her mother's transformation wasn't helping the situation any, either. Not that Hilary wasn't pleased Nellie'd stopped drinking. But it was too little, too late. Though a very large part of her wanted to, Hilary knew she'd never be able to completely trust her mother. There was another part of her—God forgive her—who hated Nellie Brown.

Hilary stood in the doorway of her room, her sanctuary in Miss Nellie's House of Ill Repute. She chewed her lower lip in consternation.

Was she marrying Zach simply to escape from this place? No, she loved him, even though she was uncertain about his sanity. She'd marry him even if her mother wasn't the notorious Nellie Brown.

Besides, in all honesty, anything was better than staying at Miss Nellie's for the rest of her life.

Hilary hated herself for feeling this way, but it was true. Even though she was able to justify her decision by remembering how much she really loved Zach, she couldn't shake the niggling voice in the back of her mind—an accusing voice.

The memory of the way he'd touched her, kissed her, taken her virginity, came back to torment and tantalize her. A flash of heat flew to her toes, then settled in her middle, a nudging reminder of the ecstasy she'd found— and was sure to find again—in the arms of Zach Ryan.

She took a deep breath and closed her eyes for a moment. "I am doing the right thing."

With a nod, she walked out of her room and closed the door—auspiciously, for the last time.

The stairs seemed longer and steeper than ever before as Hilary made her way down. When she reached the landing, a wave of dizziness swept over her. She gripped the bannister and froze, closed her eyes against an image that flashed through her mind.

She saw herself—standing in this very spot. Yet the woman who looked so much like her couldn't be Hilary. She seemed so different. This Hilary wore nothing but a red and blue shirt—a man's shirt. Her bare legs were brazenly displayed.

But it was *her* face. The blond hair hanging free in disarray was hers. She'd never have left her room dressed in such a manner. It was scandalous.

Yet the image was persistent. Then she saw another face. In her mind's eye, she gazed down toward the bar and saw Zach. He was wiping the bar with a rag, then he looked up at her.

I love you, Hilary Brown, the image said.

Hilary's heart lurched. It must be her imagination. What else could it be? She opened her eyes and took a deep breath.

The saloon looked the same as it had before the image

flashed to her mind. There were a few midday customers and Ned behind the bar. Nothing unusual.

"Hilary."

She turned toward the voice. It was Zach, standing in the kitchen doorway staring up at her. His hair was neatly trimmed and his handsome face freshly shaven. He looked wonderful.

A sensation of warmth swept through her as she gazed at the man who would become her husband. He smiled at her and her heart swelled with love. Just like in the image—the vision.

"Zach." She ran the rest of the way down the steps, then paused right in front of him. There was a part of her who wanted to run away—from him and from the strange dreams. But a far more powerful need coursed through her—the need to be near Zach forever.

"You look beautiful," he said quietly, reaching for her hand. "Elliot found the preacher. They're waiting down at the schoolhouse."

She nodded and lowered her gaze. Heat flooded her face as she considered what would certainly happen when they were alone again as man and wife. The open desire in his eyes was undeniable.

"I'm ready." She permitted him to lead her through the back door and out into the autumn sunshine. It was a beautiful day for a wedding.

Perfect.

Then why did panic lurk just beneath her calm exterior? Why did she feel as if she was running away from something, when in fact she was racing toward love and marriage? She turned a smile in Zach's direction. She wouldn't let these silly nightmares and effigies dampen her wedding day.

"Hey, teacher," Baird McCune said as he leapt onto the boardwalk in front of them. "My kid come home yesterday sayin' there weren't gonna be no school. Find somethin' more interestin' to do?''

Hilary's stomach lurched at the sound of that familiar voice. She felt Zach tense at her side as he tried to maneuver them around the man, only to have Baird deftly place himself in their path again.

''Excuse us. We have an appointment.'' Zach's smooth voice belied his true feelings, making Hilary love him all the more for it. ''McCune, let us pass.''

Baird stared at them for several seconds. His gaze raked Hilary, then returned to Zach's face. ''Still don't know what kinda man'd be caught without a gun.'' He shook his head in apparent disgust. ''Unless you're like Elliot. Yeah, maybe that's it. You're an idiot, too.''

Hilary wanted to claw the man's eyes out, but she simply bit her lower lip instead. Zach took several deep breaths and she noticed his lips move as if speaking to himself.

''McCune, I thank you for the compliment.'' Zach tucked Hilary's hand in the crook of his elbow as he sighed. He cast Baird a menacing smile. ''Being compared to someone as fine and good as Elliot Brown is a great honor. Now if you'll excuse us?''

Hilary bit the inside of her cheek to prevent herself from laughing out loud at Baird. His face turned red, then purple with rage as Zach led her off the boardwalk and into the street.

Their tormentor sputtered in mute rage. It was a rare moment, indeed. Baird McCune reduced to a speechless state. It was priceless.

Hilary suppressed her laughter until they paused in front of the schoolhouse. Zach turned her to face him and cupped her chin in his hand. The emotion blazing in his eyes silenced her laughter.

''I love you, Hilary Brown.''

The voice . . . the words were identical to what she'd

imagined in the saloon. Except this Zach was fully clothed and standing in the bright sunlight, as was Hilary. She swallowed convulsively, battling the raging emotions surging through her.

Love and fear mingled to form a new emotion—something she'd never felt before. It was terrifying, yet wonderful at the same time. The need burning deep in her soul would not be denied. She loved Zach Ryan and was willing to take any risk necessary to forge this union with him.

The realization was humbling.

"I love you, too." She met his lips halfway, then gasped as he pulled her against him to deepen the contact.

"We're ready," Elliot called from the doorway, ending the moment all too soon. "Ah, Ma they're kissin'."

Hilary heard her mother's laughter from inside. A part of the shell she'd formed around her heart to protect her from Nellie Brown, cracked and fell away.

Over the years, she'd forced herself to stop waiting and searching for her mother's love. She had vague recollections of a time before her father'd left them, when Nellie'd been a loving wife and mother. But they were buried so deep . . .

She took a breath, quelling her raging internal battles, at least for now. If her mother stayed away from whiskey, maybe there'd be time to work out their relationship later.

Right now, she had a wedding to attend.

Chapter Fifteen

"I'm worried about Elliot," Hilary said as she walked up the trail at her husband's side. This evening they would be alone in the cabin again. The sun was setting behind the mountain even now.

"He wanted to stay with your mother." Zach squeezed her hand, offering reassurance. He paused on the trail and took both her hands in his. "Nellie needs his moral support. He'll be all right. Besides, if he'd come with us tonight, it'd throw a damper on our wedding night."

Hilary shivered as his voice skittered along her spine. The air was cooling rapidly, compounding the effect his nearness had on her. Promise filled his tone, his expression, his utterance. She warmed with thoughts of what this evening would bring.

He pulled her against him and kissed her full on the lips. His mouth slanted hungrily across hers as his hands roamed down her back to intimately cup her buttocks through layers of skirt and petticoat.

Suddenly Hilary couldn't wait to be alone with Zach. Her heart raced and she grew languid with desire as he lifted her against his arousal. His tongue parried and stroked hers, boldly imitating a more intimate behavior which she was now able to identify.

After breaking their kiss, Zach led her up the mountain toward the cabin. Hilary trembled—this marriage was right. All her doubts and fears had been forcibly quelled with the words "I do." Her love for Zach was stronger than her misgivings and would tolerate no interruptions.

He opened the cabin door and locked it behind them. Hilary whimpered when he reached for her. There was something so powerful about this man. It tantalized her senses; it made her hungry for things she'd never even thought of before last night.

She was ravenous to feel him, taste him, love him. Hilary reached for the buttons on his shirt, releasing them quickly. He reciprocated by opening her dress and slipping it from her shoulders. It fell unheeded at her feet.

Together, they bared eager flesh to seeking fingers and voracious lips. Hilary moaned when he pulled her naked body against his own. The searing essence of his arousal promised a night of love she felt certain she'd always remember.

When he lifted her and carried her the few steps to the bunk in the corner, Hilary shook with longing. She needed this—needed him.

They fell together, with Hilary sprawled across his full length, in intimate contact with his surging manhood. She wanted him so desperately she ached.

Slowly, Hilary eased her body down the length of his. She brushed her tongue across the base of his throat, tasted the salty essence that was Zach's alone. Her bare breasts swelled with a dull ache as they rubbed against his hair-roughened chest.

Zach moaned as Hilary kissed his flat nipples and traced her tongue along the broad expanse of his chest. A rush of perverse pleasure—the power of seduction—coursed through her veins. It was a delicious sensation, but she wanted more. Much more.

Lingering to taste and caress at leisure, Hilary kissed her way down his taut abdomen to his navel. She tickled him there with her tongue until he arched against her and entwined his fingers in her hair.

"God, what are you doing to me?" His ragged whisper diminished to nothing more than an astonished gasp as she kissed her way lower and lower.

Emboldened, Hilary reached down to cup him in her hand. He was hot and swollen, as was she. Kissing her way downward, she found his smooth hot shaft and replaced her fingers with her lips.

He tensed. She felt the muscles in his thighs tighten beneath her as her breasts were teased and tantalized by the hairs on his legs. Hilary was lost in a world of sensual delight, hungry for all of him as she covered him with her lips.

Zach felt he was going to die, but what a way to go.

This woman was driving him absolutely insane with her innocent sexuality. She must have some idea what she was doing to him. Her luscious body slithering down his had nearly unhinged him. But having her warm, soft lips on him was more than he could bear.

"Hilary," he gasped, feeling as if he would explode at any moment. She was propelling him toward a point he knew she wasn't yet ready for.

She kissed her way down his shaft, then back up to cover the tip again. Zach moaned—his blood heated and pooled in his groin.

She groaned in protest when he gripped her shoulders and eased her away from his tortured sex. The cabin was dark now. He couldn't see her face, but he could imagine the provocative expression blazing in those blue eyes as she eased her way back up his body.

Zach wanted her with a desperation he could scarcely control. This woman was his wife.

No matter the century.

With a guttural growl, he rolled her to his side and pressed her to the mattress with a kiss born of savage hunger. His lips slanted across hers, possessed and promised a joy he felt certain neither of them had ever experienced before. He kissed his way down her throat, to the curve of her shoulder. His mouth tasted and tarried at the side of her breast as he cupped them both in his hands.

She gasped when his mouth found one nipple as his thumb brushed the other. Hilary arched against him, offered herself to him, but he resisted the devastating urge to bury himself within her and claim his release. Not yet.

Kissing his way lower still, he slipped her legs over his shoulders and tasted her. She was warm against him, confirming her desire equalled his.

The musky scent of her reminded Zach illogically but intrinsically of ice cream. His passion soared to an even more dangerous plane as his memories augmented reality, though no such encouragement was even remotely necessary.

He tasted and teased her until she became a quivering mass of flesh beneath him. Zach's intention, to inflict her with as much pleasure as she'd shown him, was manifest. She tilted her pelvis and pressed against him, moaning with the power of her climax.

He released her, kissing his way back up to hover between her thighs. But he hesitated, remembering another time when Hilary'd sat astride him, offering her glorious breasts to him as they'd journeyed together to sexual gratification.

He wanted that again—now. Hilary moaned in protest when he didn't enter her immediately to assuage their mutual suffering. He rolled away from her and swung her body over his again.

Her bewilderment was distinct, as she lifted her face to stare at him in the darkness. He cupped the side of her face with his hand. "Make love to *me*, Hilary." He pressed his erection against her abdomen.

Hilary gasped, then he heard her giggle. "How?" she asked.

Her simple question nearly annihilated his dwindling self-restraint. Zach moaned, running his fingers down her spine. "Woman, you drive me crazy."

She giggled again.

"Sit up," he said, his voice hoarse with passion.

She sat astride him, but hesitated. Zach groaned in agony, gravely conscious of her moist warmth pressed torturously against him.

Hungrily, he grasped her waist and lifted her until she was poised above him. "Now do you understand?" he whispered, nearly beyond control. "Take me inside you, Hilary. Let me feel you close around me." *And hurry.*

Her soft intake of breath at his words made Zach's blood rage with desire. She eased herself over his throbbing tip, down his shaft, enfolding him within her heated warmth. He winced, held his breath and clenched his teeth, trying to bring himself under control.

"Don't move," he whispered as she pressed herself even more fully against him.

"Oh, Zach." Her voice betrayed her amazement. "That feels good."

"Good," he echoed, reaching to cup her breasts in his hands as he eased himself upward and her forward to find her nipple. She rewarded his efforts with tiny quivers from deep inside her, pulsing around him. He imagined himself buried inside an electric current, with billions of tiny electrodes teasing and stimulating him until he went totally out of his mind—if he wasn't already.

Slowly, Hilary began to move against him. An age-old rhythm erupted between them, took command and ruled.

It was like music, he decided, as rational thoughts tried to elude him. They were the strings, woodwinds, brass and percussion sections all blended into a symphony Beethoven would've envied. It was a timeless harmony, as old as life itself.

Gasping, pressing, straining, they merged. She contracted around his thrusts as he fell back against the bed, too weak to hold himself up any longer. She took all he could give as he met her movement for movement.

All his strength, past, present and future, merged to bring them both to this moment. The anguish of losing his brother, the terror when Hilary'd disappeared, seemed to channel with the physical release building within him. It was as if he were ridding himself of these torments through loving Hilary. Pain and suffering battled with passion—with love—and lost.

Love was clearly the victor.

The love he felt for Hilary was eternal. He'd proven that by breaking the boundaries of time to find her again. A spiraling explosion began deep in his core as she moaned and gasped above him. Her body contorted to grip him in a vise of sexual madness he thought surely would kill them both.

Then the explosion came. He erupted within her like an earthquake shattering centuries of tension. He clenched his teeth, growled and groaned as he felt her quiver and press against him with her own orgasm.

When she fell against him, slick with sweat and love, Zach nuzzled the side of her neck. Her hair formed a veil around them, shrouded them in a cocoon of warmth and love.

"I love you," he murmured against her salty flesh. "I love you more than my own life."

Hilary sighed and lifted her head to kiss him on the lips. "I love you, too." She rolled to her side, resting her head against his shoulder.

Zach stared up at the dark ceiling. He felt complete, whole, for the first time in many years. The guilt of his years of drinking, of the accident that had taken his brother's life, all shattered and vanished as he held this woman in his arms.

It would be marvelous if he could undo his mistakes, but it wasn't possible. It was past time he accepted this. Being able to travel back through time to find Hilary was his allotted miracle. He felt quite certain mortal souls, such as his, weren't permitted more than one such event per lifetime.

"I'm going to find the mother lode, Hilary," he whispered in the darkness. An intensity, a sense of purpose, filled him. "Then we're going to leave here forever."

Hilary trembled in his arms. "What about Elliot and my mother?" She lifted her face to look at him again. "I can't just leave them."

Zach hugged her close. "We'll take them both with us."

He struggled with the memories Hilary'd tried to share with him about the Maggie-O, about Elliot. Elliot was Shorty's heir. Shorty's first partner had been murdered. Then Shorty. There was only one explanation, and there was nothing ghostly about it. Someone else knew about the mother lode.

"Of course. That's it." Zach sat up in bed so suddenly he nearly knocked Hilary out on the floor. "I'm sorry." Laughing, he pulled her against him. "I think I just figured out who murdered Shorty—and why."

Hilary gripped his hand. "What is it, Zach? Please tell me."

He looked at her, silhouetted in the darkness as moonlight came through the cracks between the logs. Dare he tell her his suspicions? She'd only worry about Elliot. But if he was right, there was a very good reason for considerably more than sisterly concern.

"I'd rather not say until I'm sure," he said carefully, stretching out beside her and pulling a quilt over them. "Besides, this is our wedding night, woman. I have other things on my mind."

Hilary sighed, then giggled. "Call it woman's intuition, but I suspect that's always lurking somewhere in your thoughts." She touched his jaw with her fingertip. "At least, I sure do hope it is."

Groaning, Zach pulled her against him, offering proof of her suspicion.

The dark void surrounded her again. She saw nothing, not even her own body as she drifted through the darkness. The light was there again, a beacon offering solace from the terror.

Hilary reached for the light, felt its pull, then the movement stopped. Something—someone—had purposely stopped her. She stood facing a strange woman holding a large white book. The woman was beautiful. She smiled and nodded.

Then Hilary was transported from the void. Again she was wearing the strange red dress, but she was no longer in darkness. She was home—in Columbine. But it was a very different Columbine than she knew.

Zach was there with her. His smiling eyes lit up her life and her heart. There was a strange ride in a wondrous machine, thrilling her with its speed.

Then there was Zach again, holding her in his arms. There was something cold—chocolate. It formed a seal of sweetness between them as they made love. But they weren't here in the cabin. Zach made love to Hilary on the bar in Miss Nellie's Saloon.

Another image formed in her dream world. She stood on the landing wearing a now familiar red and blue shirt—Zach's shirt. He stood at the bar, looking up at her. "I love you, Hilary Brown," he called up to her. His smile filled her heart with hope.

Then, just when she'd realized the happiness she'd been searching for, she found herself again in the dark void. She was alone; Hilary screamed.

"Hilary." Zach's urgent voice broke through the terror, dragged her from the paralyzing fear. "Hilary, wake up. You're having another nightmare."

She gasped as her eyes opened and she recognized the dark cabin and the warm man at her side. He pulled her against him and reminded her with his silent strength that he would protect her from harm. He loved her. Zach Ryan loved her.

Hilary trembled and wept in his arms. The dream had been so real—again. She bit her knuckles in an effort to stifle the sob which tore from her throat, but it was to no avail. She shuddered and cried, terrified for her own sanity. What was happening to her?

"Tell me about your nightmare, Hilary," he urged, stroking her hair as he held her. "It might help."

She shook her head against his shoulder. "I was so frightened, Zach." Hilary squeezed her eyes shut again, then forced them open. If she slept, the nightmare might return.

She must stay awake—fight the urge to sleep at all costs. Asleep, she was vulnerable. A wave of terror rippled down her spine. What if the dream came true? Zach's story . . .

"No." She wept against his shoulder. "Hold me, Zach. Love me. Don't let them take me."

Zach held her in the darkness, murmuring pacifying words of reassurance. He'd said he would take them all away from Columbine forever.

Hilary must cling to that hope for the future. She and Zach would make a new home for them all. Elliot and her mother would go away with them.

But she feared the dark void wasn't limited to Columbine. It was all-encompassing. There was no escape from it. Would the nightmare follow her wherever she went? Why was this happening?

"Oh, Zach." She clung to him as her tears dampened his shoulder and slipped between them. "I'm so frightened."

"What is it, Hilary?" he asked softly, still cradling her in his arms. "Tell me what you dreamed."

"I can't." She swallowed convulsively. "It might come true."

He chuckled low in his throat. "That's an old wives' tale. Dreams don't come true just because you talk about them. Things like that don't really happen."

She pulled back to stare at him through the darkness. "Like the crazy stories you told me?"

He was silent for a moment. "They weren't crazy stories, Hilary." He reached out to touch her face. "The truth. All true."

"No." She shook her head, fighting her rising nausea. "Can't be true, Zach. Don't . . ."

"Shh." He kissed her cheek, then tilted her face to meet his lips. "We won't talk about it now, since you're so upset. But sooner or later, Hilary, you must face the truth."

She bit her lower lip and squeezed her eyes shut against her tears. *Face the truth.* She couldn't, it was too terrifying. "Make love to me again, Zach. All night."

"Forever."

Nellie listened in horror to the men. Surely she hadn't heard correctly. She opened the kitchen door a bit wider, straining to hear their words more clearly.

It was very late. Only a few customers still occupied the saloon. Two of them were Sean McCune and Sheriff Tyler. They sat at the table nearest the kitchen door, obviously unaware Nellie stood less than ten feet away.

Sober and alert.

Too damned alert to Nellie's way of thinking. The trembling in her hands had increased as the day wore on. She couldn't sleep. She'd pleaded a headache to avoid Sean's company in her room tonight, then slipped down the back stairs to the kitchen for something to eat. It was all she could do to keep from grabbing an entire bottle of whiskey and taking it to her bed. Then she would sleep.

For a price.

She blinked and held her hands squeezed together, trying to keep them still as she listened. In her foggy memory, she recalled Zach saying that it suited other people for Nellie to be drunk. Was the man who'd asked her to become his wife one of those people?

Sean took a sip of his drink and she closed her eyes, imagining the burning whiskey sliding down her own throat. She licked her lips and forcibly quelled the desire to drink—again.

"You're sure about the papers, then?" Sean asked, leaning back in his chair. "Elliot has full ownership of the Maggie-O?"

Sheriff Tyler grinned wickedly and nodded. "Yep. Lock, stock and barrel."

"Hmm." Sean patted his abdomen and sighed. "That's just fine. My son owns the richest mine in this part of the Rockies."

Your son?

Nellie bit her lower lip, silencing the protest she wanted so desperately to voice. All these years of denying and berating Elliot, and now Sean McCune seemed ready to acknowledge his own flesh and blood.

Why? She must have the answer. For some reason, she knew it was crucial. Maternal instinct, after all these years? She'd had it once, but never for Elliot. She'd been too far gone by the time he was born.

"And the best part of it is, the Maggie-O will go to Elliot's sweet little mother when he's outta the way," Sheriff Tyler said with a chuckle. "Once she's married to you, it'll be all set."

Sean smacked his lips and leaned back in his chair. "That's the way of it, Sheriff."

When he's outta the way? Who? Nellie frowned, trying to make sense of their words. Why would they be concerned about . . .

"Oh, my God."

She hadn't realized she'd spoken aloud until Sean's head whipped around and he held her with his angry gaze. Nellie started to back away, but he was on his feet and grabbed her before she could escape.

"Why, Nellie," he said in a honey-coated voice. "I thought you had a headache."

She backed toward the kitchen table as he continued to stalk her. "I . . . I was thirsty."

"Need a drink, Nellie?" Sean grabbed a bottle of whiskey from the counter and waved it in front of her face. "Need a little sip to help you sleep?"

Nellie cringed away from him as he backed her against and pinned her to the table with his body. The bottle in his hand caught her attention. She was mesmerized by its glittering contents. "No, I don't want that," she whispered, remembering how proud Elliot was of her sobriety.

"Sure you do." Sean glanced over his shoulder. "Tyler, bring us a couple of glasses."

The sheriff came into the kitchen and placed the glasses on the table. "Here you go, Mr. McCune." He nodded toward the bottle. "You and Nellie gonna have a private party?"

"Oh, I think we might need you to hang around for this one, Tyler." Sean's eyes glittered with anger.

Nellie shuddered as he poured whiskey into both glasses, then held one to her lips. When she shook her head, spilling most of the contents down the front of her dress, he grabbed a handful of her hair and started pouring it into her mouth. She spit it back at him and he slapped her face, sending her sprawling to the floor.

"Never thought I'd see the day when Nellie Brown would refuse a drink." Sheriff Tyler clicked his tongue.

McCune grabbed her wrist and jerked her to her feet. "Pinch her nose, Tyler," Sean commanded, his tone low and threatening. "We're gonna get some of this down her, then she won't even know what hit her."

"No." Nellie's moan of anguish was drowned as Sean again poured whiskey into her mouth while cruelly twisting her hair in his fist. Sheriff Tyler's rough fingers pinched her nostrils, blocking off her only source of air.

In desperation, Nellie gulped the fortifying liquor, felt it burn its way down her gullet and into her stomach, which lurched in protest, then soothed itself as the familiar and coveted warmth spread throughout her terrified body.

She grabbed for the bottle as the sheriff released her nose. Her gaze met Sean's and she knew hatred. Pure, cold hatred as she tilted her head back and drained the bottle's contents of her own volition.

God forgive me.

Chapter Sixteen

Zach slipped from the bed as the sun blazed through the cracks between the logs, creating a striped pattern on the floor, the table, and across his sleeping bride. She was so beautiful, peaceful in slumber.

What kind of terrible nightmare had kept her awake most of the night? He pulled the quilt up over her bare shoulder. Slipping on his jeans, he decided to let her sleep while he went to the mine for a while. They could have breakfast later.

It was chilly outside. His breath formed a cloud of vapor in the cold mountain air. It was invigorating, but a stern reminder that winter quickly approached.

He noticed the frosty coating on everything he passed as he made his way up the steep trail to the Maggie-O. He'd left his tools in the mine the day Shorty was murdered, and hadn't been back since.

Remembering the ominous sensation he'd experienced that last morning gave him pause. Had the presence he'd felt really been a ghost? Was it possible? He wouldn't deny the existence of something he couldn't explain ever again—not after Hilary.

Zach paused on the flat area in front of the mine entrance. Something shiny caught his gaze as the sun popped over a mountain peak. Stooping, he picked up the silver button and turned it over in his hand. It wasn't his. The only buttons he'd had that were this ornate had been on his three piece suits back in Los Angeles—a century in the future. Shrugging, he dropped it into his pocket.

Exhaling a cloud of white vapor, Zach turned and walked toward the mine entrance. As he neared the dark hole in the cliff, apprehension gripped him.

He closed his eyes for a moment, thinking of Shorty. He'd been murdered in this mine. It was perfectly reasonable for Zach to be frightened. Wasn't it?

"Shit, Zach, it's not like Norman Bates is waiting inside."

Shaking his head and chuckling to himself, he walked into the mine. He took three steps beyond the mine entrance, then froze. Bile rose in his throat as he looked on the grisly scene before him.

Nellie Brown's broken body lay in a heap in the middle of the mine. He looked around frantically, then dropped to his knees to check for a pulse.

But he knew even before he felt her cold, lifeless form that there would be no thud of life's blood through her veins. She was dead.

Her neck appeared to have been twisted—her head was at a bizarre angle to her body. Just like Shorty . . . Her sightless eyes stared back at him. The stench of whiskey was clearly discernable.

"God, Nellie," he muttered. "What the hell happened to you?"

"Mama?" Hilary's trembling voice sounded from behind him. Zach leapt to his feet and ran to his wife, struggling to move her away from the mine—from the horrible sight of her mother's body. "Mama?"

"Hilary, don't." He picked her up and forcibly carried her away from the mine and to the cabin. Her screams echoed all around them as she twisted and squirmed, begging to be freed.

He kicked open the cabin door and carried her inside, falling down on the bunk with her in his arms. He held her against his body like a baby as she screamed and sobbed. She gradually quieted and the trembling began.

"Stop. Shh." He held her in his arms, sitting on the bunk in their cabin while she calmed. Her screams had given way to mere whimpers, but the trembling didn't pass. It became even more pronounced.

"Mama," she whispered again, then looked into his eyes. "She's dead?"

Zach nodded and squeezed his eyes shut against the pain he saw ravaging her beautiful face. "Hilary, I'm so sorry," he murmured, rocking her as she wept. Why would anyone want to harm Nellie Brown? She was harmless to everyone but herself. She'd finally found the inner strength to fight against alcohol's death-grip, only to end her life like this. Murdered. Just like Shorty Lamb.

By a ghost?

No, he didn't believe it. Someone had deliberately brought Nellie out to the Maggie-O and killed her. Or perhaps, they'd killed her first, then planted her body in the mine.

But why?

He held his breath as he considered the situation. First, Shorty's brother-in-law, then Shorty. Now Nellie, but what was the connection between Shorty and Nellie? Of course, there was only one answer.

Elliot. He'd inherited the mine from Shorty. Nellie was

his mother—the only connection between Shorty and Elliot. It still didn't make sense.

Oh, but it did. In an insidious way, it made a great deal of sense. Zach only had to ask himself, how would murdering Shorty and Nellie help someone take the mine away from Elliot? It wouldn't, unless they were a blood relative who stood to inherit the mine and the mother lode.

Baird McCune—Elliot's half-brother.

"Oh, my God."

Hilary sniffled and lifted her head from his shoulder. Her eyes were puffy from crying. "What is it, Zach?" she asked in a shaky voice.

He swallowed hard and patted her hair. "I just figured something out. That's all." He took a deep breath and released it. "We have to go to town for Sheriff Tyler."

She shuddered. "I don't like that man." She started to cry again. "My mother didn't like him, either. Oh, Zach, I was wrong to hate her. I did, you know. God, forgive me."

Lord knew he understood her hatred. It was the same kind of loathing he'd felt for himself. Zach nodded—Hilary's pain was palpable. He squeezed his eyes shut, remembering again that horrible night when Jake had died. But Zach had Hilary to think of now. She was alive and she needed him. He took a deep steadying breath.

"We have to go to town, Hilary."

She nodded and stood, smoothing her skirt with her hands. "We—I have to tell Elliot."

Zach nodded and avoided her gaze. How could he tell Hilary that if his suspicions were correct, Elliot might very well be the murderer's next victim? In fact, he was as certain as he could be.

The sun had melted away the frost by the time Zach and Hilary walked down the trail toward Columbine. He was worried about her. Her exhaustion didn't help matters. On top of the shock from her mother's untimely death, Hilary had a mountain of guilt to compound her sorrow. Lord knew he could understand her pain in that department.

His gut twisted as he tried again to remember something useful Hilary might have told him in the future about the Maggie-O and the murders. Try as he might, all Zach could remember was that she'd been terrified of going up to the mine, even a hundred years in the future. Why? *Had* Hilary believed the alleged ghost was the murderer?

"This will be hard for Elliot," she said in a quiet voice— a tortured voice as they neared the bottom of the trail. "He was so excited about staying with her last night. Remember?"

Zach glanced at his bride and tried to fight the emotions churning inside him. He'd tried to convince himself that there was no connection between the murders. But that was foolish. The only logical reason anyone would have for murdering Nellie had to be Elliot and the damned mine. But he couldn't tell Hilary that. It would frighten her. She had enough to deal with already.

There was no alternative. Family duty required decisive action. *Family*. Though it wasn't conducive to newlywed-type behavior, they'd have to bring Elliot to live with them at the cabin until Zach found enough gold to take them away from Columbine.

And destiny.

I'm starting to sound like a reporter for the National Enquirer.

"Why don't you go get Sheriff Tyler while I talk to Elliot," Hilary suggested, grabbing his arm when they reached the saloon.

Zach shook his head. He wasn't letting her out of his sight. "No, we'll do it all together." He gripped her hand even more tightly. "Let's go in."

Hilary nodded and followed Zach through the door. She paused to glance around. For the first time in her life, she realized the saloon had been home. In a way, she'd miss it and her mother. Despite Nellie Brown's shortcomings . . .

Her gaze went to Ned, behind the bar. He'd have to be told, too. Sean McCune would need to know, because of the management of the saloon. It was a very good thing she'd found Zach at this time. She and Elliot would have had nowhere to live after today, if . . .

Stop it, Hilary.

Taking a deep breath, she girded her resolve and led Zach to the bar. There were no customers in the saloon at this hour. At least that was something.

"Mr. Carter," she began, forcing the tremor from her voice. "Is Elliot still asleep?"

The big man inclined his head toward the kitchen door. "He's been up lookin' for Nellie for nearly an hour." He laughed and shook his head. "She must've found herself a bottle."

Hilary clenched her teeth and silenced the retort she so desperately wanted to shout at the man. More tears stung her eyes, but she blinked rapidly and drew a shaky breath. Her husband gave her hand a reassuring squeeze and she tried to smile at him, but had to bite her lip instead to prevent its quiver.

As they turned toward the back of the saloon, Zach suddenly stopped. He turned toward Ned. "When's the last time you saw Nellie?" he asked in a casual tone.

Ned chuckled again in his usual infuriating manner. "Last night around ten, I reckon."

Zach's gaze narrowed and he stiffened noticeably at her side. "And was she sober then, Ned?" There was an unmistakable challenge in his tone.

"Yeah." Ned gave a grudging nod. "She was. I'll have to grant her that. She's tryin'."

Hilary sighed as they turned again toward the kitchen door. When they went through the door, they found Elliot sitting alone at the table. His chin was in his hands, and a frown creased his brow.

"Hilary," he said, brightening when they entered the room. "I can't find Ma. She's not in her room."

Hilary's heart felt as if it would burst. Sorrow and guilt made powerful partners. It was punishment for the hatred she'd allowed to fester within her over the years.

Telling Elliot that his mother was dead would be the hardest thing Hilary'd ever had to do. Though Nellie Brown hadn't been a very good mother, she was the only one they'd had.

She sat down at the table and took her brother's hands in both of hers, grateful for Zach's presence at her side as he pulled out a chair. "Elliot, something's happened to Mama," she began, closing her eyes for a moment. *God, give me strength.* "She . . . she . . ."

More tears slipped down her cheeks and her voice broke. "Zach, can . . ." Her husband's presence surrounded her.

"Elliot, your mother's dead," he said in a steady voice—a strong voice.

"No." Elliot jerked his hands away from Hilary. "No," he repeated, looking down at the table. "She was better."

Hilary swallowed the lump in her throat. "Yes, Elliot," she said gently, touching his sleeve with her hand. "We found her this morning. Someone hurt her. We need to find out who did it."

Elliot looked up. Tears glistened in his gentle eyes, making Hilary's heart swell with love and grief.

"But she was getting better," he said pitifully, shaking his head. "I don't . . ."

"This isn't the kind of thing anyone really understands, Elliot." Hilary found his hand again and held it tight. "We have each other, though. Mama would want us to be together. That's why Zach and I want you to come home with us. Today.''

Elliot nodded slowly. ''All right.'' Silent tears trickled down his cheeks and he sniffled once.

Hilary looked up at Zach. ''Maybe Ned could go for Sheriff Tyler.''

Zach cleared his throat and looked uncertain. Finally, he sighed and pushed away from the table. ''I'll be right back. Don't either of you move from this table.''

Why was he so protective of her? It was ridiculous. But then Hilary remembered her mother's twisted body and cringed. Again, she began to wonder *why* anyone would do such a horrible thing. Why had Shorty been murdered? Nellie Brown? Why? What reason?

There had to be a connection between the incidents. She trembled, lost in thought as Zach left the room. He returned less than a minute later with Sheriff Tyler behind him.

''This better be good, Ryan,'' the lawman said in a gruff tone. ''I ain't even had my breakfast.''

''Nellie Brown's been murdered,'' Zach explained in a stoical tone. ''Hilary and I found her this morning. In the mine.''

Tyler shifted his weight from one foot to the other. For a moment, Hilary thought he actually looked sorry. But the expression passed very quickly.

''You think it was a dissatisfied customer?'' the Sheriff asked, chuckling as he walked over to the table. Then his laughter stopped as he turned toward Zach again. ''Or maybe you did it.''

''Now why the hell would I do something like that?'' Zach's fury was obvious and barely controlled. He clenched his fists at his sides and glowered at the lawman.

Tyler shrugged, continuing to shift his weight as he glanced from Hilary to Zach, then Elliot. Hilary couldn't help but think the man looked nervous—guilty? The sheriff? It couldn't be. Yet he seemed to have difficulty looking any of them straight in the eye as he spoke.

"Well, you live out there." Tyler shrugged, looping his thumbs through his belt. "If you didn't do it, maybe you know who did."

Zach stiffened. His gaze never left Tyler as he took a deep breath and released it. "Let's just say, I have some real strong suspicions."

Hilary gasped. "Zach, do you know—"

"I just said I have my suspicions," Zach interrupted, reaching for her hand to give it a squeeze.

Hilary turned cold. Her husband obviously didn't want to discuss his suspicions in front of Sheriff Tyler. Why? On a personal level, Hilary detested Jerome Tyler. But he was the only sheriff Columbine had to offer. If they couldn't trust him . . .

"Well, I'll head on up and investigate then." Tyler turned and shifted toward the door. He glanced over his shoulder once and looked directly at Elliot. "So, I reckon you'll all be movin' out to the claim."

Zach nodded almost imperceptibly, still holding Hilary's hand as they waited for Tyler to leave. "Elliot's coming with us today, as a matter of fact."

Sheriff Tyler cleared his throat and nodded. As he turned to leave the kitchen, the door swung open and Sean McCune walked in. As usual, he was impeccably dressed, with his silver hair slicked back away from his face.

"What's this I hear about Nellie?" he asked in a shaky voice. "It can't be true. She's dead?"

Hilary felt Zach flinch at her side. "How'd you know?" he asked in a low voice.

She cast her husband a sidelong glance, noticing his gaze riveted to Sean's midsection. Did he suspect Sean McCune? How strange.

"Looks like you lost a button, McCune." Zach's tone was clipped and harsh. "I can't help wondering where it might turn up."

Sean reddened as he glanced down at his vest. "So I lost a button." He gave a nervous chuckle, then shrugged. "No great loss."

Zach tilted his head to one side, then his lips formed a thin line. *What is he up to?* she wondered. Either her husband knew something he wasn't sharing about her mother's murder, or he really was crazy. So what if Sean had lost a button?

"Like I said . . . depends on where we find it, I suppose." Zach turned to face Hilary and Elliot. "Let's go, Elliot. We can come back for your things a little later."

"All right." Elliot pushed away from the table and stood. He looked down at his feet as he moved closer to Zach and Hilary.

Sean cleared his throat. "I . . . feel some obligation to Nellie and . . . and Elliot," he said slowly, without looking directly at any of them.

"Yeah, I'll bet." Zach sighed loudly and squeezed Hilary's hand again.

Sean reddened even more than before. "Well, if you ever need anything, Elliot . . ."

"Not from you, he won't." Hilary stiffened. Sean and Baird had rejected Elliot all of his life, even though it was common knowledge that Sean was the boy's father. They were ashamed of him. Fresh tears swelled in her eyes. "I'll take care of my brother, just like I always have."

Sean cleared his throat. "Well, that's fine, Hilary, but he's my flesh and blood, too."

"Fine time for you to finally remember that." Hilary's stomach burned. Her heart hammered in her chest. "We'd just as soon forget about it, actually. Why don't you just go back to pretending it isn't so . . . just like you always have?''

Elliot kept his head lowered as Hilary reached for his hand. God, she prayed her words hadn't hurt him, but she had been unable to prevent them. She didn't know why Sean was suddenly so concerned about Elliot. He'd never given the boy a second thought before.

"I'll arrange for Nellie's funeral then," Sean offered as the group turned toward the door. "That's the least I can do."

Hilary felt her husband stiffen again at her side as they all froze near the back door. Her gaze met Zach's. They were in complete agreement on this. She was certain of it without hearing him say the words—and she loved him all the more for it.

"We'll take care of Nellie's funeral," Zach said without looking back.

Hilary's heart swelled with love and pride as they stepped out into the bright sunshine, which seemed to mock her grief. She closed her eyes for a moment, trying to remind herself that her mother'd been sober for her wedding. Nellie had finally decided to try to change her life. If only she'd realized sooner how much better her life could be without whiskey.

"C'mon." Zach held Hilary's hand and Elliot took the other. "Let's go home."

Hilary watched as Zach traced something in the dirt with a stick outside the back door of the tiny cabin. Her mother had been buried in the tiny cemetery at the edge of town. It was over.

Except they still didn't know who'd murdered her. Or why.

She took a deep breath and smiled at her husband and

brother. Elliot stood beside Zach, watching intently while the figure at their feet took shape. But what shape?

"What is it?" the boy finally asked, furrowing his brow in obvious confusion. "Is it a bird?"

Zach laughed—really laughed—out loud. Hilary caught her breath at the transformation. When her husband laughed, he seemed younger and almost carefree. His eyes glittered with happiness as he looked at Elliot. Her brother absolutely worshipped Zach.

Leaning against the door frame, Hilary smiled. She took a deep breath, reminding herself that they had a future together as a family. Soon they could leave Columbine. They'd take Elliot somewhere far away and start a new life together.

"Look, Hilary." Elliot's excited voice broke into her reverie. "Flying machine."

Frowning, Hilary took a few steps out the back door to look down at the shape her husband had drawn in the dirt. It was a winged . . . object. She looked at Zach's smiling face, then shook her head.

He *was* out of his mind.

Her hopes disintegrated. Her dreams . . . She'd placed all her hopes—Elliot's future—on a man who was out of touch with reality. But only part of the time. Usually, he seemed so normal she was able to forget about his wild stories. Then her nightmares, or his words, would destroy that fantasy.

"Zach, there's no such thing."

"Not yet." He grinned and shrugged. "But there will be one day." He looked into the distance. "Let me think. This is 1886, so I should be able to . . ." His mouth fell open in obvious surprise. "By God, I know where we're going after I find enough gold to get us out of here."

"Where, Zach?" She closed her eyes for a minute. He was rambling again—lost in that world of his own creation.

"Kittyhawk, North Carolina." He furrowed his brow as if in deep thought. "No, it's way too soon."

"What?" She frowned. "North Carolina? Why would we want to go there? I was thinking more along the lines of California or Oregon."

His eyes glittered with excitement. "Two brothers are going to fly the first airplane there." He scratched his head. "I wish I'd paid better attention in history class." He laughed. "What year was it? You'd think I'd be able to remember something that important."

Hilary's hopes continued to crumble. How could she depend on Zach for herself, let alone for Elliot, too? He was so confused. She closed her eyes. She was so tired.

"1902?" He scratched his head. "Damn, I wish I could remember. Y'know? This might work out after all. Maybe I *can* fly again." He stared off into the distance at something only he and his twisted mind could see. "Anyway, we'll go find the Wright brothers and see if we can get a head start on the Space Age."

"The what?" Elliot asked, stooping to examine Zach's drawing more closely. "Space . . . age?"

"Yep." Zach looked up at the sky. "When—where I come from, Elliot, people ride on planes in the sky all the time." He slapped his thigh. "Why, we've even sent men to walk on the moon."

"The moon?" Elliot echoed, in obvious awe.

"Oh, my God." Hilary moaned and moved inside. She couldn't listen to any more of this. Zach was definitely worse off than she'd thought. She suddenly felt very old. Very tired.

The passion she felt for Zach—the love—wasn't enough, no matter how much she wanted it. She needed security, too. Elliot needed stability in his life. After growing up as the children of Nellie Brown . . .

Lord knew Elliot was faced with enough challenges

already, without having a crazy brother-in-law to add to the situation. She sighed and sat down on the bed.

Resting her head in her hands, she wept. She'd have to watch Zach very closely. If his condition grew any worse . . .

She drew a shuddering breath. If Zach became worse, then her only choice would be to take Elliot away from Columbine and try to make a life for them both somewhere else. She could find another teaching position. Other towns would probably provide her with a house in addition to her salary. She'd be able to make a home for Elliot.

Without Zach Ryan and his crazy stories, if necessary.

"Hilary." Elliot's excited voice broke into her depressing thoughts.

"What is it, Elliot?" She stood and dried her eyes with the back of her hand. Hilary stepped out the back door and forced a smile. "Did you call me?"

"Zach's gonna build a . . ." He scratched his head and looked at Zach. "What?"

"A hang glider." Zach smiled and continued to draw. "With the updraft here, I oughta be able to fly one off the cliff there near the trail head. God, it'd be great to fly again."

Hilary's stomach lurched. "Zach, stop this nonsense."

He laughed—actually *laughed*. "You're being a worry-wart, Hilary." He straightened and walked over to her. "I'm an engineer. I know how to do this."

"Zach . . ." She gave a helpless shrug. "Just don't get hurt."

Zach chuckled as she turned to go inside. "Elliot, we're going to need some pine for the spars." He rubbed his chin thoughtfully. "I haven't seen any willow trees around here for the ribs. I guess it's too dry. Aspen might work, though."

"Can I help?"

Zach smiled at his brother-in-law. "You bet you can."

He patted Elliot on the shoulder. "We'll do this together." Zach stooped beside his drawing again. "See, this is the front view of the glider. I'll hold it here, and lean from side to side to steer it."

"Do you . . . think I can fly?"

Zach looked up quickly and swallowed. "Maybe after I've tested it, Elliot," he said hesitantly. He could just picture Hilary's reaction to seeing her brother hanging from a monster kite. It wasn't a pleasant image. "First, we have to design it. Then we'll gather the materials. I saw some canvas in the mine I can use. There's also pitch and tar I can use for a sealer."

"This . . . fun." Elliot stooped beside Zach and looked down at the drawing. "Wings."

"Right." Zach traced the wings again of the glider. "See these things on the side here?" He pointed to the ends of the wings. When Elliot nodded, he said, "These are called winglets. They'll give the glider stability in the air."

"So you just hang on here?" Elliot pointed to the triangular shape at the bottom.

Zach nodded. "Right. Then I run and jump off the cliff."

Elliot's eyes grew round. "Jump?"

Zach chuckled and nodded. "It'll be all right, Elliot." He patted the boy's shoulder reassuringly. "I think your sister will be surprised at how safe this really is."

"Then . . . I can fly, too."

"Only after I test it, Elliot." Zach scratched his head and chewed his lower lip. "It'll take a couple of days for the sealer to set up, I imagine. Let's go find some small trees and that canvas."

"All right."

Zach and Elliot constructed the frame with spars cut from small pine trees. The ribs were aspen limbs, small enough to have some give to them. Zach carefully tied the frame together with strips of leather, nailed in a few tacks, then made some crude dowel pins for areas that needed more strength.

Elliot held the canvas tight while Zach stretched it across the frame and secured it on both sides with tacks. Then Zach applied the pitch and tar generously, making certain all the canvas was covered, especially where the tacks had gone through the fabric. In a couple of days he expected the entire glider would be very sturdy.

But would it fly?

He looked up at a cliff slightly above the mine. The drop wasn't as great here as it was on the cliff overlooking Columbine. In fact, he wasn't even sure it was high enough to allow the glider enough time to catch an updraft.

Then again, it was a lot less distance to fall if the glider didn't catch an updraft.

"When . . . will you fly?" Elliot asked, standing back with Zach to stare at their creation. "It sure is big."

Zach smiled, pleased. "It has to be. The more wing span it has, the better." He looked up at the cliff again. "I'll test it day after tomorrow, from that cliff there." He shrugged. "That way, if it doesn't work, the worst I might get is a broken leg." He winced. "But I'll be careful."

"Hilary'll be mad."

"If I break my leg?"

Elliot nodded.

"Well, won't she be surprised when she sees me fly like an eagle?"

"An eagle?" Elliot's eyes sparkled in anticipation. "A real eagle?"

"*Like* an eagle, Elliot." The boy's enthusiasm reminded Zach so much of the first time he'd taken Jake up in the Cessna. His heart swelled with affection. "It's gonna be great."

* * *

Hilary walked outside the next morning as the sun was beginning to peek above the mountains. A hard freeze had left everything coated with white frost. Her breath was a cloud of white vapor as she gathered some wood to carry into the cabin.

She'd noticed Elliot's pallet empty when she'd first awakened. Zach came out the door and slipped his arms around her waist from behind. His breath was warm against the back of her neck.

"Good morning," he whispered huskily. "Where's Elliot?"

Hilary sighed and leaned against her husband's warm body. She wished all her doubts would just go away and leave them in peace. Zach was so loving and giving with her and Elliot. All she wanted was a future with him.

"I haven't seen Elliot," she whispered, closing her eyes as she rested her head against her husband's shoulder.

He moved his hand up the side of her rib cage, cupping the sensitive underside of her breast. "Mmm, wonder how much time we have."

Hilary's thoughts were racing in the same direction. A few moments alone with Zach would be wonderful. That was the one drawback about having Elliot live with them in the small cabin. There was absolutely no privacy, and what she wanted to do with her husband was very private indeed.

Zach tensed behind her suddenly. "Oh, my God," he whispered, then pushed away from her and raced toward the trail leading to the mine. "Elliot!"

Hilary's blood turned cold. What was wrong? She turned and ran after Zach, wondering what he was so worried about. She was winded by the time she reached the open area in front of the mine.

"Zach, wait," she called when she saw her husband. He was looking up. Following his gaze, her heart leapt into her throat. Her brother stood on the cliff overlooking the mine holding Zach's ridiculous man-sized kite. "Elliot, no!"

"It's not ready, Elliot," Zach shouted as he climbed up the steep incline beside the mine. "No, Elliot!"

Hilary watched in horror as her brother waved. He obviously couldn't hear them. The boy held onto the bottom of the bizarre creation and took a running leap off the edge of the cliff.

"Noooooo!" Zach's scream mingled with hers as the object seemed suspended in air for a moment, then plummeted to the earth.

Elliot clutched his leg with both hands, but he was alive. Zach reached him before Hilary. Her heart thudded dangerously as she dropped to her knees beside her brother.

"Elliot, are you hurt?" she asked in a strangled whisper. She didn't want to frighten him any more than he already was.

"My leg." He groaned, then looked at Zach. "Sorry, Zach. I broke it."

Hilary glanced up at her husband's face. A fury unlike anything she'd ever known possessed her. "You did this," she accused. "You and your craziness. You stay away from Elliot, Zach Ryan. Don't you put any more foolish ideas into his head. You're dangerous."

Zach's gaze locked with hers for several agonizing moments, then she managed to drag hers away. Zach's pain at her words was palpable.

"I'll go for the doctor," he offered, helping Elliot to his feet. "I think we can get you back to the cabin this way, Elliot. Lean on me."

Elliot obeyed and Hilary went ahead of them. She had

to get her brother away from this crazy man. Elliot could have been killed.

Tears stung her eyes as she opened the cabin door and pulled the quilt back on the bunk she and Zach shared. "Put him here," she said in a strained voice, standing back as Zach did her bidding. She turned away from her husband's tortured gaze and grabbed a knife to cut Elliot's trouser leg.

She was painfully aware of Zach's presence; he stared at her, waiting for her to look at him. Well, she wasn't going to look at him. Because she knew if she did, she'd weaken. This had to end. Zach was crazy and dangerous. Her brother's pain was proof of that.

"Hilary, I—"

"I thought you were going for the doctor, Zach," she interrupted, glancing over her shoulder as he turned toward the door.

Zach took a step toward the open door. Then, without another word, he walked outside.

Hanged. Hilary couldn't breathe—she couldn't breathe. She was dead. Dead . . .

The long dark tunnel pulled her in, drew her toward the bright light until she stood before the strange woman. She spoke. Her voice echoed all around them in the dark void.

"I'm an angel. I'm called Sarah." Her voice was soft.

Hilary gulped. "I'm really dead."

Sarah smiled. "I've been assigned to your life, to determine the nature of your afterlife." She sighed and glanced upward once. "We redirect souls here."

"Redirect? I thought Saint Peter—"

"You haven't made it quite that far, Hilary."

You haven't made it quite that far, Hilary . . .

Hilary awoke with a start. Clutching at her throat, she

stared into the darkness, gasping in precious air. Zach's steady breathing at her side confirmed he was still asleep.

I have to get out of here—away from him. Little by little, the longer she remained with Zach, her own sanity was dwindling away. She was terrified. What would become of Elliot if she . . .

No. Hilary couldn't—wouldn't—let that happen. She bit her lip, choking back the sob that threatened to tear from her throat. She loved Zach so much. Leaving him would be the hardest thing she'd ever had to face in her life. And Lord knew she'd faced more than her share already. It wasn't fair.

But she had to get Elliot far away from Zach and his crazy stories. She was starting to believe some of them. It was terrifying. So many of his tales now filled her mind, making her lose sight of reality.

I have to go. For Elliot. Run, Hilary—get away.

She eased herself from the bed, glancing once at his peaceful face, barely discernable in the darkness. *God, how I love you, Zach.* If only . . .

Her heart thudded so hard it seemed a miracle its sound didn't fill the tiny cabin and wake its occupants. Biting her lower lip, Hilary slipped on her dress and shoes.

It was nothing less than a miracle that Elliot's leg hadn't been broken in his fall. The doctor had placed a splint on it anyway, to keep Elliot from bending his knee for a few days while it healed.

If they walked slowly, there was no reason why Elliot couldn't make it into town. Quietly, she stooped beside her brother's pallet near the back door and woke him. "Get up, Elliot. Shh," she whispered when he moaned. "Be very quiet. We have to leave now."

Nodding, Elliot didn't question her, bless his heart. Hilary knew that later, when he was fully awake, that he'd challenge her decision to leave Zach. Elliot adored the man, which made this decision even more difficult. But it also made it all the more necessary.

Elliot's future was more important than her own happiness.

And *her* sanity played an important role in her brother's future. The terror of reliving her own death over and over again in her dreams had to end. Hilary couldn't live like this. She'd really go insane if she stayed any longer. Besides, Elliot needed her. She quietly opened the front door and led a limping Elliot from the cabin.

Clouds blotted out the moon and stars as they walked away. Within moments, flakes of icy white began to sting her face. She hadn't taken time to collect their wraps to protect them from the cold.

She paused once before descending the twisting trail that led to Columbine. Tears trickled down her cheeks, threatening to freeze in the falling temperature. Glancing over her shoulder at the small cabin bathed in moonlight, she blew a kiss.

"I love you," she whispered into the night, watching her words turn to vapor in the frosty air.

Chapter Seventeen

"Elliot, you sleep in your old room tonight," Hilary whispered as they slipped quietly in the back door of Miss Nellie's. Loud music and laughter drifted into the kitchen from the saloon. The last thing in the world she wanted was to be seen by anyone. She wasn't prepared to answer questions. The best thing for everyone would be for her and Elliot to simply disappear.

"In the morning we'll start down the mountain," she said with far more confidence than she felt. Silently, she prayed there wouldn't be too much snow for such a venture. And with Elliot's injured leg, the going would be very slow. Well, they'd have to make do.

"Hilary," Elliot said, scratching his head as he yawned. "Is Zach coming with us?"

Hilary blinked back her tears. "No, Elliot."

He started to speak, but she touched his mouth with her fingertips. "Please just trust me, Elliot," she pleaded. "This is for the best."

"But . . ." He looked down. She saw his pain and felt it even more fiercely. "All right."

They slipped up the back stairs and into their separate rooms, directly across the hall from the one Nellie Brown had occupied. Once Elliot was in his bed, Hilary couldn't resist slipping into her mother's room. She walked around in the dark, with only the moonlight to guide her. The room smelled like Nellie—like the cheap perfume she'd always worn.

Her mother was dead. A fleeting memory of a time long ago flashed through Hilary's mind—the night her father'd left them. She'd known, even as a six-year-old, that her father would never return.

With a pain so profound she thought she'd die from it, Hilary recalled her mother's soothing voice that night. Nellie'd held her child in her arms while they both cried for the man who'd abandoned them.

Then Nellie Brown had found a means of keeping a roof over her child's head.

Not long after her mother'd started entertaining men, Hilary'd noticed Nellie's strange behavior. The peculiar odor that had always accompanied the slurred words and the stagger. Hilary chewed her lower lip. The whiskey must have numbed some of her mother's pain. Hilary realized that now.

She took a shuddering breath and wiped the tears from her eyes. In the darkness, with her mother's fragrance surrounding her, Hilary's hatred simply vanished. Her mother had loved her in her own way. She'd sacrificed her own life for her child's.

"Mama, forgive me for . . . hating you. I don't any-more—wish I never had," Hilary whispered into the empty room. She blinked and sighed, then stepped into the hall and closed the door, looking down at her feet. A part of

her life was over. The rest of it was in the future. Hers and
Elliot's.

A movement at the end of the hall caught her attention.
She glanced upward quickly, but whoever had been there
was gone. *Probably one of the girls.*

Hilary was so tired she didn't even care. She went into
her old room and closed the door with a sense of despair.
The last time she'd walked through this door had been to
go to her wedding.

Stop it, Hilary.

Quelling her thoughts of Zach and what they'd shared,
Hilary moved around the room in darkness. It was very
cold tonight, but she didn't want to light a fire. She didn't
need a lamp to change into one of the flannel gowns she'd
left behind. Shivering, she crawled into her bed.

With her quilt pulled beneath her chin, Hilary stared at
the ceiling for what seemed like hours. It was late. Most
of the customers from downstairs had gone home, or
turned in with their favorite of Miss Nellie's girls. Hilary
winced, then closed her eyes, praying for sleep to give her
temporary respite from the pain. Here, in her own bed,
perhaps she'd be spared the recurring nightmare.

She hoped.

A noise awakened Hilary with a start. She'd been sound
asleep—a mercifully dreamless sleep. She strained to see
in the dark room. A definite shape moved near the door.
Her heart raced.

Zach?

She didn't think she'd have the willpower to resist if he
asked her to come back. She already missed having him
at her side.

"Prissy teacher-lady," a drunken voice mumbled as the
intruder stumbled into the room. "Baird made me pay
extra to be first."

Hilary's pulse roared through her veins as she inched

farther beneath the quilt. Baird was running Miss Nellie's, and he'd sent a customer to her room.

Something hit the floor with a heavy thud, followed by a second identical sound. She heard the man fumble . . . with his clothing.

"Get out of my room," she said in a carefully controlled voice. "I'm not . . . not one of the girls."

The man snorted. "Huh. Baird said since you come back, you have to work for your keep. The bastard made me pay extra to go first. Heck, you got yourself hitched, so I ain't really gonna be first."

Oh, God—not this. Anything but this.

The man staggered toward the bed and Hilary screamed. Within a few moments the door flew open and Baird walked in carrying a lantern. He rolled his eyes, glowering at Hilary.

The lantern illuminated the half-naked customer. His trousers were around his ankles and his shirt was open, revealing his arousal. Hilary looked quickly away to glare at Baird.

"I'm leaving in the morning," she announced with bravado. "I'll pay you for this one night, but I will *not* work for my keep, as you put it."

Baird laughed and handed the man a wad of bills. "Here, Tom. Pick another girl—on the house."

"Damn prissy teacher-lady." The man continued to mumble drunkenly as he walked out of the room with his boots in his hands, holding his trousers up with his fingertips. "You better learn some manners, girl."

Baird's expression was lascivious. He closed the door behind the man and reached for his belt. "I'm gonna have to teach you some manners, Hilary," he said. "We can't have you treatin' the customers like this—not if you're gonna follow in your mama's footsteps."

Follow in my mama's footsteps . . .

Hilary shuddered and swallowed convulsively as Baird staggered toward the bed. He removed his gun belt and placed it on the table near the window. She inched as far to the opposite side of the bed as she could, praying for a means of escaping Baird's obvious intention.

"Gonna break you in good for the customers," he continued, unbuttoning his shirt as he moved closer to the bed. "I guess that husband of yours didn't have what it takes to do the job right, huh? Well, old Baird's got more than enough to please a gal, and then some."

His laughter made Hilary sick to her stomach. She prayed over and over in her mind for deliverance from this nightmare.

But this was no dream.

This was reality.

Zach's words came back to haunt her. My God, had he been telling the truth? Was it possible? This was all too familiar.

Baird moved closer and she screamed, leaping from the bed to stand on the far side. The bedroom door burst open and Elliot stood outlined in the door frame, his eyes wide with fear.

"Get away . . . from my sister," he demanded, straightening to his full height.

"Go back to bed, idiot," Baird said caustically. "You're interruptin' my pleasure, and I don't much like that."

Elliot took another step and Baird turned toward him. Before Hilary realized what the man was doing, he'd reached into the top of his boot and withdrawn a knife. He waved the blade in Elliot's direction. "Get out."

Elliot took a step back, but he shook his head. "No, you get out."

Baird's evil chuckle filled the room, crawled inside her with a perverse sense of foreboding, as Hilary inched around the bed. She had to protect Elliot. She knew he wouldn't leave her here with Baird, but she couldn't let the evil man hurt her brother, either. Elliot was much larger than Baird, but slow. And his injured leg would make him even slower and more awkward than usual.

Slowly, she made her way around the foot of the bed. Elliot took another limping step toward Baird, then grabbed for the knife. Baird took a step back and laughed.

"You can't take it from me, Elliot. C'mon. Try." Baird went into a half-crouch, obviously preparing to attack Elliot. "Let's save Pa the trouble and get this over with now."

"What do you mean by that?" Hilary asked, pausing between Baird and the table. The man's words echoed through her mind. "Save your pa what trouble?"

Baird snorted, but his gaze never left Elliot, who was circling the smaller man—his brother.

"The trouble of killin' this idiot." Baird chuckled again, obviously enjoying the entire sordid episode. "Don't tell me you ain't figured it out yet, Hilary? I thought teachers was supposed to be smart."

Oh, my God. Suddenly she knew what Zach had suspected. It was so obvious. Why hadn't she realized it sooner— before she'd made the biggest mistake of her life?

Hilary backed toward the table, groping behind her as she continued to stare at Baird and Elliot. The knife sliced through the air a few times, clearly a ploy to anger Elliot enough to make him move closer.

"Figured what out?" Hilary asked in mock bewilderment, praying she could keep Baird talking. Maybe that could at least postpone what the horrible man was trying to do to Elliot.

He laughed again. "C'mon, Elliot. Just a little closer." The blade arced through the air again, barely missing Elliot's arm. "Almost gotcha."

Hilary bit her lip and fumbled around the top of the

table behind her until she found the smooth, cold metal. She closed her fingers around the handle, then she eased the weapon from the holster.

"Figured out what, Baird?" she repeated, bringing the gun in front of her in one smooth motion. It was heavy. She used both hands to raise the weapon, then took careful aim.

"Old Elliot here owns the richest mine in the district." Baird's words hung in the air as Hilary pulled back the hammer of the gun. She knew. The truth had been there all along, just barely out of her grasp. Sean had murdered her mother, and planned to dispose of poor Elliot in the same heinous manner. All because Shorty'd generously bequeathed the Maggie-O to Elliot. With them both out of the way . . .

Their plan seemed so simple now. Why hadn't she seen it earlier? "Leave Elliot alone, Baird," she said with deadly calm. She'd kill the man before she'd let him harm her brother.

Zach's prediction come true?

She took a step closer when Baird continued to stalk her brother. He lunged for Elliot, but her brother stepped to the side just in time to prevent a fatal stabbing. The blade sliced into his upper arm as Elliot fell to the floor, clutching his wound with his other hand.

Time seemed to stand still as Hilary moved quickly toward Baird. The man lifted his blade as he hovered over Elliot. The expression on Baird's face was murderous. She had no choice.

She squeezed the trigger while only a few feet from her target; there was no possibility of missing. The explosion knocked her back against the dresser as Baird's head yielded to the awesome power of the bullet tearing through his skull.

Hilary and Elliot's screams mingled and filled the night

as the hideous sight played out before them. In a wild rush of memory, Hilary realized more truths. Zach's stories of angels, ghosts and time travel were all true.

She dropped the gun and backed away from the mutilated man. As she eased her way around him toward Elliot, Ned Carter appeared in the open doorway.

"What the hell . . ." The man covered his mouth and made a gagging sound as he backed away.

Hilary grabbed Elliot's uninjured arm and led him to the bed. Acting on pure instinct, she tore away his sleeve and bound his wound with a clean linen towel from her nightstand. She didn't look back at Baird. There was no point. He was dead.

And she knew there was no point in trying to run away. Her fate was inescapable. This had been her second chance. There wouldn't be another.

It was over—really over.

She'd be hanged for murder—then burn in Hell for eternity.

Zach stretched as he dragged his eyes open. "Man, it's cold." He jumped out of bed and walked over to the stove in the corner. After opening the door, he threw in a couple of logs, then stirred the embers with a long stick which served as a poker, until the new fuel caught and began to burn.

He rubbed his hands together, then turned to walk back to the bed, but froze in mid-step.

"Hilary?" He looked at the entire cabin, including the empty pallet where Elliot had gone to sleep last night. It was empty.

They were both gone.

A powerful sense of foreboding gripped him. A dull

thud started in his gut and built to a roar by the time it reached his head. It was happening again.

"Hilary."

Zach rushed to the front door and pulled it open. Snow. It reached half-way up the door. For as far as he could see, there was nothing but blinding white snow. How the hell was he going to find his way down the trail? Well, he'd just have to be careful. Because if something happened to him before he managed to save Hilary . . .

"God, no." His gut twisted as cold terror swept through him. He wouldn't lose her now. Not after everything they'd been through together.

Then he remembered the glider and turned back inside. He needed a piece of fabric large enough to patch the hole Elliot's fall had torn in the canvas. Frantic, he tore through his belongings and the few his wife had brought to the cabin with her.

A petticoat? Without hesitation, Zach took a knife and sliced open one side of Hilary's undergarment. It formed a large, flat circle.

"It won't hold long, but it might get me down the damned mountain."

He dressed warmly, continuing to feed the fire in the stove. Zach had to prevent Hilary's hanging. He'd traveled back in time to save her—he couldn't let her down now. If only there were some way to contact that frigging angel.

He ran his fingers through his hair. "Listen to yourself, Zach." He laughed nervously as he tied his Reeboks, wishing he had a pair of sturdy hiking boots instead. His eyes burned as he put on the buffalo robe Shorty'd left behind.

It smelled horrible—even worse than that bear's breath had.

Zach swallowed hard. The memory of Hilary standing in the sunshine, scaring away a hungry bear assailed him. He winced in pain as the fear of losing her swept through him, growing and building until he screamed out loud in agony.

It wasn't fair. He'd been dragged away from his own time because he loved Hilary. She deserved another chance. Being sent back to her life without her memory wasn't fair.

The truth hit him with a powerful torrent. By God, *he* was Hilary's memory, but he'd failed her. He seemed destined to fail those he loved most.

Taking a deep breath, Zach tucked the petticoat under his arm and opened the door, then took a lunging step into the snow. His shoes were immediately filled with the icy substance and his jeans were wet to mid-thigh before he reached the trail—what he hoped was the trail. If it wasn't, he was in for one hell of a wild ride.

A stout wind whistled up from the valley below. The sky was clearing.

A fine day for hang-gliding.

Exhausted by the time he reached the mine entrance, Zach pulled the glider from the snow and dragged it into the mine. Looking around for something to tie the petticoat over the hole in the glider, he groaned in frustration. Desperate, he bent down to yank the shoestrings from his Reeboks, then poked holes through the fabric with his knife. His fingers were numb from the cold as he laced his shoestrings through the holes and tied it securely.

"I don't know how you feel about prayers from old drunks like me, Lord, but I could sure use some help about now." He dragged the glider down the trail toward the cabin. He set it down, then moved closer to the cliff.

When he reached the overlook, he stared down at the sleepy town. It was blanketed in white, a pristine contrast to the dusty ghost town he'd driven into only a few weeks ago.

"Now let me think of a happy thought." He shook his

head in frustration. "It worked for Robin Williams, why not Zach Ryan?" He shrugged, wondering for a moment if Hilary might be right about him losing his mind.

"Ah, hell, Tinkerbell," he shouted, listening to his voice echo down the canyon, then rise again to mock him. "Hilary and Elliot are my happy thoughts. Just do it, Zach."

He'd take a running jump off this cliff, and float down to Columbine. To Hilary and Elliot. Simple. Taking a frosty breath, Zach forced himself to think warm thoughts along with his happy ones as he trudged back up the slippery trail to where he'd left the glider.

Hilary. Southern California sunshine. Hilary. Coffee. Hilary. Chili. Hilary . . .

Gripping the triangular-shaped handles of the glider, Zach inhaled and released several huge breaths trying to bring his nerves under control. His feet were twin blocks of ice. They felt as if they weighed at least four times their normal weight as he counted to three and ran.

A sensation of madness consumed him as he drew closer and closer to the cliff. There was no stopping now. Even if he were to change his mind at the last minute, the slippery terrain wouldn't permit such luxury.

He picked up speed as he neared the edge, holding onto the pine spars with a death grip as he took a running leap into thin, cold air. A scream tore from his throat.

He held his breath as he and the glider fell, then he felt the resistance of the wind against the glider. Hope surged through Zach as the icy updraft grew stronger, lifting the glider gradually skyward.

Thank you, God. The thrill of flying billowed through his veins again. It was an addiction with him, like drinking only not as destructive. He hoped.

"I'm flying," he sang, truly believing old Peter Pan had the right idea after all. Never to grow up, to always be a little boy and have fun.

But he was grown-up. And in love.

Zach leaned to his left, commending his decision to put the stabilizer on the top of the glider. It was a good design. He didn't have much control over the distance the glider might take him, though. He could only hope he wouldn't end up passing the town entirely.

"Hello, down there," he called to a group of several men gathered in front of the jailhouse in the center of town. Practically snow-blind and frozen, Zach squinted, trying to determine what they were doing. It certainly didn't seem like good weather for outdoor activities, as he knew all too well.

But he didn't really care what they were doing. All he wanted was to find Hilary.

Several of the men pointed at Zach. Soon all of them had stopped to stare at the glider.

A giddy sensation of power swept through Zach as he tilted to his right to steer the glider. He was beginning his descent, still hoping he didn't overshoot the town. Flying down to Columbine wouldn't do him much good if he had to turn around and climb back up.

Just when he was beginning to feel confident he wouldn't fly all the way to Denver, a loud snap preceded his very abrupt descent. He wasn't very high at this point, but it was high enough.

Instinct took over—Zach released the glider and free fell the rest of the way down. At least he might avoid having one of the pine spars run him through. He wouldn't do Hilary or Elliot much good if that happened.

His only hope was to land in the deep snowdrift near Miss Nellie's he'd spotted just before the frame snapped. Bungee-cord jumping couldn't hold a candle to this for cheap thrills.

"Shit!" he yelped as he landed, butt first in a nice soft

snowdrift. He groaned as a pair of men dragged his half-frozen body from the snow.

"Damn, what the hell was you doin'?" one man asked, brushing snow off Zach's back. "I ain't never seen nothin' like that before in my life."

Zach's teeth were chattering and shivers racked his body. "C-cold," he stammered. "H-Hilary."

As the men dragged him around to the front of Miss Nellie's, Zach said a silent prayer that he'd find Hilary and Elliot inside and safe. But as they neared the door, something caught his attention and he jerked himself from his rescuers' grip.

For some reason, he needed to know what the men he'd noticed earlier were doing. They were building something. Zach gulped—hard. The structure took shape right before his eyes.

Gallows.

"Hilary," he whispered, then started running on his frozen feet. When he paused in front of the jail to stare at the harbinger of disaster, pure terror swept through him. He embraced the frigid air in an attempt to bring his panic under control. He wouldn't be any use to Hilary if he lost his head.

"Hey, ain't you the fella who married the schoolteacher?" one of his rescuers asked as Zach moved toward the jail entrance.

"Yeah."

Another man snorted in obvious disgust. "Couldn't keep her home last night, huh?"

Several men laughed uproariously as they returned their attention to the heinous implement of death.

"What do you mean?" Though Zach knew in his gut what had happened, he had to hear someone say the words. It wouldn't seem real to him until he heard it as fact. "What happened?"

"Dang if that teacher didn't blow Baird McCune's head plumb off," the man explained with a shake of his head. "We're fixin' to have the hangin' as soon as the trial's over."

"Trial?" Zach felt suspended in slow motion while he listened to the man. "Where?"

"Miss Nellie's is the only place in Columbine big enough for a trial."

Zach turned and rushed back up the street. He couldn't feel his feet at all by the time he reached Miss Nellie's. Frozen and terrified, he threw open the door and tried to rush inside, but a pair of strong arms gripped him and held him near the door.

"Ain't room for no more spectators. Judge says ever'-body else should go help build the gallows."

Zach's head spun. "My wife's in here." God, this couldn't be happening. If only he'd listened.

"Oh, you're Ryan, ain't you?" The hairy man stepped aside and permitted Zach to limp into Miss Nellie's. Heads turned to stare at him as he limped slowly toward the proceedings near the bar.

A tall man sat in a chair behind the bar. Zach had never seen him before. He glanced up once, but he still didn't look familiar. His dark robe identified him as a judge.

Zach's gaze swept the group nearest the bar until he found her. Her golden head was bowed. The red dress she'd worn when he'd first met her barely covered her shivering body. Anger boiled within Zach as he rushed toward her.

"Hilary," he shouted, fighting his way through the crowd toward her. "Hilary!"

She looked up and their gazes locked. His heart broke— right then and there. It was like the San Andreas fault cracking through his middle as he watched the expression of total devastation cross her beautiful face.

"Face the bench," the man behind the bar commanded. When Hilary didn't immediately comply, Sheriff Tyler grabbed her head and forced her to turn toward the judge.

Zach clenched his fists at his sides as he tried to fight his way through the crowd to Hilary. But another set of strong arms restrained him. His gaze scanned the crowd, searching for Elliot. Where was the boy—Sean's next victim?

"We find you, Hilary Brown—er, Ryan—guilty of murder," the judge said in a stern voice. "You're to be hanged by the neck until you are dead. Dawn tomorrow. Let's just hope some of this snow melts before then."

"Jesus, tomorrow?" Zach lunged, breaking free to rush to his bride. He gathered her in his arms and held her trembling body. She looked up into his eyes and he remembered so many things in a fierce, sweet rush of joy mingled with despair. "I love you, Hilary. I'll find a way to—"

"Get away from the prisoner," Sheriff Tyler ordered gruffly, reaching for Zach's arm as he spoke.

"Don't even think it, Tyler." Zach's rage threatened his resolve. Maintaining control at this moment was one of the greatest challenges of his life. He shuddered as he continued to hold his bride. "And don't you touch my wife."

The man laughed. "The only time I intend to touch your wife is when I slip the noose over her pretty head—tomorrow morning."

Hilary swayed against him. "Zach," she whispered in a wretched voice. "Take care of Elliot for me."

Zach was helpless to prevent the men from taking Hilary away. Tyler led her out the door. Fighting the urge to follow, Zach turned in a circle. What was he supposed to do? How could he stop this horrible mistake from happening—again?

He needed to talk to the judge. He was probably an intelligent man. Educated . . . reasonable?

But he couldn't speak to the judge at the moment.

Because Sean McCune was deep in conversation with the man who held Hilary's life in his hands.

Rage continued to build within Zach as he walked toward the bar. "McCune," he said in an ominous tone. "You know this is wrong."

"Wrong?" Sean's expression was one of total outrage and bewilderment at Zach's words. "The wrong was in murdering my son. But your wife will pay."

Zach grabbed Sean's arm. "I know you murdered Shorty Lamb *and* Nellie Brown." He looked at the judge to make certain the man was listening. He was.

"That's ridiculous." Sean laughed, but it was a nervous—guilty—sound.

"What's the meaning of this?" the judge demanded, getting to his feet to move closer to Sean and Zach. "This man is in mourning."

"Your Honor, I'm Zach Ryan." He offered his hand to the judge. "Hilary's husband. She didn't murder Baird. It was self-defense."

"And how would you know that?" The man shook his head. "You weren't there. She admitted to shooting Baird."

"I said it was self-defense." Zach gritted his teeth. "Your Honor . . . Sean McCune and Sheriff Tyler murdered Shorty Lamb and Nellie Brown."

The judge's gaze narrowed, but to his credit, he ignored Sean's sputtering and cursing at his side. "Go on."

"I found a button from Sean's vest in front of the mine the same morning we found Nellie's body." Zach reached inside his buffalo robe and retrieved the button from his pocket. "Sean and the sheriff want the mine. Elliot inherited it from Shorty."

The judge turned toward Sean. "Is this true, Sean? Did Elliot inherit the mine?"

McCune shrugged. "How the hell would I know?"

The judge reddened slightly. "Everyone in the district knows you're the boy's father," the judge said in a low tone. "I haven't seen any papers come across my desk about his inheritance, though."

"My son—my only son—is dead." Sean trembled. His face turned red, then purple as he glowered at Zach. "Don't *ever* say anything like that again."

Zach grabbed the judge's arm when he turned to leave. "You have to listen to me, sir." He sighed. "Please."

"Son, your wife's been found guilty of murder." The judge looked down for a moment, then faced Zach again. He looked sad. "She confessed. It's done. You'd better just accept it."

Zach stared in horror as the man walked away. His gaze swept the room, searching for Elliot. A familiar face in the kitchen door drew his attention. Matilda, the cook.

He rushed to the kitchen as she vanished inside. "Where's Elliot?" Zach asked as he rushed into the warm room.

The woman pointed to a figure slumped over the table. It was Elliot. He rocked and stared, but made no effort to look up at Zach. "Elliot?"

The boy stopped rocking, but didn't lift his gaze.

"Elliot?" Zach dropped to his knees beside the youth. "We're going to help Hilary. I need your help."

Slowly, Elliot lifted his gaze to Zach's. The boy's eyes were filled with a sadness Zach had known before. When Jake . . .

God, why do people have to hurt this way?

Elliot was such a good, gentle person. He didn't deserve this kind of pain. Zach closed his eyes for a moment, wondering what had happened to Elliot in the first history.

He knew.

Elliot would be murdered so his father could inherit the Maggie-O.

Zach wouldn't let that happen. He didn't give a damn about the mine or the gold anymore. All he'd ever wanted was enough to give them all a fresh start away from Columbine. Away from this.

"I'll help you, Zach."

Zach embraced Elliot and held him for a few moments. He patted the boy on the back and helped him to his feet. "First thing we have to do is get up to the cabin," Zach said, thinking his plan through as he spoke. "We're going to liven this place up a bit."

"Huh?" Elliot scratched his head and frowned.

"You'll see." Zach hoped he knew what he was doing. "Oh, one thing, Elliot. Do you have a pair of boots I can borrow?"

Zach worked all afternoon. The sun had the decency to shine while he and Elliot worked out their plan. While Zach returned to rescue Hilary, Elliot was to remain at the cabin. Once Hilary was safe, they'd all leave Columbine together. Forever.

Time was short. Zach gathered up the sticks of dynamite Shorty'd left behind and went to the mine. He positioned the explosives at various spots around the mine, then stood back to examine his efforts.

That eerie sensation he'd noticed the day Shorty'd been killed gripped Zach again. He felt a slight breeze move around him, almost encircle him, then a tingling sensation crept up his spine. He knew—somehow—that the spirit didn't mean him any harm. Maybe it was because he was now certain the murders had been committed by Sean and Tyler—not by any ghost.

He continued to stare at the wall where he'd planted the explosives, noticing some shifting of the stones in the center. It was as if someone—or something—was picking away at the rock.

Zach fought the urge to run. Though he wasn't exactly frightened, his natural fight or flight instinct threatened his resolve. The stones fell in growing numbers, crumbling away to reveal a wide streak of glittering gold that ran up the side of the wall, into the mountain.

"The mother lode," Zach whispered, feeling a surge of awe mingled with regret sweep through him. He'd made—been shown—the very discovery that signaled the beginning of the end for Columbine.

The crumbling ceased as Zach's perception of the spirit's presence grew stronger. He took a step toward the golden wall, touched it with his trembling hands, and knew why the ghost had given him this gift.

It was for Hilary and Elliot.

Was the Maggie-O ghost really Hilary's angel, Sarah? Could it be?

A shape emerged deeper into the dark mine. Unafraid, Zach turned toward the shimmering light that surrounded the form. It was a beautiful woman in a white robe. He knew who she was. She smiled, then simply vanished. His perception of her presence grew stronger, then passed altogether.

A sense of purpose filled Zach. He broke enough gold loose from the wall to partially fill a burlap bag with nuggets. There was no surge of gold fever coursing through his veins. Strange. He would have expected to feel excitement and greed at the sight of so much gold. There was a vast fortune to be had. It was here for the taking, beckoning to him.

He had to laugh. Zach Ryan, recovering alcoholic, former creator of grandiose schemes, wasn't the least bit interested. All he wanted was enough gold to give him and his family a fresh start.

My family.

He'd seen the worst there was to see in life. Buried his parents, killed his own brother through his personal weakness—his addiction. Zach Ryan had seen enough to know what really mattered.

Hilary—his wife. And Elliot.

He took a shuddering breath and checked the wall again. The dynamite was in place and he had enough gold for his new family to go anywhere they wished. He stood in the mine entrance for several moments, staring into the darkness.

"Thank you," he whispered, then walked quickly away, knowing what he must do.

Chapter Eighteen

Hilary paced her small cell like a caged animal. She was fresh out of miracles. Bitterly, she laughed, then swiped at the hot tears streaming down her cheeks. Why hadn't she listened to Zach?

She bit her lower lip and held her abdomen as wave after wave of pure agony washed through her. She'd been given a reprieve, a second chance at life, only to lose it without ever realizing what a miracle it was . . . until it was too late. Blinking, she sank down to the foul-smelling bunk to hold her head in her hands.

Her tears were wasted. There was no one to hear her—no one who cared. She stood and walked over to the small window and pushed her hand between the bars, opening the shutters to peer out at the darkness. The sky had cleared, permitting the moon and stars to illuminate the dark shape of the gallows, newly constructed for her execution. It was an ominous silhouette against the moonlight—a harbinger of death.

Hers.

She didn't want to sleep. This was her last night on earth and she wanted to have every minute of it. Closing her eyes, she considered how she'd liked to have spent her last night among the living.

In her husband's arms. But that wasn't to be—not ever again.

If only she could remember more. Fragments of memory had started flashing through her mind as Baird's life ebbed out on her bedroom floor. What a shame it had taken such a tragic catalyst to make her believe Zach's stories.

She'd already died once. The memory of her hanging was vivid. At least, this time, she knew what to expect. Her hand touched her throat. She'd fallen through the trap door as the rope went taut.

That was it. No memories of choking, or terrible pain came to mind. Perhaps she'd simply forgotten that part, as she had so many other things.

It didn't matter. Nothing mattered.

Except Elliot and Zach. She brightened a little, knowing that at least this time Elliot wouldn't be left alone. He'd have Zach Ryan to take care of him, to guide and teach him. To love him as a brother.

And she remembered the future. What a paradox— remembering things that hadn't happened yet. Or had they?

How could she have forgotten the century of loneliness after all the residents of Columbine had drifted away. She closed her eyes as another memory tore at her. Elliot. Her mother'd been alive when Hilary was hanged the first time.

Then Elliot was murdered. Just like Shorty. But not by a ghost. That was obvious now.

Hilary started to pace again, trying to sort through her

jumbled memories. Zach had known for some time. She should have realized the reasons he'd tried so hard to protect her. Zach had already determined the murderer's identity.

But that was good. Now he'd be able to protect Elliot— just like he'd tried to prevent her from repeating the act of violence which would lead to her premature death. But there was one significant difference this time.

There would be no Transition. Hell awaited her.

Her stomach lurched and she bit her knuckles, trying to hold back the scream of terror that threatened to rip from her throat, from her very soul. It was over. She'd die at dawn.

Covering her face in her hands, she dropped to her knees.

"Tears aren't gonna save you," Tyler's taunting voice called from the door to her cell. "Besides, you got a visitor." He opened the cell door and stepped to the side.

Hilary leapt to her feet and waited. One last time, she'd get to see Zach's face. But the man who entered her dark cell wasn't her husband.

It was Sean McCune.

"You're going to pay, Hilary," he said with a measure of certainty that sent chills down her spine. "Today, for taking my son's life, you will pay . . . with your own."

Hilary tried to look away, but the man's gaze held her prisoner. "What do you want from me now?" she asked shakily. "You're getting what you want at dawn, so can't you leave me in peace?"

He chuckled cynically. "No. Not until I've told you exactly what's going to happen to your precious brother once you're out of my way."

Hilary went cold, terrified, as she stared at the man's

evil gaze. "Leave Elliot alone." She shook her head. "He's never done anything to anyone."

"Ah, that's probably true," Sean allowed, nodding as he walked over to look out the window. "But he inherited the Maggie-O from Shorty."

Hilary covered her mouth with her hands as more memories flooded her. "I know." Squeezing her eyes closed, she suddenly realized that after her first hanging, she'd never been positive about the identity of her brother's killer. Not even during her century in Transition.

"You'd murder your own son?"

"Son? Not hardly." Sean turned to face her again. "I don't think of it as murder. It's retribution. Elliot, the idiot, lives, while my real son is dead . . . because of you."

Hilary trembled as she backed toward the wall opposite this maniac. Though some things were different this time, the end would be the same. The order of their deaths was different—that was really the only difference. Sean would still win. "And my mother, too?"

Sean chuckled. "Nellie did something foolish." He sighed and shook his head. "For some insane reason, she decided to stop drinking. As long as she was inebriated most of the time, and oblivious to what was happening around her, she was manageable. But when she sobered up . . . well, she got in my way."

"May your soul burn in Hell for all eternity," Hilary said, clenching her fists at her sides. "And I'll be there to fan the flames."

"Do you understand, Elliot?" Zach asked the young man with a sigh. "You need to stay here and wait while I rescue Hilary."

Zach dropped to his knees in front of Elliot and looked up at the boy's face. Elliot was seated at the small table in Shorty's cabin, staring down at the dirt floor. Finally, the youth lifted his gaze and met Zach's.

"I understand," he said, then sighed as Zach got to his feet. "But I wanna help."

"I know you do." Zach ground his teeth in frustration. He was torn between responsibilities. He really shouldn't leave Elliot alone, yet he had to detonate the dynamite and get to Columbine before dawn.

Before it was too late.

"Listen, Elliot." He paced the dirt floor, looking up every few seconds at Elliot's face. The lantern flickered in the wind that sifted in between the logs. Zach was glad he wouldn't have the opportunity to find out how cold it could really get at this altitude. Just this little taste was plenty.

"What?"

Zach opened the door of the stove and tossed in more wood. "Damn, it's cold."

"Yeah, but snow's stopped." Elliot blinked when Zach turned to stare at him. "Tell me how."

Rubbing his hands together, Zach paced in front of the stove. "You can help Hilary by staying here."

The boy started to protest, but Zach paused in front of him again. "I'm serious, Elliot." He chewed his lower lip in frustration. "After I rescue Hilary, we'll come back here for you. Then we're going down the far side of the mountain. Do you know the way?"

Elliot nodded, then he brightened considerably. "I went down with Shorty once."

"Good. That's the kind of help Hilary and I will need more than anything." Zach fell silent while he considered what he should tell Elliot to do in the event that he and Hilary never returned.

That was still a distinct possibility, though Zach didn't want to dwell on the negative at the moment. "Positive vibes, Zach," he whispered aloud, rewarded with a curious frown from his brother-in-law. He had to tell Elliot *something*. "If . . ."

Elliot's eyes glistened. "I know."

Tilting his head to one side, Zach studied Elliot's expression. The young man had far more intelligence than most people—excluding Hilary and Shorty—had given him credit for. "If the worst happens, and we don't make it back . . ." He sighed and closed his eyes for a moment. What should Elliot do if that occurs? He shrugged in frustration. "I don't know, Elliot."

"I do."

Again, Zach shot Elliot a questioning glance. "What?"

"Go down the mountain by myself." Elliot wiped a tear away from his eye with the back of his beefy hand. "I know the . . . way."

Zach nodded in satisfaction. "You're pretty smart, Elliot," he said, and meant it.

"I am?" The boy's face brightened again.

Zach patted Elliot on the shoulder and remembered his own brother for a precious moment. "You're my brother now, Elliot," he said with conviction. "I promised Hilary I'd take care of you, but sometimes I might need you to help take care of me." *Like if Hilary doesn't make it, but I do—God forbid—then I'll need you to keep me away from the bottle.* Zach prayed it wouldn't come to that. He wasn't sure he could handle it.

Looking into Elliot's trusting eyes, he knew he had to handle anything fate dished out over the next few hours. He'd been thrust back in time to help Hilary, and he damned well intended to. But Elliot needed him, too. Zach had a purpose—a reason for being who and where he was. "I'll be damned."

"What is it, Zach?"

"Never mind." Zach took a deep breath, then released it with a sigh. "After I set off the dynamite, people will probably come up here right away. At least, that's what I'm counting on."

Elliot nodded, waiting patiently for Zach to continue. How long should he let the boy wait if he and Hilary . . . ? *Stop it, Zach. Positive vibes, man.*

"I want you to stay in the cabin, Elliot." He placed his hand on the boy's shoulder again. "This is hard, for both of us. But if Hilary and I don't make it back, you must go down the mountain. Understand?"

Elliot nodded. "I'll go to . . . Maggie's sister."

"Maggie's sister?"

Elliot nodded. "Shorty took me there."

"And you can find it?"

"Yeah."

"Good." Zach breathed a huge sigh of relief. He dug into his pocket for the silver button he'd picked up the morning they'd discovered Nellie's body. Holding it out to Elliot, he said, "Keep this for me. Don't let anything happen to it."

"Why?" Elliot turned the item over in his hand, examining it closely. "Whose is it?"

Zach swallowed hard. Did Elliot understand who his father was? What that meant? "It belongs to the man who . . . killed your mother and Shorty, Elliot." *And will try to kill you . . . given the opportunity.*

Elliot looked up sharply. His eyes darkened from blue to cobalt. "My . . . father."

"You've know all along." He shook his head in amazement. "Yeah, Sean McCune killed your mother. But I'd

bet my eye teeth that Sheriff Tyler helped him. You mustn't
trust either of them. Understand?"

"So, what do I do with this, if . . ."

"If . . ." Zach took a deep, steadying breath. "If we don't
make it back, you take that button to the law in another
town. And do you remember where I hid the bag of gold?"

Elliot nodded.

"You get it and take it with you when you leave."

The boy's face reddened and he sighed, obviously carrying burdens a youth his age shouldn't have to even consider. "I will, but you'll be back."

Zach nodded, though a premonition forced its way into
his mind. He tried to fight it, but for some reason he felt
an overwhelming sense of doom. "Yeah, we'll be back." *I
hope.*

"It'll be light soon." Elliot stood and embraced Zach.
"My brother."

Zach choked back the sob that nearly strangled him as
his other brother's face flashed through his mind. *Jake . . .*
"I love you, Elliot." *I love you, Jake.*

After tearing himself away from his new brother and
pocketing the tin box of sulphur matches, Zach wrapped
the buffalo robe around himself again, steeling himself to
its foul stench. He had a wife to save—a miscarriage of
justice to prevent.

And a damned mountain to blow up.

Hilary remembered.

The first time Elliot had been present at her execution.
She breathed a sigh of relief as she looked through the
barred window at the gathering crowd. The first violet
smudges of dawn streaked the eastern sky.

Elliot's face wasn't among the spectators. Nor was Zach's.

Relief mingled with her disappointment. She would've liked a few more moments with her husband before the end. But it was more important that he keep Elliot away and safe.

Protect my brother from his own father, Zach. My love . . .

She squeezed her eyes shut again, then fell to the dirt floor of her cell as a huge explosion rocked the earth beneath her feet. She struggled to her feet, gripping the bars to see what was happening. The crowd began to disperse, turning toward the mountain from where the explosion had resounded.

Just as a few people began to run toward the far end of town, another explosion, then two more, rent the morning air. Hilary bit her knuckles as she stared toward the smoke drifting upward to dissipate in the pinkening sky.

The explosions had come from the Maggie-O. She was positive. Zach. Elliot. Were they all right? She gripped the bars until her knuckles turned white, straining to see, to hear. But there was only silence and the near-panic of the crowd gathered for the grisly performance she was scheduled for this morning.

Hilary tore her gaze from the still-smoking mountain. The gallows still stood. Unfortunately, not even an exploding mountain was enough to prevent her execution. Sean McCune stood there, staring toward the jail window, obviously waiting to watch Hilary take her last thirteen steps. He was apparently oblivious to the chaos which had erupted following the explosions.

Hilary gulped as Sheriff Tyler jerked open the door of her cell. "C'mon, Hilary," he growled, grabbing her arm and dragging her away from the window. "I dunno what the hell's goin' on up at the Maggie-O, but I'd be willing to bet your husband's got somethin' to do with it."

My husband. Hilary's heart did a little flip-flop as she permitted her executioner to lead her from the cell. She had no coat, nor was one offered to her. The frosty air stung her bare arms and shoulders, a mocking reminder of how hot her new home would be.

As Sheriff Tyler led her toward the steps, Hilary's gaze riveted to the trail leading to the Maggie-O. The blood-lusting crowd had vanished, except for one old man, her executioner and Sean McCune.

If Zach had blown up the mine to keep people from watching Hilary in her darkest hour, she would be eternally grateful. Still, she would liked to have seen his face once more.

Sheriff Tyler gave her a shove when she hesitated again to stare at the mountain. The line of curious spectators had vanished, leaving only one figure on the trail now. Except this one was coming down the trail. One tall man.

Zach.

Hilary's heart swelled. She needed to give him more time to reach her before . . .

But did she really want him to watch her die? Her blood turned cold and her empty stomach protested. Stumbling, she tripped on the first step, earning herself the executioner's harsh bark and a brutal hand on her upper arm.

"Get up, whore." But the voice didn't belong to Tyler. Hilary glanced up into the glittering, hate-filled gaze of Sean McCune. "Get up and pay your penance."

Hilary struggled to her feet, but made no effort to rush the proceedings. She took a deep breath and glanced once more to her right, hoping against hope, even as she prayed he would be gone.

There was no sign of Zach.

"Now you'll pay for murdering my son." Sean sighed, emitting a huge cloud of white vapor as he did.

When the fog dissipated, she saw Zach. Hilary's heart

swelled. He was there for only a moment, then he vanished again.

"C'mon, Hilary," Sheriff Tyler urged, giving her another shove. "Twelve more steps and this'll be over."

"You treat her too kindly, Tyler." Sean's tone was full of hate. "My only regret is that there's no longer a crowd to witness justice being done."

Tyler glanced toward the mountain. "I wonder what blew up." He scratched his head.

A voice provided the answer. It seemed to come from every direction at once. "Gold. It's the mother lode."

Hilary's breath caught in her throat. Her heart hammered in her chest at that familiar voice. It *was* Zach. Biting her lower lip, she tried to see him, looked in every direction before her executioner's voice interfered again.

"Gold?" Tyler looked at Sean.

Sean's eyes narrowed as he looked toward the mountain as well. "They may walk away with some of it, but most of it'll still be mine."

"Ours," Tyler reminded as he took a few more steps with Hilary in tow. "You'd best not be forgettin' that, Sean. If you know what's good for you."

Sean arched a silvery brow. "Is that a threat, Sheriff?"

"Call it what you want." Tyler gripped Hilary's arm even tighter. "Get on up there, Hilary. Let's get this over with."

Over with. She swallowed convulsively as Tyler slipped the noose over her head. The rope felt rough against her bare flesh. When he tied a blindfold over her eyes, she fought the urge to cry again. It was useless.

God, don't let Zach see me die, she prayed, still grateful for Elliot's absence.

"Well, it's time justice was done," Tyler said quietly. There was an odd catch in his voice, then it dropped to a faint whisper, obviously intended for her alone. "Dammit, Hilary, why'd you have to go and blow Baird's head off?"

She ignored the man's question, not feeling an answer was necessary. Even if she were to try, she doubted her voice would work at this point. Her throat was so clogged with misery, no room remained for words to pass.

Good-bye, Zach. Elliot.

Zach crept toward the gallows as stealthily as possible. He was running out of time—fast. When he'd finally fought his way through the crowd and down the mountain, shouting to the world as he did that he'd unearthed the mother lode, Hilary'd already been climbing the steps. He shuddered to think what another few moments could have cost.

And still could if he didn't get up there fast.

God, if only he had a gun. For once, he wished he'd listened to Baird's taunts and bought himself a gun. But it was too late now.

He waited until Tyler moved to the far side of Hilary, then bounded up the steps. The entire scene seemed to play in slow motion. He was living Hollywood's most dramatic special effects as he watched with horror as Tyler gripped the lever that would drop Hilary to her death.

From the corner of his eye, he clearly saw Sean McCune's look of uncontrolled rage—saw the gun in the older man's hand aimed directly at Zach. His blood pounded violently in his veins to the rhythm of his terror. He must reach Hilary before it was too late.

Zach screamed and lunged for Hilary as Tyler pulled the handle.

As they plunged through the trap door together, a deafening explosion resounded all around. Zach felt as if time had stopped. A searing pain ripped through flesh and bone, rendering his chest a useless mass of goo. He was barely conscious of his pain—death took a long time coming. Even Steven Spielberg couldn't have made it any more sensational.

Simultaneously, he heard another sound—a sharp crack which seemed even louder than the gun's discharge. As blackness enveloped him, Zach identified the other hideous noise.

It was the merciful snap of Hilary's neck.

Chapter Nineteen

Swirling blackness tugged at the fringes of Zach's consciousness as he floated with Hilary at his side. Though he couldn't see her, he sensed her.

A bright light appeared far above them, reminding Zach of when he'd broken the mirror behind the bar. God, that seemed like an eternity ago. Only this was far more pleasant than his trip through time had been.

There was no pain or fear. In fact, he didn't even feel the pain in his chest any longer. Strange. He couldn't be certain that his body still existed, as they grew ever-closer to the radiant glow. Was he having an out of body experience? With Hilary?

As long as they were together . . .

Just when he thought he'd be able to reach out and touch the light with his hand—if he still had one—it vanished. A momentary sensation of panic gripped him. Were they going to Hell? Hilary'd been so certain that would be

her fate if she failed to prevent the events which had led
to her death.

As they obviously had.

"Well . . ."

A woman's voice surrounded them as Zach strained to
see. There was nothing but darkness, yet he felt as if they
were standing on something solid.

He glanced to his right and saw Hilary—his Hilary.
Reaching for her hand, he sent her what he hoped was
an encouraging smile, then turned again in search of the
voice and its source.

"It took much longer than we thought, Hilary," the
voice said as a glow illuminated a beautiful woman in a
white robe. "The space and time continuum wasn't very
cooperative, nor was the population of Columbine."

Hilary shook her head. "Sarah."

Sarah. Zach squeezed Hilary's hand and swallowed hard.
"Are we dead?" he asked, knowing the answer before he'd
spoken. But he had to ask—had to hear the words before
he would accept them.

"I'm afraid so." Sarah shrugged. "The circumstances
were very peculiar—again." She sighed and faced Hilary.
"When we placed you in Transition, Hilary, there was no
way to predict so many things would go wrong." The
woman laughed—actually *laughed.*

"I don't see anything funny about this," Zach said with
a sigh. He was beginning to feel pretty angry about the
entire situation. How could this angel be so casual about
their lives—and deaths? "Enlighten me, please."

Sarah pursed her lips and nodded. There was a twinkle
in her blue eyes, though her expression was solemn. "Very
well, Zach." She held two large books in her lap. "I'm quite
certain you've heard most of this from Hilary already."

"Yeah, but I didn't believe her when I should have."

He glanced at the silent woman at his side. "And I sure wish I had."

"Yes, I know." Sarah smiled sweetly. "Hilary, you did everything just as you were supposed to. You served some-one in need—Zach. But something went wrong with the space and time continuum. There must have been a flaw in the system." She cleared her throat. "When you were transported back to 1886, you should have kept your mem-ory." She laughed again. "Nothing like this has ever hap-pened before, to my knowledge. A glitch in a miracle is very rare."

"Gee, that's encouraging." Zach rolled his eyes and waited for her to explain.

"I understand your anger, Zach," Sarah said quietly, her expression serious. "It wasn't your time."

"Time?" Zach laughed, but it wasn't a happy sound by any means. *"Time?"*

Sarah's lips twitched as she leafed through the pages of Zach's book. "Time isn't relevant here. In Heaven."

Hilary shifted slightly. "Heaven? Really?" She glanced at Zach. "Both of us?"

Sarah shook her head. "This is very complicated, Hilary. Nothing is as simple as it seems." She opened the other book and leafed through the pages. "It doesn't seem fair to . . ." Sarah rubbed her eyes and glanced upward, then smiled and nodded.

Zach could've kicked himself. Here he stood on the threshold of Heaven—the pearly gates—and what did he do? Shot off his big mouth to an angel. *An angel.* "God."

"You've come to the right place," Sarah said when Zach looked up sharply. "Even angels have a sense of humor, Zach."

"I'm glad." He sighed and looked directly at the angel. "You say Hilary's situation is complicated, and it isn't my time, whatever that means. What's going on, then? We're both dead, right?''

Sarah nodded and placed both books in her lap. She folded her hands over the books and tilted her head to one side as if listening to someone. "As I said . . . it's complicated, but not impossible. Let's just say, you both have someone very influential on your side."

Again Zach followed the angel's upward gaze. *Someone influential? In Heaven? You're losin' it, Zach.*

"Not at all, Zach."

"Excuse me?"

Hilary giggled—actually *giggled*—at his side. "Zach, I remember from when I was here the *first* time."

"What?" he demanded when she didn't finish her statement.

"Sarah read my mind then, too."

"Okay." Zach whistled low. "Hey, I can breathe."

"In a way, yes." Sarah was silent for a few moments, then nodded again. "All right. It's set. We have approval."

"Approval?" Zach was beginning to think this entire situation was a secret mission of NASA. "For what, liftoff?"

Sarah cocked a challenging brow. "Careful, Zach." She faced Hilary. "There have been so many complications in your Transition, Hilary, we've decided to reverse your death."

"What?" Hilary trembled at his side and he squeezed her hand again. "Reverse?"

Zach closed his eyes for a moment and counted to ten, waiting for Sarah to finish her explanation. Zach knew for certain Hilary didn't deserve to go to Hell. She'd tried so hard to do what was expected of her in Transition, only *he* hadn't cooperated. *I wish I could always protect her . . . and Elliot.*

"Oh, we can grant your wish, too, Zach," Sarah stated

matter-of-factly, then laughed again. It was a musical sound, seeming to mock the solemnness of their situation.

"My wish?"

"To tak care of Hilary and Elliot."

Zach was afraid to ask. This was all so bizarre. He thought of Jimmie Stewart and Clarence, the angel, from *It's a Wonderful Life*. The analogy made him laugh. He felt just like George Bailey must have. Hollywood'd love this entire scenario. What a great movie it would make—a real blockbuster.

"What are you saying, Sarah?" Hilary finally asked, squeezing his hand as they waited for the angel to answer.

"You've both been given a reprieve." She smiled openly. "That sounds like you've done something wrong, which really isn't so. You've both been victims of a curious twist in the space and time continuum. And Columbine becoming a ghost town . . . well . . ."

"A reprieve? The space and time continuum?" Zach repeated, feeling there might be hope for them both, after all. "What . . . what does that mean? Exactly?"

"This is complicated, but there aren't any conditions on it like there were the other time, Hilary," Sarah said carefully, looking from Hilary to Zach. "We're sending you both back."

"Back?" Hilary gasped. "To Elliot?"

Sarah nodded. "You'll return to Elliot, but can't stay in Columbine. You must move far away from there, for the people of Columbine think you're dead. It would be rather complicated."

"I should say," Zach said with a sinking feeling in the pit of his stomach. "Does this mean I'm going back to . . . the twentieth century?"

Sarah stared long and hard at Zach. "What do you want, Zach?" She tilted her head to the side and waited. "Your own time . . . with airplanes and cars? Or the nineteenth century, with Hilary and Elliot?''

Zach didn't hesitate with his answer. ''Hilary and Elliot—always.''

Sarah gave a knowing smile. ''Remember, you'll both return to a place *near* Columbine, but you cannot remain. You'll have twenty-four hours of invisibility to find Elliot, then I can't protect you any longer. You must move away from there, quickly.''

''Invisibility?'' Zach's mind churned. ''What about McCune and Tyler?''

Sarah narrowed her eyes. ''They'll pay for their sins,'' she assured them, then cast Hilary a sheepish grin. ''You might like to know, that because of the great effort your mother made near the end, she's been placed in Transition, despite her unsavory lifestyle.''

Hilary gasped. Her joy was palpable and Zach shared it. Questions popped into his mind about his own family. He looked up at Sarah, who stared at him with a brilliant smile on her face.

''They're all here, Zach.''

''Thank you.'' He looked at Hilary. ''We're ready.''

''Don't thank me.'' She glanced upward. ''It wasn't *my* decision. I'm simply the messenger.''

''Invisibility has its advantages,'' Zach whispered as he and Hilary hid outside the cabin.

''I wonder if people can hear us, though.'' She giggled and squeezed his hand. It was good to be with Zach again. They were going to live as man and wife, in spite of everything. It was nothing less than a miracle—another one. What a wonderful world, to allow them both another chance.

''I'm going to sneak up to the window and check on

Elliot.'' Zach squeezed her hand. "I told him to wait here, unless we didn't make it back. Then he was supposed to go to Maggie's sister."

She nodded. "I understand. It's dark. He wouldn't start down the mountain in the dark."

Zach squeezed her hand in reassurance, then ran up to the window. Hilary held her breath while he peered through the small window. The shutters were closed against the cold night, but there was a small space where the two halves didn't meet evenly. With the moonlight, perhaps he'd be able to see Elliot inside.

He ran back to crouch beside her. "I don't know why we're hiding. No one can see us." They both laughed quietly.

"Yes, but we don't know if we can be heard, Zach," she reminded him. "Did you see him?"

Zach nodded. "He's asleep."

Uncertainty flashed through her mind. "There's no need to wake him." She touched Zach's shoulder and felt a tingle start low in her belly. "What are we going to do until dawn?"

Zach rubbed his chin with his thumb and forefinger. "We're invisible." He looked up at the sky. "It's weird, but I don't feel the cold either. There's even some snow left, but I don't feel it." He chuckled.

"That's how I felt in Transition. I didn't feel cold then either." Hilary bit her lower lip and felt her face flood with heat. "Like the night I found you in the snow."

"You remember everything now?" Zach ran his hand along the back of her neck, then pulled her face close to his. His eyes glittered with a feral light. "That night—our *first* time?"

She nodded. His face was so near, his breath was a caress against her cheek. "I remember everything," she whispered. "That time and the others." She sighed. "And Zach?"

"Hmm?"

"I *adore* chocolate ice cream."

His sharp intake of breath was a wondrous sound as he lowered his mouth to cover hers. They might be invisible to the rest of the world, but there was nothing unreal or intangible about the way he made her feel. Her blood thickened in her veins as he slanted his mouth across hers, coaxed her lips into a more pliant line.

Miracles did happen—more than once sometimes. Hilary was swept away, in her husband's arms again after thinking all was lost.

Beneath the shelter of a towering pine tree, he eased her back on the snow. No cold touched her back. All she felt was Zach and the spectacular sensations his touch awakened within her. His lips were warm and caressing, sculpting her passion to a fevered pitch within seconds.

The red harlot's gown was soon released at the waist. She remembered the first time, when she'd removed it herself for their mutual pleasure. What a wondrous night that had been.

But this time was even better. They were alive and together. He was her husband—they loved each other. What could be better?

It was fabulous to lounge beneath the night sky with no fear of being seen by prying eyes, naked to the elements without feeling their harshness. Zach removed all her clothing, slipped the striped stockings from her feet, then bared himself within moments.

Moonlight bathed him in a celestial glow that stole her breath as he knelt beside her. He was beautiful—all male and hers. Her husband. He'd risked everything to help her, because he loved her.

Hilary reached for him with open arms, drew him against her when he covered her with his warmth.

The bare branches of an aspen tree entwined over their heads with the heavily laden boughs of pine, creating an intimate confederation much like the merging of human bodies below.

"I love you, Hilary," he whispered as he slumped against her.

Hilary sighed in contentment, gathering him against her to kiss the top of his head. "And I love you, husband."

"Husband?" Zach chuckled and kissed the tip of her nose as he rolled to his side. "Y'know, I never thought I'd like that, but I do when you say it . . . wife."

"I'm glad." Hilary sat up beside him. "The sun will be up before long." A mixture of emotions filled her. Part of her couldn't wait to take her brother away from Columbine to begin their new life with Zach. But another part of her would miss the town and its people—most of its people.

He nodded. "We'd better dress and wake Elliot so we can get a head start."

They pulled on their clothing in silence. Zach placed the buffalo robe over her bare shoulders. "We'll find you something else to wear before we leave." He raised a mischievous brow. "Do you remember wearing my jeans before?"

She nodded and reddened, recalling how vividly her breasts had been displayed through his shirt. "Anything would be better than this."

"The bad days are all behind us now, Hilary," he promised, pulling her to stand before him. "This dress is beautiful to me, because it's what you were wearing that first day."

She smiled suddenly. "I remember."

Zach shook his head as he recalled that day. "I owe that

bear a lot." They laughed together as he pulled her close to cradle her head against his shoulder. "By the way, bears *do* hibernate, don't they?"

Hilary giggled. "Yes, Zach. They sleep through the winter. But it's still pretty early."

"Oh." He swallowed hard and glanced around. "But bears aren't nocturnal creatures, are they?"

She laughed again. "You're invisible. Remember?" She touched his face and lifted her gaze to meet his in the moonlight. "You've lived up here for weeks without worrying about bears."

He chuckled and stroked her golden hair. "I had other things on my mind. Now that things are calming down for us, I remember things like bears and . . . mountain lions." He gulped. "Unfortunately, I think they *are* nocturnal creatures."

She laughed again. It was a delightful sound. "Yes, they are."

"All right, time to wake Elliot." Zach gripped Hilary's hand, then froze as a perplexing thought crossed his mind. "Hilary."

"What's wrong?"

"How are we going to talk to Elliot if he can't see or hear us?"

"Oh." Hilary covered her mouth with her hand. "I never thought of that." She looked up at the sky. "Sarah said twenty-four hours."

Zach nodded. "That means we should stay invisible until around noon, I think." He scratched his head. "Not that I've been real concerned about time recently."

"I know what you mean." She squeezed his hand and looked toward the cabin. "We can still try. He may be able to hear us, after all."

Zach's gaze darted to the building. A movement near

the side of the cabin caught his eye. "What's that?" Not a mountain lion—he hoped.

They both remained silent, watching the shadowy figure sneak around the side of the cabin. "It's a man," Zach said with a sinking feeling. Or Big Foot? No. His heart thudded in his chest. Somehow, he knew the identity of the intruder.

Reminding himself that he and Hilary couldn't be seen, Zach took a step toward the cabin, leading her along with him. "I wonder."

"Wonder what?" she whispered.

"If we *can* be heard." Zach paused to rub his chin as the first faint smudges of daylight showed promise in the eastern sky, far beyond the mountains. "If that's who I think it is . . ."

"Sean McCune," Hilary said with a shaky voice. "He'll hurt Elliot. We have to stop him."

"C'mon. If that son-of-a-bitch can hear us, we're going to scare the hell out of him." Zach pulled her along until they saw the figure before the front door. His back was to them as he tried to open the door.

A burst of protectiveness gripped Zach. He released his wife's hand and lunged for the threatening figure. His body, apparently more solid than it appeared, slammed into McCune and sent the older man tumbling into the snow.

"What the hell . . ." McCune struggled to his feet as he looked frantically around in a circle. "Who did that? Dammit, I said who's there?"

Zach laughed. It was a menacing sound, as evil and threatening as he could muster. Maybe Sarah'd grant them one more little miracle. Let Sean McCune hear them, think they were ghosts, and be scared out of his wits.

Then another thought gripped Zach. Justice should be served. For Nellie, Shorty and Abe. He grabbed Sean by the back of his collar and kicked open the cabin door. "C'mon, Hilary," he called over his shoulder.

His wife rushed into the cabin to her brother's side. Zach struggled with the squirming, confused Sean McCune, truly enjoying his invisibility at the moment.

"So, McCune," he said, praying again that he could be heard. "Thought you were rid of me, didn't you?"

"Wh-who . . ." The man's face turned bright red as sunlight flooded the cabin through the open door. "I don't see you, but I sure as hell hear you."

"Good. I'm real glad to know that." Zach chuckled menacingly. What a paradox. He'd been dead and now he was alive. But he was still being granted the marvelous opportunity of being a ghost to haunt someone deserving of such an experience. "You're going to write a confession, McCune."

The man's eyes widened with fright as he continued to look around the room while Zach shoved him back into a chair at the crude table. "Hilary, there's paper and a pencil in that bag beside the bed."

Elliot sat up in bed, scratching his head while his sister went through a burlap bag beside the bed. Zach reminded himself that he and Hilary were invisible to Elliot as well. He would see the objects he and Hilary picked up move around as if under their own power.

"Elliot, Hilary and Zach are here," he said in a reassuring voice. "We're here to help you."

"Zach?" Elliot swung his legs over the side of the bed. "I can't see you."

"Elliot." Hilary's soft voice responded to her brother's obvious confusion.

Zach watched her kneel beside Elliot and whisper in his ear. Good. She'd be reassuring the boy that they weren't dead, while he enjoyed tormenting McCune just a bit longer.

"All right, Sean," he said in a patronizing tone. "Pick up that pencil and start writing."

"What . . . do you want me to write?" The man's Adam's apple bobbed up and down in his throat, and his face was still very red.

"The truth. That you murdered Nellie Brown, Shorty and Abe." Zach thrust the tablet and pencil into the man's shaking hand. *"Now."*

Trembling, Sean took the proffered writing utensil and paper. He wrote for several moments, then dropped the tablet.

Zach reached down to scoop up the object, smiling in victory when he saw the words. "Ah, implicated Sheriff Tyler in your little game, too." He whistled in appreciation. "Now we'll just make sure the right people get this."

"I don't believe in ghosts," McCune whispered, clutching at his throat. "The ghost story was . . . was a fake."

Zach laughed loud. "Sometimes we tell lies until they come true, Sean." He watched as the man struggled with the simple effort of breathing. "Feeling a bit puny, McCune?"

"Gotta get outta here." Sean stood and moved toward the door. "Can't breathe."

"Kind of like having a noose around your neck, huh?" Zach cast Hilary an apologetic smile when she gasped. "It's just as well you get used to it now. When the law gets wind of how many people's lives you've taken because of that wretched gold, you'll hang for sure."

"Yes, that's right." Hilary moved closer to them. "I don't believe in anyone being hanged. It's a horrible waste of life," she said in a trembling voice. "But if there's an exception to that, Mr. McCune . . . you're it."

"You're dead." Sean moved closer to the door, but Zach blocked the exit. When Zach gripped Sean's arm, the older man screamed in terror and jerked free.

Sean ran toward the trail head like Darth Vader, Robocop and The Terminator were in hot pursuit. Patches of ice and snow made the trail treacherous, but the terrified man didn't slow, even when he neared the edge of the cliff.

Hilary stood in the cabin door beside Zach as they watched Sean try to slow his retreat at the last minute. McCune slipped and fell, skidding along the ice on his backside until he vanished over the edge of the cliff. His scream echoed through the countryside, signaling a certain end to his miserable life.

They were silent for several moments as Zach pondered the natural justice in this world. Sarah'd said as much before they left Heaven. With a sigh, he turned to face Elliot. He reached out and gave the boy an encouraging pat on the shoulder, reminding himself that Elliot had been aware of his ambiguous relationship to Sean McCune.

"I'm sorry, Elliot," he said with all sincerity, though he felt justice had been served by Sean's death.

Elliot looked over their heads at something Zach felt only the boy could see. "I'm not," Elliot said at last. "Let's go away."

"There's one more thing I'd like to see happen first," Zach said, recalling the way Columbine had been in the twentieth century. "Can you write, Elliot?"

"Of course he can write," Hilary supplied, placing her hand on her hip as she turned to face Zach. "His sister's a teacher, remember?"

Properly chagrined, Zach cast her a sheepish grin. "Sorry."

"What do you want me to write, Zach?"

Elliot took the tablet and pencil from Zach's hands and glanced down at the page Sean had scribbled on. "He killed Ma."

"And Shorty." Zach sighed as he watched Hilary slip her arm around her brother's shoulders.

Elliot took a deep breath and sat on the edge of the bunk. "I'm ready."

Zach walked back and forth in front of the door, wondering if they should send Elliot into town to tell them about Sean. Then he recalled the man's blood-curdling scream and realized Sean had heralded his own demise. How generous.

"We have the gold I hid," Zach explained as he stared at Elliot. "I'd like to leave the Maggie-O and all its wealth to the town."

Hilary touched his arm. "That's a wonderful idea, Zach."

His gaze met hers and he knew she was also remembering the sad, lonely town of the twentieth century. "It's best," he said, not regretting the loss of their personal wealth, even for a moment. "We don't need all that gold. And if it's tied up with the town's treasury, maybe Columbine won't become a ghost town at all."

"Ghost town? Are you ghosts?" Elliot glanced up, though they were still invisible.

"No, we're alive. It's a long story, Elliot," Zach said with a chuckle and patted his new brother on the shoulder. His gaze met Hilary's. "Remind me to tell you all about it after we reach Ohio."

"Ohio?" Hilary frowned. "What's in Ohio?"

"I finally remembered where Orville and Wilbur Wright should be living about now." Zach sighed in wonder at what the future might hold in store for him. "I'm not going to waste the gift of life—ever again."

Hilary blinked. There were unshed tears glistening in her eyes. "Neither will I."

"And while I'm telling you all about the future, Elliot,

remind me to tell you about my other brother." He blinked back the stinging sensation behind his eyes. "Jake."

Hilary touched his face. "We'd better get that note written to the people of Columbine," she said in a quiet voice.

When he looked at her lovely face, Zach knew their future would be filled with love and hope. "And find you some clothes to wear down the mountain."

"I'm ready," Elliot said, holding out the piece of paper he'd been printing on.

Zach and Hilary bent their heads over Elliot's block-style letters.

Elliot Brown wants Columbine to have the Maggie-O.

Hilary took the pencil and wrote the date at the top of the page.

"We'll make a special invisible delivery on our way out of town." Zach felt a sense of closure on the entire situation.

Past and future.

"Elliot." Zach pulled a pair of jeans and a flannel shirt from the bag beside the bed and handed them to Hilary with a wink. "Do you think you'll like flying?"

Hilary gave him an indulgent smile. "I don't know about Elliot," she said in a quiet voice as she gazed into his eyes. "But I'm looking forward to it."

Zach raised both eyebrows in surprise. "Oh?" He pulled her into his arms and delivered a kiss to her lips. "And chocolate ice cream?"

"Ice cream?" Elliot's eager voice intruded on the moment.

"Yes, Elliot. Ice cream." Zach burned with love for his wife as he met her suggestive gaze and returned her smile. "I know what we'll spend most of that gold on now."

Hilary laughed and smiled up at him. "No, we won't need it." She kissed him softly, then sighed. "Just the memory will be enough for me."

Zach's hormones waged a frontal assault that nearly

knocked him senseless. He pulled her closer, displaying the results of her sensuous promise.

"I think maybe dairy farming might be in the cards for me," he said in wonder. "In a cold, northern climate . . . where there's plenty of ice."

Dear Reader:

This book is about two kinds of miracles—those over which we have some control, and those ordained by forces beyond the scope of human understanding. *Almost an Angel* is about love and courage. Zach and Hilary face challenges most humans never have to endure, yet they do so with courage and conviction, with love as their ultimate reward.

I hope you've enjoyed reading *Almost an Angel,* and that you close this book with renewed understanding and respect for people who battle the disease of alcoholism. May the wisdom and unconditional love shown by and for Zach, Hilary and Elliot live on in all our hearts.

I love to hear from readers. Please visit my home page at http://www.netforward.com/poboxes/?debstover/, or write to me at:

PO Box 1196
Monument, Colorado 80132-1196

May all your days include a bit of magic. . . .

ROMANCE FROM HANNAH HOWELL

MY VALIANT KNIGHT	(0-8217-5186-7, $5.50)
ONLY FOR YOU	(0-8217-4993-5, $4.99)
UNCONQUERED	(0-8217-5417-3, $5.99)
WILD ROSES	(0-8217-5677-X, $5.99)